Up-hill all the way /
FIC THO

3713000057471

Thompson, Jean,
Sanilac District Library

12·00

UP-HILL ALL THE WAY

UP-HILL ALL THE WAY

Jean Thompson

Five Star
Unity, Maine

This novel is a work of fiction. Names, characters, places, and incidents are either the product of the author's imagination, or, if real, used fictitiously.

Five Star First Edition Romance Series.
Published in 2000 in conjunction with Jean Thompson.

Cover photography by Geraldine Cyr.

Set in 11 pt. Plantin by Rick Gundberg.

Printed in the United States on permanent paper.

Library of Congress Cataloging-in-Publication Data

Thompson, Jean, 1933–
    Up-hill all the way / by Jean Thompson.
        p.   cm. — (Five Star first edition romance series)
    ISBN 0-7862-2714-1 (hc : alk. paper)
    1. Oregon — Fiction. I. Title. II. Series.
PS3570.H624 U7   2000
    813'.54—dc21   00-044284

For Clint and Jan
Whose grandparents knew the country and the people

Up-hill

Does the road wind up-hill all the way?
Yes, to the very end.
Will the day's journey take the whole long day?
From morn to night, my friend.

—Christina Georgina Rossetti

Chapter 1

LEE

Late March, Wednesday and Thursday

Sometimes it seemed that Lee Jamison's entire life could be defined by the spinning of wheels. When he was young, wheels had turned on tractors and farm machinery as they worked up and down the fields. The greater wheel of the seasons—planting, harvest and fallow—circled around him. The spinning wheels on the freight train that first carried Lee away from home sparked and thundered in his memory. Other wheels revolved in recollection . . . the gleaming spokes on a Pierce Arrow automobile; metal-rimmed ranch wagon wheels; threadbare pickup tires; as well as carefully engineered, high-speed tires that hummed confidently over the highways. Almost fifty years of wheels spun in a galaxy inside Lee's head.

The road undulated in front of his weary eyes as it curved across the northern California landscape. Over the hills to the west, a late March sun feebly colored the chill pearly sky.

Lee pushed the year-old, black '49 Mercury as hard as he dared, considering the safety of the horse in the rented trailer. The Mercury had a big motor and handled the load well enough. He'd paid a pretty penny for the mare, but he'd fallen in love with her just as he might fall in love with a woman. She could run on his brother's ranch until he decided what to do with her—and with the rest of his life.

The powerful engine throbbed beneath the dusty hood as he followed the hypnotic rise and fall of the road. He pressed against fatigue, pressed against the years. God, he was nearly half a century old. On his left, a dark ridge reached slowly toward the sun. Beyond the immediate night, he felt the advance of another, more final night that threatened to close, too soon, around him.

The road seemed to have a life of its own. It humped up and flattened out, rolled and twisted like a snake. As the car sailed over the crest of a hill, for a breathtaking instant, Lee saw nothing ahead except empty space. His stomach muscles contracted in the absurd belief that he'd run the Mercury off the edge of the earth. The world was flat, after all. He'd just soared over the rim, with the horse and trailer hanging behind like an exclamation point, and they were on their way down to whatever waited at the bottom of the sky.

The hood dropped. Hills speckled with live-oak trees arose in the distance. The wheels gripped the descending road. The shocks jolted and groaned as the car raced down into a valley. A sign flashed past: "Redding, 20 miles." Lee eased up on the accelerator and restacked the books that had skidded across the seat beside him. A well-worn copy of George Bird Grinnell's *Pawnee Hero Stories and Folk Tales* topped the pile.

He pulled in at a Flying A gas station with a phone booth. While two attendants filled the tank, measured engine oil and checked tire pressure, Lee dialed a number.

"Hello?" Joanne's voice was deceptively little-girlish.

"Good evening, ma'am. Is this the lady of the house?" It was his standard, cautious greeting, in case she was not alone.

"Lee, honey, where are you?"

"Just got into town. I'd like to see you, if the coast is clear."

There was a pause. Lee felt oddly disoriented. When he was on the road, moving over mountain passes, along river valleys and cultivated lands, he flowed through towns and past houses as a man apart, feeling almost invisible. Now he was leaving his phantom state, making a human connection. It was jarring, too mundane. Why had he stopped? He regretted the phone call. He should have kept on driving. He should have kept the wheels spinning, remained in that detached state that was a kind of grace. Instead he'd descended from the purity of the road into the condition of the ordinary man—a less-than-admirable ordinary man.

The pause had gone on too long. He had a feeling that Joanne was waiting for a reply. "Sorry. Would you repeat that?"

"I said that Don was here yesterday."

"Do you think he's still around?"

"He said that he was leaving early this morning. He never has come back after he said he was leaving, but I don't know. God, it would be so awful if he showed up while you were here."

"Yeah, I've no doubt it would be embarrassing."

"Embarrassing! God, he might kill us. I mean it. He's . . . he's funny sometimes. And I don't mean funny ha-ha."

"It's up to you, baby. I'd like to see you, but you have to feel okay about it. If you don't—well, we'll wait til next time."

There shouldn't be a next time, his road self said. You don't belong here. You complicate things and Joanne has problems enough already.

"When will next time be?" she asked.

"I'm not sure. I bought a dandy little mare that I'm taking to my brother's place in Oregon. And I've got a deal cooking

9

in Reno. I'll call the guy from Bob's and, if it works out, I'll be back this way in a couple of days." The wheels had stopped turning. His feet touched solid ground now. He felt vaguely soiled.

"And if the Reno deal doesn't work out, then what?"

"I've been thinking about Alaska." Alaska was a good thought, white, distant, pure.

"Oh, God, Lee. Alaska. I'll never see you then. Why don't you get a job here in town?"

"That'd be real poor planning. We'd never know when the boy friend might show up."

"If you were here, maybe I wouldn't need the boy friend."

"Don't forget that he makes your mortgage payments."

"I'd give that up for you."

Damn. Was she going to talk about marriage again?

Lee looked toward the highway as the silence lengthened.

Then Joanne said, "Oh, hell . . . come on over. I'm sure he's gone. We'll live dangerously, right?" She laughed, but it sounded forced.

"Right. I'll be there in a few minutes." He hung up and lit a cigarette as the attendants finished cleaning the car windows. Down the street, at a drive-in restaurant, a carhop on roller skates glided across the asphalt with a tray full of food. Her short majorette skirt swirled around her thighs. She smiled at the people in the car as she hooked the serving tray over the open window.

Lee liked Joanne—she was a lot of fun and the sex was great—but their occasional meetings were enough for him. He'd never been married, didn't want marriage and, even if he did, it would not be with her.

A divorced hairdresser, Joanne had an arrangement with a man from out of state. In return for financial assistance, he expected her to be available whenever he was in town and to travel with him when he wanted a companion. He insisted on complete secrecy and Joanne had revealed nothing, not even his name. Lee had the feeling that she herself knew very little about her secretive visitor.

Apparently the man expected exclusiveness in return for the mortgage payment. Lee thought him a fool. His visits were only occasional and one look at Joanne should convince him that she wasn't the type to stay home alone for long. Lee did not want such consideration. He'd been dismayed when, the last time he'd passed through Redding, Joanne had introduced the subject of marriage. It had almost scared him off—almost, but not quite.

The sun and the horizon inched closer together as he drove past small bungalows on perpetually green California lawns. Three little girls played hopscotch on a driveway. One hopped along the squares—bounce, feet together; bounce, feet apart. Her long hair flopped up and down in rhythm.

Three more blocks and the lots got larger. The houses were still modest, but had a country look with rail fences and patches of forest between the homes. He turned into a driveway that curved back into the trees.

Joanne bounced off the porch just as Lee's boot heel touched the ground. She was in her late thirties, a bottle blonde with glossy tanned skin and wide brown eyes surrounded by a thick fringe of dark lashes.

"Lee, honey. God, I'm glad to see you."

Her body was large, firm, lush. He pulled her against him. There was no doubt at all why he'd turned off the road. It was for the most ancient and earthy of reasons.

"You look great," he said sincerely. She always did, carefully groomed and made up. They kissed.

She took off his cowboy hat and ran her fingers through his

hair. "If I didn't know better, I'd think you bleached your hair to make it so pretty and silver."

"It's gray, honey. Been gray for years."

"No, it's platinum silver. Most women would kill for hair naturally this color."

Hoofs thumped impatiently on the floor of the trailer behind Lee.

"Oh, there's your horsie. Let me see him."

"Her. A mare. I'll get her out. She needs to be fed and watered and walked around a little."

He stepped the horse backward to the ground and she tossed her head up and down as though nodding in approval.

"She's so pretty, with that nice white spot on her forehead. What's her name?"

"Gypsy."

Lee tended the mare as Joanne petted and fussed over her. They went into the house, as immaculately maintained as Joanne herself. Later, after drinks and dinner, Lee led her into the bedroom. She followed slowly, reluctantly, without her usual eagerness. He unfastened the top button on her shirt, but she put her hands over his, stopping him.

"What's wrong?" he asked.

"I don't want you to be mad."

"About what?"

She looked away, biting her full lower lip.

"What is it? You can tell me."

"Last time you got really angry. Please don't this time, because it doesn't do any good."

Lee's lips tightened. He unbuttoned the cuff on Joanne's long-sleeved shirt and turned it back. A red line, raw and painful-looking, circled her wrist. Joanne didn't meet his eyes as he unbuttoned the other cuff and revealed an identical mark.

"What the hell's the matter with him anyway?"

"I knew you'd get mad."

"You're damn right I'm mad. Why does he do it? Why do you let him tie you up like an animal and hurt you?"

"It doesn't hurt much, really. Not so much I can't put up with it." Joanne wrapped her arms around Lee and laid her head on his shoulder. "All men aren't as good as you are. My husband used to beat me up when he got drunk. I was always lying to my friends, telling them I fell down the stairs or ran into the door in the dark. They must have thought I was the clumsiest person in the world. What this man does isn't as bad as that."

Lee cupped his hands on each side of her face and lifted it so that he could look into her eyes. "Joanne, you shouldn't put up with it. Tell him to get lost."

"Then I'd have to work a lot more hours. I couldn't keep my house without the help he gives me. I'd have to move into a noisy apartment or a dumpy trailer in a crowded park. I love my house and all the trees. I love waking up in the morning and hearing the birds and seeing the little rabbits and squirrels."

Lee shook his head. "This guy worries me. He's a creep."

"Well, he . . . he is kinda strange sometimes. And I don't like some of his ideas. Sometimes he . . ."

"He what?"

"Oh, I don't want to talk about him. I just want us to have a good time together. Please, honey. I don't get to see you very often. Just do what it is you do so well . . . make me feel good."

Lee caressed her, moving his hands gently over her body. Anger smouldered, a hard little lump inside him. But it was bridled by the knowledge that he did not want responsibility for Joanne. If he protested too much, she might misunder-

13

stand, might expect more than he would ever give her. Joanne was an experienced adult. If she was willing to submit to a sadist in return for her mortgage payments—well, that was her choice. She'd stayed married for fourteen years to a man who beat her. There must be something in her that drew her to such men.

And why did she like Lee so well—love him, she said? The question jolted him. Certainly he'd never hurt her physically, but she'd cried the last two times when he left. Was he abusing her in a different way? What made her so willingly accept pain of one kind or another?

"Why are you looking at me like that?" she asked.

He didn't answer. Instead he kissed her tenderly, careful not to look at the rope burns or the ugly round prints where a lit cigarette had unmistakably touched her flesh.

Later he slept, worn out with sex, whiskey, and the long hours of driving. Joanne woke him, too suddenly, too soon. Her fingers dug painfully into his bare shoulder.

"Lee! Lee! Wake up! Oh, my God!"

"What? What's wrong?"

"He was here. I just saw him. He was in the hall."

Lee sat up. "Who? Who was here?"

"Him. I saw him. He was looking at us. Oh, God, Lee, what'll he do?"

Lee's eyes strained to penetrate the darkness of the hallway as he swung his feet to the floor. His brain felt clogged with sleep, his reflexes as slow and thick as glue.

"I don't see anyone."

"I saw him. He was looking right at us. Oh, God."

Lee pulled on his jeans. Barefooted, he stumbled down the hall into the dimly lit living room. Glasses, cups, an overflowing ashtray crowded the coffee table. It was completely dark outside. The wall clock said 12:45. He opened the door to the porch.

A car motor throbbed faintly, seeming to originate in the shadows down the driveway. He saw no headlights. Was the bastard driving with them turned off? He sprinted across the parking area, wincing and swearing as sharp gravel stabbed his tender soles. The motor receded ahead of him, invisible in the darkness under the thick trees and bushes.

Something jabbed or bruised his feet at every step. It felt as though he were running on chunks of iron, punctuated with dull knife points. "Oh, shit! Jesus Christ!" It was a nightmare—or a bad comedy at which the audience laughed uneasily, ashamed even while they jeered. He floundered to a stop at the junction of the driveway and the narrow county road. Two dim red taillights hummed away and faded in the distance.

He hobbled slowly back to the house. When he reached the porch steps, blessedly smooth beneath his tortured feet, he saw Joanne huddled against the wall. As he moved toward her, light from the window illuminated her eyes, glazed and blind with terror like those of a trapped animal. He took her in his arms. Her body was mannequin-stiff and cold.

"I didn't see a car in the driveway," Lee said, searching for comfort without lying. "I did see taillights on the road, but the car could have been just passing by."

"He was here," Joanne said dully.

"Come inside." He steered her to the living room. Obediently as a doll, her legs folded to lower her to the couch. He poured a little whiskey. "Here, maybe this will help."

She gulped at it and coughed. A trickle ran down her chin. Lee wiped it away with his finger.

"There was nobody on your property. And I got out the door pretty fast." Fast enough, he wondered, to catch a man

15

already wide awake, with his pants and shoes on, and his car parked down the driveway? A cautious man might stop when he saw the Mercury and the horse trailer, and approach the house on foot.

Lee went on. "But let's suppose the worst. Let's suppose he walked in and saw us in bed together. He didn't pull a gun and shoot us or even start yelling. Instead he drove quietly away, like a man who didn't want trouble. It might be disappointing, as far as money is concerned, if he ends the arrangement, but you'll be better off in other ways. You can find somebody with regular tastes, instead of bent like this guy."

"That's it. He's bent. He's twisted. That's why I'm so afraid. With most men, it might be a good sign that he left without a word. But not with Don. I've never told you even a tenth of what he's done to me, the things he likes to do. When Phil used to hit me, it was right out in the open, on the face or arm. But Don knows how to do things without marks or else leave them where nobody can see, if I wear long sleeves and no shorts. Oh, God, Lee. What'll he do? What am I going to do?"

"What's his last name?"

"I can't tell you that."

"You already told me his first name—Don. Tell me his name and where he lives and I'll go talk to him, warn him to leave you alone."

"Don isn't his real name. I promised I'd never tell anyone his real name. And I never have—not you or Gloria, my best friend. I don't break promises."

"Why do you call him Don?" Lee fished, hoping she'd give away something.

"It's a Spanish title of honor. And it's short for the first name of some French nobleman that lived a long time ago. He believed, and Don does, too, that pain makes sex better.

16

Pain is a natural part of life, he says, just like sex, so it's natural to combine the two. Pain doubles pleasure. He says that a lot." Her voice quavered. "Maybe it does for him, but not for me."

"Joanne, think about this. You've got to protect yourself. Tell me who he is."

"I don't know what to do. I'm so tired I can't think straight. Help me push some furniture against the door. Maybe I can sleep and we'll decide in the morning."

The sound of the shower woke Lee a little before 7:00 on Thursday morning. He followed the smell of coffee out to the kitchen. Joanne had been up for awhile. The living room was picked up; glasses washed, ashtrays emptied, the coffee table polished. The sofa, an unpleasant reminder, backed up against the front door where Joanne had insisted it be moved. Don had a key to that door and she couldn't sleep, she said, unless it was blockaded.

Lee filled a cup and looked out the window. Two of the squirrels that Joanne enjoyed so much chased each other through the branches of a tree. They leaped recklessly from limb to limb. One dashed headfirst down the trunk to the ground and then vanished up another tree.

Joanne entered the kitchen. Her makeup was already in place and her hair, the impossible beauty-shop gold of ripe corn, neatly combed.

"Hello, gorgeous. How do you feel this morning?"

"Not as bad as last night."

"I've been thinking. You need to get away for a few days. I'm stuck with the mare. But I'll hustle up to Oregon, unload her, and come back. I'd like to stay the weekend with Bob and his family, as long as I'm there. Could you stay with Gloria until Monday? Then we'll go to Reno for a few days. By the time we get back, Don—or whatever the hell his name is—will be long gone."

If he was here at all, Lee thought to himself.

Guilt nibbled at him as he saw the way Joanne's face lit up, first with a little glow of hope and then brighter and brighter until she shone. He felt stuck, certainly, not with Gypsy, but with Joanne. And he'd suggested something that would encourage her to count on him more than he wanted. He couldn't bring himself to take her to his brother's house to meet the family, but neither could he ignore her fear.

"Will you really do that for me, come right back and take me to Reno?"

"Sure. Now call Gloria or somebody. I don't want to leave you here alone."

"You're so good to me. No wonder I love you."

"I'm not good," he said roughly. "Don't ever call me that." He peeled her arms from around his neck. "I'm going to take a shower while you phone."

"Gloria doesn't get up this early. I'll call her later. She and Bud are going to the coast this weekend. I know they won't mind if I go along. I'll call LaVerne first and see if she'll take my Saturday appointments. She owes me. And she gets up early."

At eight-fifteen, Gypsy had been in the trailer for almost twenty minutes. "Joanne, I want to get going. Call the woman now."

"Gloria takes the phone off the hook sometimes so she can sleep. I'll go to the Red Rooster and drink coffee awhile. I'll call her from there."

"Okay, let's roll. I'll put your bag in your car." He stowed it in the trunk and lit a cigarette. What the hell was she doing now? She'd already cleaned half the house. He'd never known a woman so obsessed with neatness.

He beeped the horn. Joanne appeared around the corner of the house. "I've got to water my plants back here. We've had a real dry winter."

"For God's sake, I could be almost to Dunsmuir by now." He couldn't, but annoyance caused him to exaggerate.

"I don't want you to get mad at me. You go ahead. This will only take five minutes."

"Joanne . . ."

She ran to him, wrapped her arms around his neck. Her wide eyes sparkled under dark lashes heavy with mascara. She kissed him, smudging him, he was sure, with lipstick.

"Lee, honey, I just love it that you're worried about me. And I feel sort of silly about last night. Maybe I did dream the whole thing. I'll be done here in a jiff. So go. And I'll see you Monday."

She hurried around to the backyard. Gypsy whickered softly from the trailer. A bird darted low overhead, swooping after its shadow on the ground. The place was as secluded and quiet as though they were a hundred miles, instead of only a quarter of a mile, from the next house. No wonder she loved it.

Lee started the car and drove slowly down the driveway. The main road was empty. He paused, motor idling, and looked both ways. No cars went by. Nothing moved under the trees. He pulled out, accelerated, and settled himself in the seat. In five or six hours, he'd be at his brother's ranch in Oregon.

Lee turned off the radio that had pounded cowboy songs into his head for most of the last two hundred miles. They'd been slow miles, on a narrow road that wound through the mountains. Half the time he'd been stuck behind a loaded truck laboring up a grade or some farmer poking along. Normally Lee was absorbed by the endlessly changing scenes beyond the cubicle of the car, but other thoughts had intruded upon him.

It was odd how certain patterns repeated themselves. Joanne had found him standing beside a stalled car with his thumb out. Years ago, another car had stopped beside another road and ordained his meeting with Rosalind. Not Roza-lind, but Rose-a-lind, a name like a poem. The remembered scent of honeysuckle drifted into his mind. Would it have made a difference if he hadn't been so young? He still had the sapphire and diamond ring. Bob kept it for him, in his safe deposit box in Woodbridge, Oregon.

Long after Rosalind, another woman—Doris—had taken Lee home from a bus station. His life and his loves seemed connected to wheels, endlessly spinning. He'd always liked movement, change. The women in his life changed, too. Sometimes he wondered about that . . . did it represent a flaw in his character? But if a man wanted to live in a variety of places and he didn't get married, of course he would know many different places—and many women.

In 1922, twenty-eight years before, Lee had been the same age as the century when he left the family farm in Illinois and headed west. He had already made several sorties around the Midwest, but this time he intended to go all the way to the Pacific Ocean.

He said his farewells to his family—his distant, preoccupied father and his regal mother. His father shook hands as though he were going to Chicago for the weekend and his mother gave him a cool dry kiss. Yet he knew that they loved him and wished he would not go. He hugged his three little sisters who clamoured and teased for him to bring something

20

for them when he came back, not realizing how long he intended to be gone.

It was hardest to leave Bob. He was fifteen and, as nearly as possible, every time Lee took a step, Bob took one right behind him. Lee was his mentor, his favorite companion, and his judge. Bob sometimes resented or disregarded his father's words, but never his older brother's. Lee's lifelong habit of presenting himself differently to Bob than to anyone else was already established. As they shook hands in farewell, Bob looked bravely into his eyes.

"I'll miss you, kid," Lee said.

His brother's Adam's apple bobbed as he swallowed noisily.

Lee said, "You'll be old enough to go with me next time."

Bob didn't say, "Let me go, anyway," or "Why don't you wait?" They'd been though all that. Lee hugged him roughly and Bob turned away, hiding the quick tears that fifteen was too old to reveal. Lee swung up beside the neighbor who had offered him a ride in his horse-drawn wagon. The team moved out of the yard. Lee waved one last time at the people who stood beside the big white house.

The enormous house on the prairie, holding his parents, Bob, his sisters, a maiden aunt, and the live-in housekeeper, had become a torment to him. Sometimes he felt as though he lived in a giant birdhouse. The little girls rushed around with shrill piping cries, interspersed with the dove-like notes of his mother and aunt and the strident cawing of the young domestic. The air rustled with the sound of plumage. Skirts swished; linen popped as it was shaken out and folded; dustcloths flipped; brooms, mops, and carpet sweepers swished along the halls and up and down the front and back stairs.

Even the big farm seemed confining—the fields marked

off with neat fences, each square containing its crop of corn, oats, soybeans, or pasture for the placid dairy cows, endlessly working their jaws. The days were marked out in yearly rhythm, molded to the march of the seasons. In fifty years, if he were still there, Lee knew that he would do essentially the same things during the same months of each and every year. The rich, endlessly demanding land, by its very bounty, held men in merciless bonds of slavery.

So he escaped down the road with his bedroll on his back and a few changes of clothing rolled up inside. He also carried two books. They were heavy, but the extra weight was minor, compared with Lee's fear of being without something to read. He intended to use *Seeing the West* as a guide. The other book, *Lord Jim*, he'd picked from the shelves of the family library.

The neighbor left Lee at a crossing where the county road intersected the railway. Lee wouldn't spend money on a train ticket. When his father learned of his intention to hop a freight, he refused to drop him off "like a bum." But Lee found a ride with a neighbor headed in the right direction at the right time.

His clothes clung damply to his skin. Stock flies, drowsy and clinging from the heat, pestered him. But he didn't have long to wait. When the train slowed down, blowing for the crossing, he threw his pack through an open door and swung neatly aboard.

He lay on his side, his head propped on his hand, and watched the countryside click past. Cornfields drooped in the sun. Their soldier-straight rows flicked open and shut before his eyes. Dairy cattle stood knee-deep in fields of grass.

At a crossing, Lee glimpsed a team of skittish black horses rearing as the train racketed past. A wild-eyed boy hauled on the reins while the stout farmwife beside him clutched her straw hat with one hand and a basket in her lap with the other. Then they were left behind in a blink.

The train crossed a river. Water lay brown and sluggish beneath the bridge. Roots and sticks, encrusted with dried mud, thrust through the opaque surface. Ugly whiskered catfish fed on the sludgy bottom. A big turtle sunned on a flat rock and stretched its skinny neck toward the sun. Trees crowded thick along the riverbanks and only the faintest of clouds tinged the pale blue of the sky.

The farms slid by, each house with its assortment of dairy barns, machine sheds, and silos. The train glided through small towns, their courthouses and church steeples rising above the trees. Lee saw ice cream parlors, feed stores, children waving grubby hands, busy trotting dogs. A few automobiles chugged down sleepy streets.

Lee almost made the Missouri border before he was kicked off the train by an intolerant brakeman. He slept that night in a hay field, alternately dozing and swatting mosquitos. A chatty salesman gave him a ride to St. Louis.

The next afternoon, Lee came upon a car beside the road. It was a Pierce Arrow, a gleaming jewel of a car, as golden as topaz, and trimmed with a black stripe, black top and fenders. A woman struggled to change a flat tire while another watched from beside the road. They turned as he approached.

"It looks as though you ladies have a problem," he said as he slipped off his pack.

"We certainly do. I simply can't manage this silly thing."

"Let me help you."

The girl fluttered around him as he worked. She was probably his age, neither plump nor slender, but quite short. Her reddish-brown hair was freshly marcelled under the brim of her hat. Damp pink skin showed in streaks through a thick layer of powder. Her dress appeared more suitable for a city evening than a drive down country roads. She made small ineffectual gestures to help him, almost brushing him with her pale plump hands.

Lee found her unattractive. He liked being flirted with, he didn't mind her faintly tawdry look, he could even tolerate the fake southern accent. But while each individual thing might have been acceptable, together it was all too much. Even as he replied to her constant stream of remarks, he was aware of the other woman. The sun at her back revealed nothing more than a slender silhouette. Lee finished the job and wiped his hands on the cloth the girl handed him.

"I declare, you got so hot changing that stubborn thing. I do wish I could offer you a nice glass of lemonade to cool off."

She half-raised her hands as though she might actually wipe away the beads of perspiration that stood on his tanned skin. Then she quickly put her hands behind her back, like a child who has been warned about touching a forbidden treasure. At the same time, she shot him a calculating look, measuring the effect of her action.

Lee turned to the other woman as she came forward, rippling through the heat and dust. Her head was swathed in a close-fitting turban of thin, soft beige fabric, pleated into folds. She wore a dress of the same material and it flowed around her body with every graceful movement.

"You've been very kind, sir." Her voice was low and resonant. "May we offer you a ride?"

"Thank you. I'd appreciate it."

"We're going to Des Moines."

"Then if it's all right with you, I'll ride as far as the junction to Kansas City."

"That will be fine. And if you can drive, perhaps you would? I think Melba needs a rest."

24

She slid into the back seat. Lee stowed his pack among their bags. Melba bounced in beside him and fussily arranged her skirt. Lee couldn't resist turning around to look into the back seat. He wanted to see again the incredible dark eyes that had met his too briefly, but the woman was turned away and he saw only a remote profile.

Melba chattered as he drove. They were actresses with a touring company. She filled the ingenue roles and Rosalind Shores was the leading lady. Normally they traveled by train, but Miss Shores had recently acquired the Pierce Arrow. The trip had gone well at first, but she was afraid it really would have turned out quite dreadfully if he hadn't come along at just the right moment.

Melba asked Lee questions about himself and hung on his answers with wide-eyed interest. He guessed that many of her mannerisms were copied from her stage roles and that she performed for him as though he were an audience of one. Miss Shores remained disinterested in their conversation.

They stopped at a tourist park, a cluster of small cabins in a semicircle, around seven o'clock. For dinner, Miss Shores changed into a plain black dress and removed her turban. Black hair coiled in a heavy knot at the back of her long neck. She wore no jewelry except three enormous glittering rings.

Images from childhood fairy tales floated in Lee's head. He thought of gray stone castles, lute songs and snow-white steeds, of words like sorceress and enchantress. Those eyes, those long graceful hands could weave spells, charm snakes, cast out devils or call forth demons. Once or twice, he felt she looked at him with interest, but the light was dim in the shadowy roadhouse and the candle flickered so faintly on the table between them that he wasn't sure.

Nor could he guess her age—perhaps thirty or forty years. Her skin was so smooth it seemed nearly poreless and gave

25

her the timeless look of one for whom age is only a minor matter.

As they left the building through the narrow entrance hall, a noisy group of people barged in. Melba darted out the door as quickly as a child, but Miss Shores paused. Lee stepped between her and the rude crowd, bracing his arm against the wall as the others jostled past.

Miss Shores looked at his large work-hardened hand beside her shoulder. Her glance traveled up his protecting arm to his face. Something changed. Light refracted differently in her eyes. Lee thought of far-off fireworks in a dark summer sky. An answering surge went through his body and he felt a response leap into his own eyes. He may have stopped breathing. After a moment, they went out to where Melba gazed raptly at the moon.

"Just look at that. Isn't it a beautiful night?"

She stumbled as she crossed the road and clutched at Lee's arm. She did not release him as they walked the short distance to the cabins.

"I declare, it's too pretty to waste. I feel like taking a walk."

"You go ahead," Miss Shores said. "Maybe Mr. Jamison will join you."

Lee extricated his arm from Melba's grip and stretched mightily. "You're younger than I am, Melba honey. I've had a long day."

"Oh, come on. You don't look as though you'd be so dull."

"Dull or not, you ladies will have to excuse me. Good night."

He hurried to his cabin and shut the door. Through the window, he saw the two women enter the cabin they shared. He felt not the least bit tired, but wild, restless, and frustrated. He paced around the small room. He wanted to howl at the moon, sing a wild song, leap into an arena to meet an unknown gladiator in combat. More than anything, he wanted to stride to the other cabin and say, "Miss Shores, if Melba will leave us alone, walk with me by the light of the moon."

Instead he stripped off his shirt, splashed water on his face, and brushed his teeth. He turned off the light and flopped naked on the bed. He stared at the ceiling while he smoked a cigarette. Nearly uncontrollable currents surged through him. A warm breeze blew in the open screened windows. Music drifted faintly from the roadhouse and the throbbing beat increased the hunger in his body.

Footsteps on the graveled drive crunched softly toward his cabin. Oh, God . . . Melba. He sat up and pulled the sheet to his waist as she rapped lightly on the unlocked door.

The coil spring squeaked as she stepped inside, but it wasn't Melba in the clear light of the moon. She wore a lemon-yellow and white print wrapper, held closed with one hand. She crossed to the bed and looked at him with enigmatic Egyptian eyes.

"I hope I am not unwelcome."

Dazed, he flung back the sheet. She dropped the silk wrapper to the floor and loosened her hair so that it spilled halfway down her back. She lay naked beside him. He touched her cautiously, smoothed his hand over her pale shoulder, and watched her eyes for clues. Just as gently, her hand moved on him. It traced up his flat ridged stomach, across his chest and shoulder, along the line of his jaw.

Honeysuckle vines grew outside the window. Their thick sweet scent permeated the softly stirring air. Forever afterwards, as long as he lived, that scent recalled Rosalind and memories of her fine-boned body, warm and slippery with sweat.

He awakened early in the morning in time to see her vanish out the door. He dozed awhile, content as the proverbial tomcat. As he shaved and dressed, a provocative thought occurred. What conversation had passed between Rosalind and Melba the night before and, even more intriguing, what would they say to each other this morning? He was still smiling to himself when he went out to wait for them.

They emerged together, Melba subdued, Rosalind as detached as ever. Lee quickly took his cue and was careful that no hint of familiarity crept into his manner. When they got into the car, however, Rosalind sat beside him and Melba slouched grumpily in the back.

All too soon for Lee, they reached the junction where he was to leave them for Kansas City. Carefully, hoping the slight trembling in his hand would not be noticed, he took the key from the ignition. Longing ached inside him, in the place where his heart must be. If only Melba were not there, then he might speak. If only Rosalind looked at him differently, less haughtily, then he might say that he did not want this to end so soon. His eyes locked on hers, but there was no help there. He felt as though he might suffocate.

There was nothing to do but get out of the car. He did and closed the door gently. He had to say something. The words sounded gravelly, scraping past his throat.

"Ladies, it's been unforgettable. I wish we could go further together." He dropped the keys in Rosalind's lap.

She flung back her head and laughed. "You really are quite lovely. And it can go on. Come to Des Moines."

Relief, exultation, triumph—his body charged with electric emotions. He tried not to grin too broadly as he held out his hand for the keys.

Lee found himself smiling as he remembered—indeed, relived—the emotions of his young self. Sometimes those days seemed as recent as last month, other times a hundred years ago.

He shifted his position. Time had passed quickly as he revisited the past. The town of Woodbridge lay only a few miles ahead and then he'd take the turnoff up the river twenty-five more miles, through the tiny community of Whistler's Bend, to Bob's ranch on the Little Nezzac River.

A man in jeans and a plaid shirt stood by the road, wiggling his thumb. Lee slowed to a stop. He'd done his share of hitchhiking and, besides, he was tired of his own company and his own thoughts.

Lee scooted the pile of books to the middle of the seat, as a short muscular figure slid into the car. His profile was classic Native American, the beaked-nose severity relieved by a generous mouth. He looked to be seventeen or eighteen years old when he smiled.

"Thanks. It looks like rain coming."

"Doesn't it always, in Oregon? You going into Wood-bridge?"

"Up the Little Nezzac. Aren't you Lee Jamison?"

"Yeah." Lee looked at him. "Should I know you?"

"We've never met, but I know who you are. I live just a couple of miles from your brother's place."

"No kidding? Well, happy to meet you." Lee thrust out his right hand and steered with his left.

"I'm Charles Balleau." The young man's hand bore a long white scar across the knuckles.

"Oh, sure. I've heard the name."

"I'm in the class ahead of Katie. And her mom tried to teach me English."

They talked about Lee's niece, two nephews and his sister-in-law who taught at the high school. Then the conversation moved to fishing and horses. They soon entered Wood-bridge, a town of about ten thousand people. It straddled the main Nezzac River and had grown beyond the river flats and up into the encircling hills. Farms and ranches filled the valley, extravagantly green with early spring growth. There was no shortage of rain here. The streets hummed with traffic: cars, farm vehicles, loaded logging trucks and those that were empty and carried their trailers piggyback.

Lee pulled up at a stoplight. Several people crossed in front of them. One, a slender woman with dark hair and silver-rimmed glasses, seemed startled as she noticed Lee. She leaned down to the open car window.

Lee pushed back his Stetson and gave her his best grin. "How are you, Doris?"

"Just fine." She glanced at Charles and smiled. "I've seen you in the store."

"This is Charles Balleau. You may know Mrs. Gooding."

Doris spoke to Lee again. "I saw Bob and Vivian the other day. They said you were going on a wild horse hunt."

"That's a little later on. I've got a couple of other deals cooking right now."

Her lips moved in what might have been a smile. "Of course. Nice to see you, Lee."

She went on across the street, back straight, head high. Lee shifted too fast as the light changed. Tires squealed as the Mercury tried to leap ahead, but was held back by the weight of the horse and trailer.

"Shit!" He shook out a cigarette and jammed it into his mouth. "Want a smoke?"

"Sure." They both lit up.

"Mrs. Gooding is a nice lady," Charles said.

"Yeah."

Lee turned east. In a few blocks they passed the cone sawdust burner at the edge of town. A plume of smoke rose toward the sky, fading quickly into the gray cloud cover. Raindrops splattered against the windshield and soon became a steady drizzle.

Doris had been so cool, so remote. Somehow he'd thought that she might be more . . . more what? Just what did he expect, anyway?

The hitchhiker spoke. "So you're going to hunt wild horses?"

Lee was glad to think about something else. "I've got a friend on a ranch near Rock Springs in southern Wyoming. We get together every couple of years and round up a few mustangs. We maybe make a few bucks, but mostly we have a hell of a good time."

"I bet. I'd sure like to see a herd of real wild horses. There's some stock up the river that runs loose on the open range, but that's different."

"Not really," said Lee. "The true mustang pretty well disappeared before 1920. The wild herds that are left are mostly made up of animals that once belonged to cattlemen or to your people—the Indian tribes. Some of the horses have run free for generations. But they're not quite the same as the originals that descended from Spanish stock. The history is all in here." Lee tapped a book in the pile.

Charles picked it up and read aloud. "*The Mustangs.* J. Frank Dobie."

"A damn good writer," Lee said. "I like wild horses, even though a lot of them are ugly little brutes, not the romantic beauties you hear about in stories. But they're tough. Those grass-fed nags can run a grain-fed horse right into the ground. Wild horses are tougher and more resilient than anything I know, except coyotes."

"It'd be great to look for them." Charles's voice was wistful.

31

"Hell, come along," Lee said expansively. "Just bring your saddle. Art's got plenty of riding horses. You probably won't get any money out of it, but it might be interesting."

"I shouldn't skip school," Charles said regretfully. As Lee glanced at him, he added, "Yeah, I skipped today, but I had a job to do for my old man."

"Well, if you change your mind, Bob has Baxter's address and he'll know the dates, too. Bob went along once, but he's too busy most of the time."

They soon passed the little settlement of Whistler's Bend. The road narrowed and curves increased.

After about ten miles, Charles said, "The store's just ahead. I gotta get some groceries, so let me off there."

Lee pulled in by the gas pumps. A sign advertised "Fishing Tackle" and another "Cold Pop." The Nezzac River store served the locals, as well as fishermen and hunters in season.

"Shall I wait for you?" Lee asked.

Charles shook his head. "There'll be a neighbor along to take me the rest of the way. But thanks for the ride. Tell Bob and the family I said hello."

A nice friendly kid, Lee thought as he pulled away. Talking to him had kept Lee from thinking about other things, about Doris, about Joanne. As soon as the first flurry of greetings and conversation with Bob and the family were over, he'd phone Gloria and assure himself that Joanne had made connections with her.

No one answered when he called early in the evening. He let it ring eight times. Then, just to be sure, he tried Joanne's house. The phone rang and rang.

He felt a sense of relief. They'd gone to the coast together. Now he could enjoy a weekend on the ranch and postpone thinking about Joanne until Monday.

Chapter 2

DORIS

Thursday afternoon to Friday morning

Back straight, head high, Doris marched across the street after her brief conversation with Lee and Charles at the intersection. The light changed as she reached the curb. Tires squealed behind her. She knew that it was Lee's Mercury that had leaped ahead too fast and caused the screech. How adolescent of him.

"Hello, Mrs. Gooding."

Who was that? She'd barely noticed a figure approaching her. Oh, well. Failure to return one greeting would hardly cause a slump in business.

"How are you, Doris?"

"Fine, thanks. And you?"

There was another one that she hadn't even seen. What a relief it would be to live in a city where no one knew her, where she could walk for miles along unfamiliar streets and never encounter a single person who recognized her. If she strode along muttering to herself, cursing or crying, others might think her a madwoman, but they would soon forget her. In Woodbridge, this small town where she'd lived her entire life, everyone knew her. Everyone knew everything. In a little while, today or tomorrow, someone was sure to say, "I saw Lee Jamison. Did you know that he's back?"

Here came someone she recognized. "Hello, Fred. How's Betty?" She hurried on before he could tell her about Betty. The hardware store, a refuge of sorts, was half a block away. But then she remembered that her landlord, Warren Stonebraker, would be waiting. The lease payments were mailed to his office in Portland, but Warren came on the same date every other month to check on things. Such attention to detail might have been welcome, if Warren were different.

The odd combination of boredom and unease that her landlord created in her began to form as she pushed open the door. A quick glance around the interior showed her that he was not there. Keith, the young sales assistant, talked into the phone. He motioned her back to the desk.

"It's the Wilson Company in Seattle. There's a problem with the last order we sent in."

She took the receiver with a sense of relief. At least she had a little time to compose herself before Warren arrived. She felt almost normal by the time the call was completed. The store was busy enough to engage her attention for the rest of the day. She rode home on the tide of busyness. It swept her through the door and left her in the middle of an empty house. And then she realized Warren hadn't come. How odd. How very unlike him. But it was just as well. Seeing Lee had thrown her off-balance. She'd be better able to cope with Warren on another day.

Doris made a cup of tea. She sipped at it too soon and scalded her lip. She took off her shoes and put both feet up on the sofa. Running a business was hard work, both mentally and physically. She'd had no idea what she was getting into when she'd married Carl.

She was eighteen and barely out of high school at their wedding in 1930. He was eleven years older and a partner in his father's hardware store. When her father-in-law died in 1940, Doris made the transition from part-time clerk to full-time partner, although neither Carl nor his mother accorded her recognition as such. She simply "helped out at the store," eight to ten hours a day, six days a week, from then on.

Bob and Vivian Jamison bought their ranch on the Nezzac River in the early years of World War II and became regular customers. Lee came early in the spring of 1946 and opened a shop around the corner from the hardware store. He sold leather goods, bridles, saddles, boots, and belts. A friendship quickly developed between Carl and Lee. Doris sometimes wondered why, as they were so different. But perhaps that was the appeal. Carl avoided outdoor activities, while Lee had the lean rawhide look of a ranch hand. Bespectacled Carl appeared bookish beside him, but Lee was the one who read, while Carl said he had no time for books.

Lee also liked honky-tonks and dancing. Doris and Carl, usually homebodies, surprised themselves sometimes and went along. Doris felt uncomfortable with the women Lee dated. They wore flashy clothes and too much makeup. They touched Lee too often and too boldly. Doris felt awkward in the presence of these alien women, so unlike her own friends. She knew they thought her dull and prudish, and had an uneasy feeling that they were right. Even her name had a prissy sound—Gooding.

Doris paused in her thoughts to study herself in the mirror and did not like what she saw. She was too thin. Her skin was smooth and unlined, a plus. But newly needed, silver-rimmed glasses gave her a spinsterish look. Her dark hair was all right, but she saw where a few gray ones crept in. She looked boring, plain and boring.

In a drugstore where she hoped no one knew her, she bought a selection of cosmetics, which she'd never worn. She tried them while Carl was at work. Lipstick accentuated the narrow lines of her mouth and blue shadow made her large eyes look cavernous. She washed her face and berated herself for being a fool. Everything went into the trash, except the rouge. It lent a soft, becoming color to her pale features.

The next time she saw Lee, he said, "You're looking mighty pretty today, Doris."

He noticed! Carl hadn't, but Lee had immediately noticed even that subtle difference. He was amazing. It was wonderful to be noticed, to be complimented. She felt young and almost pretty and . . . A shocking knowledge erupted through her euphoria: I'm in love with him.

She hurried to the back room and moved things aimlessly from shelf to shelf. It was awful and ridiculous—the feeling of giddiness in his presence, the nearly uncontrollable urge to touch him as did the women she despised, the need to say his name. She'd never felt this for Carl. He was more a friend, a "good catch," her friends had called him. When she looked at Lee, she didn't think "friend" or "good." She didn't think at all. She only felt and wanted and imagined.

Portions of a story Doris had read came into her mind as she hid in the back room that day. It concerned an untouched young man who fell in love with a girl whose life had been full of pain. She may have been a displaced person or a World War II prison camp survivor. The sentence Doris remembered was this: "He loved her for the sorrows she had borne." Not because she was young, virginal or beautiful, but for her sorrows. So Doris was drawn to Lee for the marks that time had made upon him, for the wild years at which she could only guess, but which had indelibly stamped him with a red sign that blinked "Danger" to conventional women like herself.

She had long ago learned concealment. It seemed a primary requirement for females, judging from the admonishments she'd received from parents and advice columnists as soon as she reached puberty. "Pull down your skirt and keep your knees together." "That neckline is too low." "Smile and pretend that you don't care." "Don't talk about your interests. Encourage him to talk about his." After years of this, it was easy to pretend that she was Lee's friend and nothing more. She did it for several months, and then was stunned when Lee announced that he'd sold his shop.

He said, "You know that my business has been slow. There's not much market anymore for saddles, harness— stuff like that. A young fellow came in today from New Jersey. He wants to open a record shop and likes my location. Old man Farrell's going to buy my leftover stock."

Doris's throat constricted so that she could barely speak. "You haven't had the store a year yet. It takes time to build a business. Maybe you should consider it awhile."

"I did. For five whole minutes, which is longer than I needed. I'm not a storekeeper. I've signed the papers and I'll be out by the end of the week. I heard from a friend in Mexico. He's got a deal cooking there that . . ."

Doris didn't hear the rest. After a bit, as Carl nodded in agreement, she broached, as tactfully as she could, the subject of wasted potential. Lee was not offended and his reply showed that he'd given it some thought.

"Most people work all their lives and hope to have a few years at the end to live the way I live right now. I work only as long as a job or an area interests me or until I have enough money for a stake. Then I go camping and fishing. Or take a horse into the back country. Sometimes I just lie on the beach in Mexico." He grinned. "Look at it this way. I'm living my life in reverse."

All too soon, the day came when he shook Carl's hand,

kissed her in a brotherly way, and drove off with a final wave. It hurt to get up in the morning. As soon as she opened her eyes, realization flooded her, as fresh and sharp as though it had never come before . . . he's gone.

Carl suffered attacks of angina, like his father before him. He stopped going to the store as his heart condition worsened. He puttered at home while Doris tended to business. He was only forty-six, but heavy glasses and early hair loss gave him a grandfatherly air. He spent hours in the kitchen fussing over recipes for Swiss steak, molded noodle ring filled with creamed chicken, chiffon cake, all the new and popular dishes. His mother came to dinner once a week and Carl beamed when she or Doris praised his cooking.

On a hot August morning in 1947, Doris kissed him quickly on top of his head. He smiled as he looked up from the newspaper.

Doris said, "I won't be home for lunch. Feldmans have put their summer shoes on sale and I want a pair of sandals."

She hurried out the door. The hardware store was running a sale, too, and it was a busy morning. At eleven o'clock, Doris sat down with the mail and a cup of coffee. She sorted quickly, stacking material into one pile for immediate attention and another pile that could wait. There was a letter from Lee bearing stamps from Mexico. It was a "How are you? I am fine," sort of message, without a return address.

"Doris."

She looked up. Her neighbor, Anna Stegner, stood before her. Doris struggled to focus attention on her friend.

"Hello, Anna. Would you like some coffee?"

"Doris, it's Carl."

It was difficult to switch her attention from Lee's letter and all the emotions that flooded her as she read it. "What about Carl?"

Anna took her hands and held them tightly. "It's not good. He must have had a heart attack. It's very serious." She swallowed noisily. "Doris, Carl's dead."

She heard the words, but they had no meaning. They jumbled senselessly in her head.

Anna went on. "I took over some sweet corn. I knew Carl was there, but he didn't answer the door. When I looked in, I saw him lying on the floor. He was already dead. Maybe I should have called you then, but I didn't want you to hear over the phone. I left the house at the same time the ambulance did. I'm so sorry, Doris."

It was odd, but she felt no lonelier without Carl than she often had with him. It was terrible that she couldn't miss him more. They'd lived together, eaten together, slept and worked together for seventeen years, and yet the amiable distance between them had never closed.

The next year passed quickly, but at a distance. I could make changes, she told herself. But if I sold my share of the store, I'd have to get a job. What would I do? If I moved, where would I go?

The door to the hardware store opened on a rainy afternoon early in the winter of 1948. A familiar figure approached her, a tall, wide-shouldered shadow against the falling rain. Lee came around the end of the counter. She leaned against him, inhaling the well-remembered odors of cigarettes, bourbon, and his own faint personal scent. Before she was ready, he released her and stepped backward, holding her upper arms in his hands.

"Bob told me about Carl. Did you get my note?"

She nodded, surprised by a sudden sprinkling of tears. She rubbed at them. "Let's talk about something else. Tell me where you've been."

"It's a long story. If you can take a break, I'll buy the coffee."

When they were seated opposite each other under the harsh lights of the cafe, she had her first good look at him. He wore a wrinkled shirt and faded denim jacket. His Stetson looked as though it had been stepped on and then reshaped as best he could. The lines on his face had deepened. Red rimmed his pale gray eyes and there was something hard, almost desperate, in them. If she had met him on the street without knowing him, she would have been wary and not let him come too near. A spasm of pain and pity welled up in her throat.

"Lee, you look so tired."

"Hell, I am," he said glibly. "I rode a bus all the way from El Centro, where I sold my car. But now I've got a deal cooking in Montana. It sounds pretty good. I'll head up there in the morning."

By now, she'd learned that he always had a deal cooking somewhere, patched together in long distance phone conversations or scribbled notes.

She asked, "What about Bob and Vivian? Aren't you going to see them?"

He shook his head. "They're in Illinois. My father died."

"I'm sorry, Lee."

"Yeah, me, too. I was camping on the desert and didn't get word until I got back in. Then it was too late to make the funeral. But Bob and Vivian went and my sisters are there, of course, so Mother isn't alone. I'm glad I visited the folks last year."

Doris took him home with her. She suspected he was short of money and glad to use her second bedroom. In the morning, she fixed a big breakfast and drove him to the bus depot. It was still raining. Lee moved sluggishly, as though

40

the night's sleep hadn't done much good. He checked his suitcase and they stood a bit awkwardly together.

His mouth twisted in a bleak smile that didn't reach his eyes. "This rain reminds me of another time, years ago when I was a young man. I saw the Pacific Ocean for the first time and felt about as depressed then as I do now."

A harsh voice announced passenger boarding time. The sound went through Doris like an arrow. Her stomach hollowed. "Don't go," she croaked. She tried it again, a little louder, a little steadier. "Don't go. I want you to stay with me."

He looked at her for a long time. She thought that it was the first time he had ever really looked at her, reading her, seeing the woman behind the pale, composed features and the silver-rimmed glasses.

His hand moved softly on her shoulder. "You're too good for me."

"That's what men say when they're not interested."

He smiled a little. "You can surprise me, Doris. But it wouldn't be fair. I never stay long in one place."

"Maybe I won't want you for very long. But I do now."

A shift of emotion made him look suddenly vulnerable, almost young, beneath the jaunty set of his cowboy hat. "Are you sure?"

"Yes, I'm sure."

The bus driver leaned out impatiently. "Hey, buddy, you going or not?"

"No, I'm not. And I've got five bucks if you'll find my suitcase for me."

The driver got down, grumbling, and Doris breathed again. The feeling of relief and euphoria lasted until they stepped through the door of her house. Lee set down his suitcase and looked around as though he'd never seen the room before.

41

Oh, God, what's he thinking? What have I done?

She thought she might faint. Or throw up. Or gibber like an idiot.

Lee took her clammy hand and drew her to the sofa. "Sit down a minute. Let's talk. I know some things about you, but there are lots of things I don't know."

His fingers remained linked with hers, but there was nothing sexual in the clasp. It was friendly, companionable. His eyes were friendly, too, and intent. He looked at women, no matter their age or appearance, in a way that made each feel special. Anna Stegner had once said, "Lee has a gift for noticing women, but not in an offensive way."

He said to Doris, "Tell me what you were like when you were a little girl."

"Well . . . I was skinny. And gawky. Just like I am now."

"If you were just like you are now, you were good-looking. And competent, but shy. Not nearly as self-confident as you should be, considering your abilities."

"I don't have many abilities. No, erase that. I'm not fishing for compliments. What were you like when you were a little boy?"

"I was surrounded by women. Bob wasn't born until I was seven years old and Dad was too busy tending to the farm to spend much time with me. Two of his sisters lived with us. They were much younger than he was. They made me their pet. They took me everywhere, like a puppy. They probably put ribbons on me, too."

Doris laughed at the image of a small boy in short pants, cossetted and teased by young women in pale organdy dresses and garden hats. Her tension vanished. It was several days later before she realized how skillfully he had disarmed her. He gently guided the transition from friends to lovers and made it seem so spontaneous that Doris could almost believe it had been his idea instead of hers. Her neighbor was right—Lee had a gift with women.

Whatever else she might be—or not be—to Lee, she knew that she provided a resting place, perhaps even a hand-hold when he was falling, when the next deal, the next job, had not materialized as he expected. She watched him recover, saw the redness leave his eyes, the tight lines of his mouth relax. Under her care, he grew fit and sleek again. Even though she didn't ask, he cut his drinking to just one bourbon and water before dinner.

I'm good for him. Does he know that? Does he know that he needs me?

Woodbridge was too small to keep secrets and conservative enough so that Doris knew many disapproved when Lee stayed on in her house. It had not been easy to tell her parents, even though she was thirty-six years old.

"You may not find another husband," her father warned. "A lot of men won't marry a woman who steps outside the line."

"I don't care about lines," Doris said. In fact, she wished she knew of another one that she could cross.

It wasn't long until Mrs. Gooding came to the hardware store. After Carl died, Doris had conscientiously continued to invite her for dinner once a week. At first, her mother-in-law came, but soon she began to find excuses. Their phone calls and visits became less frequent until they saw one another only accidentally or concerning store business.

Mrs. Gooding, looking heavier and more corseted, advanced grimly to the back of the store. Her attack was immediate. "Doris, I hear you have a man living with you."

As Doris thought about how to respond, Mrs. Gooding went on. "Don't try to deny it. It's that wild cowboy who used to own the saddle shop."

"I'm not denying it."

"How could you do this to Carl?"

"Carl's dead. I'm not doing anything to him."

"You're degrading and demeaning the years you had together."

"I don't feel that way. There's no connection."

"Carl could have married anyone in town. I never understood why he chose you. I'm afraid he wasn't a good judge of character."

"What I do is no longer any concern of yours," Doris told her, struggling to remain civilized.

"But it is. You have the Gooding name. You're embarrassing me in front of my friends. They all know about you. Everyone knows. How can you be so shameless?"

Doris sighed and looked at her pale bare hands. She'd taken off her wedding ring the day that Lee moved in.

"Mrs. Gooding, I'm sorry that I've upset you. But I'm not so sorry that I'll make changes in my personal life just because you disapprove."

"It's not as if I don't know what it's like to be alone. I've been widowed longer than you and it isn't easy. But I have a sense of what is decent and proper and what is not. Your parents must be ashamed of you, too."

Doris's anger rose. "Since you mentioned shame, you've always been ashamed that my father, your son's father-in-law, is only a hired hand on other people's farms. You barely speak to my parents because they've never been good enough for you. Why do you suddenly care what they think?"

Mrs. Gooding flushed bright red. "If you don't tell that man to leave, I'll take legal steps to remove the store from your hands."

"You go right ahead and try," Doris said. "But my legal right to the store doesn't depend on your narrow-minded version of morality. Now, excuse me. I have a customer."

Stiffly, like a wind-up toy on tiny feet, Mrs. Gooding marched out of the store. Glenn Draper, vice-president of the Woodbridge Bank two doors away, looked at Doris admiringly.

"You certainly put her in her place. I didn't know you were such a spitfire."

"What can I do for you, Glenn?"

"Just a few odds and ends."

He followed her around as she gathered the items on his list. "You're very attractive when you're angry. I've heard the expression 'eyes blazing' many times, but I never before knew exactly what it meant."

He stood uncomfortably close to her. Doris moved away as she dropped a few screws into a small brown bag.

"We've worked almost next door to one another for years. I'm sorry I never made an attempt to know you better."

"You've had a good reason. You're married."

"Not for long. Phyllis and I have separated. She's gone back to California."

"I'm sorry to hear that. You'll miss your little boy."

"I do miss him. But Redding is close enough so that I can see him fairly often. Phyllis's parents are there. And we own some property—which might soon be all hers, I suppose, when the lawyers get through."

Doris rang up the order. "That'll be $7.45."

He gave her a ten-dollar bill. He deliberately turned his hand so that his fingers caressed hers. She made change, slapped it on the counter, and retreated a step.

He smiled, unabashed. "Keep me in mind. When you get tired of your friend, remember that I'm right down the street—very easy to find. Did the cowboy ever tell you that you have beautiful eyes?"

45

Doris slumped against the counter after he left. She'd been right. She'd sensed that Glenn's attitude toward her had changed since Lee moved in, or maybe since Phyllis moved out. She'd noticed a difference in some other men, too. They'd become a little more familiar, a little less respectful. Now that she loved a man outside of marriage, she was a "soiled dove"—a phrase she'd heard from her grandfather—and thus fair game. Men should know better. This was 1948, not 1898, and she could do what she damn well pleased.

She said it aloud. "I'll do what I damn well please, Mrs. Gooding." And laughed. Oh, it felt fine to be wicked.

During the following weeks, Doris occasionally wondered if Mrs. Gooding had gone so far as to speak to a lawyer. She must realize that profits had increased since Doris had taken over sole management of the store. Once a month, she deposited her mother-in-law's share of the business into her account. Even though she might resent it, Mrs. Gooding was dependent upon Doris for much of her income.

Lee scrupulously paid his share of expenses. He was selling cars and did well. Success in sales largely depended on making people like him and he was very good at that. He picked up Doris at closing time and they drove home together. If a customer kept him late, he called to say that he'd be delayed. In spring, when green fuzz appeared on fields and trees and the endless winter rains turned into the intermittent showers of spring, Lee's late evenings increased. She smelled liquor on his breath on those days. One morning he suggested that she drive her own car to work. The dinners she prepared congealed in the pans. She waited a few times and then she ate alone.

One evening Doris sat in the big flowered chair, her feet curled under her, and an open book on her lap. She read a few sentences, then her glance drifted to her wristwatch. Lights shone from the kitchen and the dining room, as well as the living room, so that the house glowed brightly. She thought it sad with only one light in the evening. It signalled that the person inside was alone and didn't expect anyone else. Many lights radiated welcome and the presence or at least the expectation of others.

A kitten, offspring of Anna's cat next door, lay beside her. He sprawled on his back. Doris absently rubbed his white stomach and he roused enough to purr sleepily. She shifted her cramped legs. The kitten grabbed her hand with prickly little paws, gnawed on her thumb, and then licked her a few times in apology before he went back to sleep.

It was 10:30. It seemed as though more than ten minutes had passed since she'd last looked at her watch. Her eyes went to the top of the page and she began the same words again. ". . . left Raintree County for the first time in his life, crossed the river that divided North from South, and came to his marriage bed at last a long way from home and in an alien earth." When she'd started the book, it had been like slipping into a long dark dream, entering a land both strange and familiar. The words had pierced her, stabbed her to the heart with their beauty. Now they rolled off the opaque surface of her mind like beads of water from a pane of glass and trickled away, unabsorbed.

Headlights flashed on the wall. She jumped. The kitten sat up, looked resentfully at her and licked his rumpled coat. Doris stretched her legs cautiously and felt the prickles of returning circulation.

Lee entered and crossed the room a little too carefully. "Hi, baby. Sorry to keep you waiting. I hope you went ahead and ate."

"I did." She hated being called "baby" no matter how

47

many leading men in the movies used it as a term of endearment. Lee knew she didn't like it and the fact that he used the word said something about the state of his mind. She shifted and grimaced as blood stabbed like thousands of tiny needles through both legs.

"A funny thing happened today. I went over to the Pine Tavern for a quick beer after work and who should I see there but Ed Graham. You've heard me talk about him. He has a ranch near Santa Rosa."

Doris nodded.

"His ranch hand got smashed up in an auto accident. Ed asked if I'd help out for a couple of months, until his man comes back to work. I'm thinking of it. It'd be good to work with horses and livestock again."

"I see." She massaged her calf, flinching from the excruciating touch of her own hand.

"Do you mind? It won't be for long."

"It's all right."

Lee had selected a dark corner of the room to sit in. The shadow of his hat brim concealed his face, but she felt his eyes upon her.

"It's okay," she said, lying as firmly as she could, knowing it wouldn't make any difference what she said. "If I sound funny, it's because both my legs fell asleep from sitting on them. The prickling is driving me wild."

He rose and stepped into the light, relieved and smiling. "Okay. We'll talk about it tomorrow. I'm going to bed. Are you coming?"

"In a few minutes. As soon as I can walk."

Lee chuckled and squeezed her shoulder. The odor of whiskey surrounded him in an invisible cloud. He bumped into a floor lamp as he crossed the room and into the wall as he went down the hall. The bathroom door closed behind him. She knew she'd done the best she could, put up a good front and agreed to his plans. He was already gone in spirit, if not in body.

She stayed home from work on the day that he left. She leaned against the bedroom door, sipped a cup of tea, and watched him pack. He snapped the suitcase shut.

"You didn't take all your shirts. And you left your good gray pants."

"There's no room in the suitcase."

"You can hang them in the car."

"I don't need them this trip."

"Don't pretend. Take the clothes."

She went to the kitchen and poured the tepid tea down the drain. He followed her. Her hand slipped inside his shirt collar and pressed into the warm joining of neck and shoulder. His body had become familiar. She rested against him, wishing that she could be absorbed into him, bone, flesh, and blood, so that they would be one forever.

"You're a terrific woman, Doris. The best ever and that's no lie."

"I know."

There was that quick little smile, the one that meant she'd surprised him. He kissed her for a long time. He pulled back and looked into her eyes. Something in his changed, revealing the same flickering expression of uncertainty and vulnerability that she had seen only once before, in the bus station. His mouth softened and she sensed emotions surge up inside him like water behind a wall. Her breath caught. The beat of her heart seemed to suspend and a great dazzle of emotion sizzled through her.

But too soon. His eyes left hers and went to the shiny new black Mercury that waited in the driveway, seductive in its promise of miles and speed and unknown roads to follow. Lee released her. Cold and emptiness rushed in where his warmth had been. He stroked her cheek lightly with his finger and walked to the car.

Doris followed, carrying the clothes he foolishly refused to take. She opened the door on the passenger side and draped them over his shopping bag full of books. She even noticed the title on top, *Across the Wide Missouri*. Her eyes briefly met Lee's over the roof of the car, then she went back to the house.

She hauled the vacuum out of the closet. After all the rugs were done, she dusted, washed the kitchen floor, polished furniture. She spun the dial on the radio away from the station that Lee liked—the one that twanged out cowboy tunes—to one that played classical music. She turned up the volume. Violins soared. Sound filled the house like rising water that would sweep everything away and leave it as clean and as empty as it had been before.

Doris remembered all this as she mechanically prepared for work on the morning after she'd seen Lee and the Balleau boy in the black Mercury with a horse trailer behind them.

She wondered, why do women always believe we can change men? A year ago she had believed, up until the moment when Lee headed for Santa Rosa, that he might do for her what he had never done for anyone—change. It should have been perfectly obvious that he refused to be the man she knew he could be, yet she had hoped for, perhaps even anticipated, a transformation: the domestication of a man she had initially admired for his free spirit.

As she drove toward the store, she remembered that her landlord had not come yesterday. Warren Stonebraker was precise, even rigid, in his attention to business. Although he lived in Portland, he had interests in several locations. He visited each one every sixty days, cruising the highways in a big Cadillac, a new one every second year.

She'd never liked Warren, finding him boring and self-important. He made frequent references to his "properties," a favorite term, and to the responsibilities of managing them and his money. When Carl was living, he had dealt with the landlord, as it was obvious that Warren had a low opinion of women in business.

One of his favorite topics, on which he droned at length to Carl, was the breakdown of morality in the modern world. "It started with the war. When the men left, women became overly independent. They lost their sense of propriety, of right and wrong."

Carl nodded and murmured, which Warren seemed to take as agreement. Her husband was careful never to look at Doris during these monologues.

She'd been shocked when Warren had asked her to join him for dinner after Carl's death. She'd declined as politely as she could, saying that she preferred to keep business relations purely business. That had been all right, until Lee entered her life.

While some men had exhibited a changed attitude, none made her feel as uneasy as Warren, yet she could not place a finger on any one incident or remark that explained those feelings. She read a different expression in his eyes—or was it only that she recalled his self-righteous remarks about the "proper place" of women? At any rate, she wished there was a way to avoid his visits.

As she unlocked the store, Lila Prentiss, who worked at the Woodbridge Bank, paused to speak to her.

"I hope it's nice today. I'm so tired of the rain."

Doris glanced at the sky where a smothered luminescence in the east suggested the presence of the sun. "Maybe it will clear up. I saw Sherry for a few minutes last Saturday. She gets prettier every day."

Lila's usual chilly expression warmed at the mention of her daughter. "Oh, thank you. I think I told you that she's a cheerleader this year?"

"Yes, you did. What fun for her . . . and you, too."

"It is fun. Although it keeps her busy, with practice and schoolwork, as well as helping at home. But Sherry has always been happiest when she's busy." She looked over Doris's shoulder. "Hello, Mrs. Gooding. How are you today?"

Doris turned to see her mother-in-law's suspicious face. "I'm not sure, Lila. Yesterday I saw Lee Jamison driving down Main Street. I hope that doesn't mean my daughter-in-law is going to lose her head again."

"Lee is here to visit his brother," Doris said as evenly as she could manage. "I doubt that I'll even speak to him again."

Mrs. Gooding's lips pinched together. "You've already seen him?"

"Here comes Warren," Lila whispered. "For heaven's sake, Alice, don't make a scene. Warren would hate it."

Mrs. Gooding turned quickly. "Good morning, Mr. Stonebraker," she said sweetly. "How nice to see you."

Warren nodded. His cold eyes passed over her without interest, then a smile briefly touched his face as he looked at the other woman. "Hello, Lila."

"Good morning, Warren," Lila said primly. But her face warmed as it had when Doris had mentioned her daughter.

Not for the first time, Doris wondered at the relationship between them. Warren frequently visited Whistler's Bend, where his brother owned a sawmill. Warren maintained a remote cabin on the Nezzac River road beyond the Jamison ranch. His niece, Marlene, and Sherry Prentiss were best friends, Lila proudly told Doris, and the families were often

52

seen in one another's company. Doris had also seen Warren, Lila, and Sherry at the movies or dining out together.

Surely it was an unlikely friendship, not a romance. It was almost impossible to imagine Lila involved with a man. Although obviously there had once been a Mr. Prentiss to father her child. Somehow Lila gave Doris the impression that it was a mistake she'd made once and would never make again. As for Warren, he was younger than Lila, but that didn't preclude . . .

She looked up to find his eyes on her. She read contempt and an arrogant assessment of her worth—or lack of it—that made her hackles rise.

"Come in, Warren," she said briskly. As he followed her into the building, she was aware of his massive bulk just behind her. "I expected you yesterday. I hope you didn't have car trouble."

"No, not car trouble. One of my other properties took a little extra attention. But it's resolved now."

There was a note of self-satisfaction in his voice. In fact, he sounded so uncharacteristically cheerful that she turned to look at him. Warren was smiling, a full-fledged, lip-stretching smile, almost a grin. She'd never before seen him really smile. Usually his lips moved in a perfunctory grimace that didn't reach his eyes. The sight of Warren glowing, triumphant, was so astonishing that she bumped into a counter.

"Be careful, Doris. You'll get hurt." His voice was soft as his thick fingers closed gently on her upper arm.

She moved on toward her desk. He trod so close behind that she felt him brush against her skirt. She imagined that blazing smile still on his face and glanced back again, into the force of it.

"Doris, there's much about me that you don't know." He

seemed to struggle to suppress excitement. "If you knew, you would . . ."

The front door opened. "Hello, Mrs. Gooding, Mr. Stonebraker."

"Oh, good morning, Keith," Doris said too gaily, too loudly.

When she looked again at Warren, the smile was gone from his lips, but traces lingered in his eyes, of amusement, of a private and satisfying knowledge. With another man, she might have asked, "What is it? What's happened?" But she did not ask him.

Chapter 3

CHARLES

Thursday to Monday

On Thursday afternoon, Charles Balleau got out of Lee Jamison's Mercury in front of the Nezzac River store. The chilly wind blew a handful of rain into his face. He hunched his shoulders as he thanked Lee for the ride, then hurried into the store. He took a bottle of Grapette soda out of the case and drank from it as he selected a loaf of bread, a pound of ground beef, four oranges, and a handful of Hershey bars, five cents each.

"I'll take a pouch of Beechnut, too," he said to Mrs. Furman.

She turned to the shelves behind the counter. "I'll have to get some out of the storeroom." She disappeared through a back door.

Mrs. Domingo came in while Charles waited, sipping from the pop bottle. She was a tall lean woman in bib overalls, a man's jacket and a battered, broad-brimmed hat. Long gray hair, gathered into a rubber band, dangled to her shoulder blades. She lived alone in the last house, except for Warren Stonebraker's vacation cabin, on the river road. The narrow gravel road wound on farther into the mountains, providing access to logging operations and the fire

55

lookout on Carmody Butte.

"Hello, Charles. How's school?"

"Not bad," he answered. In his mind, he saw Sherry Prentiss with her blonde hair radiant in the sunshine and a pencil between her parted lips. School itself didn't interest him. He would have quit last year when he turned sixteen and could legally drop out if it weren't for the fact that he wouldn't see Sherry anymore.

"You're a senior, aren't you?"

"Yep. I'll be all through in a few months."

Mrs. Furman returned with her daughter, Loretta. "Hello, Miz Domingo. Hello, Charles. We got your tobacco," the girl said. She formed the words with concentration. Loretta was sixteen, but had the mental capacity of perhaps a five-year-old.

Charles took the pouch. "It's not my tobacco. It's my old man's. Do you ever chew, Loretta?"

She giggled. "No, it's nasty."

"It sure is. You and me got more sense than to get bad habits like that."

"That's right." She gazed at him adoringly. "You're nice, Charles. Some boys are mean, but you're always nice."

"Some people don't think so." The pinched face of Sherry's mother floated into his mind. She'd never spoken to Charles, but he didn't expect that she would like him.

"Well, I do. And people who think you're not nice aren't very nice."

Mrs. Domingo laughed. She sounded surprisingly young, almost girlish.

Loretta laughed with her. "Miz Domingo's nice, too," she added generously. "But I like Charles best."

"You're okay, too, Loretta," he said awkwardly. "I gotta go. My old man will be wanting his chew."

"If you wait til I get my groceries, I'll give you a ride," said Mrs. Domingo.

The rain pelted down as they hurried out to her old pickup. Charles listened to her talk about ponies. She left the county road and drove the half-mile up to his house, instead of letting him off to walk the shortcut as he had expected. His dog, Blackie, rushed out to greet him, his thin tail whipping back and forth in delight.

"Come visit me," Mrs. Domingo said, as Charles got out of the pickup. She was an old woman of at least eighty and she showed every year of her long difficult life, but her eyes were still beautiful. They were startling in her weather-beaten face, a remarkable color, more gold than brown and flecked with darker lines like the eyes of a lioness. They looked at him with real interest and, it seemed, even affection.

"Thanks, I'd like to." He watched her drive away. She must have glanced in the rearview mirror and seen him looking after her because she gave two cheerful little beeps on the horn. He grinned and waved.

Charles had only one grandparent, his father's mother. She lived on the reservation near Pendleton and he usually saw her once a year, during his summer vacation. His grandfather had died when Charles was a baby. He had never known his mother's parents and thought that they must be dead, too.

It would be nice to have a grandmother like Mrs. Domingo nearby. He could visit whenever he wanted and she'd listen to every word he said. Her eyes would be warm and approving and she'd smile now and then. She'd cook good suppers for him, crispy fried chicken and maybe bake a fruit pie. They'd eat together in the warm yellow glow of the kerosene lamplight and afterward . . .

Charles was suddenly aware that he still stood in the drizzling rain. He hurried inside, Blackie at his heels. He built a fire in the cookstove. Mrs. Domingo faded from his mind as he watched the first flames lick upward at the wood.

He thought of Sherry, of the way she'd looked earlier that afternoon when a brief flash of sunlight had slanted through the smudged classroom windows. The rays had touched her pale hair and ignited it into a glowing halo. Her head bent over her desk, so Charles saw only the curve of her creamy cheek and lowered dark gold lashes.

She stopped writing, put the eraser end of her pencil between her lips and raised her head. He was powerless to look away. Their eyes met. Sherry Prentiss smiled at everyone. She was the friendliest girl in school, as well as the prettiest. Her smiles touched her schoolmates as easily and impersonally as the sunbeams shining through the windows.

But she did not smile at Charles. There had been a time when she had. When their eyes had met in the past, she had smiled casually, turned away, and Charles knew that he was forgotten almost before he was out of sight. Now she looked at him soberly, attentively, until Charles felt dizzy with the pressure of the blood that drummed through his veins. He wanted to smile back instead of just staring, stupefied, but he couldn't. His face was too stiff and the longing in his heart too intense for anything so frivolous.

Finally Sherry did give him a half-smile, a look that was intimate and almost shy, before she turned away. Charles felt as if he'd been jolted by an electric charge. He kept looking at her, hoping she'd turn to him again, but she wrote studiously. Suddenly he remembered that he was in the middle of a classroom. He'd no doubt his feelings were written all over his face. Indians were supposed to be impassive, but he felt exposed, as if he had shouted, "I love Sherry." He glanced around to see if anyone had noticed, but no one paid attention.

When the bell rang, signalling the end of the school day, he'd tried to time his exit so that he could walk beside her. But he was too late. Big red-haired Marlene Stonebraker and other girls surrounded her. Charles watched Sherry get on her bus, but she didn't look his way again.

Charles's name, Balleau, was a legacy from a French trapper who had ventured into Umatilla country over one hundred years before. He had married an Indian woman and then, after a few years, went away and left her with her people. Their dark-eyed, dark-haired offspring were unnoticeable among the pure Native American children, but the French name stayed with them. Charles's mother was white, of Italian descent.

The shack where he lived with his father, Asa, had walls and floors of unfinished wood. Tattered curtains, grimed and faded to a neutral grayish shade, hung forlornly at the windows. A battered table and four chairs, one of them broken and never repaired, a sagging couch, the black woodstove crusted with grease and smoke, furnished the room that served as both kitchen and living area. Storage cupboards hung on one wall and a kerosene lamp provided meager light.

The bedroom contained a double bed for Asa and a cot for Charles. A wooden pole across one end of the room acted as a closet. A ladder nailed to the wall led up to a loft above the kitchen. Two rifles, hats, a washbasin, a cloudy mirror, and other miscellaneous items hung from nails driven randomly into the walls of both rooms.

There were some people on the river who had better houses with more furniture. There were others whose cabins were similar to his own. It didn't matter to Charles, who noticed, but didn't care, how other people lived. Most of the neighbors didn't care much, either.

* * * * *

On an autumn day when Charles was six years old and had just started first grade, he followed the shortcut up the hill after the bus had dropped him off by the trail. It was warm and sunny. The air smelled sweetly of old fir needles. A warm gusty wind blew from the high cloudless sky.

Charles sang breathlessly to himself as he trudged along. He watched his feet as he walked, admiring his too-big, but new and shiny, school shoes. When he was little, before he started school, he had gone barefoot much of the time. Now it was satisfying to listen to the solid thunking of his shoes on the hard-packed trail.

It had been a good day. He carried a grubby paper wrinkled in his hand. He had made all his letters correctly. His teacher had said he'd done a fine job. He felt warm and full of pride. Mama would be proud, too. There were times when she didn't listen to what he said. She looked off into space as though she saw things visible only to her eyes. Sometimes tears ran silently down her cheeks, sometimes she smiled, but she never told anyone what she saw. Today, though, Charles knew that she would be pleased. The teacher had written 100% with a red pencil on his paper. That was very good. He'd never had 100% before.

Blackie, an indeterminate sort of hound, waited where he always did, at the point where the trail came out of the timber and into the clearing where the cabin stood. The rutted road which his father drove up with the car followed a longer route.

"Hey, Blackie, look at this." Charles waved the paper and the dog jumped around with enthusiasm. The boy ran the last few steps and flung open the door.

"Mama! Hi, Mama!"

The room was quiet and empty. Dishes from breakfast still

littered the table. Mama was probably taking a nap. She often slept in the afternoon. He put his head cautiously into the bedroom. She did not like to be awakened suddenly. The sheet and blanket were tangled together at the foot of the empty bed.

"Mama, I'm home. Are you in the loft?"

There was no answer, but he climbed up and looked anyway. It was also empty. There were two pallets on the floor where he and Juanita, his ten-year-old sister, slept. Juanita had gone to the reservation for a week to stay with their grandmother, who was sick and needed her help.

Charles went outside. "Mama," he called as he walked toward the wooden privy that stood near the edge of the clearing. Fat black flies buzzed upward, lazily disturbed, fanning the effluent air with their wings. He closed the door and looked around.

Across from the cabin, an old wooden shed leaned close to the point of collapse. A number of boards were missing and Charles could see the empty interior through the cracks. The car wasn't there, so his father hadn't come home from work yet.

The shadowy forest circled the clearing. It was thick with ferns, underbrush, and rotting, moss-covered logs. A black buzzard soared out over the trees. It made two long lazy loops above the clearing, as it looked down at the boy and the dog. It slanted its wings and slipped sideways out of sight.

"Mama," Charles called again. His voice sounded tiny and unsure, lost in the trees and the empty spaces. "Mama, where are you?"

He trotted across the clearing and peered down the road. A squirrel sat in the middle, paws folded in front of its chest. It flicked its tail and scuttled off into the brush. Then the road was empty as far as Charles could see, down to the curve into

61

the deep shade of the Douglas firs.

He went back into the house. "Where is she, Blackie?" The dog looked at him with sorrowful brown eyes.

Charles still carried his 100% paper. He unfolded it and looked at the red figures again, then sighed and laid it on the table. Another piece of paper was already there, propped against a cup half-filled with cold coffee. Charles's heart began to pound as he looked at it. There was something ominous about that folded paper. It waited in the middle of the cluttered table like a coiled snake among the dishes. It had been there when he first came in and he hadn't even seen it. How long had it been there? For only a little while? Or all day long, since right after he left for school in the morning?

He took it in his hand. He unfolded it and looked at the black marks scratched above the pale blue lines. He knew what the letters were, but he did not know how they went together to make words and sentences. He sat in one of the hard chairs and held the paper.

His mother was always home. She didn't drive and almost never went anywhere, except with his father. Now and then, he went off for a few days to celebrate payday. Mama would walk down to ask Mrs. Graham, a neighbor, to take her to the store to buy food. But his father had been home this morning and Charles had seen Mrs. Graham in her yard when the school bus went by. Where would his mother go that she would leave this piece of paper in her place?

"Aaa ess aaa." His lips moved as he softly read the first three letters to himself. They were followed by a large crooked *I* and then a lot of unsteady little letters, so poorly printed that he could barely tell one from another. He moved his stubby finger slowly across the page, pausing on the letters he recognized and saying them out loud. "Cee. Tee. Em. Oh. Tee."

His name was in the middle of the page. His teacher had printed it for him on the first day of school. He knew the way the shapes went together after the big curved *C*. He sometimes made a little stick figure out of it and the letter *C* formed the head, mouth wide open, yelling things that no one ever heard.

He sat on the chair and looked at the paper for a long time. He heard the sound of the car as it came up the steep road. The engine labored and complained; various loose parts squeaked and rattled. Blackie raced out to bark in greeting and Charles went to the door. His father put the car into the shed and came toward the house, carrying his tin hat in his hand. His face was streaked with dirt and he looked tired.

Charles stepped aside as he entered. His father flopped on a chair and pushed the dishes aside with his arm. The coffee cup tipped over and brown liquid spilled onto the table.

"Charles, run down to the spring and get me a cold beer. Lucia," he yelled. "Lucia, where the hell are you?"

He frowned at his son. "Charlie, move your lazy little ass."

Charles looked at him mutely.

"Where's your mama? Hey, Lucia."

"I couldn't find her."

"What do you mean?"

"She ain't here. I found this on the table."

He handed the paper to his father and watched as he read it. The feeling of dread and fear that had been in the air of the cabin thickened and congealed in his stomach as he watched his father read. The lines in Asa's face hardened and deepened, all seeming to run downward like a wax mask melting in the heat.

"Goddamn her! Goddamn woman!" He crumpled the paper and threw it on the floor. He jumped to his feet, jarring the table. Charles's school paper fluttered down and settled near the letter. Asa savaged the note with his caulk boots. He ripped and pawed like an enraged bull. He shouted and swore as he gouged holes in the wooden floor. The spikes ripped up splinters and shredded both papers until nothing was left but scattered bits.

"She ain't coming back, Charles," he shouted at the little boy huddled by the door. "She didn't say where she was going, but she did say she ain't never coming back. Never. Goddamn it, get me a beer."

As Charles fled out the door, a white scrap with a red zero on it fluttered beneath his feet.

Nobody saw my 100% paper, he thought.

Juanita came back from the reservation. She cooked and took care of the cabin about as well as his mother had done, which didn't mean that she did a very good job, but only that his mother had done so little. They often went to school un-combed, unwashed, unmended. Sometimes the girl who sat behind Charles complained that he smelled bad and then the teacher suggested that he take a bath.

Bathing was not easy. Water had to be carried from the spring, heated on the woodstove, poured into the enamel basin, and smeared over his body with a washcloth. It was es-pecially unpleasant in winter. The cabin was never warm enough. Cold air whistled under the door and through the many cracks in the walls and windows. It was easier just to forget about washing until the teacher reminded him.

By the time she was thirteen years old, Juanita didn't mind taking baths, even in cold weather. She arranged the chairs near the stove, draped a blanket around them, and crouched down inside the little shelter with the washbasin and soap. She combed her shiny black hair and applied bright red Woolworth's lipstick. Sometimes she asked Charles, "How do I look?"

"Okay," he'd tell her. But the true answer, which he was too embarrassed to say, was "pretty."

The firewood shifted in the stove and fell against the side with a small thud. Charles jumped like a startled cat. Shit! He didn't want to think about Juanita. He hated it when she slipped into his mind.

The horses should be fed. He looked out the window before he opened the door. There was no one there. Of course there was no one there. As he hurried toward the shed, he couldn't keep from glancing into the shadows beneath the surrounding trees.

The three horses, in from the open range, waited for him. One nickered softly and Charles rubbed his nose. They were peaceful, not edgy as they would be if a stranger were near. A stranger . . . had it been a stranger? A faint cry came from the woods. Charles flinched and spun in his tracks.

Asshole! Asshole! Grow up. You're almost a man, not twelve years old anymore. That cry was a bird. It was a bird, you asshole.

The horses shifted nervously as they picked up his unease. The mare whinnied shrilly and backed away from him. She tossed her head. Her long black mane swirled around her neck.

"It's okay, Star. Take it easy, girl."

The need to calm the horses calmed him. He took a deep breath and let the sound of the rain, the gentle stirring of the trees, flow into him. After a moment, he opened the shed door. The horses stepped closer. Blackie rushed inside and sniffed eagerly around.

"No varmints today," Charles told him.

He gave each of the horses a small ration of oats. He fed them just enough to keep them coming in. Otherwise, they could wander for miles over the unfenced range and it might

65

take a long time to find them when he wanted them.

He carried two pails of water from the creek and put one on the stove to heat. The skillet sat at the back, the bottom covered with congealed bacon grease left from breakfast. Charles took dry bread crusts from an old loaf and wiped them around in the grease. He tossed in a cold potato, a few scraps of carrot, and dumped it into Blackie's dish outside by the door. The dog gobbled it down in a few bites. He'd nearly finished by the time Charles closed the door.

Blackie woofed a little later, not his warning bark, but a greeting sound. Charles heard the car coming up the hill. The water in the pail had warmed and he quickly swabbed off the dirty plates from breakfast. His father entered, still in his caulk boots. He hung his dripping tin hat on a nail and peeled off his rain gear.

"Hell of a day," he growled.

"No worse than usual." The memory of the way that Sherry had looked at him warmed Charles deep inside. She hadn't smiled. Emotion had been so thick in him that he couldn't have smiled if his life depended on it. Had she felt a little of that, too? Was that why she hadn't smiled in her usual friendly, meaningless way?

As much as he wanted it to be true, it wasn't likely. Sherry was the most popular girl in Whistler's Bend high school. She had dated Jim Parrish, the only son of the area's wealthiest rancher. Jim was still crazy about her, but she'd lost interest in him. She'd dated Wally Jenkins, a hotshot athlete, popular with everyone. She could have her pick, so why would she be interested in Charles?

"Hey!" His father's voice was rough. "Answer me when I talk to you."

"Sorry. What did you say?"

"Did you get the money from Dolan?"

"Yeah. He gave me a check."

He handed it to his father, who scowled at it suspiciously, then put it in his pocket. "I'm not sure woodcutting's worth what I get out of it."

Charles said, "I got a ride from Lee Jamison, Bob's brother. He asked me to go wild horse hunting with him."

"You better stay in school." His dad stretched gingerly. "I twisted my back today. Cook up that meat, Charles. I'm hungry."

After they'd eaten, Charles gathered dirty clothes from the corner of the bedroom where he'd thrown them on the floor. He poured warm water and soap into the washtub. He scrubbed and rinsed his clothes and hung them on hangers behind the stove to dry. It didn't matter that water dripped down onto the floorboards.

He heated more water, stripped and stood naked by the stove. As the chilly wind crawled up his legs and back, he scoured his brown muscular body, remembering how Juanita had done the same.

His father watched him. "You've been taking a lot of baths lately. You must have a girlfriend."

"Nope."

"Then you're wanting one. No other reason to freeze your butt off in this cold house."

Charles ignored his father's cynical smile. He thought about Sherry, who was easier to think about than anything else in his life. Her mother had brought her to Whistler's Bend five years ago. Mrs. Prentiss seemed like a town person and she'd made few friends in the community, only the Stonebrakers and the Parrishes. Rich people. She couldn't be bothered with anyone else.

Charles went to bed early and stared up into the darkness as rain splashed onto the roof. His stomach fluttered when he thought of the way Sherry had looked at him, a way no girl had looked at him before. And she spoke to him, too. They'd talked more in the last few days than they had in all the previous years.

When the school bell rang for lunch the next day, Friday, Charles dawdled at his desk as Sherry piled her books neatly one on the other. Casually he stood up just as she did and followed her down the aisle. He tried to think of something to say, something easy and friendly, but his mind remained a blank. All he could think of was how pale and pretty her hair looked against her navy blue sweater.

She turned to him. "I have a terrible time in history. I never can remember all those dates."

"Neither can I."

"I try to memorize them just until the tests are over. I don't suppose anyone but Mr. Konschak will ever ask me how long the Roman Empire lasted."

"Who cares, anyway? It was so long ago."

She leaned against the wall and looked at him with her head tilted to one side. She was so cool and sweet, like vanilla ice cream with butterscotch sauce. His whole body ached with wanting to touch her, yet he couldn't bring himself to do it. The inches between them were as difficult to cross as a thousand miles.

"Where did you get that scar?" The tip of her finger almost touched the back of his hand, sending shock waves tingling all through his body.

He rubbed the scar with his other palm. "My old man did it."

"How?"

"He rapped me a good one with a kitchen knife."

"That's terrible!"

"He didn't mean to. He was just mad. He was sorry later." Charles left out the fact that his father had been drunk. He regretted that he'd said anything. He didn't want Sherry feeling sorry for him.

Maybe Sherry sensed his feelings, because she said, "I'm starving. Are you going to eat in the cafeteria?"

"Naw. I hardly ever eat lunch."

"Don't you get hungry?"

He shook his head. He didn't have money enough to buy lunch at school and it seemed too much trouble to fix a sandwich in the mornings.

After a moment, she asked, "Will you be at the game tonight?"

"Yeah." Even as he answered, he wondered how he'd manage a ride.

"Well, I'll see you there."

He watched her walk away, narrow shoulders, rounded hips under the navy pleated skirt, slim legs. God, she looked so good. And she acted as if she liked him, really liked him. He ran down the stairs, grinning to himself.

Wally Jenkins, the school's star athlete, and one of Sherry's former boyfriends, lived up the Little Nezzac just beyond where the shortcut left the road. He and Charles were friendly without being real friends. Charles hated to ask favors, but he was determined to find a way to the game. Asa had always refused to let him use the car, unless he wanted Charles to run errands for him.

Wally readily agreed to pick him up if he'd walk down to the road. Then he eyed Charles speculatively. "You don't come to many games. My guess is you're more interested in a certain cheerleader than basketball."

"Maybe."

"You're lucky if Sherry likes you, but don't expect it to

last more than a few weeks. It never does."

Charles shrugged, jarred by the suggestion that he was only another in a succession of unimportant boys.

Wally went on, "She's good-looking, no doubt of that. Jim Parrish would give his left nut to get her back. You don't seem her type, if you don't mind my saying so. What did you do to get her interested?"

Wally grinned when Charles didn't answer. "Don't be bashful. Hell, half the guys in Whistler's Bend have got a crush on Sherry."

Charles got away from Wally as soon as he could. Even though he didn't want to talk about it, he wondered himself why she'd begun to pay attention to him, since he wasn't rich or an athlete or even smart in school. All he'd done was look at her with longing in his eyes and one day, instead of turning away, she'd looked back. Now a force as strong as gravity kept pulling them together, so that they always seemed to be in the same place at the same time.

When the boys arrived at the gym in the evening, Wally went to the locker room to suit up. Charles saw Sherry with the other cheerleaders in front of the stands. They wore dark green pleated skirts, yellow letter sweaters, and bobby socks. Just looking at her was a pleasure so acute it hurt.

When she saw him, she hurried over. "Hi, Charles. I can't talk much because Mother is here." She sounded breathless. "When I asked if you could come tonight, I didn't expect her. She was sick. But she feels better now."

If Charles was uncertain about what to say, he usually didn't say anything.

Sherry went on. "I'll try to come outside at halftime. Wait for me at the back corner of the gym by the fence."

She hurried to rejoin the other cheerleaders. Charles searched the bleachers with his eyes, row by row, until he saw

70

Mrs. Prentiss. She sat up straight, head and back erect, feet crossed at the ankles, hands neatly folded on her lap. Sherry resembled her mother, but Lila's face was sharp and cold, with a discontented droop to her mouth. It seemed that she looked at Charles. His impulse was to stare back defiantly, to send her a challenge, but why aggravate Sherry's mother? He forced his eyes to drift on by.

He watched the skinny, long-legged boys on the team warm up. Their feet thudded on the polished wooden floor. Wally ran with them, shorter and heavier, but quick. His blocky body already glistened with sweat.

Charles found a seat. Several times during the game, he glanced at Mrs. Prentiss who sat above him and toward the center. Her eyes were always on Sherry as she jumped and pranced back and forth in front of the crowd. A few minutes before the half, Charles slipped from his seat and out the door.

The chill of the night touched him. He was glad he'd worn the heavy old black and white plaid shirt that belonged to his father. A dwarf moon the size of a dime hung over the roof of the gym. One gray tattered cloud swirled out, like a frazzled scarf trailing in the wind. However much the wind gusted in space, the air below was still.

Behind the walls of the gym, the crowd roared and bellowed with the voice of a single giant animal as they cheered the last game of the tournament. The sound swelled and subsided according to the rhythms of play. He heard the referee's whistle, followed by the shaking and thumping of many feet as the half ended.

As he turned the corner by the gym, two small boys in silhouette, laughing giddily, pounded toward him. He stepped out of the way and they ran past him, on down the dark corridor between the gym wall and the high wire fence that

71

marked the boundaries of school property. Soon Sherry came around the corner, another silhouette, identified by bright hair illuminated from the lights behind her.

"Charles?" She sounded uncertain.

"I'm here." He took her arm and guided her into the shadows.

"I can only stay a few minutes."

"Because of your mom?"

"Yes."

"Why is she so strict?"

"She doesn't want me to make the same mistake she did."

"What was that?"

"She married a man who never made any money, who couldn't provide for his family the way a man should."

He heard the flavor of recitation in her voice, as she mouthed words someone else had put there.

He asked, "Where is your dad?"

"He's dead." After a moment, she moved uneasily. "Well, my mother considers him dead." Her voice was defensive.

"What difference does it make? He's gone, one way or another." The darkness inspired intimacy. "My mother went away, too."

"I know. Some of the kids told me a long time ago."

Her face was pale and soft in the dim light, her eyes shadowy. The moon outlined her hair . His hand went out of its own volition and his fingers slid into the silky mass.

"You've got pretty hair." His voice sounded as if it belonged to someone else.

She leaned closer. A hollow twisting sensation, like the beginnings of pain, moved through his guts. His chest, his stomach, his heart, were filled with something like fear and yet it felt so good at the same time, so awful and so incredibly delicious.

His fingers drifted from her hair down to her cheek. His hand and arm began to tremble. He wondered if she could feel it. He willed it to stop, but the shaking went on, a small shivering like the leaves of an aspen in an almost imperceptible movement of air. Sherry looked at him with such soft eyes. He'd never seen a girl with that expression before, everything soft as though she were melting inside, eyes, hair, skin, mouth, all melting.

God, she was sweet; marshmallows and ice cream and spun sugar from a summer carnival. He put one arm around her shoulder and the other slipped over her ribs. He felt the neatly aligned bones under her sweater, under her skin. She lifted her face. He had never kissed a girl. He put his mouth gently, tentatively, on hers. A great surge poured through him. His arms tightened convulsively and his mouth clamped down. Sherry's lips opened and she made a small sound.

"I'm sorry." Charles at once relaxed his grip. He held her loosely, but he surged with tension and unreleased power—all of his body, his legs, his arms. He felt it vibrate and shake him, demanding release, but he didn't want Sherry to know. She might be frightened or disgusted and not like him anymore.

He kissed her again, experimenting a little, moving his mouth, tasting hers. All of her body was against all of his. He felt the soft mounds of her breasts, her stomach, her pelvis pressing against the swelling in his jeans.

Oh, God, she'll know I've got a hard-on.

He stepped back. "You're too pretty," he said hoarsely. "I'm afraid I'll scare you."

"I have to go in, anyway. I don't want Mother to wonder where I am. I don't want to lie to her."

As she turned, he took her hand. "Sherry, you do like me, don't you?"

Her fingers moved lightly down his face, traced his high curved cheekbone and moved across his lower lip. "Yes, Charles. I do like you."

On Monday afternoon, going home from school, Charles slumped on the bus with his face toward the window. The laughter and strident voices of the other passengers came as distantly to him as the sound of wind in the trees. He smiled as he remembered his arrival at school that morning. Sherry had been talking to another girl in the hallway, but her eyes searched the crowd of incoming students. As soon as she saw Charles, she came to meet him. He'd been dizzy with delight.

On Saturday morning, while his father slept, Charles had taken a few dollars from his pocket. He'd never pilfered from Asa, but he needed money to eat in the school cafeteria with Sherry. He'd been aware of the looks the other students gave them—some surprised and disbelieving. He understood that and yet it felt so right to be with her. For all their apparent differences, they meshed together like two cogs turning in opposite directions, perfectly aligned with one another.

The bus slowed and moved toward the center of the road. Charles saw a pickup parked along the side. A woman in a battered hat and leather jacket crouched beside one of the wheels.

Charles hurried to the front of the bus. "Let me off at the next turnout, Eddie. It looks like Mrs. Domingo's got a flat tire."

"I didn't know you were a Boy Scout."

The driver pulled over and opened the door. Charles trotted back toward Mrs. Domingo, who stood scowling as she watched him come.

"I can't get the damn lug nuts off. They're stuck on tighter than ticks."

"Let me try." Charles bore down on the wrench. The nut refused to yield. He gritted his teeth and applied more pressure. Slowly the nut gave a little and then a little more. Mrs. Domingo grunted with approval. In a little while, they rattled along the road on the spare.

"That was neighborly of you to stop," she said. "I baked an apple pie this morning. When your dad comes home from work, how about the two of you coming over for supper?"

"I don't think he'll be home. Friday was payday and he hasn't come home yet. Sometimes it takes him a few days to find his way back."

"Then we'll go to my place right now, if you've got nothing else to do."

Charles noticed that her house wasn't any cleaner than his own. Stacked newspapers, a tangle of string, a pair of pliers, and cotton work gloves cluttered the kitchen table. A pair of muddy boots lay underneath, along with chunks of dried mud crumbled on the floor beside them. Dogs circled underfoot and the house smelled of them. Matted tufts of hair, twigs and burrs lay where the animals had pulled them out of their coats and dropped them on the floor.

Mrs. Domingo swept everything off the table and piled it on a chair. "You like chicken-fried steak?"

"Sounds good." His mouth watered at the thought. Anything would be better than the boiled beans, with or without meat, that were a staple of his diet.

"Give me a hand with the chores and I'll get cookin' faster."

Charles followed her to the barn and they tended the animals. Later he sat at the table, replete with the taste of apple pie still sweet in his mouth. One of the dogs sprawled by his foot and he felt its warmth against his ankle. A battery radio played softly in the background. The kerosene lamp cast a yellow glow, just the way he'd imagined it. He'd got his apple pie, and the steak, pounded thin and tender, floured and pan-fried, accompanied with creamy mashed potatoes, was maybe even better than chicken.

"That sure was good," he said contentedly.

Mrs. Domingo smiled. "Johnny, my husband, he always liked fruit pie. Peach was his favorite, but he liked apple, too. And cherry."

She sighed and looked toward the shadows in the corner of the room. Charles knew she wasn't seeing anything there, but just remembering. Her face was softened by the lamp-light, the harsh weathered lines blurred and smoothed out.

She'd been an old woman as long as he'd known her, which was his entire life. It seemed strange to think that she'd been in love, years ago. Maybe she'd felt some of the same emotions that he felt now.

A woman who'd lived so long, who ran her ranch without help from anyone, must understand a lot. Charles felt an urge to talk about Sherry. But Mrs. Domingo might think him foolish, mooning over a girl. She'd probably forgotten all about things like that. She was a no-nonsense kind of woman and he didn't want her to laugh at him.

He shifted his feet. She switched her eyes to him, blank for a moment, as though she wasn't quite sure who he was. Then they focused and she stood up briskly.

"Here I sit in a trance while the dishes are getting sticky. Do you want to wash or dry?"

"I'll dry," Charles said. "And then I should head home. I get up early for school."

Charles awoke suddenly in the darkness. Blackie barked outside the cabin. Charles listened as the dog woofed again. He didn't sound excited—probably a raccoon or a bobcat had come too close to the house. Or it might be a cougar prowling off in the woods. At any rate, Blackie wasn't too worked up, not the way he'd been the night that Juanita . . .

It hurt to think of her, but she kept coming into his head. He knew why. It had happened five years ago tonight. Maybe he should allow himself to remember. After all, she was his sister. It wasn't her fault that she was pretty. Maybe it wasn't even her choice to be wild and hungry. Sometimes Charles felt hungry, too, for all the experiences that life could offer. Maybe Juanita would have been a little less wild if their mother had stayed with them.

When she was fourteen, a great number of cars began the steep climb to the cabin. They were rarely boys she knew in high school, but young men of eighteen or nineteen, already out of school and at work in the woods or mills.

Asa stomped around the cabin. He yelled and knocked over chairs. "You're like a bitch in heat. Good thing your mother's not here to see the kind of girl you've become."

Sometimes he rushed at the cars, carrying a rifle, and then no young men came for awhile. Juanita didn't sulk or argue with him. If she wanted to go someplace, she simply walked down to the main road. She flagged a logging truck and the driver gave her a ride to town. Occasionally her father slapped her around when she came home, but it didn't stop her from going again.

When she was sixteen, she began to date someone special. The cars stopped coming, but she still went out. She walked down the road to meet him.

Charles could tell that he excited her, whoever he was. Juanita bathed before every date. She brushed her dark hair until it was glossy. When she thought Charles wasn't looking, she pouted her lips and made sexy faces at herself in the mirror.

"Who are you going out with?" he asked.

Her eyes sparkled. "You'd be surprised if I told you. He's a man, not one of those kids I used to date."

"Tell me."

"Not yet. I can't talk about him yet. But he's different from anybody else."

When Charles got up one Sunday morning, Juanita was already at the table, slumped over a cup of coffee.

Charles poured half a cup for himself and added enough milk to fill it. "You're up early for as late as you got in last night." Then he saw her face. "Jeez, what happened?"

She tried to cover the huge bruise on her cheek, the cut and swollen lip. "It was so stupid. I was walking fast. I opened a door and it stuck. I walked right into it. I know I look like hell."

"You sure do," Charles agreed.

She told Asa the same story. About this time, he seemed to give up on his daughter. He ceased to question her or pay any attention to her activities. He was involved with a woman and stayed weekends with her in Woodbridge. Charles and Juanita were left alone most of the time.

As she dressed one morning, Charles saw big ugly bruises on her back and upper arms and what looked like a bite mark on one shoulder.

"You didn't bump into a door this time," Charles said. "You better stop seeing him."

"He's so nice afterward. And look at this." She reached inside her blouse and pulled out a chain with a heart pendant attached. "It's solid gold. So is the locket."

"So what? It's not worth getting beat up."

"He's going to take me on a trip. Maybe San Francisco. He travels a lot. He's real sophisticated."

The next time she hobbled stiffly around the house, even

more slowly and carefully than Grandmother moved when her arthritis was especially bad.

"You're crazy to put up with this. Why do you do it?"

"I'm not going to, not anymore. I told him that. He thinks I should like the rough stuff, but I don't. If he tries it again, he might be surprised at how tough I can be. I've got this." She showed Charles a small knife, then tucked it into her purse. Her eyes glittered confidently. She seemed almost eager for the challenge.

Charles knew that she was tough. He'd fought with her several times. He had a scar on the side of his head, covered by hair, where she'd bashed him with a stick of firewood.

She went out on Saturday night, sashaying down the hill in her tight black skirt and red sweater. Charles fed the horses and threw sticks for Blackie until it was dark. He opened a can of soup for supper. The wind raced through the tops of the trees. Stars faded as the moon came up. He lay on his pallet in the loft, but he couldn't sleep. A fir cone thumped on the roof and then rattled down the steep pitch.

He must have dozed, because he awoke with a violent twitch. His eyes flew open. He heard Blackie's fierce barking. Juanita's pallet was still empty. Charles crawled to the edge of the loft and looked over. Bright moonlight flooded through the uncurtained window into the room below. Asa's bed was also empty. Blackie barked without pause. Charles climbed down the ladder and thumped on the windowpane.

"Shut up, Blackie."

Something screamed out in the darkness. A second later, Blackie passed the window, running fast. He flew down the road.

"You fool dog," Charles yelled. "That cougar will kill you."

He'd heard cougars scream before. They sounded just like

79

a woman. He snatched the .30-06 Winchester from where it hung on the wall. He rushed outside and down the hill.

He heard Blackie's frenzied barking. And screams. Lots of screaming. Terror iced his blood. There were words mixed in the screams. He couldn't quite understand them, but there was no doubt that there were words half-strangled in the shrill, throat-shredding cries.

The screaming stopped. Suddenly. Blackie's barking went on and on. Then he yelped—a sharp, shocked sound. He yelped again like a hurt puppy. Then silence overwhelmed the night. The abrupt stillness was eerie, unsettling.

Charles slowed. He scurried from the middle of the road and edged into the deep shadows beneath the trees. If he couldn't see whatever was out there, he didn't want it to see him. He was a target in the middle of the road in the bright moonlight. He slipped through the trees as silently as any other forest creature.

Something moved out in the road. It was Blackie, hobbling painfully toward home. He panted and whined softly. He smelled or sensed Charles and crept to him on his belly, ashamed that he'd been hurt. He whimpered and licked Charles's hand.

"Shh. Be quiet," Charles whispered. Something came up the hill toward them, something big and heavy. Maybe it tried to be quiet, but it did not belong in the forest. Twigs cracked, bushes rustled. And it breathed—noisy, uneven, gasping.

Charles glimpsed movement on the hill below. He froze. There was a shadow under the trees. It was big, as big as a bear. He watched it loom closer. Blackie whined. The shadow paused.

Shit! The dog would give away his position. Charles had the impression of a head that swung toward him, of eyes like searchlights. Blackie trembled against Charles's leg and whimpered softly. Charles levered a round into the chamber. The loud, metallic snap-crack was unmistakable to anyone who knew anything about firearms.

Charles raised the rifle and pointed it at the center of the shadow. He had hunted with his father since he was nine years old. He'd shot his first deer last year when he was eleven. There were certain rules that Asa had drummed into his head. The rules were as much a part of Charles as his ability to ride a horse, to tell a cougar track from that of a dog, to read a newspaper.

"Don't shoot at anything you can't see clear. That shape in the brush might be the neighbor's cow. It might be the neighbor. It might be me. If you can't see it plain, don't shoot it."

The rifle barrel, centered on the target, did not waver. The breathing from down the hill had stopped. Did he also hold his breath to listen? All at once, the shadow shifted. It slipped sideways behind a tree. As it went, the moonlight picked up something bright in the middle of the shadow, something that glinted back the light of the moon.

Charles heard, but did not see, the shadow retreat down the hill. He listened and kept the rifle ready. After a few moments, a car motor started up and then receded softly into the night. Blackie ceased trembling. He whined and looked at the boy. Charles lowered the gun, but he waited at least five more minutes. Sometime during the wait, Blackie sighed heavily and lay down.

At last Charles crept on down the hill, hugging the shadows banked along the edge of the road. Blackie limped ahead and then broke into a shuffling, crab-wise trot. He turned into the brush. The dog made strange, soft, crying sounds, almost human.

Charles followed. The dog stood over something on the

ground. He snuffled at it, cried again, and looked toward Charles. The boy knew what he would find, even before he saw the inky hair spilled across the moonlit forest floor.

He knelt beside her. "Nita," he whispered."Juanita . . ."

He slid his hand over her shoulder, her neck. She felt warm. He couldn't find a pulse, but something sticky clung to his fingertips. Charles knew. He'd known the instant the screams stopped, so abruptly, so finally.

Blackie licked his face. Charles slumped on the ground beside his sister. He leaned back against a tree and held the cocked rifle across his knees. Blackie settled beside him. Charles put his hand on the dog and plainly felt his broken ribs beneath the skin. The dog dozed. Charles watched the moon creep across the sky and vanish.

As soon as it was light, he left Blackie to guard his sister. He walked to the road and flagged down the first vehicle that passed, a crummy full of Carnes and Baylor loggers headed upriver.

The sheriff said that Juanita had been beaten, strangled, and ultimately her neck was broken. "She put up a hell of a fight."

"She would. She was tough," Charles said.

"I wonder what caused that?" He pointed at the bloody groove cut into one side of her neck.

"I know what it was," Charles said.

The sheriff waited.

"He gave her a necklace, a gold heart on a chain. He ripped it off her. He took it back."

In the five years since Juanita's death, no substantial leads were found. Her killer was still unknown.

Chapter 4

CHARLOTTE

Tuesday to Wednesday morning

Charlotte Domingo drove her aged pickup carefully along the road. Fence posts and wire loaded the back end. The body squeaked and rattled, but the motor purred like a barn cat with its stomach full of mouse and warm milk. She approached the Whistler's Bend community school just at noon. Students thronged the sunny yard.

Her heart filled with an old familiar sadness as she slowed to look at them. Even after all these years, she still ached inside when she thought of Alejandro, her son, her only child. He'd died in a fall from the haymow when he was twelve years old. If he had lived—if Johnny had lived—how different her life would have been.

There was Charles Balleau by the fence. She slowed a little more. She'd enjoyed having him for supper last night. He didn't look like Johnny, except for the Indian dark hair and skin, yet there was something about Charles that reminded her of her husband.

She tooted the horn, but Charles didn't look up. His eyes were fixed on the girl with him, who gazed back intently with her head tilted to one side and her blonde hair bright in the sunlight. Charlotte recognized her—the Prentiss girl,

83

daughter of that pickle-faced woman who worked in the bank in Woodbridge. Her mother had given her some fancy name that wasn't a real name at all, something fluffy-sounding, like Candy or Fifi. She didn't seem like Charles's kind of girl, too soft and glossy for someone as tough and earthy as he. But what did Charlotte know about the girl or who Charles would find attractive?

He looked so young standing in the school yard, but he was seventeen, a year younger than she had been when she became engaged to Howard Pope. Being young didn't mean that you couldn't be in love. Being young meant that you felt it was the only time in your life that you would ever love anyone as much. And sometimes it was the only time.

The pickup had lugged down. The motor struggled and bucked. She shoved in the clutch, shifted, and picked up speed. The school and the young faces reminded her of her own youth and of scenes and people from long ago.

Her parents had died the year that she turned thirteen. Her father, thin-faced, red-haired and freckled, returned in memory and looked at her in his sober way. She recalled her mother, before she got the fever. Mama wore a flour-sack apron as she tended the red rose bush that grew by the sagging back porch. Miss Edgerton also came to mind, the fat schoolteacher who'd smacked Charlotte's hands with a ruler for sassing her. And Sadie, who'd been her best friend, returned as if she'd seen her only yesterday. They'd traded lunches and giggled together, sharing what small secrets they had. Sadie had wanted to grow up quickly so that she could marry Howard Pope and have five children. Instead she'd got pneumonia and died at the age of sixteen. Howard had come courting Charlotte instead and they'd been engaged for almost a year . . . that last year before Johnny.

In the back of her mind stood Howard's mother, Hannah,

of the sad eyes and generous heart. Charlotte's lips moved in the small prayer that always followed thoughts of the woman who'd nearly become her mother-in-law.

A weathered garage loomed up through the windshield. Charlotte stepped on the brake and looked around in surprise. She was home. It seemed only a minute ago that she'd passed the school. Fifteen curving miles had slid under the wheels and she hadn't even noticed their passage.

"Good thing you know the way," she said out loud to the pickup.

Her pack of reddish hounds surged around the truck. She opened the door and stepped into the middle of them, kneeing those that crowded too close.

"Get out of my way, you mutts. Move back, damn it."

She should get rid of some of them. But sometimes the females had puppies before she got them spayed. They were so cute and lovable when they were little. She managed to give some away, but no one wanted them after they grew up. She knew people who drowned or shot unwanted puppies. Even worse, some took them to an isolated spot and dumped them. The puppies wandered, bewildered, until they died slowly of starvation and thirst. She could never do that.

She pushed her way through the dogs and opened the tailgate. She pulled on heavy canvas gloves and tugged at the wire. She could use help unloading, but as in so many other things, she'd have to manage by herself. Her back hurt clear through to her chest, but she ignored it and hauled out a post. The chores on the ranch never ended. There was the fence to mend, the ponies to feed, the roof on the barn leaked again. God, it was tough to live alone.

If she had a grandson like Charles . . . he was a good boy, a good neighbor, even if he did have a streak of wildness in him. She felt it humming through him like electricity, ready to come crackling and flashing into life under the right circumstances. She'd lived with a man like that and she knew.

She leaned on the pickup. Her vision blurred and slipped out of focus. She looked beyond the pasture where the ponies grazed, beyond the circling trees and the hills, beyond the years, to Johnny. He was always there, dark and shining, beyond her reach and yet so near, so near.

Minutes passed. The dogs settled around her feet. A small brown sparrow lit on a fence post and groomed its feathers. Charlotte sighed, straightened up, and finished unloading. As much as her back hurt already, she'd surely be stiff tomorrow. She closed the tailgate and went to the house. The dogs stirred and followed her. Some of them flopped on the porch. Others came inside, squeezing through the door before it closed. They collapsed upon the floor as though they had walked miles instead of only a few yards.

She built the fire, moved the coffeepot to the front of the stove and sat down at the kitchen table to record her purchases in the account book. It was good that spring was here and new grass coming in. The hay was almost gone. She could turn the ponies into the south pasture a little early. She'd run short of cash when Dolly got the strangles—equine distemper, Dr. Miller called it. She'd had to have him come out from town, but he'd saved the mare and the unborn colt, too, so it had been worth the expense.

Her dividend check would be in at the end of the month. If it weren't for those checks coming regularly, she couldn't keep the place. She and Johnny had worked hard to save money to buy the ranch. But marginal land wasn't profitable unless there was enough to carry a good-sized herd. There wasn't much money in raising ponies, anyway. They ate almost more than they brought when they were sold. But Johnny had loved horses and she couldn't give them up.

Charlotte did not raise Shetlands. She believed them too often stubborn, bad-tempered, and unsuitable for young children. Her ponies were full-sized horses, but small. They were usually no more than fourteen hands high and weighed 800 to 850 pounds. They were fast, responsive, and made good cow ponies as well as children's mounts.

She'd never told Johnny about her investment in stocks. It was the only thing she'd kept from him, but it was her own money. He didn't think a married woman should work off their own place, but their neighbor, Mr. Greeley, needed help after his wife died and he got so stove-up with rheumatism. He'd lived right across the field from them. It had been easy to walk over and do his chores. He had been a clean and orderly old man, except he would not wear his teeth. He kept them in a Mason jar in the kitchen. He changed the water every day and put them in before he went to town or if he expected special company like his daughter. But his teeth were usually in the jar, not in his mouth.

Charlotte had cleaned his house, which was never really dirty, did his laundry, and took a generous plate over to him when she cooked the evening meal. He paid her more than it was worth, but he insisted. He also insisted that she invest part of her earnings every month in the same companies in which he had his own small investments. Johnny wouldn't have understood that. He understood horses and land, but wouldn't have accepted the idea that little pieces of paper could be worth more than either one. But he never asked what she did with her earnings; they belonged to her to use as she pleased. Those small bits, five dollars, ten dollars, now and then twenty, added up over the years.

Mr. Greeley was a wise man, a good neighbor and friend. It was a real loss when he'd died near Christmastime while visiting his daughter in Grants Pass. She'd kept the property;

it was only three acres and maybe she thought she'd retire there someday. But she'd passed on, too, and her daughter, Mr. Greeley's granddaughter, also left the land neglected. The empty house had burned and brush grew over the foundations, so that a stranger passing by would never know a house had once been there.

Well, people died all the time. Like flowers, they grew up and bloomed for their brief time in the sun. Young people thought that eighty years was a long time, but it passed quickly, much too soon.

Charlotte idly looked at the advertisements in the newspaper. Bacon was fifty-five cents a pound, coffee seventy-nine cents. Soon it would be too expensive to drink. Eggs were forty-three cents a dozen, but she had her own chickens and didn't need to buy them.

Costs kept going up. Grain for the ponies, dog food, repairs on the house and ranch buildings. The older she got, the more often she had to hire someone else to do work she had once done herself. She didn't like to think about the future, except in specifics of how much grain and hay to buy, how many mares to breed, how many acres of alfalfa to plant. You couldn't count on tomorrows, anyway. They were slippery, always sliding around, turning out differently than you expected. Tomorrow was a day you couldn't depend on, not at all.

She glanced at the alarm clock ticking away on the sideboard shelf. It was five o'clock. Where had the afternoon gone? Time had a habit of getting away from her lately. Whole hours slid by during what she thought was only a moment's inattention.

She rose stiffly to her feet, startling the chicken that sat comfortably on the chair next to her. She opened the door and shooed it out. A dog went out and two other dogs slipped in to replace it. She fixed supper, sliced up cold boiled potatoes left from the night before and fried them in the skillet with chopped ham. She opened a jar of peaches, one of the few still left from last summer.

She bit into a peach and summer ran down inside her. Johnny had a sweet tooth and she baked often when he was alive. She could see him as he inhaled the sugary aroma of fruit and crust, smiling at her. She smiled back as she watched his hands cut the pie. Some men were clumsy and awkward with things around the house. They could split a fence post or throw a bale of hay on the back of a wagon, plunge with gusto into anything that took energy or brute strength, but they were rough and uncoordinated when it came to small movements. Johnny had remarkable grace, an elegance of movement that turned the simplest act into a ballet. Oh, God, he had been so beautiful.

She clashed dishes together, piled them into the dish-pan, slopped a little water over the top, and went to milk the cow, feed the horses, dogs, cats, chickens, pigs. It was easier not to think while she moved around. She murmured to the animals and they murmured back, a contented, affectionate chorus of grunts, clucks, meows, and whinnies.

Charlotte heard the chickens squawk while she was in the barn. She peered out. Something bothered them, but none of the dogs barked. She looked up and saw the pair of hawks against the evening sky. They'd taken one of the pullets a few days ago. She hurried to the house and took the .22 out of the coat closet.

The hawks sailed above her, looking things over. Their wings didn't seem to move. She squinted along the rifle barrel, got one of them in the sights, tracked for an instant, and squeezed the trigger. The rifle cracked. At the last second, just before she pulled the trigger, she let the barrel waver to one side.

She fired twice more, to make sure they were scared enough. The hawks streaked toward the trees high on the hill above the house. Charlotte felt a small tremor in her hands as she lowered the gun. She loathed that sound, the crack of a rifle. She should be used to it, considering that she'd heard dozens of guns fired since that one terrible shot.

But she never got used to it. Every one seemed to go right through her center, right to the heart of her where it echoed and echoed inside her soul. She would hear the sound of that one shot for as long as she lived, whenever others awoke its reverberation.

Later she went to bed in the cluttered room off the kitchen. It was really too small to be a bedroom. She and Johnny had used it for storage, but she couldn't sleep alone upstairs in the double bed they had shared. She slid beneath the covers. They felt cold and damp. The room never warmed up until summer, even though she left the door open into the heated kitchen. She pulled the frayed nine-patch quilt around her shoulders. She arranged herself so that she could see the rocking chair by the window.

It was the nicest thing Charlotte had ever owned. She remembered the day Johnny had given it to her. He'd carried it through the door, smiling in a shy, pleased way. "This is for our child," he'd said. "Babies should be rocked to sleep."

"But I'm not pregnant yet."

"It is my hope and my prayer that you will be soon. That we will rock our child in this chair."

It was golden oak with a single rose carved in the back. She had rocked their baby in it, but all the love in the world hadn't kept him safe for long. Or Johnny, either. Charlotte thought that she was a person for whom nothing was destined to last for long, except her life. She just kept on living, like a weed tenaciously sprouting beside the road, surviving dust, drought and neglect, while the beautiful flowers withered and died before their time.

The night was dark and the window only a little paler than the dark walls around it. As her eyes adjusted, she saw the dim oblong of the glass and . . . yes, he was there. Part of and yet separate from the flat shadows of the wall was the definite outline of a man in the rocking chair. She saw the dim silhouette of his head turned toward the bed, the line of his shoulder, and his arm that rested on the arm of the chair.

She lay quietly, careful not to look too intently. If she got up to investigate as she had done long years ago in the early days of her loss, trembling with eagerness and disbelief, he went away. He simply faded and she was left in an agony of loneliness. She had learned to keep her distance and then, sometimes, he stayed until morning.

The chair began rocking gently. It squeaked on the backward movement and, in counterpoint, she heard a delicate clinking, the almost inaudible metallic jingling of a spur. Johnny had come back again.

And with him came memory of the way it had been, so many years ago. Or was it just yesterday? It was difficult to remember, sometimes, how much time had passed. But it was easy to remember the way it had been.

Her name was Charlotte Blakely then and she lived on one of the big ranches east of the Cascade Mountains. William Mosher had a distant family connection with Charlotte's father and he had taken her in after the fever killed both her parents. She scrubbed floors, carried water, tended the three children, and helped with the cooking.

She became engaged to Howard Pope, who had been so admired by her friend, Sadie, before her early death. His family lived in a big house on the banks of the river. Cattle and horses grazed in the surrounding meadows. Roses, iris, and sweet honeysuckle grew by the long shaded porch. Soon Charlotte would enter that house and another girl would scrub the floors for her.

The mirrors told her why. Her long thick hair was the color of pale copper. Fine skin, dusted with a faint powdering of golden freckles, stretched smoothly over prominent facial bones. She saw the curves of her body, full and strong. She didn't look pretty to herself, as little Sadie had, but rather unusual. And enough heads turned to convince Charlotte that it wasn't a bad way to look.

William Mosher was interested in horse breeding and prided himself on his stock. He went on an extensive trip once a year to look for new blood.

"He'll be back today." Elsie, his wife, sounded confident. "He said this week sometime. And I feel it in my bones. It'll be today."

Charlotte smiled. Elsie felt a lot things in her bones. Sometimes they happened; sometimes they didn't.

"We'd better fry a chicken, just in case he gets here for noon dinner. I'll kill it as soon as I finish this sleeve." Elsie sat at the sewing machine, stitching a shirt for her son. Her foot rocked rhythmically up and down on the treadle as her fingers guided the fabric under the needle.

Charlotte went to the back porch. It wasn't right that Elsie always had to kill the chickens just because Charlotte was squeamish. She was eighteen years old, soon to be married, and it was time she stopped being so silly.

She took the hatchet and marched resolutely to the chicken pen. She lay the hatchet on the chopping block, careful not to look at the stained, axe-scarred surface. She cornered a young rooster and grabbed him by one leg. He squawked and flapped wildly. She scrabbled for the other leg and managed to get a grip on it.

When he was arranged with both legs in one hand, she carried him out of the pen. His beak hung open and the eye that she could see rolled fearfully. He panted like a dog on a hot day.

She grabbed the hatchet and tried to place the rooster's head on the block. His wings beat against her arm and his legs jerked in her grip. She lifted the hatchet. One round wild eye stared at her from the upward side of his head. She gagged. The hatchet dropped from her fingers. The rooster beat free and dashed off, wings outspread, leaning forward as though he fled into a wind.

Someone laughed. Howard stood between her and the house. He threw back his head and laughed harder when he saw her expression.

"Charlotte, you're such a tender-hearted girl."

He swooped after the rooster, covering the distance in a few long strides. He cornered him against the wire pen and snagged him quickly with one big hand. The rooster squawked and flailed. Howard strode to the chopping block and slammed the chicken's head down. He seized the hatchet. It rose and fell with a solid thunk.

The head dropped to the ground, the eye still round and scared, still rolling. The rooster's body flopped off the other side of the freshly bloodied block. It pushed up onto its legs. The breast and bloody neck rested on the ground. The wings flapped; the legs churned. The headless rooster scooted through the dirt, first one way, then another.

Charlotte covered her eyes. She swallowed quickly, once, twice, forcing back the fluid that rose into her throat.

She heard the quick thump of Howard's boots. She opened her eyes. He came toward her, one hand outstretched, the bloody chicken head held in his fingers. His blue eyes glittered with laughter. "It's time you were baptized, honey."

Charlotte screamed and struck blindly at him. Her hand hit his arm. She struck again, this time at air. She ran toward the house. She tripped on her long skirt and nearly fell as she struggled up the porch steps. She heard Howard behind her, still laughing, getting closer. She screamed again.

The door opened and Elsie stepped out. She thrust Charlotte behind her. "Howard, what are you doing?"

"Just a little baptism ceremony."

"You stay away from her. Why are you so cruel? Why are men such bullies?" She encircled Charlotte in her arms, pulled her close. "You take that chicken head out to the trash where it belongs."

"It's first blood, Elsie. None of us like it. I was only ten years old when my daddy dipped my hand in antelope blood . . ."

"I don't care what your mean old daddy did. You leave Charlotte alone. She can't help it that she's sickened by the sight of blood."

"I don't want to make her sick." Howard wasn't laughing anymore. "But she's got to learn to kill a chicken. How can she be a ranch wife if she can't kill a damn chicken?"

"We'll worry about that another time. Now if you plan to stay for dinner, you go clean that bird. I don't want you coming in the kitchen until it's all ready for the skillet and you've washed your hands good."

She drew Charlotte inside and sat her down at the table. "Honestly, I don't know what's the matter with some of these men. They never grow up. They're just mean little boys until the day they die."

Howard stood on the porch, blocking the sunlight. "I'm sorry, Charlotte. I didn't know you'd be upset so bad."

She swallowed again. She felt ashamed, inadequate. Howard was right. She'd be a poor ranch wife if she couldn't kill a chicken. "I'm all right now."

But Elsie did not relent. "You do as I said before you set foot in my kitchen, Howard Pope. I still think you're a big bully."

She stalked toward the door. Howard meekly retreated. Charlotte saw him stoop to pick up the rooster's head where he'd dropped it on the ground by the porch. She quickly looked away.

Howard, Elsie, and the children ate chicken for their noon meal. Charlotte put a wing on her plate, but couldn't lift it to her lips. No matter that she'd eaten chicken in the past and knew that she would eat it again.

She walked with Howard when he went to his horse. He looked sheepishly at her. "I didn't know a little teasing would upset you so much. I'm really sorry."

"I have to get over it. And I will."

He moved toward her, tentatively, half expecting to be rejected. She let him take her in his arms. She let him kiss her, although she couldn't forget the sight of the rooster's head held between his ungloved fingers.

"God, Charlotte, I can't wait until we're married. I can't wait until I can . . ."

She pulled away. "The children are watching out the window." She saw them giggling, pointing.

Howard took off his hat and bowed to them. They erupted into shrieks of laughter and fell out of sight below the windowsill. Howard grinned as he mounted his horse. He winked at Charlotte and nudged the animal into a trot. She watched him ride away. Elsie was right. Howard was almost thirty years old and over six feet tall, yet sometimes he was still a cruel and clumsy boy.

This time, Elsie's bones were right. Her husband and his hired hands arrived late in the afternoon, several bearded, trail-weary men and a caravan of dusty horses. They plodded through the gates and into the corral nearest the house.

"They're here! They're here!" shrieked the children. Everyone dashed to the porch. The dogs, roused from sleep in the cool backyard, raced to the front and barked ferociously, as if they'd been on guard all the time. The noise partially aroused the new horses. They milled around halfheartedly and then stood quietly in a bunch. The children shouted and clutched at their father. Elsie clutched at him, too. The men sat in their saddles, grinning, as Charlotte watched from the porch.

"Lord, am I dry," one of the men said. Charlotte went to the well. She pumped water, letting it run a few minutes so that it would be cold, and filled the dipper. The men clustered around her, smiling and dust-covered, reeking with sweat, and drank in turn.

Then Charlotte saw him by the trough, watering his horse. He was the most barbaric creature she had ever seen. His glossy black hair hung long and straight beneath a high-crowned black hat. He wore a dark shirt and high moccasins laced like leggings instead of boots. Round hammered bits of shining metal crisscrossed the front of his shirt. Shiny bits decorated his hat, his knife scabbard, his horse's saddle and bridle. He glittered and dazzled in the sunlight, exotic among the drab, nondescript men.

She stared at him until he looked back. She filled the dipper and took it to him.

"You'd better have some water, too."

His mouth appeared sensual in contrast to the rest of his spare carved face. He said thank-you in a husky, whispery voice. Charlotte's eyes were riveted by the dazzle, by the exotic look of him, and he was the first to turn away. Released, she started toward the porch.

"Hey, Charlotte," William said. "I brought that horse I promised you."

She'd temporarily forgotten all about it. "That's wonderful. Which one is it?" A horse was a generous gift and she must show the appreciation that she truly felt.

"Right there. The red chestnut with the white foot."

"He's beautiful."

"He's not broke yet. Johnny here will gentle him for you."

She turned to the stranger. He took off his hat and held it in front of his chest. His hair was parted in the middle and he wore a red cloth band around his forehead.

"This is Johnny Domingo," William said. "He's going to lend a hand for awhile."

Like the sun, she dared not look at him too long. She lowered her eyes. Then a wave of giddiness passed through her. She saw the front of her dress, splattered with dried drops of blood.

Early the next morning, Charlotte went to the corral where Johnny was already working with her horse. He held a halter rope in one hand, a saddle blanket in the other. He rubbed the gelding's neck and shoulders with it, let it flap gently around his legs, lay it over his back. At the same time, Johnny murmured to the horse in a combination of soft whistles, hisses, and words that she couldn't understand. The chestnut flinched and trembled. His eyes rolled back. His ears worked nervously, but he stood still. After awhile, Johnny dropped the blanket over the horse's back, led him around a few steps, and then to where Charlotte stood.

"He is a pretty one," he said in a heavily accented voice. "I will take extra care with him and he will learn well."

Two other men came to the corral. Charlotte petted the

horse and returned to the house. Mrs. Mosher was looking out the window.

"That new man is wild-looking. What is he—Indian?"

"Part Apache, part Mexican, I believe," said her husband. "He knows horses. I swear they understand him when he makes those crazy noises."

During the day, Charlotte was frequently drawn to the window from which she could see the corral. Domingo roped and handled each animal, assessing them in turn. Then he singled out a big dark bay gelding. The horse didn't respond to the gentle approach, but bit, shied, and kicked unreasonably. Finally the wrangler stepped back, folded his arms, and stared at the animal with what Charlotte felt must be exasperation. The horse glared in return. His ears lay back and his feet shifted threateningly.

Charlotte hurried toward the corral. Johnny harshly twisted the gelding's ear, gathered up the reins, and swung into the saddle. The bay didn't move for an instant, apparently shocked by pain and surprise. Then he squealed in outrage and sprang into the air. His long body snapped and sunfished like a hooked trout. His stiff legs jolted dust upward in spurts and puffs. Saddle leather creaked. The horse grunted with effort. The slender figure of the rider moved easily with the horse, following as flexibly as though he were an extension of the animal.

The angry explosions of the horse's breath turned to wheezes. His jarring leaps diminished. He crow-hopped across the corral and stopped. Legs spread wide, he trembled with exhaustion. His nose almost touched the ground.

Johnny pulled his head up, nudged him with his spurs, and the bay moved slowly around the corral. He turned to the right, turned to the left, halted, broke into a tired trot—obeying signals from the man on his back. Johnny jogged him over to Charlotte, stepped from the stirrup to the corral bars, and dropped to the ground beside her.

Dust and perspiration streaked his face. He was younger than she'd first thought, probably close to her own age. A strange constriction blocked her throat and she could only gaze mutely at him.

He smiled. "Hey, copperhead." His brown hand stroked lightly down her hair.

"What the hell do you think you're doing, cowboy?" A voice spoke sharply behind Charlotte. She whirled to see Howard. He looked big and bulky, his face bright red with rage.

She managed to keep her voice matter-of-fact. "Howard, this is Johnny Domingo. He works for William now."

"Okay, Domingo, you better learn one thing right away and that is to keep your place. Don't you ever touch Charlotte again."

"Does this man have a right to speak for you?" Johnny asked her politely.

"We are engaged," she said stiffly.

He looked at Howard. "I am sorry. I did not know she was spoken for."

"Even if she wasn't, it shouldn't make any difference to you. You should know enough to keep your distance from a white woman."

A flush burned under Johnny Domingo's dark skin. His lips pulled briefly back from his teeth in a grimace of pain or anger. He looked at the ground, frowning thoughtfully. There was something so peculiarly menacing in his silence that Howard moved quickly away from Charlotte and braced himself. Domingo's expression altered. He glanced briefly at both of them and then walked away.

Howard gripped Charlotte roughly by the arm and propelled her toward the house. "That damn savage!"

"He's not a savage."

"You keep away from him. He's trouble, I can tell."

"He behaved better than you did."

He stopped and faced her. "Are you thinking thoughts about him that you shouldn't?"

"Let's not fight. He's not that important." She put her hand on his arm.

"Okay. Maybe I was a little quick. But I couldn't stand seeing his dirty hands on you."

The words jarred something inside her. *His hands are as clean as yours.* But she did not speak the words aloud.

It was several days before Charlotte saw Johnny Domingo again, except at a distance. She dreaded a meeting, sure that he would be angry and resentful. She'd already passed through the gate on her way to the well when she saw him by the trough, with the gnarly-muscled buckskin that was his own horse. He'd already seen her, so she went resolutely on.

"Good morning," he said easily. He took the pails and pumped them full of water. "Your horse is coming on fine. You have not seen him lately."

"No, I've been busy."

"You should get acquainted with him. Isn't he to be your friend?"

She smiled, relieved by his manner. "I hope so."

Johnny carried the pails to the house and set them on the porch.

She said, "I won't neglect him anymore. What's his name?"

"That is for you to decide."

"What do you call him?"

"To myself, I call him Foxy, because he is red and because he is smart."

"I like that. I'll keep it."

He touched his hat and left her.

They were interrupted at breakfast the following Sunday morning. One of the men came to the door to speak to William, who frowned as he listened.

"What's the matter?" Elsie asked when he returned to the table.

"It's that half-breed. He's in jail."

"Whatever for?"

"He got in a scrap in town last night. The sheriff locked up him and the other fella, too." He shoveled in a mouthful of fried eggs and hash brown potatoes. "I hope that boy won't cause me problems. I'll let him lay in jail until Monday morning. Maybe it'll cool him off a little."

Later Charlotte saw one of the other riders, a gnomish older man, sitting on the tack room steps and holding his head in his hands.

"What's the matter, Moss? Too much Saturday night?"

"Oh, honey, you women have a lot of advantages over men and one of the biggest is that you won't ever have to be cowboys and endure those Saturday nights."

"I thought they were fun."

"I can't remember too good, right now, whether it was fun or not."

"What happened? I heard something about a fight."

"Oh, Johnny had a little run-in with one of the Fish Hook boys. This fella objected to the way Johnny cuts his hair. He didn't like all those pretty shiny things he hangs on his clothes, either. Come to think of it, there wasn't much about Johnny he did like and he let it be known in a loud and impolite way.

"Well, Johnny doesn't say much, but he riles easy. One

101

little poke and he's up, hissin' like a snake." Moss chuckled and slapped his hand against his thigh. "That Johnny! He ain't a big guy, but he's a regular tornado. Reckon he could tie little red ribbons in his hair now and nobody would object."

"It wasn't serious, then?"

"Serious, hell! It was dee-lightful. Best fight we've had in a long time. Makes me feel better just settin' here thinkin' about it."

William and Johnny Domingo returned to the ranch a little before noon on Monday. Charlotte sat with Elsie on the porch, snapping beans. Johnny's face was cut and bruised and his left hand bandaged. He removed his hat and nodded gravely as they rode by toward the bunkhouse.

Charlotte shuffled out to the back porch. Even though it was late March, it was as warm and sunny as a June morning. Memories of the past still hovered in the corners of her mind, as she eased her old bones into the creaky wicker chair. She carried a cup of coffee and an over-sized biscuit cut in half and stuffed with bacon. Dogs gathered, drooling and hopeful, on the steps. For all their pleading eyes, they knew better than to come too close while she was eating.

A calico cat lay on the railing. Her tail and one paw hung down. She looked at the biscuit, then closed her eyes, too disdainful to beg. A small flock of band-tailed pigeons rustled about, picking up seeds from the ground beyond the back fence. The cat raised her head, stared intently for a moment, then closed her eyes and sank down again.

Charlotte chuckled. "You're smart, Patches. You know when to try and when to take it easy."

Cleared and fenced pastures lay on both sides of the house. The road passed in front, beyond the garden. Hills rose just over the back fence. Most of the first slopes had been cleared, although stumps remained among the grass where the ponies grazed. One area had never been cleared. An arm of old-growth Douglas fir grew untouched, an extension of the vast miles of virgin forest beyond. It reached almost to the house itself.

Charlotte liked it most of the time. It was pleasant to see the line of tall old trees so near, to hear them rustle and sigh in the wind. Other times, when she was lonesome for the wide-open sagebrush plains of her youth, where the trees gathered decently along watercourses and in isolated groves, these trees seemed vaguely threatening. It seemed that the old forest had yielded reluctantly to the saws and axes of men. It waited, for the opportunity to gather the wooden buildings and corrals back into itself again.

Something moved in the shadowy trees. It shifted and paused, shifted and halted again. Charlotte sensed herself observed. The dogs, drooling steadily, focused on the remaining bites of food. One of the puppies whined. Patches dozed, having chosen to withdraw from all distractions. The ponies grazed, heads down and oblivious, among the stumps in the pasture.

Charlotte had long been aware that the forest had another life, beyond the obvious one of trees, undergrowth, birds, and animals. Sometimes she sensed ancient stirrings, perhaps formed from the collective energy generated by many living things crowded together for undisturbed centuries. It seemed a neutral form of energy, indifferent to but not unaware of her or other humans, who were so young, so insignificant to Them.

One of the dogs turned suddenly. His jaws closed with a snap as he stared up the hill. He whined deep in his throat. The other dogs turned, the bacon forgotten. They shifted restlessly as they looked toward the old forest, but not one of them barked.

Charlotte nodded. Her voice was soft and dreamy. "You're right, you pesky mutts. They're out there this morning."

Chapter 5

LEE

Monday and Tuesday

It had been a mixed weekend. Lee always enjoyed being with Bob, Vivian, and the kids at the ranch. But a phone call to Reno revealed that the business deal which had sounded so promising was nothing more than pie in the sky. Fortunately, he had a decent cash reserve so that there was no immediate financial pressure.

But there was an immediate responsibility which he did not welcome. Bob was hurt and disappointed when Lee told him that he had to return at once to Redding. Lee was forced to go into some detail about Joanne. Bob didn't say much. He never criticized. Rather he continued a younger-brother idealization that Lee knew he did not deserve. At the same time, Lee fed it, as he told Bob anecdotes of his life. He cleaned them up, gave them a slight twist to make them funny or picaresque. He edited in another way by leaving out entire episodes that didn't lend themselves to glorification.

It was difficult to sanitize the situation with Joanne and the brutal and mysterious Don. "I promised her I'd come back," Lee said. Bob accepted that he must keep his promise, although he looked speculatively at Lee when he left.

He felt sulky and tired on the tedious trip south. He lit one cigarette after another, increasing the henhouse taste in his mouth. He told himself that he should quit smoking. He'd made a halfhearted attempt when he lived with Doris. She was another reason for him to feel guilty and diminished, as he thought of the way he'd let her down. The bouts of self-scorn came often of late and he didn't like them at all.

He found a phone booth on the outskirts of Redding. A man answered when he dialed Gloria's number.

"Is this . . . uh . . ." Lee fished around, trying to remember the name of her husband, a long-haul trucker who was rarely home. He couldn't. "Uh . . . Mr. Hahn?"

"Yeah?"

"This is Lee Jamison. You may remember me. I'm a friend of Joanne Johnson. Is she there?"

"No, she's not."

"Do you know where she is?"

"No, I ain't seen her this trip."

Uneasiness poked at Lee. "Didn't she go to the coast with you and Gloria?"

"No. What's going on?"

"Let me speak to Gloria, please."

"She's gone to the grocery store. What's going on?"

"I'm not sure. I saw Joanne on Thursday morning and she was nervous about being alone. She said that Gloria had asked her to go to the coast with you. I thought she did."

"Just the two of us went. Gloria called Joanne, but she wasn't home. She'd told Gloria that her other friend was in town. You know about him. So we thought maybe they'd . . . well, sometimes he takes her on trips and . . . ."

"I'll get back to you." Lee cut him off. He dropped in more coins and dialed Joanne's number. He didn't let it ring long nor did he call the salon where she worked. Instead he hurried to his car and sped to her house.

106

The Mercury slid to a stop in the graveled drive. The sun hung just above the trees to the west of the house. They looked thicker than they had only four days before as buds swelled in the spring sunshine. Five or six birds, silhouetted like Victorian cutout figures, perched on the upper branches of a tree. They seemed to look curiously down at him. An airplane droned far overhead.

Lee stepped out of the car and looked around the clearing. Joanne's car was in the carport. Except for the position of the sun, everything seemed as it had when he left four days ago. He might have merely turned the Mercury around and never gone to Oregon at all. Except for the crawling feeling that lurked in his stomach.

A curious reluctance slowed his movements. He forced himself up the steps. His boot heels thudded, too loudly, on the porch. He pressed the bell and heard faint chimes inside. He tried the knob. The door was locked.

He walked around to the back, where Joanne had been watering when he left. The kitchen door was also locked. A squirrel chittered irritably at him from one of the trees. He peered through the glass into the neat kitchen. A single coffee cup sat on the counter.

He pounded on the door. "Joanne. Joanne." The sound of his own loud voice was startling. "Joanne!"

A mixture of fear and anger gripped him. He looked wildly around. Joanne was so goddamned neat. She never left anything out of place. Finally, he picked up a heavy pot of geraniums and hurled it at the window in the kitchen door. Glass shattered. Jagged bits, along with dried earth, fell to the steps.

Lee reached gingerly past broken shards to the lock and let himself in. His feet crunched on the glass and pottery shards that littered the gleaming floor. He walked as quietly as cowboy boots allowed through the house—kitchen, dining area, living room, hall. The door to Joanne's bedroom was closed, but not latched. Slowly, he pushed it open.

"Oh, God."

It was as bad as he feared. Joanne lay naked on her stomach on the bed, her hands loosely bound behind her. Most of her face was concealed by tangled and matted hair. Darkened puddles of blood had soaked into the flowered bedspread. Her flesh had been gouged in places with something both sharp and heavy, something that smashed as well as cut.

Lee was not squeamish, but it took real effort to touch her arm. She was cold and stiff as a mannequin; all that was human had fled days ago. He stumbled from the room to the phone in the kitchen.

Hours later, he sat in another kitchen with Gloria and Bud Hahn. She dabbed at her tears with a sodden tissue, smearing more black mascara beneath her eyes. Bud held one plump white hand and frowned at her with an expression of intense concern.

Gloria's voice sounded thick with weeping. "I told her. I warned her over and over. Dump that bastard, I said. He's a creep. He's not normal."

Bud nodded. "I heard you say it, more than once."

Lee sighed and sipped at his bourbon and branch. Inwardly, he thanked God for Gloria. Her semi-hysterical testimony to the police had assured that no suspicion fell on Lee. His head ached dully. Exhuastion, shock, and guilt caused them to repeat the same thoughts and words over and over again.

Bud asked, "Do you suppose that guy was at Joanne's place, watching you? Those woods are pretty thick, even now. It would be easy to hide."

The thought had already occurred to Lee and he regretted

that he hadn't thought of it before he left Joanne alone. If he'd only looked, he might have found Don in the woods and prevented Joanne's death. There were many "ifs" in her pathetic story and his less-than-honorable contributions were only part of it.

"Tell me again about the belt," Lee said.

"It's heavy," Gloria answered. "Silver with a phony coat of arms and a big ram's head on it. He had a thing about it, Joanne told me. Sometimes it was all he wore when they were together—you know what I mean. He almost always wore it when he got rough with her. Rough! We went skinny-dipping once and I saw the marks on her butt from that belt. That's why she was so cut up. He beat her with it before he strangled her."

She burst into sobs. Bud put his arm around her and patted her shoulder. "There was nothing you could have done. She was a grown woman. I heard her say she'd do anything to keep her house."

"I knew it was worse than she let on," Gloria sobbed. "But even I didn't know how bad it was. I'd have done something if I'd known. I would have."

Lee pushed back his chair and stood up. "I've got to find a motel and get some sleep. I'll head back to Woodbridge tomorrow, stay with my brother a few days and . . ."

"Woodbridge?" Gloria pulled a fresh tissue from the box and smudged her eyes again. "That's in Oregon, isn't it?"

"Yeah."

"Joanne said something once about Woodbridge. She almost never talked about this Don creep, you know. She was so scared of him and he'd made her promise. But once, when she had a few drinks, she said something about him and Woodbridge."

"He lives there?" The thought jolted Lee.

"She didn't say that. More like—he'd be driving down from Woodbridge."

"Did you tell the police?"

"I didn't remember it until just now when I heard you say the name. I'll call them first thing in the morning. That's kind of a coincidence, isn't it? Him driving from the same place you're going."

Lee agreed. It was quite a coincidence. One he didn't like.

Bud expressed another thought, even as it also occurred to Lee, one he liked even less. Bud said, "Better watch your back. If that guy was out in the woods waiting for you to leave, he's seen you pretty clear. He knows who you are."

Gloria followed him to the door when he left. "Joanne told me a lot about you. She really loved you."

He nodded, the knowledge weighing heavily on him.

"You came right back after her when you thought she was in danger. That means something. Maybe you loved her, too."

"Maybe so. Maybe more than I knew." He kissed Gloria quickly on her tear-wet cheek and hurried to his car.

It was a lie. He knew that what he'd felt for Joanne was not love. But Gloria was her closest friend, her surrogate. If a lie made her feel better, maybe—somehow—Joanne might be comforted, too.

He knows who you are.

Lee thought about that as he drove north the next morning. He would not forget Bud's warning—watch your back—even though he didn't expect to be in Oregon more than a few days, just long enough to make things right with Bob. And then he would go—where? He had no idea. Maybe Wyoming, even though he'd be in advance of the scheduled wild horse hunt. For some reason, the coming weeks stretched emptily ahead of him, instead of being filled with a sense of possibility.

The ugliness of Joanne's death hovered around him as persistently as a fly that refused to be brushed away. It traveled north with him . . . awful images that he could not erase, accompanied by the dull headache he couldn't shake and a faintly sickish feeling in the pit of his stomach. The rational part of his mind said that what had happened was not his fault. But that was the smallest, least effectual, part. The larger punishing part cried, "Shame! It was your fault. You're to blame."

He rolled down the window and fiddled with the radio until he found a cowboy music station. But the songs were sad and wailing and did nothing to lift his mood. On the last trip to Woodbridge on Thursday—only four days ago—he'd thought about Illinois and his meeting with Rosalind. Those early years had been the springboard for many actions and reactions, some like arrows pointing the way to Joanne.

But be honest about it, he admonished himself. You made the choices. After Rosalind, you made all the choices.

The theatrical troupe coursed back and forth across the Midwest, East, and South. Rosalind refused to perform west of Topeka. "They're all barbarians out there," she proclaimed.

Lee carried props and luggage, shifted scenery, sold tickets. His favorite job was driving Rosalind's car. His father was progressive enough to own an automobile, but it was a conservative Buick, boring when compared to the Pierce Arrow with its gleaming headlights growing like crystals out of the front fenders. The golden car spoke of money, freedom, adventure. Heads turned as he drove it down streets and country roads.

Sometimes he had small parts in the plays, but pretending emotions, pretending to be someone else, didn't hold much appeal for him. Nor did Rosalind take it very seriously. She lacked the interest to delve into the characters she played and give them any real life. She did have enormous charisma and most of the others, mediocre performers anyway, faded into the background as soon she appeared on stage. Occasionally, a part or a scene caught fire, and then she was completely compelling. She only shrugged if anyone mentioned the variations in her work.

She seemed remote and detached much of the time. Now and then she turned feverishly animated and euphoric. At other times, a playful and gentle Rosalind appeared. Like a shy little girl playing hide-and-seek, the child emerged from behind the other, more powerful personalities. Somehow this seemed the most genuine of all the Rosalinds, but stronger forces pushed her into the background and she surfaced only rarely.

Lee soon connected one of the moods, the unnatural exhilaration, to a white powder that she carried in a little box. Whenever she took it into the bathroom and closed the door, he knew what reaction would follow.

"What is that stuff?" he once asked, although he had a pretty good idea.

Her chin lifted and her voice was hard and challenging. "Do you want to try it?"

"No, thanks." From then on, he pretended not to notice.

Uncertainty kept Lee quiet. Rosalind was so unlike any woman he had known that sometimes he wondered if she was even human. A dark mystery brooded at the heart of her. He saw it in her long, blank-eyed silences. He knew it when he felt, more than heard, her crying in the night, nearly silent sobs that convulsed her body and yet left her without tears.

"What is it?" He asked the first time—and the second. He pulled her against him, cradled her close, offered the comforting warmth of his body. "Tell me what's wrong."

She didn't answer. He held and stroked her until she slept. In the morning it was as though it had never happened. After the second time, he didn't ask questions, but simply held her and murmured words of solace, words of love. He circumspectly questioned members of the troupe, but no one knew anything about her past.

"Rosalind is different," they said. "She's been with us three years and never said a word about herself. She doesn't like it if we ask."

Lee did not ask, either. If she tired of his questions, she could say "go" as easily as she had once said "come." He was fascinated by all that he knew and all that he did not know about her. He was lost in the boneless, cat-like compliance of her body and the way he felt whenever he looked into her eyes, captured all over again. Lee teetered uncertainly in the palm of Rosalind's pale hand, her possession to keep or throw away.

Lee had felt confined in his family-filled house on the prairie and it sometimes seemed that he had exchanged one kind of bondage for another. As the troupe moved from place to place, he was locked into their close-knit, quarrelsome, somehow incestuous life. There were rivalries, intrigues and jealousies among them, but they presented a closed front to the rest of the world. Birds of passage, they roosted only briefly in the towns they played. In spite of the traveling, it was a regimen with little freedom.

The company teetered constantly on the edge of bankruptcy and the performers complained of lack of funds, all except Rosalind. She traveled with trunks of clothes and, in addition, provided her own lavish costumes for her roles. Lee had sisters and a mother who loved clothes, as well as a father who was willing and able to indulge their tastes. He knew how much such things cost.

Rosalind's trunks yielded a seemingly endless supply of nightgowns, camisoles, and knickers, made of silk or fine cotton, delicately hand-embroidered. There were dozens of pairs of soft leather shoes and handbags; dresses of silk, wool jersey, crepe de chine. There was the car, which she scrupulously maintained. The other performers sought bargain lodgings; Rosalind went directly to the best hotels. This lavishness led to more questions, unanswered, unasked.

She loaned her books to Lee—*The Forsyte Saga*, novels by Henry James and Jane Austen. He devoured them all, hoping they might tell him something about her.

They'd been together for a little less than two years. It was April in Kansas City. Frail green blades of new grass pushed through the muddy earth. Lingering patches of dirty snow soon disappeared in the strengthening sunlight. Flowering shrubs produced brilliant yellow, white and pink blossoms to decorate winter's dull brown sticks.

Lee felt the pull of distant lands, of places he'd never seen. He dreamed of mountains. Sometimes he stared toward the west, imagining that if his vision were better, he might see mountains against the sky. Wild horses galloped through his dreams. Wolves and buffalo circled his sleep at night. An odd pungent scent he knew was sagebrush faded as he awoke.

"Let's go to San Francisco, Rosalind. That's a real city. Or Seattle. I'll bet you could get all kinds of bookings in Seattle."

She shook her head.

"I hear it's beautiful on the West Coast. How do you know you won't like it, if you don't go?"

"You go, Lee."

That silenced him. The westward fantasy went into the

114

closet of silence along with all the other things. But he rode a dappled horse through mountains in his dreams.

Lee perfected his card playing along the way. He was especially skilled at poker and accumulated a fat wad of bills, so much that it surprised him. As he added to it, he thought about how far it might take him. With this much money, he would even ride a train.

Then he saw the ring in the window of an antique store. Diamonds, like little ice cubes enhancing an exotic fruit, surrounded a dazzling blue sapphire. He only half-listened as the old proprietor launched into a complicated tale of how he'd managed to acquire such a remarkable ring.

"The setting is platinum," he told Lee. "That and the quality of the diamonds makes it even more choice. And it is a wonderful sapphire. Old Persian tales say that the world rests on a giant sapphire. Other legends tell that the Ten Commandments were written on slabs of sapphire."

"That's interesting," Lee murmured, as he envisioned the ring on Rosalind's hand. It was a fit adornment for her, equal in quality and showiness to the others she wore. Lee offered something less than the asking price and the dealer accepted. It took all of his poker winnings.

Rosalind had been distant and moody for several days, the result, he believed, of his rash suggestion that she break her long-standing rule and travel to the West Coast. Maybe the ring would put things right between them. Maybe she would recognize the ring as an indication of the depth and seriousness of his feelings.

He waited until an evening when she had performed well and seemed approachable again. Still, apprehension nibbled at him. He delayed as she changed into her favorite lemon and white silk kimono. She uncoiled her hair and allowed it to fall down her back. She sat at the dressing table and watched herself as she stroked her hair with a brush. Then she transferred her gaze to Lee in the mirror.

"What is it, Lee? What are you fidgeting about?"

"I've got something for you," he blurted. "I saw it in a window and . . . and I wanted it for you." This wasn't what he'd planned to say. He'd rehearsed a cool, clever little speech, but the words scattered like bats beneath the impact of her eyes. He dug in his pocket and held the ring toward her image in the mirror, toward her back as she sat on the bench.

She glanced at it without turning around. "It's lovely, Lee. I can see that it's very expensive, much too expensive for you to give to me."

"I want to give it to you. I want you to have it."

"No, thank you."

Of all the scenarios he had imagined when he presented the ring to her, "No, thank you," had never entered his mind. All possibility of speech left him.

Rosalind's cool gaze did not falter. "The timing is a bit awkward since you've offered such a generous gift, but I've thought seriously about this. I've thoroughly enjoyed your company, but I think it's time for us to separate for awhile. You want to go west and you should. I've distracted you long enough from your dreams. Take back the ring and you'll have enough money to travel for weeks."

It hurt, as though he'd been kicked in the stomach. "I'd rather stay."

"Perhaps we'll meet again, if we both want it. But right now, I'm not good for you. I'm not good for anyone, including myself."

"Rosalind, I don't care. I don't care about anything, except being with you. I love you. Don't you know how much I love you?"

She frowned. A hint of impatience entered her voice.

"You're over your head. And you're young enough so that you don't even realize how deep the water."

"I can swim. And I'll get older."

"Yes. But not with me." There was no mercy, no wavering in her eyes. "I understand that you're upset now. But you have no idea how complicated things are. Someday perhaps you'll recognize at least a little of what I did for you when I set you free. And you'll be grateful."

"You're wrong, Rosalind." There was absolute conviction in his voice. "I'll never be grateful. Besides that, no one else will ever love you as much as I do—or in the way I do—just letting you be yourself, without criticizing or trying to change you. Just loving you without demands. If you kick me out, you'll never find anyone like me again."

Her eyes changed. The remoteness disappeared. Surprise and realization dawned, a recognition that what he said was true. For the first time, she looked away, as though she could not bear what she saw in his eyes.

"I . . . I know." Her voice trembled.

Lee took a long step forward. He pulled her to her feet, turning her so that she faced him directly rather than through the distancing mirror. He noticed, as always, the fragility of the bones beneath his hands. She seemed little more substantial than a bird.

"Rosalind, tell me what troubles you. Tell me what's wrong in your life. I don't care what it is. We'll work it out together. Tell me."

She shook her head, wordless with shock as he had been a few moments before.

"I've seen you talking on the phone. I know you call someone from wherever we are. Are you married? Do you have a child? A parent who's dependent on you? I'll help any way I can. Just tell me. Please, please trust me."

117

Something happened to her face. Fear, shock, confusion . . . emotions crumbled the clean lines of her features. Her eyes seemed as enormous and staring as those of an owl. She struck wildly at his face as she struggled to twist out of his arms.

"Let . . . go!" she screamed. "Let go! Don't say those things. You don't know. You don't know anything."

She was so frantic that, as he held her, Lee imagined bones snapping beneath his hands. He released her. She stumbled to the closet and dragged his clothes off the hangers. She wrenched open the door and threw them out into the hall.

"Rosalind, wait. Don't . . ."

An ashtray sailed across the room. He ducked. It whizzed past his head and smashed into the wall. She rushed to the dressing table and snatched up cosmetic jars. They bounced off his chest and shoulders. He flung up an arm as one came directly at his face and it struck his elbow.

"Rosalind . . ."

"Get out. Get out. Get out!"

A door opened across the hall and a rumpled man stared out. A woman on tiptoe peered over his shoulder. Lee's shaving supplies thudded onto the floor of the hall. His toothpaste whacked the opposite wall. A riding boot followed.

Rosalind's fingers dug into his arm as she propelled him out the door. She shrieked with the frenzy of a terrified bird. "Go! Don't come back. Just leave me alone."

The door slammed. From behind it, Lee heard long, anguished wails. "Ohhh . . . ohhhh."

Another door opened down the hall. "What's going on?" a man's gruff voice asked.

Dazed, Lee gathered his belongings into a pile. "I'll get the bellboy to help me," he said to no one in particular. The doors shut after a moment and he was left alone in a hallway of closed doors.

He didn't return the ring, but tucked it into a corner of his pack. Early in the morning, he managed to find a ride that took him out of town, west toward the mountains that filled the topography of his dreams. Sometimes, in the weeks that followed, he took out the ring and looked at it. It was beautiful, perfect for Rosalind.

What happened? What did I do wrong?

The first time he saw the Rocky Mountains rising sheathed in ice against the sky, he knew he'd been born one hundred years too late. He should have been a mountain man back in the early days with Jim Bridger or Louis Bonneville or mapped the trails with Lewis and Clark. He made his journey too late. The fur trade was gone. Many of the Indians had turned into reservation dwellers on the fringes of white man's society. Service stations, junkyards, and billboards blemished the historic westward trails. Lines for phones and electricity as well as highways crept across the landscape in proliferating numbers. The mythical West of his dreams vanished even as he approached it.

Cowboying came naturally to Lee, after years of experience with animals and agriculture. His first job was on a small ranch near Farmington, New Mexico. In early November, in spite of the lectures he regularly gave himself, the sense of unfinished business could no longer be denied. Before he'd left the theatre company, he'd had the foresight to copy the address of their booking agency. He telegraphed the number in St. Louis and found out where they were performing. He managed to reach Melba, as he stood in front of a hand-cranked, wall-mounted phone. It was Rosalind he wanted, of course, but he feared she would not speak to him.

"Lee, honey, we sure miss you." Melba's voice wasn't as southern these days, but it was as syrupy-sweet as ever. "It's been really boring since you and Rosalind left."

"Rosalind left? When was that?"

"About a month after you did. You should have seen the way she moped around. You broke her heart, Lee."

"I didn't go by choice. She kicked me out."

"Well, she was sorry later."

"Did she say so?"

"No, but I could tell."

"Where is she now?"

"I don't know. It was the strangest thing, even for Rosalind. It was after we closed in . . . let me see, was it Memphis or . . ."

"It doesn't matter," Lee interrupted.

"No, I guess not. We'd closed and were ready to move on to the next booking. I was going to drive for Rosalind. I went to her room in the morning and she was gone. The desk clerk said she'd checked out the night before, about 1:00 A.M. She left a note saying she wouldn't be back. Then she drove off all by herself. And you know how she hated to drive. No one's heard a word from her since."

"Do you know if she got any phone calls or maybe a telegram before she left?"

"I don't have the slightest idea. But you know she was always calling or wiring someone. It was quite mysterious, really."

There didn't seem much else to say. Lee extracted a promise from Melba that she would write to him at his parents' address in Illinois if she heard anything from or about Rosalind. Melba assured him she would be happy to do that for him.

"Why don't you come back, Lee? You could work with us

again. And things might be easier this time. We aren't all as difficult as Rosalind."

There was promise in her voice. The southern accent had crept back. Melba apparently equated southern with seduction. Lee murmured gallant though vague phrases. He didn't want to alienate Melba as she was his only link with Rosalind.

Where Lee had once dreamed of mountains, afterwards he dreamed of Rosalind. He stood beside a road, hitchhiking. He'd see Rosalind approach in her golden jewel of a car. Sometimes she looked at him with her incomparable eyes. Other times she didn't give him a glance. But she always drove on by. Always she drove away and left him without a word. She passed like a phantom from an unknown land on her way to an unimaginable future.

Each time, after he awoke, Lee felt the pain of her loss as sharply as though it occurred for the first time. Each time he vowed that never—never again—would he allow any other woman to hurt him as much.

He soon grew tired of New Mexico and drifted west. He hired on at a large ranch in eastern Oregon. According to the other employees, Hartley Dietsch was a fair man to work for. Lee settled in, preparing to pass the summer and maybe the winter, too, if he was kept on.

Dietsch had a nineteen-year-old daughter named Hallie, wide-hipped and big-boned like her father. She was awkward, boisterous, neither plain nor pretty. She would not have received much notice in another society, but men vastly outnumbered women on the ranches and women were consequently a prime commodity. Hallie was feminine enough to enjoy the men flirting and competing for her attention and naive enough to think she really was as special as they said.

Soon after Lee's arrival in Oregon, he bought a horse that resembled the one in his dreams—a beautifully built, dapple-gray gelding with a creamy white mane and tail. Hallie often stopped to pet and fuss over him. She asked to ride him and Lee complied. Hallie was as good a rider as anyone he knew. After the third time, two of the men approached him as he unsaddled the horse.

"Hey, Lee," one said. "Me and Jimmy would like to know what brand of shaving lotion you use."

"Why's that?"

"Hell, don't be so modest. You get more attention from Hallie than anybody else. She follows you around like a puppy dog."

"Aw, shit. She likes old Smoky better than me." He pretended to throw his saddle at them. They laughed and scurried off awkwardly in their high-heeled boots.

But Lee knew that they were right. Hallie used Smoky as an excuse to approach him. He'd never been anything but polite to her and maybe that was the trouble. The others chased after her and maybe she considered it a challenge to get his attention. But if he pretended to be attracted and she responded, he'd be worse off than he was now. There was no question of a casual romance with her. She was "a good girl," according to bunkhouse conversation. A good girl—and the boss's daughter—could be approached only if he were interested in marriage. And that was the last thing in his mind, especially when he compared the graceless girl with his memories of Rosalind.

It was impossible to avoid Hallie. Her blue eyes watched him hopefully, expectantly. She touched him in ways that seemed accidental. She showed off like a child, making her horse rear and cut up. The other men teased Lee as they mistook his reluctance for shyness and became amused at his constant retreats. They offered encouragement and told him to go get her—the old man needed a son-in-law and pretty soon they'd all be working for him.

"She scares me half to death," Lee said. They thought it hilarious, not understanding why.

He considered leaving, but the pay and working conditions were good and he needed to build up his grubstake. He mended fence one day in an isolated part of the ranch. In the middle of the afternoon, Smoky turned his head, pointed his ears, and nickered. Hallie trotted her horse along the fence line.

"Well, hi there, Jamison," she said as though she were surprised.

"You're a long way from home, Miss Dietsch."

"I keep telling you to call me Hallie. Everybody else does."

She dismounted and stood close beside him as he tightened the wire and refastened it to the post. She was so near that he heard her breathing. When he was through, he looked down at her—not far, for she was a tall girl. In spite of himself, he smiled at the look in her eyes.

"You always smile like that. As though you know some secret nobody else does. What's the secret? Tell me."

"Hallie, the secret is—we're all damn fools."

"Well, at least you called me Hallie."

He turned away to hang the fence-mending equipment on his saddle.

"Why don't you like me?"

"I do like you."

"You sure don't act like it."

"You've got so many beaus around you all the time, what's one more or less."

She tilted her head coquettishly. "I didn't think you ever noticed whether I had any beaus or not. I didn't think you ever noticed anything about me."

Oh, hell, he thought. Maybe I can scare her off. "You're a

123

nice kid," he said, deliberately harsh. "But if you fool around with me, you're going to get into trouble."

She made a purring sound in her throat and her smile widened. "What kind of trouble?"

His arms and hands closed roughly on her and he clamped his mouth on hers. He was as brutal as he knew how to be. To his surprise, her hands clutched his shoulders and she thrust her body against his. He seized one breast. She gasped, but clung more tightly to him. Her mouth was hot and eager. She hung on him, the heavy weight of her body pulling him down.

He staggered backward, breaking her hold. "Jesus Christ."

She laughed. "You are shy. That's what the boys have been telling me. I think that's adorable."

She reached for him again and he grabbed her wrists, holding her off while she laughed and struggled to reach him.

"Hallie, you're crazy. You don't know what you're doing."

"Oh, yes, I do. Don't be scared. I won't hurt you."

"I may hurt you," he yelled. "I'm not staying around."

She stopped pushing. "What do you mean?"

"Just that. I'm only passing through. I'll be gone in a few months."

A hint of her smile came back. "People change their minds."

"I won't. I know myself. I won't stay."

She looked at him, smiling, and he knew that she was sure she could change that. The local cowboys had always told her, one way or another, that she was irresistible and she had no reason to doubt her power.

"Besides that, I'm sort of engaged," he lied.

The smile disappeared again. "Who is she?"

"She's an actress."

"An actress! I suppose she's one of those smart modern

women with bobbed hair."

"No, Rosalind's not like that."

"What is she like?"

He answered truthfully, hurtfully. "She's beautiful. She's the most fascinating woman I've ever known."

Hallie turned away, but not before he saw tears well up in her eyes. She went clumsily to her horse and mounted. She hauled him roughly around and kicked him into a gallop back the way she'd come.

After that, she kept her distance and seemed to try as hard to avoid Lee as he did to avoid her. She was tense and abrupt when they had occasion to speak, while Lee remained carefully respectful.

August came with burning days and scorching sun. The men hayed stripped to the waist until they were burned dark as pirates. Lee saw himself in the mirror when he shaved—his fair hair sun-bleached lighter than the hay, his pale eyes glinting against dark skin. Not bad-looking, he thought, without false modesty.

Hallie watched him whenever she thought herself unobserved. He knew his problem was not resolved, but as long as they both kept their distance, he felt safe.

A small river ran through one section of the Dietsch land. It formed a sandy bar where the men went to swim when work was over. One day Lee finished later than the others. He'd already missed supper in the bunkhouse, so he detoured by the swimming hole before he went in to see what the cook might be coaxed to feed him. He cut in close to the river as Smoky jogged eagerly toward home.

The sun went down in a shimmer of gold. Long gilt clouds stretched across the horizon, fading into pearly translucence above. Bushes, earth, and trees ripened with the fullness of life and thick, polleny odors weighted the evening air.

Lee saw another pool, smaller than the one he knew, and without a sandy edge. The bank was open on the near side, but a dense growth of cottonwood crowded the other shore, masking it in shadow. The water looked deep and cool.

He sent Smoky down the bank and the horse splashed shoulder-deep into the water. Smoky buried his nose and shook his head back and forth, blowing bubbles. Still perched on the saddle, Lee took off boots, socks and shirt and threw them to the shore. He plunged into the water. The heavy jeans dragged at him, so he peeled to his skin. He turned over and over, luxuriating in the silken ripple of the water.

When he stood up, wiping water out of his eyes, he saw Hallie by the opposite bank. She'd been there before him, hidden in the shade of the cottonwoods. She stood in the sunlight, thigh-deep in the pool, aureate in the glow of sunset. Unclothed, she had a disproportionate voluptuousness—heavy thighs, broad hips, small waist, and little delicate breasts that seemed to belong to another body. She glowed in the golden light against the dark green trees, Venus in a sylvan setting, as painted by one of the romantic Old Masters.

She didn't move or speak, but even at that distance, Lee felt the hunger in her eyes. His maleness responded, rising and hardening beneath the water that lapped around his waist. Almost unwillingly, he moved toward her until, gently this time, their bodies touched.

Afterwards they met as often as they could, coupling like animals in hidden corners, on the ground or in the hay, anyplace where they could be alone. Hallie was in love. She repeated the words over and over, her adoring eyes begging him to say the same. He couldn't do it. She was no more than a physical indulgence to him.

He knew that he gave up another small bit of honor each time he lay with her. It was the first time he'd ever continued on a course that he knew to be unethical, the first time he'd made his own selfish desires more important than his sense of right and wrong. He'd turned a corner that he never thought he'd take. But he didn't stop. Hallie was too eager, too hungry. It felt too good to indulge himself in her passion.

Hallie had a cousin named Conrad, a pimply boy of sixteen who stayed on the ranch in the summers. He was supposed to work, but he did as little as possible while eating as much as he could. He hung around the bunkhouse, irritating the men with his lordly ways and his unbelievable tales of himself as a dashing young man in the city where he lived. He was tolerated only because he was the boss's nephew.

One afternoon, Lee and Hallie arranged to meet in a barn far from the house. A storm had been building all morning. Thunder rumbled distantly and towering white clouds piled up in billowy columns. The sky changed from shiny metallic blue to a deeper hue. A strange intense light, almost yellow, suffused the earth. Thunder crept closer as lightning flickered uneasily and the sky darkened with expectancy.

The first drops of rain fell as Lee approached the barn. He nudged Smoky into a gallop and ducked his head as the horse shot through the open door. The gelding swirled to a stop in the half-dark interior. Bits of dust and straw rose around his hoofs. Hallie's horse was already there, tethered to a beam. Lee scrambled up the ladder to the loft just as the full onslaught of rain struck the building.

Hallie lay in the middle of the fresh hay, naked, on a blanket. She smiled and reached for him. He stripped off his clothes and was barely down beside her when her strong arms and legs clamped around him. She had no finesse and little gentleness, as desire swept over them in a jarring wave. When the sexual act was over, then she became soft and flirting. She

127

wanted to be petted and reassured; she hinted for words he could not speak.

They lay close together, tension gone, bare limbs entwined. Rain drummed on the roof, closing them into their cocoon. As the air cooled, Lee rose up on one elbow and reached for their shirts to spread over them.

He looked into Conrad's eyes. The boy stood on the ladder a few feet away, only his head and shoulders above the level of the loft. His spotted face wore an expression of avid shock. It was impossible to know how long he'd been there, the sounds of his presence masked in the drenching storm, but it was more than long enough. Lee glared at him. He felt his eyes harden. A long silent moment passed and Conrad's expression became unsure. He opened his mouth as though he would speak.

"Get the hell out of here," Lee grated. "And if you say one word to anyone, I'll beat the shit out of you."

Conrad's head sank wordlessly below the loft. Neither Lee nor Hallie moved until, straining their ears, they heard the quick drumming of hoofs rush away into the rain. For the first time since he had seen Conrad, Lee looked at Hallie. Her eyes blazed with triumph. An unpleasant shock ran through him as she lowered her head and concealed her victorious smile against his bare chest.

"Oh, my God, Lee. What will Daddy do?"

He stroked her automatically and murmured words of reassurance. He felt sick with angry disgust, both for himself and for Hallie, with her smug assumption of victory. They dressed in silence. There was no point in returning separately as they had done in the past. They rode to the ranch under a clearing sky, without a word spoken. She looked expectantly at him after they'd dismounted.

He managed a small smile. "Don't say anything unless you

have to. I'll do the talking tomorrow, after I make some plans tonight."

Her face lit up with joy and the smile blazed forth, unhidden. "Oh, Lee, I knew you would. I love you so much." Heedlessly, she flung her arms around him and kissed him on the mouth. She thrust the reins into his hand and ran toward the house, head down, heavy hips bobbling from side to side.

Lee lay awake most of the night. He stared at the ceiling as he backtracked down the roads of remorse, regret, and if-only-I-had-not. Before it was light, he slipped his hand under the mattress and extracted the money he had accumulated. He crept out of the bunkhouse in stocking feet and saddled Smoky in the dark. He guided the horse away from the slumbering ranch. When the first light came, he rode hard and fast across the sagebrush. Now and then he looked over his shoulder, like a legendary cowboy on the run.

After that, he learned gentler ways of running out. The result was the same, but the methods were more subtle. When he was older, he occasionally thought of going back to find out what had happened to Hallie and thought of lies he might tell to make her feel better. She remained an uncomfortable and persistent memory. The loss of his honor was a hard price to pay for escape and the guilt was part of his burden of freedom.

Close to two months after his inglorious retreat, Lee stood on a beach on the Oregon coast. It was raining again—or maybe it was still raining. It seemed to him that the skies had dumped on him ever since his dawn ride away from the Dietsch ranch. Driving rain pummeled the hard gray sand, while the slate-gray ocean heaved beneath a dreary sky.

He had arrived three days before, descending stiffly from the truck, with its friendly driver, that had carried him unnumbered miles through the rain. Through water that spread and shivered on the truck's windshield, he'd glimpsed steep dark green hills. Only their bases were visible beneath the lowering clouds, but the long symmetrical trunks of the trees that stretched up into the mist suggested great height. He imagined invisible mountains hanging above the narrow winding road and the tiny, toy-like truck that crept along it.

The ride had ended in a small gray village, a dejected cluster of weather-beaten, haphazard buildings that seemed to have been washed up by the ocean and left on the beach with the rest of the tidal debris. The air smelled of fish, salt water, and rotting wood. Street lights came on in early afternoon and cast puddles of yellowish light. He found a boardinghouse, another gray nondescript building, encircled by a scraggly lawn blotched with patches of mud. His room was drafty and well-populated with assorted insects.

He had less than thirty dollars, no job, and no prospects. Smoky was gone, sold from desperate necessity. He had the sapphire ring, worn on a chain around his neck, but he didn't even consider selling it. He was cold and tired. His bones ached; his blood moved sluggishly. He was twenty-seven years old and had been on the road for over five years.

He yearned for Illinois, for home. The neatly fenced fields, the slow rivers winding through thick summer trees, the dairy pastures, all glowed nostalgically in his mind. He was tired of raw lands populated with strangers. He wanted to see his mother, his little sisters who he feared he might not even recognize . . . and Bobby. Bobby was twenty years old now and even he might be a stranger.

Lee hunched his shoulders against the rain and hiked back to town to find a telephone or telegraph. It hurt his pride that he must ask for money. He made certain it never happened again, that afterwards he went home only when things were going well and stayed away when they were not.

He put Rosalind's ring—he still thought of it as hers—in the family safety-deposit box and didn't see it for years. The year that Lee turned forty-five, during a visit to Illinois, he asked his dad to open the box. His father watched as he removed the ring. The sapphire appeared dull and the stones around it looked more like rhinestones than diamonds.

"It needs cleaning," said his father.

Lee nodded. The elder Jamison was too circumspect to ask, so Lee told him. "I bought this for a woman who wouldn't accept it. There was a time when I thought I might find her again. Then I thought I might find someone else. Now I don't know why the hell I keep it."

His father said, "It's not too late. You still may find someone."

Lee took the ring to Oregon where Bob had settled with Vivian, a librarian he'd wooed among the bookstacks. Bob allowed him to keep it in his box at the bank in Woodbridge.

Sometimes Rosalind returned when Lee lay in that shifting place between waking and sleeping. She haunted him as someone or something had haunted her. She'd passed on obsession like a curse. He could never be sure how much she had marked him and how much was his own nature. But whatever the reason, he cultivated an interior switch. When life began to get too real, too serious, the switch turned on. Lee changed gears, pulled out, did whatever it took to keep things light and easy.

If he got a little lonely, a little depressed now and then, especially as years went by, it was only natural. Being down was temporary, like everything else. And someday, maybe, if he were lucky, one of the roads he followed would lead him straight on to the base of the Big Rock Candy Mountain.

Chapter 6

CHARLES

April to early May

Charles and Sherry sat side by side on the back steps of the school. Their fingers entwined, shoulders and thighs touched.

"Someone told Mother about you. She's been asking a lot of questions," Sherry said.

"What kind of questions?"

"Oh, how much do I like you . . . why am I wasting my time with you? That kind of thing."

"Why are you wasting your time with me?"

"Because you're different. Because I like you. Because you're sweet." She laughed at the expression on his face. "You are sweet. Before I really knew you, I thought you were sort of hard and tough, but you're not. Not at all."

It had rained in the night and an uncertain sun hovered above the thinning clouds. In addition to the school, Whistler's Bend contained a lumber mill, two churches, a gas station, and a combination store and post office. Charles's eyes drifted to the hills beyond the small community. They were part of the Cascade Mountains that extended for miles eastward until they dwindled into the arid basins and plateaus of central Oregon. Habitation dwindled, too. Whistler's Bend, on a curve of the Little Nezzac, was the last name on the map.

132

The untouched forest beyond the cleared and logged areas still sheltered many inhabitants, although power saws and logging equipment forced them into constant retreat. The cougar were hard-pressed and shy, threatened by bounty hunters who collected sixty dollars for each big cat killed. Their range kept shrinking and they competed with hunters for the deer that were their main food source. They killed rabbits, squirrels, and other rodents, but little animals were hard to catch and didn't go far toward sustaining a big hungry cat.

On occasion Charles saw bobcat in the woods, like bright-eyed overgrown tabbies. There were black bear, which actually had brownish fur. Black-tailed deer thrived on the cut-over lands with plenty of browse. Small creatures—raccoons, squirrels, muskrat, beaver, and rabbits—still bred and died in multitudes.

Sherry shifted her body closer to Charles and brought him back to the school yard. He held her hand in his lap, cradled in both of his. It looked slim and white against his blunt dark fingers.

"What did you tell your mother about me?" he asked.

"I had to tell her that I don't like you better than anyone else, that we're just friends."

The fingers of his left hand slid restlessly up under the tight-fitting cuff of her sweater and back to circle her fragile wrist.

"I've never lied to her before. I felt terrible. She never lets me forget how hard she works. She hardly ever buys clothes for herself, just for me. Last week, she laid away a cashmere sweater. It's powder blue. She said she had to get it because the color is so perfect for me."

The sweater she wore was cashmere. It felt soft and expensive against Charles' hand. It was dusty rose and perfect for

Sherry, too, complementing her clear fair skin and buttery hair.

"Sometimes I wish she'd do something for herself and forget about me, just once."

"At least your mother cares about you. That's better than not caring at all."

Where was his mother? Did she ever think about him? Did she even know that Juanita was dead? Or were Charles, his sister and their father put out of her mind forever, left behind without a thought?

It was easy to imagine Mama living alone, pursuing her private thoughts without interference from anyone. But she might have other children by now. It gave Charles a strange feeling to think that he might have little brothers or sisters somewhere. Would she smile at the others, cuddle them the way he had seen mothers cuddle their children? Maybe she was happy with someone else. Maybe there'd been something wrong with Asa, Charles, and Juanita, something that drove her away, first into herself and then, at last, away all together. That thought hurt, cutting deep and sharp as a knife blade.

What could I do different, Mama? I was only a little kid.

Four years ago, when he was thirteen, a letter came for him. He recognized the printing, even though he had seen it only once before, on another September day. The school bus had just dropped him off. He stuck the letter inside his shirt and hiked up the trail. Blackie waited at the edge of the clearing. He was older and didn't jump around as much. Charles sat on a log and scratched the dog behind the ears.

When his heart wasn't pounding quite so hard—not from the climb—he took out the letter. There was no return address, but it was postmarked Seattle. He opened it carefully and removed the single sheet of paper. It was almost painfully neat, as though it had been written once for practice and then copied without a blemish.

Dear Charles —
 I know you will be surprised to hear from me after all these years. I think of you often and Juanita, too. Your father is a good man in many ways, but he gave up before he even tried. I hope you will understand that I could not stay. I had to try to find a better life. Please try to understand.

With love,
Your mother

Charles put the letter back into his pocket. Blackie followed him across the clearing and into the cabin. Crusted dishes piled up on the table. They could have been there for seven years. It was rare to see the table completely cleared. He took a Coke out of the six-pack on the floor and lifted it for a long drink. It was fizzy and warm, but not bad. A dirty shirt of his father's lay wadded on a chair. He threw it into a corner and sat down. He took another drink and tilted the chair back on two wobbly legs as he looked around the room.

Why didn't you tell me, Mama? Did you find a better life?

An awful thought occurred to Charles as he sat on the steps of the school, with Sherry silent beside him, absorbed in thoughts of her own.

Mama might be dead. Even if she lived apart from him, she was still his mother. If she were dead, then who was left for him? Juanita was gone. He couldn't count on his father. He clutched at the thought of his grandmother, Asa's mother. They didn't see one another often, but it was comforting to think of her and her affection for him.

For a long time, Charles had believed that his mother would come back. He imagined her reappearing as suddenly as she had disappeared. It would be like her, to return without any explanation. But then the letter came. It was as though Charles had been waiting beside a door. He waited and waited, even when he wasn't actually thinking about her. There were no sounds or movements, no clues as to what went on beyond the door. But a sound had come along with the letter from his mother. It was the sound of the door closing. It was not loud or dramatic, just a gentle little click. But he knew it had closed forever.

He remembered his mother's face, broad cheekbones and thick hair falling straight on each side. She was nearly as dark as her Indian husband. Her rare smiles transformed her somber face, turning her suddenly dazzling. When Charles's father was angry at him, he said that Charles looked like her, as though it were an insult.

Sherry had an absent parent, too. For all the ways they were different, they shared this in common.

"Do you ever think about your old man?" he asked her, breaking the long, comfortable silence. "Do you remember him at all?"

"No, he left when I was a baby. Mother says he's not worth thinking about. She was young and made a bad choice. But sometimes I wonder what he was like."

"I remember my mom."

Sherry turned to look at him and the shifting of her body left a chill empty place against his side where she had been warm and close. "Tell me about her."

How could he tell Sherry what he didn't know himself? He put his arm around her and pulled her back against him. "She left because she wanted to go. That's enough."

Sherry and Mrs. Prentiss were friendly with Marlene Stonebraker and her family. Marvin Stonebraker had inherited money from his father and increased it through his own successful lumber business. Marlene, his daughter, was a large formidable redhead, harsh-voiced and domineering.

She took a possessive interest in Sherry's popularity. There was more than a hint of superiority in the way she treated Sherry's boyfriends. It annoyed Charles that Marlene acted as though she had a special claim to Sherry, one that excluded him.

At first, she regarded Charles with her usual scornful pity, but that soon changed. He felt the malevolent weight of her eyes upon him. She didn't call him by name, but "Chief" or "Scout." He sensed that she tried to dissuade Sherry from dating him—if holding hands at school and clandestine kissing at games could be called dating. His father refused to let him borrow his old junker and Charles wasn't too sorry. He would have been embarrassed to take Sherry anywhere in that car, even if Mrs. Prentiss would let her go, even if he had money enough to take her to a movie or anywhere else.

There were many if-onlys in his life. If only he had a little money, even pocket change. If only he had access to a decent car. If only Mrs. Prentiss weren't so set on Sherry dating boys that met her strict standards. If only he were older, instead of not quite eighteen.

Charles saw Sherry and Marlene in the hall between classes. Sherry shook her head, her face set and stubborn, while Marlene, red-faced with anger, berated her. Charles paused. Should he interfere or not?

"It's gone far enough." Marlene's voice carried clearly. "You two are so obvious that your mother has asked me questions. Even my mom asked. I keep telling them it's not important, but I'm not going to lie any longer."

Sherry's soft voice said something that Charles couldn't hear.

"You can't expect me to keep on covering for you, not with my own family. Don't forget what you owe them, especially him."

Another low reply.

"Even if I don't tell, somebody else might, without even meaning to. And you know he won't like it. High school dates were fine, he said. But this is different. You know it's different."

Charles moved closer. "Is something wrong, Sherry?"

Marlene swung on him. "Go make an arrow, Chief. We're busy talking."

"There's nothing more to say," Sherry said. She sounded tired and her usually sunny face was pale and subdued. "I just need a little more time, Marlene."

"If you're not smart enough to think about yourself, think about your mother." Marlene's voice was hard.

Sherry walked away without replying.

"You're ruining her life." Marlene spoke fiercely to Charles. "Don't you have sense enough to know that she's too good for you?"

When he didn't answer, Marlene stalked toward him, holding herself as tall and straight as she could. She was the same height as Charles, 5'6", and a good deal heavier. She stretched whenever she was near him, as she tried to look down upon him physically, to reduce him to someone small and insignificant, to intimidate him as she intimidated nearly everyone.

Sudden rage exploded in Charles. She thought she was so Goddamned good, so special that she could tell other people what to do, so damned smart that she knew what was best for Sherry. His eyes narrowed and he almost smiled, just a small chilly movement of his lips. He ached to drive his fists into that superior face, to pummel her pale chunky body until tears of pain filled her contemptuous eyes.

"Damn it, Marlene." His voice was soft. "Too bad you're not a boy instead of a poor excuse for a female."

The desire to hit her was so strong that he could barely control it. Both hands clenched into fists and his whole body telegraphed his hard-held rage. Marlene blinked and drew back a step.

"Don't let my sex bother you, Sitting Bull. I might still be able to clean your clock." But her voice was uncertain, all bravado.

Charles glared at her a moment more before he followed Sherry. His knees felt weak as the rage flowed away as swiftly as it had come.

Sherry waited by the outside door, looking anxiously at him. "I'm sorry she says such terrible things to you. She can be really mean sometimes."

"Who cares? Usually she doesn't bother me." He opened the door and Sherry went through. "She wants you to break up with me, right?"

"Right."

"Why does she care? What business is it of hers?"

"My mother is very close to her family."

Charles had a feeling that Sherry had stopped herself from saying more.

"Who's the 'him' she kept talking about?"

There was a long pause. "Marlene's Uncle Warren, I guess."

The pause bothered him. He had a feeling that he stood outside another door and could only guess what might lie beyond. If he rushed at the door and tried to push through, it would slam in his face. He was sure of that, even though he wasn't sure of anything else.

Charles thought about Warren Stonebraker. He must be

nearly forty years old. The family's red hair washed out to a grayed brick color on him. His body was thick and his neck so short that his head seemed to sit right on his shoulders. He often accompanied Marlene's family, and Sherry and her mother, to community activities. The women fussed over him as though he were a ruling caliph and they were part of his retinue. He was rich, even richer than his older brother, according to gossip, and that was no doubt why he got so much attention.

"Why does Marlene's uncle care anything about us?"

"Warren loaned her money to buy our house and pay off some debts. I guess they feel the way Mother does . . . that I should do everything just right. And just right means exactly the way they want." Resentment flavored her voice.

"If it's not what you want, tell them to go to hell."

But even as Charles spoke, he knew it wasn't that easy. He might talk big, but how much control did he have? He couldn't bring back his mother or Juanita; he couldn't change his father. He couldn't earn money as long as he stayed in school. And if he left school to work, he would lose daily contact with Sherry.

Sherry's words echoed his own hopeless thoughts. "You don't know what it's like at home. Mother makes me feel so guilty. She has so many hopes and plans for me and I'm risking it all. And what for? What good will it do me?"

Her face twisted. She squeezed her eyes shut and tried to hold back the tears that poured down her cheeks.

The words he'd never dared to say erupted from him. "Sherry, I love you. Let's run away. We'll . . ."

But she'd already turned to hurry toward the building. Terror weakened him. When the words spilled out, they left a great quivering hollow inside. He felt empty and fragile, like a figure made of brown paper. There was nothing to him except a thin shell, so easily crumpled and thrown away.

The bell rang a few moments later. Sherry's seat remained empty. He glanced at Marlene and met an angry glare. In a moment, a wadded-up paper lit on his desk. He smoothed it out and read it.

"Sherry got sick and had to go home. You're the one making her sick. How does that make you feel, Tonto?"

Sherry wasn't at school the next morning. The long hours dragged by, each minute as heavy as a block of lead. At noon Charles could bear it no longer. He left school and walked the five miles to her house. Mrs. Prentiss's car was parked in the carport. Charles slipped into the bushes by the fence. He willed Sherry's mother to leave, to go to work. Why was she home, anyway? Was Sherry really sick, so ill that her mother had to stay with her?

The door remained closed. The windows opaquely reflected the light, giving away nothing, not a silhouette nor a flicker of movement. Charles edged farther into the thick bushes so that he would be out of sight from the road. He stood until his legs grew numb. When he shifted his weight, a bird flew off with a squawk. He'd been unmoving for so long that even the birds didn't know he was there. A sour smile twisted his mouth. He made a pretty good Indian.

A familiar motor rumbled in Charles's ears as the school bus passed. It was later than he realized, too late for Mrs. Prentiss to be likely to leave the house. He crossed the road and hitchhiked home.

The next morning, he waited for Sherry's bus. His heart lightened as she stepped down. But as she approached, he saw her set face and strained eyes. The words he had prepared dissolved unspoken on his tongue.

"I can't see you anymore."

He'd never heard her voice so harsh, so abrupt. A sickish feeling formed in the pit of his stomach. "Why not?"

"There's no point in it. We're two different kinds of people. We'll break up eventually, anyway, so we may as well do it now before one of us gets hurt." She recited words that she had learned from more determined lips.

"What makes you think I won't be hurt now?"

"Oh, Charles, I don't want to do this. But I have to." Her voice trembled. She sounded like Sherry again, instead of a parrot.

"Your mother is making you say this, isn't she?"

"I have obligations to my mother and to . . . to other people. Nobody at school understands, except Marlene."

There was Marlene's name again, illustrating the Stonebrakers' power over Sherry, showing that they could intrude even between her and Charles.

"What's going on between you and those people?"

Sherry drew a deep breath and visibly took control of herself. "I'm really sorry. I like you a lot. I hope we can be friends."

The school bell rang. To Charles it was a distant sound from another, unimportant world, but Sherry flinched.

"It's time for class."

"Wait. I'll quit school. I'll get a job and we can . . ."

"No, it's over." All emotion had left her. Her voice was flat, her eyes dull and resigned. "It was all decided a long time ago. I forgot for a little while, that's all."

She brushed past without looking at him. Charles stared off at the hills beyond the river. Her words made little sense. The only thing he understood was the finality of her voice and the distance in her eyes.

He left the school and hiked along the road. When he heard a logging truck behind him, he turned and held up his thumb. The driver took him to town.

A friend of Asa's lived in a shack on the north end of Woodbridge. Charles rapped on the door, but there was no response. Good. If Bill was out this early, it meant that he was working. The door was not locked. A sour smell struck him as he stepped inside. Molding newspapers, crumpled magazines and dirty clothes littered the house.

He went into the bedroom and pulled up a loose board in one corner. He felt around underneath and brought out a wooden cigar box. He'd seen old Bill take his "happy money" out of there before and he wasn't disappointed. Two ten dollar bills lay inside. He put one in his pocket and walked to town. He'd pay Bill back as soon as he could.

Charles soon found an old wino shuffling down the street. "Hey, Pop, want to make a buck?"

The man squinted at him, making quick chewing movements with his empty mouth. "What ya want?"

"Go to the liquor store and buy me a bottle of whiskey. I'll wait outside."

"Kid, you're too young to drink."

"And you're too old. So what the hell? Let's get some whiskey."

The old man cackled and took the bill. "What the hell? You're right."

Charles had never liked the taste or smell of whiskey. He'd seen his father sick too many times, puking his guts out, groaning and sweating. The times when Asa felt good didn't seem worth the times when he felt rotten. But now drink presented a temporary respite in a situation that had no real solution. It gave a purpose, at least for a day, to an endless series of days that stretched away without any purpose at all.

The wino took Charles to the riverbank, down a narrow trail to a hidden spot in the brush. The ground was dry and sandy with a pile of driftwood to lean against. Through the willow screen in front of them, the Nezzac flowed past, dark and swift in the sun. It was as warm as summer and Charles was reminded of playing with Juanita, when they were little and she would still play with him. There was a place in the woods near their cabin, a cozy spot with fir needles thick on the ground, surrounded by walls of fallen logs. It had been their hideaway, their secret place.

Charles twisted off the bottle cap and took a careful sip. It was no better than he remembered, medicinal and corrosive on his tongue. He swallowed and felt the whiskey slide down his throat and warm his stomach. He sipped again and passed the bottle to the man beside him.

He said his name was Rinky. He talked incessantly, but in a monotone that blended soothingly with the sound of the river. He didn't expect Charles to listen. Just the presence of another person was enough to wind him like a tinny clock and he ticked away in the background of Charles's attention with the same lack of intrusion.

Charles knew that Sherry had gone beyond his reach. The fact that her mother spoke through her made little difference now that Sherry had accepted the decision as her own. The tie that bound mother and daughter was too strong for him to break. And in addition, the Stonebraker family, with all their money, stood behind Mrs. Prentiss in an unknown relationship. It was money that gave them their mysterious power over the Prentiss women. But a simple loan wasn't reason enough. There was something else, something more, if only Charles could figure it out.

He gulped from the bottle. Even if he knew what was going on, it wouldn't make any difference. Except for that one moment of insanity—"Let's run away. I'll get a job—" he'd never dared think of any future with Sherry.

At the moment, he felt almost indifferent to her loss, but pain lurked beneath the surface. Once he'd smashed his thumb with a hammer. There had been an instant when it didn't hurt, a suspension of feeling as nerve endings gathered information, assessed damage, and sent reports off to the correct parts of his brain. He'd almost heard his body clicking and shuttling as it prepared to send messages of agony back to his injured thumb.

It was the same now. The pain waited for damage to be processed and assimilated. Then the hurting would begin. But alcohol was suppressive. It replaced the emotional suspension of feeling with a spreading numbness of its own. All feeling floated off on a hazy rocking sea that surged gently up and down at the edge of his vision. He'd never been in a boat on the ocean, but he knew it must be a similar feeling, a loss of equilibrium and the knowledge that solid ground had been replaced with something much less stable.

"Man the lifeboats," Charles said loudly. The old man laughed shrilly and nudged his shoulder.

The liquid in the bottle went down. Rinky talked and talked, long rambling sentences and disconnected anecdotes. His aggrieved voice spun away the hours as easily as his whole life had been lost. Finally, there was someplace they must go and something they must do, but Charles could never remember what it was that seemed so urgent. He did recall stumbling up through the brush and down alleys, ricocheting off walls as he went. He remembered shouting, "Man the lifeboats," several more times. They met some of Rinky's buddies and Charles had never before known such easy, amiable men. He was sure they'd be friends until they died. He made them repeat their names several times so that he wouldn't forget.

It became more and more difficult to stay on his feet. The

friendly seas that had bobbed around him now seemed threatening. Any minute he might go under and drown. He reached out to take his good buddy Rinky's arm for just a moment of support and reassurance, but there was no one there. He stumbled over a tin can and it clattered to one side. He floundered against the brick side of a building.

"Hey, Rinky," he yelled. "Where are you? I can't see anything."

His vision cleared for a moment. He was alone in an alley. Three dim figures moved at the other end. Were they going off without him?

"Hey, wait a minute."

Charles lurched after them, keeping balance by running one hand along the wall. It ended abruptly and he blundered across the sidewalk and off the curb. The pavement was inches lower than he expected. He fell forward like a scarecrow, boneless and flopping. His cheekbone smashed into concrete. Skin and flesh shredded off like carrot on a grater. Something screeched in his ear and nudged against his body. He rolled over groggily. A car bumper hung directly above his head and a tire pressed against his ribs.

"Oh, shit." He closed his eyes and sank into darkness.

In the city jail, two days later, Charles looked up when he heard footsteps outside the cell. He met his father's eyes. The guard watched from the end of the hall.

"You got a smoke?" Charles asked after a moment. His father passed him a cigarette.

"Boy, I thought you had better sense."

"I thought I'd try it your way once."

Asa glanced away and then back again. "You look like hell. What happened to your face?"

"I missed a step."

"Looks like you might have to set here a few days longer. Why'd you kick that deputy when they picked you up off the street?"

"I don't remember."

"The sheriff said he'll let you out next weekend, if you behave yourself." He dragged on his cigarette and coughed. "Before I go, I gotta tell you. You'll find out when you get home, anyway. Your dog died."

"What?"

"Old Blackie. I found him dead this morning when I got up. It's a wonder he lived this long. I know it's tough, but I had to tell you."

Asa walked heavily away. Charles sank to the bunk, his face still, hands loose between his knees. Blackie. God, he was old. Charles could hardly remember a time without him. Miserable skinny old mutt, always underfoot, slurping at Charles with his sloppy tongue, looking up at him with eager eyes. He always waited for Charles to come home from school, sitting by the stump where the trail came out of the woods.

He'd been slow getting up all winter and moved stiffly from one sunny spot to another. It had been a long time since he had chased squirrels or crashed off through the brush in pursuit of a deer, but it had happened so gradually that Charles hardly noticed until he looked back.

Blackie had come out of the woods when Charles was five years old. He remembered the dog creeping from the brush, hesitant on awkward puppy feet, trembling with fear and hunger. He'd licked Charles's hand and looked at him with pleading eyes. His mother was in a good mood that day. She'd given the starving pup a bowl of leftover mush and another of water. After that, he was their dog.

And now he was dead. Charles's eyes stung. His throat ached. Surely those weren't tears that slid down his face. He rubbed his hands over his eyes, wincing as he touched the abrasions on his cheek, tasting the salt that leaked into the corners of his mouth.

Old Blackie. Damn worthless dog . . .

Two weeks later, Charles stopped in Furman's store. He picked up bread, a can of sardines, a six-pack of Coke. The outside door opened and Wally Jenkins, the school's star athlete, came in.

"Hey, Charles, how are you doing?"

"Not bad." A knot formed in the pit of his stomach. He longed to ask about Sherry, but didn't want Wally to know how much he cared.

"You're lucky, in a way, that you can quit school. It's more boring than ever, but my dad would kill me if I even thought about it. He expects me to go to college."

"That might be all right," Charles answered doubtfully. The thought of college was like the notion of being rich, so remote that it was uninteresting. What he wanted to know about was Sherry. Tell me about Sherry, Wally. Does she care that I'm gone?

"I'll probably be a coach," Wally went on. "That way I'll still be involved with sports even when I can't play anymore myself."

"Sounds pretty good." Damn it, don't make me ask.

But Wally rambled on about baseball practice just as though Charles were interested in the stupid baseball team.

"We're having a game this Friday afternoon. You ought to stop by, see everybody."

"I can't. I got a job."

"Oh, yeah? What are you doing?"

"Pulling slabs on the green chain at Pacific Plywood Mill."

"It's probably no worse than school. At least, you get paid."

"I gotta go," Charles said. Damn you, Wally, for not telling me.

"I think Sherry misses you," Wally said. "She's quiet and she doesn't smile much. Jim Parrish hangs around her, trying to get her back. But she hardly looks at him."

Gratefulness flooded Charles. "She'll get over it," he said. But he'd heard all that he could hope to hear.

"She really liked you." Wally sounded faintly surprised. "But her mom has a lot of power over that girl. And then there's that bitch Marlene, who thinks she's better than anyone."

"What's going on with them? I saw Sherry and Marlene in town on Saturday with her Uncle Warren." They hadn't seen Charles; he'd quickly dodged into a store so they wouldn't.

"It's weird how they hang around together, isn't it?" Loretta Furman came through the door at the back, carrying a gray, tiger-striped kitten in her arms. "Charles, lookie what I got. Miz Domingo gave him to me."

"He's cute." Charles rubbed one finger along the kitten's bony back. It closed its eyes and purred.

"See, Wally. Isn't he cute?" Loretta burbled.

Wally drew back, grimacing. "Cats give me the creeps."

"He isn't creepy. He's soft. Touch him and you'll see." She thrust the kitten toward Wally and he stepped backwards. Loretta advanced. The usual placid expression on her face changed. She giggled, a high-edged sound.

Her mother glanced quickly at her, but continued to ring up purchases for another customer.

Charles said, "Let me hold the kitten, Loretta. What's his name?"

Loretta waved the cat up and down in front of Wally, who

had backed into a corner of the shelves. The kitten mewed and clutched at his shirt with tiny claws.

"You're going to make the cat dizzy. Better take it easy," Charles said.

She clutched it to her chest and stroked it gently. "Oh, poor kitty. Poor little Charlie. I won't make you dizzy."

"Is Charlie named for Charlotte?" Charles scratched the kitten behind one ear.

"It's for her. And for you, Charles. My two best friends. Your names are almost the same, so he's named for both of you."

Mrs. Furman came with a pint of milk. She looked gratefully at Charles, but spoke to her daughter. "Here's some milk for the kitten. Let's go pour it into his bowl."

"Good-bye, Charles. I have to feed my kitty now. I have to take good care of him."

"Okay, Loretta. See you next time."

"I can't stand cats," Wally's voice was defensive. "I know it's not normal. One must have scared me when I was a baby or something."

Charles grinned. "I always thought you were such a tough guy."

"It's a phobia. Some people have it for snakes or bugs or small spaces. I've got it for cats. I'm glad no damn cat is named after me."

"He's named after Mrs. Domingo, too."

"Oh, yeah. Her husband was Indian, wasn't he? Are you related?"

"No. I heard he was from the Southwest. He was part Spanish or Mexican. My father is Umatilla—it's a small tribe." Charles explained patiently.

"You know, we talked more today than we ever did at school. Let's do it again." Wally slapped his shoulder.

He's a pretty good guy, Charles thought as Wally left. He always seemed stuck-up at school, too busy and important to bother with me.

He didn't hold it against Wally that, like many whites, he lumped all Native Americans under the same label—Indian—and thought of them as one homogeneous people. In fact, some tribes were as different from other tribes as Swedes were different from Frenchmen. People like Charles, with white blood mixed in, further complicated an already rich and complex stew.

Charles rarely bothered to mention that his mother was Italian nor did he give much consideration to his mixed heritage. His ancestory seemed less important than the problems of daily life.

Mrs. Furman smiled warmly as Charles paid for his groceries. "You're so good with Loretta. Most young men your age don't take the time."

"She's a nice kid," he mumbled, feeling both pleased and embarrassed. He'd be eighteen in August. Maybe he was a young man and not a kid anymore.

The dirty blue Plymouth tore up the furrowed logging road. Its overworked motor whined and knocked in protest. Charles nearly always drove at the outer limits of the vehicle's capacity for speed and his own ability to control. The bald tires whirled in the powdery soil which dried quickly from mud to dust.

The narrow track had been hastily punched out of a hillside mutilated by clear-cut logging. The majestic old-growth trees were gone. A few scrubby trees and saplings, pitiful survivors, clung to a hillside littered with stumps and rejected logs. Brush filled in, flourishing in the empty spaces left by the death of kings.

151

Charles slowed the Plymouth as he saw what he'd hoped to find—a car parked beside the road. He cruised slowly past the other vehicle and into the shade of second-growth timber farther along the road. He turned off the motor and listened.

A power saw droned far up the hill, little more than a faint hum vibrating the air. A tree creaked and popped. A brown and white towhee flickered from one thicket to another. The logger on the power saw probably worked alone, salvaging what remnant timber he could find after the big operators had moved on.

Charles turned the Plymouth and drove back to the other car. He took an empty gas can and a length of rubber hose out of his trunk. He unscrewed the cap of the other gas tank and thrust the hose down inside. He sucked on the free end. Gasoline rose up and burned his tongue. Quickly, he jammed the hose into the can on the ground and spat several times, rubbing the back of his hand across his numbed lips.

When the can was full, Charles stowed it in his trunk. He saw a pair of leather gloves and a fair-sized toolbox on the back seat. The door was locked. He smashed the window with a fist-sized rock. The glove compartment was empty of anything interesting, except two packs of Camels. He took them, the gloves, and the toolbox.

He ricocheted back down the way he'd come and skidded out onto the Nezzac River road with only the briefest glance to check for oncoming traffic. Loose gravel gnawed at the tires as the Plymouth slid sideways. The wheels scrabbled in one spot, then the Plymouth hurtled forward and whirled around the next corner. A loaded logging truck, as big as a boxcar, loomed up ahead. Truck and car rushed past each other with a whoosh and a roar, separated by only a foot or two of windy space.

Charles slowed down, feeling mildly contented. Stealing

was a lot more fun than working. He'd been fired two weeks ago for talking back to the boss, but he'd kept his gas tank full and a few bucks in his pocket by picking up anything that wasn't nailed down. He sold his loot to a contact in Woodbridge. He'd have to look for another job soon, but this was okay for now. His father and Bill had gone to Portland on the bus last week. They'd got in some kind of trouble on Burnside and were in jail, so Charles lived alone in the cabin and drove the car whenever he wanted.

Asa's presence was hardly missed. Days passed and he might not say much more than, "Hand me the coffeepot, boy." Most of the time he didn't even look at Charles. He looked at his plate as he shoveled in beans and beef boiled together. He looked at the wall as he listened to the battery radio at night. He looked at his rifle while he cleaned and oiled it or at his caulk boots as he saddle-soaped them and put on waterproofing. A lot of the time, he looked at nothing, just off into space with his eyes glazed over.

When Charles's mother drifted off that way, he was sure that she saw something. There were things out there—memories, desires—that engaged her attention. They were real and absorbing to her even though no one else saw them. But when Asa stared, there was only emptiness. If there ever had been anything, it was gone, eroded by the slow dripping of days that slipped like water from the roof.

Charles passed the covered wooden bridge, one of the few left in the United States, he'd been told. Mail delivery had stopped at the bridge until recently. So had the phone and electric power lines. But now poles marched slowly up the river, a few houses at a time.

Another two miles and the Jamison place appeared on Charles's left. The house sat back from the road, withdrawn against the side of the hill. Most of the people on the river had been born within a few miles of where they lived, as were their parents and grandparents before them. The Jamisons had arrived less than ten years ago, not long enough to raise their status much above that of newcomer.

Bob was friendly and talked about all the right things—weather, logging, horses, government interference—but some felt that he held himself to be a little better than his neighbors. Mrs. Jamison taught at the high school and was considered tough, but fair. Katie, a year younger than Charles, was cute, but overly studious. She always had her nose buried in a book, reading even if she wasn't studying. Her brother, Justin, was two years older, so Charles hadn't known him much at all. No one else did, either. He'd joined the army right out of high school and was stationed in Japan. Rumor said that his parents were unhappy with his decision. Andy, the little one, was young enough for Charles to disregard.

A figure on horseback jogged down the long straight lane toward the road. It was Bob's brother, Lee. As he approached the wooden gate that closed off ranch property, he turned his horse sideways. He touched the mare with one heel and she sidestepped perkily up to the gate. He leaned down and opened it without having to dismount.

Charles had stopped when he saw Lee and he leaned out the window as the man approached. "Do you remember me?"

Lee's attractive, leathery face creased in a smile. "Sure do. How are you, Charles?"

They talked about Lee's mare, about the weather. Then Charles said, "I thought you'd be chasing wild horses."

"That's coming up. I've been helping Bob around his place."

"Where'd you say you're going?"

"Wyoming. Not far from Rock Springs. A friend named

Art Baxter found a good-sized herd running near his place."

"Last time we talked you said maybe you could use another rider."

"Did I? Well, hell, why not? If you don't mind not getting paid. I can't cut anyone in without clearing it with Art."

"It was just a thought. This old junker probably wouldn't make it that far."

Lee looked critically at the cloud of oil smoke that rolled out of the back of the chugging Plymouth. "You might be right."

"Well, I gotta go. So long."

Charles shifted and accelerated. In the rearview mirror, he saw Lee and his horse cross the road. Charles wondered if he'd saddled the mare to ride a quarter of a mile after the mail. He'd heard jokes about old-time cowboys who would catch and saddle a horse rather than walk a hundred yards. He had no doubt that Lee was an old-time cowboy.

Charles drove another mile to a turnout by a Douglas fir stump about ten feet high. It was weathered and furrowed, left over from the early days of logging when trees were felled with axes and crosscut saws. The loggers inserted spring boards into the trunks in order to avoid the flaring base and the sticky pitch that often collected there. Men balanced on the narrow boards as they made their undercut, sometimes ten to fifteen feet above the forest floor. They worked in pairs, facing one another, each perched on his own board. One swung his double-bladed axe right-handed, the other left-handed, alternately chopping. After the undercut—a notch about one-third through the trunk—was completed, they moved their springboards to the other side. With a man on each end of the long narrow saw, they sawed until the tree lost its support and fell toward the undercut side.

For many years, before mail delivery was extended beyond

the covered bridge, the aging stump had been an informal
post office for people who lived on up the river. Enlarged
from its original size, the old springboard notch held money,
letters, small packages, invitations, a varied assortment of
items. Anyone who lived beyond the stump checked it on the
way upriver and picked up whatever needed delivering to the
houses on the way home. In spite of the row of mailboxes by
the covered bridge, there were still a few people who preferred to use the old stump.

Charles stepped up on the base where it swelled into the
ground to become roots. He pulled a folded piece of brown
paper out of the notch. There was a twenty-dollar bill inside
and a scrawled note that said, "For Charlotte Domingo.
Money I owe, from Tom Cummings."

Charles thrust the money into his pocket next to the stolen
cigarettes and drove on. He hadn't thought about Mrs.
Domingo for awhile. So many things had happened since the
night he'd had supper at her house that she'd been driven
from his mind.

He cruised slowly, glancing down into the river that
turned and twisted on his right, sometimes close to the road,
sometimes far below. It ran high and murky with spring melt,
roiling brown and thick through dark-splashed rocks. The
banks were scarred by drifting logs and hung with sweepers.
On the road, loaded logging trucks boomed steadily past.
The heavy chains bit into high-piled stacks of logs.

A horn blasted behind him. An empty truck was right on
his tail. The back half of the trailer sat piggyback on the front
half. When the trucks went up empty, they carried their own
trailers. Charles pulled over at the next wide spot and the
truck roared past with a thank-you beep on the horn.
Truckers were paid by the number of board feet they hauled,
so they always drove as fast as they could.

The road split a little farther on. The old Nezzac road continued on the left bank of the river, while a new bridge crossed the water to the right. That was where the trucks came from, where the logging company worked. Charles drove up the old road. Soon he saw the unpainted shakes of the house and barns and the corrals that belonged to Charlotte Domingo.

She was out in the garden in front. She waved and Charles pulled over to the left side of the road. As he stepped out, her pack of big red dogs rose up from the shade near the porch. They charged across the garden and hurled themselves against the wire fence. They bellowed and snapped their teeth.

"Shut up, you miserable hounds. Shut up!" Mrs. Domingo flailed at them with a spade. They yelped and snapped a moment more and then subsided to lie panting by the fence.

"I don't know why I keep all these mangy mutts," she complained. "I ought to shoot half of them. All they do is bark and eat. They're no damn good, except once in awhile they chase deer out of the garden."

"Everybody needs a dog or two." An image of Blackie with his thin ribs and eternally hopeful eyes flashed through Charles's mind.

"One or two, sure, but not eight or nine. Aren't you working today?"

"Nope. Got fired."

"Well, a fella can always find a job if he wants one. There's always work in the woods."

"I'll look in a week or two."

Charlotte nodded. "I'm late gettin' my garden in. It's been so wet, I only got a few things planted."

It looked like a lot to Charles, laid out in neat rows with seed packets impaled on little sticks to indicate the vegetables. He saw saw tiny pictures of peas, lettuce, beets, carrots, green onions.

"There was something in the stump for you." Charles fumbled in his pocket, groped past the stolen Camels, and brought out the note with the twenty dollars folded inside.

"Why, thank you, Charles. That's sure nice of you. I hope you didn't come all the way up here just for that."

"Had nuthin' else to do." Charles smiled farewell and got into the battered car. Mrs. Domingo waved the spade as he drove away.

Charles would never steal from friends or neighbors, his own people. But to steal from strangers or from people he disliked was to play an exciting game. The fact that it was illegal and dangerous only made it more of a challenge, more of an exercise in skill and daring. It was a game that seemed to get a little easier all the time.

Chapter 7

CHARLOTTE

Late April

The axe lifted and dropped. Wood split cleanly and the sticks piled up on the ground. The sharp blade chunked again and again into the crisscrossed chopping block. Charlotte straightened and stretched her sore back.

Woodcutting was a year-around job, although in the warm months it took much less for cooking alone than was required for both cooking and heating during cold weather. In spite of the ache in her back, she forced herself to cut a little extra every time. She stacked it on the back porch, planning ahead for the winter months to come. It wasn't a job about which she could say: "There, I'm finished—at least for this year."

Chickens scratched and pecked at the ground nearby, paying no attention to the sound of the axe.

Fools, Charlotte thought. You'd think they'd figure out that one day that axe will fall on them. You'd think they'd be just a little nervous at the sound of chopping.

But people were not much different. Everyone walked around every day under the shadow of the axe. For human beings, the axe took the form of disease, auto accidents, old age. And guns. Sometimes it was a gun.

Charlotte rested the axe blade on the wooden block. She

159

closed her eyes. Once again, she heard the shot. It reverberated inside her head as it had a thousand times before, as it would reverberate over and over until the moment of her death. Each time, it was as loud and shocking as it had been the first time. Each time, it stunned her with its enormity. The sound of a bullet propelled from a barrel. A bullet that once sent on its way could never be deflected nor called back.

Immediately after the sound of the shot came the image of Johnny's face, of his eyes, of the way he had looked at her. Oh, my dear. My darling Johnny. The things people do in the name of love.

Charlotte lifted the axe and brought it down again. Wood tumbled and piled at her feet. She stacked a load in her arms, carried it to the porch, and added to the pile along the wall.

Bob Jamison had once told her that it wasn't wise to stack wood on the porch. "If there's a forest fire, that will make your house burn all the faster. It'll act as kindling."

But it was easier to get wood from the porch, handy to the stove, and no need to go out into the winter rain. If there was a forest fire close by, her old shake-roofed house would likely go up, anyway. A little wood on the back porch wouldn't make much difference.

Her thoughts lingered on the Jamisons. For some fool reason that nobody could figure out, young Justin, normally smart as a whip, had joined the army instead of going to college as his parents expected. The military didn't seem a safe place to be, as Charlotte considered the state of the world. Actually, there was hardly a safe place left. The Russians had got The Bomb last year and no one knew what Communists might do with such terrifying power.

During her long life, Charlotte had lived through a number of wars, always at a safe distance. Faraway countries constantly squabbled among themselves. While it was horrible for those involved, most had no more impact on her than children quarreling on a distant playground. World War III would be very different, according to the radio and newspapers. Fallout from atomic bombs could reach anywhere in the world, even to a remote river valley in western Oregon.

Some of her neighbors stockpiled dried and canned food in secret places in the hills. They kept jugs of water, refilled regularly to stay fresh. And guns and ammunition, to fight off the less prudent who hadn't stored food for the coming Armageddon. Charlotte felt herself too old for that kind of silliness. If she couldn't sustain herself with naturally grown food, if the rivers and creeks were poisoned with nuclear waste, she'd just have to die and get it over with.

But, although she would never admit it to anyone, she was afraid of death, afraid to die alone and terrified of what might come afterward. She thought of those who'd gone before— her parents, Sadie and Mr. Greeley, Alejandro, Johnny. The names struck her like stones, each name a blow in her long and painful life. She wondered, as she had before, if they had gone somewhere else or if they had simply ceased to exist.

To think of death was to stand before a portal which could not be opened from this side, only from the other. For those who'd died young, like Sadie, Alejandro, Johnny, an afterlife would make up for all they'd missed by leaving earth so soon. But oblivion was the best she could hope for herself.

Thoughts of death made her faintly queasy. That was one reason why she raised ponies instead of beef or sheep. Nothing had to die before she made a profit. She had finally learned to kill the chickens, but that didn't mean she liked it. As for the sound of guns, every shot went through her, as the bullet had gone . . .

The axe blade hit a knot and glanced to one side. She'd cut herself if she wasn't careful. Thoughts of blood and death might become an immediate reality and she didn't want to bleed to death from an axe wound. She buried the blade in the chopping block. Enough for today. Enough for her back; enough if she was getting careless. She carried the last of the wood to the porch and added it to the stack.

The dogs in front began a racket. The dogs in back raced wildly to the front yard, barking before they knew why. Charlotte walked through the house and peered out the cloudy windowpane.

Down at the end of the pasture, a shiny new convertible had pulled under the trees on the river side of the road. A man stood beside the car, fiddling with something he held in his hand. She recognized Glenn Draper and knew he carried a fishing rod. He'd bought that fancy car, another kind of bait, after his wife left him. He liked to fish the Nezzac. Charlotte wouldn't have thought a banker would be such an out-doorsman, but she'd seen him for years, fishing and hiking up and down the river, always alone. He'd asked her, nice and polite, if she minded him fishing across the road from her house. She didn't.

The hullaballoo from the dogs was deafening. Charlotte flung open the screen door. "Shut up!" she bellowed. Encouraged by her presence, the dogs increased their clamour. She marched onto the porch, grabbed the broom that leaned against the wall, and walloped right and left. Yelps followed. Some dogs dodged and collided with others, who snapped at the offenders. A crescendo of yelps, growls, and barks filled the air. Charlotte cursed and yelled as the broom thumped in all directions.

In a few moments, the last yelping dog raced around the house to the back, in a rush to escape the dreadful broom. Charlotte leaned against the porch rail to get her breath. Glenn Draper, fishing rod held erect like a lance, stared toward the house. When he saw that she was looking at him, he took off his hat and waved it. She knew that he was smiling. He always smiled, a great big grin. He was a friendly fellow, maybe too friendly. Charlotte thought that every time Glenn grinned, he hoped it would bring more business to the bank.

Still, it was better to be too friendly than not sociable at all, like that other big shot, the Stonebraker brother from Portland. The turn-off to his cabin was not far past Charlotte's place. He cruised along in his big white Cadillac, smack-dab in the middle of the road as though he owned it. He moved over for logging trucks, but not much else. And he never looked at anyone, either, as if the sight of poor people might damage his rich eyes.

Charlotte noticed that Glenn's arm still pumped up and down. He was determined that his greeting be noticed. She raised the broom and brandished it at him. Satisfied, he turned and disappeared into the brush along the river.

Later in the evening, she stood on the back porch with her arms folded, looking at the moon-washed hill that rose behind the house. The dark arm of the old forest draped itself along the line of the fence to the east. It was prepared to encircle the house, but discreet about its intentions. The trees rustled and chittered softly together, busy with their secret life. Moving things shifted and brushed against other moving things, a vague vast host that whispered and murmured together.

She went inside, turned on the battery-operated radio and sat in a chair by the window without lighting the lamp. "Irene, good ni-ight," sang the Weavers. A man's voice followed, encouraging listeners to send for plans to build a backyard bomb shelter. "This program can save thousands of lives in the event of a national emergency." A short news broadcast followed and Charlotte listened sourly.

Communist agents may have infiltrated the State Department and were feared to present a major security risk. The Soviet Union continued to boycott meetings of the U.N. Security Council.

Always fussing and squabbling. As far as Charlotte could tell, most of it was over territory, like kids in the back seat of the car. "He's on my side." "No, she crowded me first." There was no world-sized Mom or Dad to straighten things out, so the kids squabbled on with the aid of ever more dangerous toys.

The announcer said something about Indian tribes, capturing her attention again. "The senator supports termination of federal services to Indians and advocates placing them instead under the jurisdiction of the states. In a related issue, some tribal leaders objected to a proposal to repeal the federal law that forbids the sale of alcoholic beverages to Indians. They believe that they should have local options in regard to sales on reservations."

Charlotte knew that the war years had been difficult for the native people in many different ways. Most funding had been diverted to the war effort and many reservation schools and agencies had closed. After the war, a large number of better-educated and more ambitious young men who had served in the military declined to return to reservation life and took their families elsewhere, creating a vacuum in tribal leadership.

People like Johnny, like Charles, were often caught between two cultures, cut off from the old ways, uninterested in or excluded from the new. She feared that Charles was headed for trouble—no supervision and too much time on his hands. She was sorry he'd quit school. She hadn't liked it herself and Johnny hadn't gone beyond grade school. But the world was changing and a person needed schooling these days. She'd didn't want Charles to waste his life, as Asa had done. Charles needed an opportunity, someone to believe in him, to show him how things could be better. If he were her grandson, she could tell him so much . . .

She sighed. Night tucked itself around the house. The arm of the ancient forest seemed to creep a little closer. In the dusky bedroom behind her, the rocking chair squeaked. Floorboards creaked gently as if someone stepped upon them. She turned off the radio. Slowly, dreamily, she slipped through the half-open door into the shadows and the memories that awaited her there.

Foxy, the horse that William Mosher had given to Charlotte, quickly learned his lessons. She'd ridden all her life and enjoyed working with him herself, helping teach him to neck rein.

She saw little of Johnny. When he first came, he had stayed close to the main house, working with the new stock. He was courteous and formal, careful to keep a distance between them. Later, as chores took him away, she saw him only occasionally. But even if he was not in her sight, his image burned in her mind. She recalled the softness of his eyes, the line of his mouth, the grace of his slender body. She imagined his voice whispering things no man had ever said to her.

And all the time she was betrothed to Howard. Their wedding was planned for the fall. A definite date had not been set, but Howard pressed to make it as soon as possible. Even before she saw Johnny, Charlotte had delayed and delayed again. Marriage was so final. Once those vows were spoken, her life was settled forever. She wished . . . she wished for a little more time. And then into that small space which she had stubbornly preserved rode Johnny Domingo.

Sunday was Charlotte's day off. Sometimes she went to church with the Moshers, riding in the buggy down the road along the river. Sometimes she stayed home, enjoying the unaccustomed privacy of the place all to herself. Sometimes she rode horseback, with Howard or alone. She set out early one morning, taking along a lunch of cold meat and biscuit.

"I'll go to Big Bend," she told gnomish Moss as he saddled Foxy.

The day was warm and windy. Thick white clouds dolloped the distant sky. Foxy fretted at the bit, moved it around in his mouth, and tossed his head up and down. Now and then he skittered along sideways. She kept him in check, half-enjoying his bouncy, fidgety gait.

The river soon made a sharp bend to the left. Off to the right, far across a jumble of rocks, a long line of rimrock broke in the middle to form a sort of gate. Charlotte had been told that there was a pretty little valley and spring beyond, called Flat Rock. She'd never seen it, although she had started twice with Howard. Once his horse's shoe had come loose. Another time they had lingered along the way, dawdling over lunch, talking and kissing, so they'd had to turn back before dark.

On a sudden impulse, she turned off the road. It wasn't wise. She'd told Moss that she was going to Big Bend and, in case of accident, that was where they would look for her. But it was early and the opening in the rampart appeared alluring. They went across a stretch of rock, through a dry, steep-sided gulch, up a long gradual slope. The gateway was much farther than it looked. She ate part of her biscuits and meat on the way.

At last Charlotte passed through the rocky shoulders and paused to look back the way she'd come. The land slanted down to the silvery-gray ribbon of the river, fringed with a scribble of green trees. The ranch buildings were out of sight and so was the road. She was all alone in the wide windy land.

As she passed between the rocks and started down the other side, she moved from sunshine to shadow. Great clouds loomed above her, through which the sun gleamed in ever-changing patterns. Below lay the little patch of green that marked the spring. A sudden gust of cool wind whipped up into her face. Foxy broke into a gallop down the hill, then bogged his head and erupted into exuberant bucking. Charlotte grabbed for the saddle horn, but it was too late. She hit the ground with bone-jarring force.

As she wobbled to her feet, the world revolved slowly around her. The sky didn't stay where it belonged. First it was above her and then sickeningly far below, deep as a well. She teetered and fell, but upwards into the dirt. Suspended far above, she saw Foxy with his nose in the spring. She hung on as long as she could, her fingers digging into the earth, but she slipped helplessly backwards, backwards into the sky.

It was cloudy and much cooler when Charlotte opened her eyes again. Her head hurt. She sat up carefully. As soon as she could, she staggered to the spring and sank to her knees. She drank and splashed water on her face and neck. Foxy was not in sight. He hadn't learned to ground tie.

Someone will find me, she thought woozily. She lay down and promptly fell asleep.

When she awoke again it was to darkness and the sound of the sky breaking apart overhead. Great pieces tumbled heavily around her. The blackness split open and a long crackling reach of lightning flickered nearby. Fat drops of water plumped onto her.

"It's raining." she said aloud. She crawled on her hands and knees under the partial shelter of a big rock. The rain came down harder, beating into the thirsty land, washing away dust and the tracks of horses.

Nobody will find me now. I'll have to walk out.

Perhaps she dozed again. Then she heard a sound not belonging to the rain. A horse put his nose down to her and snorted.

"Foxy?" She clutched at him. Instead of a horse, she gripped a poncho and someone said her name.

"Johnny, is that you?"

It rained most of the night. They crowded together under his rain gear and what small shelter the rocks provided. She slept fitfully, shifting on the rough ground. Each time she awoke, Johnny Domingo spoke to her in a language she did not understand, but the sounds were soothing. With her back against him, warmed by the heat of his body, she slept again.

Morning dawned gray and damp. He built a small fire and made tea. She nibbled on hardtack, but her stomach roiled uneasily and dizziness returned every time she sat up. She wrapped herself in Domingo's bedroll and, between showers, he dried her wet clothes over the little fire.

Foxy grazed with the buckskin beside the spring. Johnny had been on his way back to the ranch. As he passed the bend in the river, he saw the little speck that was Foxy coming down from the gap. He waited to see who it was and soon saw Charlotte's horse heading home, saddle empty, reins trailing on the ground.

Johnny had backtracked on Foxy's trail. Charlotte imagined him leaning down from the saddle, dismounting when the prints were dim on the hard ground. By the time it started to rain, he guessed where the horse had come from and he jog-trotted swiftly along, leading Foxy, following his instinct when the trail was washed away.

All that day, Charlotte passed in and out of sleep. Johnny flickered shadow-like before her, tending the reluctant fire.

Now and then he crouched beside her and lay his hand on her head. He gave her more tea to which he added a bitter herb he took from his saddlebag.

Once he asked, "Do you feel like riding."

"No." It made her head spin to think of it.

At last she awoke again. Her head felt nearly normal. The slow washing waves of nausea had subsided. She felt as though all the bones were drawn out of her body and stacked away in a pile, leaving her as limp as a scarecrow.

Night had come again and the rain had stopped. Far above, stars shone bright and cold, chips of shattered ice. Johnny Domingo lay dark and glinting beside the fire, composed of shadow and scintillating bits of brightness from the flames. His head rested on his arm and his velvety eyes were fixed upon her.

She sat up cautiously and he rose with her.

"Are you better now?"

"Yes."

"Then perhaps you will eat."

They talked later. "I will not stay long at this ranch," he said. "I want to go over the mountains to western Oregon. Once I met a man from there. He said that the trees are so tall and so green that they grow on the mountains like wheat in the field, each one two hundred feet tall. Do you not think it would be fine to see so many trees so tall?"

"Yes. It would be fine." Fierce longing pierced her like an arrow. "But I probably never will. Howard hates to go very far from home."

"You are truly promised to him?"

"Yes, I am." She spoke quickly, firmly, to still the doubts and the fantasies that shimmered inside her. She had promised. She had given her word, a serious and binding promise to marry, not only to Howard but to the community, to the

169

Moshers, to Howard's parents. Howard's mother, Hannah, had welcomed Charlotte warmly into her home and into her heart. Hannah must have dreamed of someone like herself for her oldest son, someone from a prominent family, certainly not an orphan—little more than a hired girl. But Charlotte saw no criticism in Hannah's eyes and only warmth in her frequent hugs and touches. She would not repay such generosity with faithlessness nor lightly change her mind, no matter how tempted by the beauty of a stranger.

"Yes, I have promised," she repeated firmly, even if her heart and her body trembled.

Johnny ran one finger lightly down the curve of her cheek. "So be it." He walked from the circle of firelight.

When he didn't come back, Charlotte slept again. She awoke several times to the scent of sage and wet earth. She heard the wind moving softly on the desert, the sound of the horses chewing grass and once, far away, the wailing of a coyote woke its lonely painful echo in her heart.

At dawn she heard leather creak as Johnny saddled the horses. They spoke little, but mounted and rode toward the ranch in the chill of early day. The sun drenched across the land in a steadily advancing wave, leaving pockets of shadow behind. Before they reached the ranch, they met the riders coming out, beginning their second day of search.

Charlotte was put to bed at the ranch, while Elsie fussed over her. It was lovely to be pampered and she enjoyed it for an entire day. But guilt—she was supposed to help Elsie, not the other way around—drove her to rise early the second morning. She felt slightly dizzy as she mixed up biscuit dough.

Elsie soon joined her. She set out cups, saucers, and plates with little thumps. She clucked continuously like a nervous hen, a mixture of domestic comments and maternal fussings.

Charlotte felt the weight of unasked questions and understood her friend's curiousity. She had, after all, stayed two nights in the desert with Johnny Domingo. But she had little to say. All details and explanations seemed insignificant as she struggled with the sense that she'd lost control of her life, that she was in the grip of wheels set in motion long ago and was now merely dragged along by offstage machinery.

I want to change it. I do. I do. But the cost . . . the cost to us all . . .

The outside door banged open and William thudded into the room. He threw a leather drawstring bag onto the table. "We've lost our wrangler."

Charlotte and Elsie looked at him in surprise.

He said, "Domingo drew his time. He's getting his horse now." As the silence lengthened, he looked at Charlotte. "He asked about you. When I told him that you were up and around this morning, he said it was time to move on."

Charlotte went out on the porch. Johnny saddled his muscular buckskin gelding by the corral. He tightened the cinch, checked the bedroll, swung up into the saddle. The horse moved toward the house.

He saw Charlotte and took off his hat as he approached. The early light shone on his hair, glossing it black as the wings of a raven. He looked somberly at her as he rode by. A little whirlwind snatched up dust raised by the buckskin's hoofs. It spun into a brief gritty cloud that sifted against the fence and back to the ground. Horse and rider were the color of earth and the coppery morning sky. As silently as figures from a dream, they dissolved into the shimmering desert day and vanished within moments.

Charlotte became aware of the Moshers peering out the window behind her. When she went back into the house, the smell of burning biscuits filled the kitchen. She scraped them into the woodbox and began to mix a new batch.

"You'd better have some coffee while you wait," Charlotte said, stubbornly ignoring the dull pressure in her head and the other, unlocalized agony that engulfed her.

William and Elsie sat down at the table. From somewhere outside, a meadowlark warbled a salutation to the day.

Howard had been with the riders going out to search as Charlotte returned. He had greeted her thankfully, adding his bass obbligato to the confusion of sounds that welcomed her back. When she was hustled home and into bed, Howard had been left outside her room with his hat in his hand.

He arrived the next day and greeted her stiffly. "Charlotte, will you come outside? I need to talk to you."

There was no one else at home, but she slowly followed him to the gate. He took off his hat and put it on again. He cleared his throat twice and looked around the yard as if in search of something.

"What is it, Howard?"

"This isn't easy to say. But—here it is. I'm breaking our engagement." His face flushed with the effort of speech and then paled as he heard the words he'd blurted out.

"Why?" Her hands trembled suddenly and she clasped them together.

"You must know."

"I think it's fair you tell me."

He shifted uneasily and repeated himself. "It's not easy to say, when you stand there looking at me like that." After a pause, he went on. The words seemed to hurt his mouth, like bits of broken glass, but he said them anyway. "You spent two nights out on the desert with that Goddamned Indian."

"There wasn't anything happened out there you or anyone

else couldn't have watched."

"Don't you think I want to believe that? But the whole thing was so fishy. You said you were riding one way and then you went another. And why'd you stay out two nights? You weren't so far away that you couldn't have come in after the first night."

"I was sick. I didn't feel like riding."

"You made an awful fast recovery for being so sick."

She didn't tell him that her head still ached.

He went on. "Why didn't you signal? Domingo had a rifle. You must have known everybody would be out looking for you. A couple of shots in the air, just so somebody could find you, and everything would have been all right."

"I never thought of that." Why hadn't she? It would have been a perfectly logical, sensible thing to do.

"What about your half-breed friend? He's plenty cagey. Why didn't he think of it?"

"I don't know."

"Maybe I'll ask him. Where is he?"

"He left yesterday morning."

"Left? You mean for good?"

"Yes."

"Where'd he go?"

"I don't know. Maybe western Oregon."

Howard seemed surprised and turned the information over in his mind. "It wouldn't be so bad if it had been somebody else. But he's no more than a sneaky savage . . ."

"He's not sneaky or a savage."

"See, you're stickin' up for him again. I know better than anybody else the kind of girl you've always been, but you act different when he's around. And I saw how he touched you that time. You were going to be my wife. I can't have people think that you were fooling around with someone like

Domingo while you were engaged to me. I've got more pride than that."

She smiled a little. "Yes, Howard. Let's save your pride."

"Well, I had to tell you right out how I feel."

"I've told you the truth," she said composedly. "As you said, you know me pretty well by now. If you don't believe what I say, it's only right we don't go on."

He glared at her, baffled. "All right, then. Good-bye, Charlotte."

"Good-bye, Howard."

She watched as he went awkwardly through the gate and mounted his horse. He hauled the bay roughly around and looked at her once more from his red miserable face. Then he jog-trotted out of the compound and away down the rutted road.

Charlotte looked after him. She knew, as surely as she knew the sun would rise tomorrow, that he would return to her. She would continue to live her blameless life, to work hard without complaint. She'd go with the Moshers and their children to Sunday school picnics, to dances at the neighboring ranches, to town on Saturday. As Howard watched her, he would begin to doubt the possibility of her guilt. Even now, he was not sure.

Maybe he'd wanted her to cry and so assure him of her womanly weakness and dependence on him, of his worth and her gratitude. Maybe he'd wanted her to cling and plead, to give him the opportunity to be strong and generous.

But even if she never did, he would come back. There wasn't another girl like her for a hundred miles around. Howard had told her so often enough and it might be true, although Charlotte felt she deserved no more credit than a pinto mare deserved credit for the pretty markings she received at birth.

She could still live in the big house by the river. She could still have a hired girl and new clothes even when she didn't need them. She could still have Howard Mosher, a rich rancher's eldest son. All she had to do was wait.

Howard was a tiny dot in the distance. She felt hollow with indecision. She closed her eyes and then it came . . . at first a gentle seeping, then a great flood poured into her, until she was suffused with excitement. How much of a choice was there, really, between the certainty of a dull circumscribed life with Howard and all the wild possibilities with the man she loved?

Charlotte skimmed to the house like a bird in flight. She sorted swiftly through her few belongings and divided them into two piles on the bed. She stacked the smallest pile on a folded blanket. She gathered coffee, dried fruit, oatmeal, matches, and a few other supplies into a clean flour sack. She rolled everything into a lightweight canvas tarp. She wrote a hasty note to Elsie and left it on the kitchen table. She caught and saddled Foxy, tied the tarp on behind, and added a feed bag full of oats for him.

In a few minutes, Foxy jogged down the road. Charlotte didn't once look back. In town, she withdrew her small savings from the bank, ignoring the half-curious, half-friendly questions of the teller.

She took the road that led west, pushing Foxy harder than was wise for the journey that lay ahead. Oregon was a big territory. There were a thousand trails, mountains, and valleys into which Johnny could vanish. He'd said "western Oregon," but he could blow before the wind like thistledown, following the fading tracks of his ancestors from Mexico to Canada and all across the wide lands between.

Darkness approached too soon. Charlotte knew that she should find a campsite, but she was reluctant to end the steady ticking-off of miles beneath Foxy's feet. The last of the sunset glowed in the sky ahead, dark rose-pink splotched with the serrated blackness of clouds. As she hurried through the advancing night, she saw a campfire twinkling in a clump of trees.

A horse nickered. Foxy answered. As she drew closer, she saw Johnny Domingo standing by the fire. He waited for her beside the trail, following that mysterious instinct stronger than reason. He took off his hat and held it in front of his chest. The firelight kindled on his darkness and all his glittering metallic adornments. Foxy trotted eagerly toward him and Charlotte saw that he was smiling.

Chapter 8

LEE

Early May to mid-May

"Thanks, Lee." His slim, dark-haired sister-in-law accepted the mail on the day that Lee had spoken to Charles at the mailbox. "You had a phone call while you were gone. He didn't give his name."

"I wonder if it could have been Art. Not many people know I'm here."

"He said he'd call back. Here, do you want to look at the new *Argosy?*"

Lee flipped through the magazine. The lead article was about hunting for pirate treasure under the waters of the Caribbean. He read part of it. The phone rang.

"Maybe it's for you," Vivian said as she picked it up. She listened a moment. "Yes, he's here now."

Lee took the phone. "Hello?"

No one responded. "Hello?" he said again.

The silence lengthened. Then a man's muffled voice said, "I know who you are."

"Sorry, I don't understand."

The voice sounded a little louder, but still indistinct, unnatural. "I saw you with Joanne. I know who you are."

Lee, stunned into silence, didn't answer. He had a sudden

image of lips moving in a self-satisfied smile. He made his voice cool, indifferent, a poker-playing voice. "Oh, really? We should talk about that. Where can we meet?"

He sensed the smile disappear from the other end of the phone connection. The voice was harsh, clear. "You wouldn't want to meet me. I don't think you'd like me." The phone went dead.

Lee replaced the receiver. "Has this guy ever called before?" Lee asked Vivian, who looked at him with questions in her eyes.

"I don't know. I don't think so. What did he say?"

Lee hesitated. He'd given Bob and Vivian a sanitized version of Joanne's death, little more than the fact that a woman he occasionally dated had been murdered by someone who might have a link to the Woodbridge area. But now the man had connected Lee to Bob and Vivian. He'd called their house. Whether Lee liked it or not, they were involved.

He said, "It was an anonymous call. The man said he saw me with Joanne, the woman who was killed in Redding. He said he knows who I am."

Vivian's eyes widened. "Oh, my God. You'd better call the sheriff. That sounds like a threat."

"I'm not sure it was a threat. Maybe just a . . . a . . ."

"If a man who might be a killer calls and says he knows who you are, I'd call that a threat."

"Yeah, you're right."

Vivian looked up the number and Lee talked to a deputy sheriff. After some questions, the man said that he would contact the authorities in Redding and inform them of the call. He asked that Lee contact him if he received any more. Then he said, "If I were you, Mr. Jamison, I'd be cautious for awhile. Cautious and watchful."

As he hung up, Vivian said, "I hear Katie and Andy

coming in. Let's not say anything in front of them."

"All right. I'm sorry about this, Vivian."

"It's not your fault."

Lee retreated to his room, the one that had been Justin's before he joined the army. Lee took the bourbon bottle from the closet shelf and poured a good-sized jolt.

Vivian said it wasn't his fault, but he knew better. If he were choosier about the women he dated, if he had not become involved with a foolish woman with a dangerous "friend," then no peculiar phone calls would have come to his brother's house. Lee had pulled his family, including his sixteen-year-old niece and her little brother, into an ugly and dangerous situation. He'd brought them all to the attention of a vicious and unpredictable man.

The dusty black Mercury clattered at eighty miles an hour down long, gently curving Wyoming roads. The radio blared a catchy cowboy tune. Lee whistled and boop-de-diddled along with it. It felt good to be on the road again.

He'd left Whistler's Bend earlier than planned. He'd told Mrs. Furman at the Nezzac River store, as well as every neighbor he happened to meet, of his intended departure. He created every opportunity for word that he was no longer at the ranch to reach the anonymous caller. Since Art didn't expect him so soon, Lee had camped and fished in Idaho.

The peaceful days had somewhat eased his mind and taken away a little of the guilt and apprehension. The changing images that flashed by the car windows and the sense of imminent encounter were as addictive as a drug. The old anticipation returned at every bend and hill, a subliminal notion that something totally unexpected might wait just out of sight.

He'd long ago discovered that going to a place was almost

always better than actually being there. After the first few days at any destination, Lee often experienced a feeling of disappointment. Things were rarely quite the way he'd expected. Contentment was like the foot of the rainbow, he guessed. No matter how fast he moved, it always seemed to be somewhere else.

His thoughts wandered to Doris. It had been like coming home when she took him in after his return from Mexico. That had been a bad time, when a life of change and adventure had suddenly seemed more like one of aimless drifting. It wasn't fun anymore. He'd immersed himself in Doris the way a thirsty man might plunge into a pool in the desert. He'd even thought about marriage, a thought so laden with words like "responsibility" and "forever" that he soon packed up and moved on. He admitted that he sometimes still missed the easy companionship he'd shared with her. Of all the women he'd known, he'd felt the most comfortable with Doris.

He hadn't been the pursuer, though. She had invited him, as women so often did, starting with one of the hired girls on the farm in Illinois. He was barely sixteen and she an "older woman" of twenty.

Later, of course, there was Rosalind. Lost love is the most memorable, he'd found. Memories of Rosalind came accompanied by the fragrance of honeysuckle, the sweep of surprisingly heavy hair that flowed like water across his skin, the tide of emotion that swept him to the moment when he'd handed her his twenty-four-year-old heart in the form of sapphire and diamonds. There'd been no time for tedium or boredom with her, no months or years of taking for granted what once seemed rare and precious, no thickening waist, fading eyes or coarsening skin. Rosalind existed beyond all of that, in a shimmering dream of endless youth.

If she were alive, she would be over sixty years old. If she were alive. It was far more likely that she was dead. Drug users as a rule did not have expectations of long, healthy lives. Chances were good that what Lee believed was cocaine had led to other abuses—alcohol, perhaps heroin. He'd seen the sort of women Rosalind might have become—old hags with harshly dyed hair, smeared scarlet lips and matching fingers like blood-dipped claws.

Knock it off, he told himself. You're not writing a dime novel. Besides, it's over, twenty-six years over. Forget her. He'd think about the next few days, about wild horses and long days in the saddle riding through untouched country where fences and suburbs were little more than ugly rumor, out of sight and out of mind.

In the evenings he would listen to Henry Baxter's stories. He was Art's father, well over seventy, but still a tough old bird. He'd chased mustangs with the legendary Pete Barnum in Nevada forty years ago. Henry had a lot of old-timer tales to tell; some of them were even true.

Originally corrals of poles or brush had been built on the spot. That limited the areas where mustangs could be hunted. If poles did not grow naturally in the area—and there were far more places in the wild horses' range where they did not grow than where they did—they could be cut and transported to the hunting area on horseback. By the time the corrals were set up, the wild horses were often spooked by the activity and retreated into even more remote country.

Barnum originated the idea of carrying in lightweight canvas, cut into sections seven feet high. It could be erected in a short time with a minimum of disturbance. Once penned, the horses couldn't see over the sides, which seemed as solid as rock to the range animals. They didn't hurl themselves at the canvas as they did at poles, trying to batter through or climb over. Fewer animals were killed or injured and horse hunting was more profitable.

The cowboy's love for his horse was a favorite topic of song and story, but for some reason it rarely extended to the wild mustang. They were more likely to be regarded as inferior pests consuming feed that would otherwise go to support more valuable stock. Cattlemen complained that wild horses clipped the grass even closer than sheep and that their sharp hoofs cut up the range. They said that they chased domestic stock away from salt licks and water holes. The mustangs were undaunted by the fences that divided their native range and often knocked them down in their attempts to reach water.

Faint but ominous sounds from the Mercury distracted Lee from thoughts of wild horses. He'd heard that worrisome clatter ever since he'd crossed the Idaho border. He hoped it wouldn't become a major problem.

Just ahead, he saw the turn-off to the Baxter ranch, marked by Art's brand burned into a piece of weathered wood hung on a post. The car bounced down the one-track lane for over a mile before he came to the small house, with out-buildings huddled around it.

Lee got out of the car and stretched. He'd heard a good story in a bar a couple of nights ago and knew it would get a laugh from Henry. The old man liked dirty stories and always had a fund of new ones. It was worth driving all the way from Oregon just to swap stories and hear old Henry laugh.

A brown dog, faintly collie, barked and sniffed his boots. The dog trotted to the car and lifted a leg to make his mark on the rear wheel. Art's wife came out of the house, pushing faded hair out of her eyes.

Lee took off his hat. "Good afternoon, Fernie." He braced himself for the oncoming torrent of words.

"Hello, Lee. Art ain't here. He had some business to tend to. He said for you to put your gear in the shed. He set up a cot for you. If you want to come to the house, I'll give you a cup of coffee."

"That sounds mighty good." He followed her inside and hung his hat on the back of a chair. "I haven't seen you for a couple of years. How have you been?"

"Not too good, since you asked." She poured coffee into a cup. "I haven't felt right since a year ago Christmas. I had surgery, female complications. An operation is bad any time, but this was just before Christmas. I'd planned to sew for Glenda's children—that's our daughter, you know—but I couldn't do hardly a thing. I was in the hospital a week, flat on my back, and in such pain. Men don't have any idea what women go through. Most men make a big fuss over nothing. There's no man in the world a bigger baby than Art when he gets a cold or some little complaint. He takes on like he was dying. But there I was, home from the hospital, so weak I could barely move, and he acted like I oughta go right out and chop wood. It woulda been nice if Glenda could have come and stayed, but she just had a little one—that makes two— and they're the cutest babies you'd ever want to see. Too bad they ain't got a better father. That man she married, not worth the powder to blow him up. I never did like him, with his shifty eyes, and he's proved I was right. He's got him a girlfriend on the side, a two-bit tavern waitress. He denies it, of course, but I know better. And all this time, Glenda sits home with the babies. It ain't easy to spend so much time waiting at home. You men got no idea how lucky you are to get out and do things the way you want. I thought I'd go crazy last winter with the old man. He got to be such a burden. Didn't know what was going on. Almost set the house on fire twice, going off and leaving his cigarettes burning. I confess it was a relief when he died. It was time, anyway. No point living on past . . ."

"Are you talking about Henry?" Lee interrupted her droning voice. "Is he dead?"

"Yes, a little more than two weeks ago. You may think I'm hard-hearted, but he didn't do much more than set around the house, smoking and reading. That man spent more money on books and magazines. And wasted more time reading. Well, I've seen you read, too, Lee—all those books you carry with you. But Daddo read lots of trash. And then his old cronies would come and they'd set on the porch and tell dirty stories, laughing like a pack of coyotes. Horrid old men, all of them. Didn't have any decency. Seems like a man should learn to have pure thoughts when he's lived seventy-seven years, but not him and not his friends, neither. I got so tired of them hanging around the house . . ."

Lee stood up. "Thanks for the coffee. I'll put my gear in the shed now."

"You do that. Art should be back before long. I might have gone with him, but then I thought, no, if I go, then sure as shootin' . . ."

Lee closed the door gently. How did Art bear living with a woman who talked so much? But maybe she didn't talk to him. Maybe she'd said everything she had to say to him a long time ago. Life wasn't easy for women on these remote ranches. Still, it didn't seem right that a good man's epitaph was buried among a flood of complaints spilled out by his fault-finding daughter-in-law. His life—any man's life—should be worth more than that.

Henry Baxter was old, messy, and dirty-minded, but he had a great sense of humor and he loved to laugh. He was a walking anthology of stories, nowhere near all of them off-color. He never stopped reading and learning, trying to expand the horizons of his world. Art's wife could have learned a lot from him, if she'd stopped complaining long enough to listen.

So now Henry was dead and all the stories were buried with him in the ground. Lee tossed his bedroll on the sagging cot and lit a cigarette. If men like Henry, settled with a family, left so little sorrow behind when they died, what about him? Would anyone mourn Lee? He sometimes thought of himself as a tumbleweed, moving on with any wind that passed. It had seemed a romantic image. But now as he thought of tumbleweed, all he could picture was a dry withered life form. It didn't take root or provide comfort or nourishment. It just blew on by, blew on by.

Early the next morning, Lee sipped good, strong coffee in the Baxters' kitchen. Fernie talked about the weather, the neighbors, her grandchildren. She was a talker, but she was also a hell of a cook. Last night's beef stew may have been the best he'd ever tasted. This morning he'd eaten so many pancakes that he'd been forced to loosen his belt a notch and, in spite of his protests, she spooned more batter into the skillet. A platter heaped with thick curling slices of bacon waited in the warming oven. A yellow bowl, half-filled with brown-shelled eggs, sat on the tin-covered surface of a cabinet by the woodstove.

Art winked at Lee and took another bite of pancake, perhaps suggesting that background noise was a price he willingly paid for other comforts.

The collie barked from the yard. Art looked out the window. "Now, who the hell is that, on foot way out here?"

Cool morning air swirled in as he opened the door. Lee rose to look over his shoulder. A sturdy figure, black-haired and hatless, hiked along the lane toward the house. He carried a small pack on his back.

Fernie was so astonished that she managed only one short sentence. "Why, it looks like an Indian."

Lee was equally surprised. "I'll be damned. It's Charles Balleau."

"A friend of yours?" asked Art.

"Well, he's my brother's neighbor. He's—I guess he's a friend. I did say something about him maybe coming along, but I didn't really expect . . ."

"Shut up, Monty," Art bellowed at the dog. "Goddamn dog. Nobody ever comes here on foot. They're always on a horse or in a vehicle of some kind. Stupid dog don't know what to make of somebody walkin'. Monty, get over here."

Monty, appearing chagrined, scooted toward the door. He woofed once more, nervously, as Charles entered the yard. The boy's longish hair scraggled around his collar. He looked ungroomed and wary, like a stray dog not at all confident of welcome.

"Come in." Art beckoned him. "Any friend of Lee's is welcome here."

Charles sidled in. Lee made the introductions, as Charles hovered by the door, ready to snap and run.

"Take off your pack. Set down and have some coffee. Fernie, pour the man a cup," Art said.

Mrs. Baxter's lips pursed suspiciously as she eked out three-quarters of a cup.

"Where's your car?" Lee asked, recalling the aging Plymouth. He thought of the knock in his own Mercury and of breakdowns along the road.

"I didn't trust that heap enough to drive it out of state," Charles answered. "I came on the bus as far as Rock Springs and hitchhiked here last night."

"Where'd you sleep?" asked Art.

Charles gestured toward the open range beyond the small house. "Out there."

They looked at his pack, too small for cooking gear. A tattered olive drab Army surplus sleeping bag, leaking feathers through several pinprick holes, hung from the bottom of the pack.

Charles looked at Art. "I don't expect a share of the money. I came to see the wild horses."

There was a hint of longing in his voice. Lee wondered if he dreamed of them as Lee had once dreamed of wolves and vast dark herds of buffalo.

"You better have some pancakes," Fernie said. She put three on a plate and sided them with eggs and bacon. She poured more coffee.

Charles took a bite. He chewed a moment, then took another and worked on it thoughtfully. He looked at Mrs. Baxter. All the hardness disappeared from his face when he smiled. "Ma'am, these are the best pancakes I ever ate in my life."

Fernie blinked, dazzled by the sudden, white-toothed smile. She wiped her hands on her faded blue and white apron. "Here, have some more." She snatched his plate and heaped it with pancakes. "Try this syrup. I made it from blueberries I got from my neighbor last summer. It's pretty good, if I do say so myself."

"Ummmm." Charles was too busy shoveling in food to use his mouth for speech.

Fernie, satisfied, watched him eat. "Don't your mother worry about you traveling around all by yourself?"

"Got no mother. Not since I was six years old."

Something happened to Fernie's face. She clutched at her apron and sank down on the chair beside Charles.

Art whispered, not softly, in Lee's ear. "He better watch it.

She'll be pettin' him in a minute."

"I heard that, Arthur Baxter. You watch your mouth." She sprang to her feet. She shifted bowls and wiped things. Then she said to Charles, "You could eat some more bacon, couldn't you? And how about another egg?"

Leather creaked as Lee shifted in the saddle. "This is not what I expected," he complained to Charles who was mounted on one of Baxter's horses. "I can't believe that Art hired a pilot and a damn airplane to look for the damn mustangs. It's not the way he used to do it. All he needed us for was to help build the damn corral."

Charles didn't answer. After breakfast, Art had tried to convince him to use his wife's saddle, but Charles refused. He'd said that he usually rode bareback.

"The horse ain't used to that," Art had said.

Charles rubbed the gelding's neck. "I don't think he'll mind."

"You can't rope without a saddle."

"Hell, I can't rope, anyway."

"What kind of a cowboy are you—can't rope?"

"In case you didn't notice, I ain't a cowboy. I'm one of the other guys—an Indian."

Art snorted. "Lee, when you get back to Oregon, you take this fella out, teach him how to rope. Here, if you won't use a saddle, take this blanket and surcingle. At least you won't get so sweaty."

Charles and Lee waited on the crest of a low hill above where they'd built the canvas corral. Two long wings fanned out on each side, camouflaged with brush, and funneled down to the narrow corral mouth.

A fly lit on Lee's cheek and he brushed it off. He heard another buzzing sound, deeper and far away.

"Here it comes," Charles said.

The metallic droning got louder. Lee squinted toward the northeast where he knew the plane would appear. The gray-blue sky was empty above hills tinged green with spring. Suddenly the airplane popped into view. It sprang up over the ridge like a child's toy, an absurd, poorly constructed thing cluttering up a sky that should belong only to birds. How the hell did it fly, anyway? Lee had never been in an airplane and flying in a heavy metal contraption seemed unnatural to him.

The plane skimmed frighteningly close to the hill's crest. As it circled, Lee saw the mustangs. They ran desperately, like chickens beneath a hawk. Their heads worked up and down; long manes and tails floated around them. They topped another little ridge and dropped out of sight into a draw.

In a few minutes, they labored over the last rise, a bay mare in the lead. It seemed that some instinct warned her of danger, for she swerved sharply to the left. The herd followed. The airplane dodged in the same direction and screamed toward the ground directly over her head. The mare whirled and led the horses into the wings of the trap.

Lee's saddle horse flinched and reared as the airplane passed overhead. Lee kicked him into a gallop behind the mustangs. Charles followed and they raced between the wings, along with Art who came from the other side. The men leaped to the ground and hauled canvas across the entrance to the corral. The wild horses, drenched with sweat and foam, jostled in a tight circle, baffled by the high walls they could not see over. The stallion, a hammer-headed roan with white-ringed eyes, bugled in rage and frustration.

"Ugly brute," Art said. "And nothing much better than the average stunted broomtail in the whole bunch. Don't look as though we'll get more than dog food and glue out of the whole herd."

"That little sorrel looks pretty good." Lee pointed to a filly with a cream-colored mane and tail.

"She's the only one. I'll check her over later on. If she still looks good, maybe I'll cut her out and see if I can sell her separate."

Charles asked, "Is that true—that they'll go for dog food?"

"Yeah. Or feed for hogs and chickens. Maybe their bones for fertilizer and fish food. Sometimes hides are made into baseball mitts or shoes," Art answered.

"It's a damn shame," said Lee. "I know scrubs like this are more trouble to break than they're worth, but it's still a shame."

"I thought wild horses would be beautiful." The wistfulness was back in Charles's voice. "And when I first saw them come over the ridge, with those long manes flying, they were pretty."

"Take a good look close up," said Art. "Disappointing. And not reliable, either. It's discouraging to ride a horse all day and then have him try to dump you off on the way home at night. With a wild one, you can never relax. Look at them as a resource, a cash crop, like steers. Nobody ever gets sentimental over a damn steer."

The next day, the men roped, threw and earmarked the horses one by one. They attached a six-foot rawhide strap to one front leg of each horse and turned them loose to graze. The trailing strap didn't bother them as long as they walked slowly, but if they tried to run, they tripped themselves by stepping on it with their hind feet. The mustangs were exhausted, sore-footed, thirsty, and hungry. But everyone put up a fight when they felt the rope.

The little sorrel chewed on it like a dog when it was her

turn to be earmarked and hobbled. Her neck was too thin, but she had a nicely shaped head and fine eyes, now distended and rolling in terror. Lee brushed the pale forelock out of her eyes and rubbed her neck. When she was released, she lunged to her feet and tried to run. The rawhide strap tangled in her legs. She stumbled and nearly fell. She made two more attempts to run before she gave up and stood head down, front legs braced, sides heaving.

"She'll catch on," Art said. "Get the gray next. Bundy will be back with another bunch tomorrow and we want the corral empty when the airplane comes over the hill."

"This is a hell of a way to hunt horses," Lee said. "Why did you hire Bundy and his flying scrap heap anyway?"

"Time and money." Art spit tobacco juice into the dirt. "Remember how long it took to do all this on horseback? Just finding the herds could take days. Now Bundy flaps out like a big buzzard and spots a band in no time. And remember all that chasing around, trying to get them into the corral? One time I broke the leg of a perfectly good saddle horse running after those little scrubs. Sometimes the old ways just ain't worth it, Lee."

"It was sure as hell more fun."

"You can talk about fun. You don't have a wife depending on you and payments on your ranch coming due. Last winter was pretty tough. Fernie had lots of medical bills. And then there was Daddo's funeral—even dying costs money."

"Okay. Let's get the gray."

It was over in a few days. Bundy, the pilot, brought in another band, no more impressive than the first. The horses were herded into town and loaded onto stock cars that would take them to Chicago. Lee watched the sorrel as she was forced up the ramp into the already packed railroad car. Art had forgotten about cutting her out for a separate sale.

The horse's small hoofs slipped on the wooden ramp. She flinched as the unfamiliar shadows closed over her head, blotting out the sky. She'd never been under a roof, never known any confinement or restriction until she was run into the corral. As she shuddered and balked, a cowhand reached through the fence and jolted her with an electric cattle prod. She jumped forward. The heavy doors rolled shut behind her. Almost immediately the train pulled slowly out of the station.

Depression descended on Lee as he collected his share of the money—it wasn't very much—and divided it with Charles. He wondered how the boy had paid for his bus ticket, as he didn't seem to have a regular job. But where Charles got his money was no business of Lee's.

"I'll run you back to Whistler's Bend," he told Charles. "I may as well go that direction as any other."

"You're lucky." Art spoke with more than a little envy. "No responsibility, no bills to pay, free to come and go as you please. Sometimes I think I should have stayed single, but then I wouldn't have Glenda and my grandkids. I wouldn't give them up for anything."

"You made a good choice. A family is worth any amount of independence."

Did he mean that or did he say it only to console Art? Lee wasn't sure. Today he almost believed his own words. Occasional loneliness was a price he'd gladly paid for freedom, but lately the loneliness had increased and the lack of responsibility and continuity in relationships felt more like emptiness than anything else.

He'd even started to think about money. Art felt the pressure of paying off loans and medical bills. Charles lived from day to day on the edge of the razor between very little and nothing at all.

Lee had always been fortunate and he knew it. A certain knowledge had traveled with him from the time he made his first trip when he was little more than a boy. He had a net beneath him. Even though there had been lean stretches between jobs, he'd never been desperate. If he really needed it, if he lost his grip and couldn't catch himself, the net would save him.

Bob and Vivian, the prosperous farm and properties in Illinois, as well as the family there, anchored Lee and supported him. Only once, years ago, had he called upon their resources and asked for money to go home, but they stood invisibly behind him. The Jamison family gave him a confidence he otherwise would not have known.

One of his sisters and her husband managed the farm since his father's death. Lee's mother, regal and straight-backed at seventy-four, lived in an apartment in town. His other two sisters had married successful men and lived nearby. He didn't know his sisters well—he never had—but relations were cordial when he visited. Of course, they did not understand him nor did he understand them, content to stay in the same place where they were born. But if he decided to go home—and in some deep part of himself, Illinois was always home—they'd find a way to fit him in.

Lee glanced at Charles as he got into the car beside him. The boy had no net, no support except whatever he managed for himself. Lee had made a choice to live the way he did; Charles had no choice. There was no sure, safe place for him anywhere in the world. And that made all the difference.

Charles cocked his head as the Mercury moved out into the street. "Something doesn't sound right. Do you hear it?"

"Yeah, but I don't want to hang around a garage in this town. We'll take it easy and, if we're lucky, we'll get back to Oregon before it becomes a real problem."

They hadn't driven far before Lee saw vehicles parked along the road at a railway crossing. Boxcars were piled haphazardly on and off the tracks, some as dented as discarded beer cans. Debris littered the roadside—tangled slats from stock cars, chunks of metal, pieces of siding appearing as insubstantial as cardboard.

An old farm truck lay crumpled beneath the locomotive. Splintered boards from the wooden bed scattered the ground like kindling. Horses wandered aimlessly, some bloody, limping, and obviously in shock. Several dead ones lay along the track. One hung half in and half out of the shattered train.

Lee and Charles approached two men who looked on. "Anybody hurt?"

"Not bad," one answered. "The truck stalled on the tracks and the kid driving it jumped out when he seen the train coming. One of the crewmen on the train broke his leg and others got some cuts and bumps, but that was all. The real casualties are the horses. Busted most of them up pretty bad."

Lee walked on; Charles followed. They searched among the bodies and the injured animals for the little sorrel. They found her lying in a shallow gully on the other side of the tracks. Both front legs were broken. She was stained with blood and sweat from her struggle to get up. Her eyes rolled fearfully toward them. Her entire body quivered with pain and exhaustion.

"Oh, shit," Charles said softly.

Lee returned to his car and took his rifle from the trunk. "Better step back," he told Charles. He quickly pumped two bullets into the little mare, into the white diamond in the middle of her forehead. Blood splashed the flaxen forelock.

Lee returned the rifle and leaned against the car to light a cigarette. It tasted harsh and bitter. He avoided looking at the battered train and the cargo that littered the clean, wind-scrubbed face of the earth, ugly garbage spilled across the ground. Instead he looked at the plains, over rock and sagebrush to the distances where earth and sky became one. Out there somewhere, the mustangs still ran, not beautiful, often despised, but still hanging on. Like coyotes, they survived in spite of all the hands against them; in spite of guns, poisons, and mercenaries like himself who hunted them down with soulless metal devices. In spite of everything, a few survivors still ran free.

Lee closed his eyes and filled his lungs with cool evening air, acrid with sage and dust. He hurt all over. His head throbbed. His guts twisted in empty spasms and he swallowed down the meager bile that rose into his aching throat.

He spoke aloud. "God, I hate machines."

He'd thought he was alone, but someone moved nearby. Charles's strong fingers gripped his arm. He didn't speak, but simply let Lee know that he was there.

They camped a couple of hundred yards off the road, behind a small hillock so that they were partially shielded from the sight of any passersby. Lee had a small tent, but they didn't bother to set it up. They built a fire out of dried sagebrush and twigs. When it was burning steadily, Lee fetched a gunnysack from the trunk of the Mercury. It contained chunks of pine with pitch pockets. They caught easily and would burn even in the rain.

Charles grinned as Lee added one to the flames. "That trunk is like a magic box. You got just about everything in there."

"I picked this up in Idaho. Lots of good wood there, but not much in this part of Wyoming. I do like a campfire. And there's one more thing in the magic box." He flourished a bottle of bourbon. He hunkered by the fire, opened the bottle, and passed it to Charles.

He shook his head. "No, thanks. When I tried it, I ended up too much like my old man."

Lee sipped at the bottle. There didn't seem to be a sound in the world except the pop and crackle of the fire. A vast darkness hovered beyond the flickering circle of light. Stars like salt sprinkled the sky. A small wind, sharp-edged as a razor blade, moved through camp.

Charles shivered in his unlined denim jacket. He hauled out his sleeping bag and draped it over his shoulders. Tiny escaping feathers joined the drifting bits of ash from the fire.

Charles looked up at the stars. "Do you suppose anybody lives up there? I saw a movie once where aliens came down and invaded the earth."

"I dunno. Scientists say it's possible. With all those millions of stars, it doesn't make sense that Earth is the only one with life." Lee drank again.

"On the car radio today, did you hear the announcer talk about the scientist who sold atomic secrets to the Russians?"

"Klaus Fuchs?"

"Yeah, him. Now the Russians have the bomb. Bob told me that he's got food stockpiled, in case of attack."

"Yeah. But it doesn't seem likely that the Russians would bother to bomb Oregon. Or Wyoming." He grinned.

But Charles remained serious. "They don't have to bomb us. They could bomb somewhere else. The wind would carry radiation to us, atomic dust, stuff like that. We'd all get sick and die, even animals. Just like those cities in Japan."

Lee didn't have an answer. It was a changed and dangerous world. He imagined America like the campfire, a small place of uncertain safety beyond which hovered vast wings of darkness.

Charles seemed to read his mind. "In the old days, we could find a safe place. A guy could leave the war zone, take his girl or wife and go someplace far away, where they'd be safe. But you can't do that anymore. There's no place in the world that's really safe. Is there?"

"I don't think so, kid. If I knew one, I'd go there with you."

No net, Lee thought. No net anywhere—not in a world with atomic bombs.

He took another nip and screwed the lid back on the bottle. Charles had confided his fears to Lee. It would cheapen his confidence if Lee drank too much and behaved like the boy's father.

A car passed on the distant road. It moved slowly, a dark shape pursuing its beam of light. When the faint sound and lights had vanished, the darkness and loneliness seemed more intense. The intimacy of the tiny campfire increased.

"Do you have a girl?" Lee asked. "Someone you'd take with you to a safe place, if you could find one?"

"I did have. Not anymore." The stern lines of Charles's face did not change, but the wistfulness was back in his voice.

"I don't, either. The woman I most wanted wouldn't go with me, anyway."

"Neither would Sherry. Go with me."

They exchanged a rueful look, part humor, mostly regret.

In Lee's mind, an unexpected image of Doris replaced that of Rosalind. Doris would go in a second. At least, somebody truly cared about him.

A chunk of wood toppled in the flames. Another one rolled out onto the sparse grass and set a few blades on fire. Lee scuffled it out with his boot. He added the last piece of Idaho wood and settled down again. But the mood had changed. The memory of Doris led Lee to Woodbridge. He followed another mental track and approached a subject that had been often in his thoughts.

"There was a woman in Redding, California, that I spent time with whenever I was there. Somebody killed her a couple of months ago, murdered her just after I left. She had a boyfriend with connections to Woodbridge.

"Some guy called a few days ago, a muffled, funny-sounding voice. He said he knew me, that he'd seen me with Joanne. It sure seems like he's from that area, if he knew enough to call me at Bob's ranch."

"That's . . . interesting." Charles spoke slowly. "Do you have any idea who it might be?"

"Not a one. I've thought back to when I lived there, when I had the saddle shop and later when I worked at the car lot." And lived with Doris, but he didn't mention that. "It was someone with money, because he made Joanne's house payments for her. He was very secretive. He made her promise never to tell anyone his name. She was afraid of him, so she kept her promise. He beat her, among other things."

Charles's eyes sharpened. An expression that Lee could not decipher crossed his face. "My sister dated somebody like that. When I asked about him, she wouldn't tell me any-thing—except that he was rich."

"God, I remember now. Your sister was murdered, wasn't she? Bob told me a few years back, but since I didn't know you then, I didn't remember. When did it happen?"

"Over five years ago."

"That long. How was she killed?"

"He broke her neck. But he beat her, too."

"Jesus. I'm sorry."

"It happened just down the road from the cabin. My dad was gone. I heard Juanita scream and thought it was a cougar.

198

Blackie, my dog, ran down, barking like crazy. I followed him with the rifle."

Charles's hands twisted together, his knuckles white with tension. "I saw the bastard, too. He came up the hill toward me. He must have followed the dog to see if anyone was there. But he heard me cock the rifle. I've wondered—if I hadn't had the rifle, would he have killed me, too, if he caught me?"

"You saw the guy? What did he look like?"

"I only saw a shadow, an outline. He looked big. But I was a kid, twelve years old. I was scared. Anybody would look big to me. I should have shot him. I had him right in my sights. But I didn't know for sure Juanita was dead until later, when I found her body. Actually, it was Blackie found her for me."

"I'm sorry," Lee said again. "That was a terrible thing for a kid, for anyone."

Charles didn't reply. Lee went on.

"Twice. Twice he's killed women. Maybe more, for all we know." He lit a cigarette and rubbed his jaw. "Joanne called him Don, even though that isn't his name. He liked it because he thought it showed respect and because of a connection with a writer who was the basis for the word sadism. Did your sister ever mention anything like that?"

Charles shook his head. "It sounds pretty strange to me."

"This guy is very strange. And scary. Sometimes he wears a fancy belt buckle with a coat of arms and a ram's head. It seems to mean something special to him."

Charles stared at Lee, but he could tell that he didn't really see him. Charles was thinking, casting back into the past, trying to pull a distant memory into the present.

"A big belt buckle," Charles said at last. "That could have been it. I saw something just before he stepped behind the tree. It shone in the moonlight, right in the middle of the

199

shadow that I knew was him. It could have been a fancy belt buckle."

Lee took off his hat and ran his fingers through his hair. "As soon as we get back, we'll go see the sheriff. It sounds as though there might be a connection. If so, whoever that guy is, he's been around Woodbridge for at least five years."

Chapter 9

DORIS

The end of May

Doris watched Glenn Draper as he approached the counter of the hardware store. Most women thought him attractive. She knew that he was well-off and soon to be single. He'd twice asked her for a date.

So why didn't she say yes?

He smiled a little tentatively and she returned her standard customer smile.

"Did you find everything you need?"

"Yes, I did." He watched as she rang up. He cleared his throat. "There's a dinner dance at the country club next weekend. I'd like to take you, if you'll go."

"No, thank you, Glenn."

"Look, I'm not a bad guy. But somehow I got off on the wrong foot with you. I'd like to start over."

"I don't want to date anyone," she said, not entirely truthfully. If an interesting stranger came to town and asked her out or, even better, offered to take her away from Woodbridge and everyone and everything in it, she'd certainly consider the offer.

"Do you mean you don't want to date anyone at all or anyone except Lee Jamison? I've seen him around town lately."

"Well, I haven't," she snapped. "I saw him once and that was accidentally. Not that it's any of your business."

"God, I've done it again. I always say the wrong thing when I'm with you. I just wanted to know if . . . I'm sorry that I annoyed you. I sure didn't intend to."

Doris studied him a moment. A lock of light brown hair fell over his forehead, giving him a boyish look. He brushed it back, but it instantly flopped forward again. She noticed his big-boned wrists and large hands, tanned and strong from golf and tennis. He was quite good-looking and certainly more appealing when he was humble than when he tried to sweep her off her feet.

Glenn sensed her softened attitude. "It's hell to be single in a small town. Everyone knows all about you—or thinks they do. Everyone jumps to conclusions—usually the wrong ones. And there's no privacy at all."

Doris sighed. "You're right about that."

"And you're right about the country club dance. It's too public. How could we get better acquainted with half the town staring at us? Maybe . . ." He paused and then went on. "Maybe we could drive to Eugene for an evening? Have dinner where no one knows us?"

Doris didn't answer as the door opened and a customer came in. She watched the man move down one of the aisles, searching for something. She transferred her gaze back to Glenn. He looked like a little boy waiting for the teacher to tell him if he'd done well or poorly on an exam.

She smiled again, genuinely this time. "Maybe we could do that. But I understand that your divorce isn't final. You may believe that things are emotionally resolved, but it took me a long time to get over my breakup with Lee."

She felt a sense of shock immediately after the words left her lips. What had possessed her to speak so frankly? She'd never discussed her feelings about Lee with anyone, except Anna Stegner, her next-door neighbor and friend.

Glenn's mouth twisted ruefully. "I got over Phyllis soon after we were married. We stayed together as long as we did only because of Tommy. But I understand what you're saying. And I can wait. You'll be seeing me." He turned to wave jauntily as he left the store.

Doris sank onto the stool behind the counter. *Why did I say those things? Was I so undone by a stray lock of hair and boyish contrition?*

She knew it was more than that. She was lonely. She'd been lonely for a long time, during the years before and after Lee. She was not quite thirty-eight years old, too young to want to spend the rest of her life alone.

She helped the other man find what he needed. She answered the phone. She discussed paint with a rancher's wife as she pondered a selection for the exterior of her house. In between chores, Doris thought of what she knew about Glenn.

He was vice-president of the Woodbridge Bank and already anointed to step in as president when elderly Mr. Stilwell retired. Glenn was active in numerous civic organizations. He wasn't much over forty. He and Phyllis had arrived seven or eight years ago, a newly married couple from northern California. There'd long been rumors of a shaky relationship. The local gossips said that Phyllis took too many private lessons from the golf pro at the country club and that Glenn consoled himself with one or more cocktail waitresses. But the golf pro left, Phyllis became pregnant and the birth of their son seemed to solidify the Draper marriage.

But then Phyllis had taken the boy and moved back to Redding with her parents. Divorce proceedings involved arguments over property and custody arrangements. Glenn was right. Everyone knew everyone else's business in a small town.

Mrs. Domingo came through the front door at the same moment that the phone rang.

"Hello. Gooding Hardware," Doris said.

There was no response. "Hello. You've reached Gooding Hardware. May I help you?"

Dead silence. She tried one more time.

"Is anyone there?"

Doris replaced the receiver with a shrug and smiled at the woman in front of her. "I guess it was a wrong number. How are you today, Mrs. Domingo?"

"Not too bad. At least my rheumatism's better now that the rain has let up. I need a few more fence posts. And other odds and ends. Here's my list."

"Keith's in the lumber yard. He'll help you with the posts and I'll gather the rest."

"The store looks real good," Mrs. Domingo said. "You've done a good job with it, Doris."

"Thank you. I appreciate you saying that. Especially since you know all about managing alone."

The two women exchanged a look of mutual respect and satisfaction.

"Oh, we can get along without men just fine," Mrs. Domingo said. "But that doesn't mean we don't like them."

Doris laughed and put her hand on Charlotte's sinewy arm. "Why, I believe you're still twenty-one years old at heart."

Later, after everything was loaded into the old pickup and Mrs. Domingo had clattered off in it, Doris went to the washroom. She soaped, rinsed, and lotioned her hands. She combed her hair and dusted her nose with powder, feeling that, like a warrior, she girded herself for battle. Her mother-in-law would soon arrive.

Alice Gooding had called a few days before and asked that Doris allow her accountant to look over the books.

"I didn't know you had an accountant," Doris had replied. "But, certainly, the books are open to you at any time."

Sometimes Doris feared for the future of the store. As manager and co-owner, she received sixty percent of the profits. The rest went to Alice. When Alice died, presumably that share would go to her remaining family. It worried Doris as she speculated on how they might intrude upon her management policies. Could she afford to buy them out if they agreed to sell? Did she want to take that step, even if she could?

Mrs. Gooding's accountant turned out to be someone with whom Doris was acquainted—a fusty old gentleman long retired from bookkeeping at one of the lumber companies and a regular bridge partner of Mrs. Gooding. Doris wondered at the conversations that led them to conclude that the books needed examining, but she turned them over with as much of a smile as she could manage.

Mr. Atchison had turned pages and scribbled little notes for some time, now and then asking a question. When he left, he'd announced rather importantly that he'd report to Mrs. Gooding and that she would soon call for an appointment with Doris. That appointment was only a few minutes away.

She went to her desk and shuffled papers. The day was not going well. She'd had two unwelcome offers from men, the other from someone much less attractive than Glenn. Warren Stonebraker had been in for his regular taking-care-of-business visit. He'd asked her for dinner, something he hadn't done in awhile. She'd refused politely, wishing, as she did whenever Warren appeared, for the protection of Carl's presence in her life.

Warren had regarded her with unblinking eyes. "You're an intelligent woman, but you underestimate me. I know that we could have interesting conversations."

Doris thought that unlikely as she remembered the monologues that he had inflicted upon Carl. Perhaps Warren believed that she would be as agreeable an audience for his opinions as her husband had been. Warren would be furious if he knew how they had laughed together later and even imitated some of his more pompous remarks.

A brief smile crossed her face in remembrance.

"Did I say something amusing?"

"I was thinking of something Carl said," she answered honestly.

"About me?"

"No," she lied. "But it was about men and women."

"Tell me. I'm very intrigued by what goes on between the sexes."

She looked at him as she tried to come up with a prudent response.

He leaned forward. "Doris, I am a man of many layers. I give much thought to important issues, to age-old questions of . . ."

The phone rang, like a blessing.

"Excuse me. Keith's gone on an errand. I'm so sorry." She gratefully picked up the phone. Even more luckily, it was a supplier in another state with several complicated questions. She'd looked at Warren and shrugged. He left the store, rigid with annoyance. There were sixty welcome days before she needed to face him again.

After the desk was tidied and she waited for the arrival of Mrs. Gooding, she turned on the radio for the hourly five-minute news broadcast, softly so customers in the store would not hear.

". . . spoke of card-carriers and fellow travelers in his speech last night. McCarthy, the Republican senator from Wisconsin, continued his attack on those he considers soft on Communism.

"From overseas, reports arrived early this morning of another border clash as troops from Communist North Korea skirmished with South Korean forces near the 38th parallel. In Seoul, Syngman Rhee said that . . ."

Doris sighed and turned it off. Would there be another war, only five years after the end of the last one?

Carl had been over age and 4F as well during the Second World War. Lee had also missed both world wars, too young for the first and too old for the second. He'd told Doris that he was disappointed at first, as war had seemed a great adventure, an opportunity for tests that he, in youthful arrogance, was sure he would not fail. Later, as he listened to stories from the men coming home, he'd begun to believe he was lucky, after all.

But many others had gone, had died—so much loss, waste and destruction. And still the frenzied race went on, for more armaments, more secret weapons, more atomic power. When Doris was first married, she'd dreamed of children, of babies to raise and cherish. But it was safer to be childless, in these years of perilous existence under the threat of The Bomb.

Doris moved around the store, checking displays. As she neared the big, plateglass window in front, she glanced toward the street. Warren stared in at her.

She felt an unpleasant jolt. She'd thought him safely on his way out of town. Her elbow struck a large camp coffeepot displayed on a small table. The pot skittered into a stack of matching speckled enamel cups and knocked them over. Metal rattled and crashed to the floor. Outside the window, Warren smiled.

Doris gritted her teeth. "Damn! Damn!"

Lila Prentiss, beside Warren, waved gaily through the glass. Lila's daughter, Sherry, and Warren's niece, Marlene, giggled together behind the adults.

Doris lifted her hand in greeting as calmly as she could and went about restoring order. Only one of the cups had chipped. It could have been a lot worse.

She hated it that Warren unnerved her as he did. He apparently didn't have that effect on either of the Prentiss women. But he didn't seem to look at them in the same way he looked at Doris. Presumably Lila was a virtuous widow— or divorcee. Whatever she might be, she was apparently without blemish, while Doris, through her open relationship with Lee, had crossed a line which Warren considered significant.

Doris watched him and the women cross the street. Lila and Sherry had fallen behind. Lila slipped her arm around Sherry, and the girl bent her bright head toward her mother as they talked together. There was something both tender and conspiratorial in the moment.

Doris felt a sharp pang of envy, in spite of her earlier rationalization about the dangerous state of the world. In theory, she could still have a child, but it was highly unlikely at her age. Carl had said that he wanted children, but Doris wondered just how deep that wish had gone. Thoughts of children brought back memories of old frustrations.

Carl's mother had disapproved of their marriage and let her daughter-in-law know that she believed her son had married beneath himself. The lack of grandchildren increased Mrs. Gooding's dissatisfaction. Doris had consulted doctors and none of them found anything wrong with her. They suggested that Carl come in for a physical, but he was always too busy. Usually reasonable and good-natured, he'd become angry when she pressed him. Doris tried to enlist her mother-in-law in her campaign to persuade Carl to see a doctor. She was sure that Alice would be on her side in this issue, if no other.

To her surprise, Mrs. Gooding had become indignant. "There's nothing wrong with Carl. The Goodings have always been strong, healthy men, just like my family. You're so pale and thin, Doris. You should eat more."

In her uncharitable moments, Doris considered the fact that the "strong, healthy" Goodings had produced only one son who, for all his virtues, had little interest in sex. Their years together had been spent in amiable companionship, but not much else.

The bell on the front door tinkled. Mrs. Gooding stumped toward her on chubby feet squeezed into high-heeled, peep-toed pumps. A beige dress with a wide woven belt gave her body the look of a lumpy burlap bag cinched in the middle with a leather strap borrowed off a saddle.

"What a pretty hat." Doris looked at the clump of flowers on her mother-in-law's head. She loved the way Alice dressed. It gave her an opportunity to feel superior.

"Thank you, Doris," Alice replied regally, not slowing in her progress toward the back.

Mr. Atchison, following behind, nodded politely. Keith appeared on cue to take over the floor. The visitors settled themselves and declined Doris's offer of coffee.

Alice plunged right in. "You'll be pleased to know that Mr. Atchison found everything in order."

"I'm glad that you're satisfied with the accounting." Doris's voice sounded stilted and she tried for a softer tone. "We've had a very good year. Our best ever, I think."

"People are feeling good about the economy," Mr. Atchison contributed. "There's been a tremendous boom in housing since the war, which certainly impacts the hardware business. And, of course, you took advantage of that by adding the lumber annex."

He stopped abruptly, as he seemed to recall that Mrs. Gooding had been opposed to that addition. She'd argued that there was a big lumberyard on the outskirts of Woodbridge and they didn't need a smaller one as part of the store. In spite of her objections, Doris had bought the building directly behind them. With Warren's permission—and a raise in the rent—she'd put a door through to the alley and built a portico to keep off rain, so that customers could easily pass from one building to the other.

"The trend in retail seems to be toward one-stop shopping," Doris said mildly.

"I still don't like that shed roof over the alley," Mrs. Gooding complained. "It looks so tacky, so Dogpatchy."

"I agree," Doris said. "When Warren was here this morning, I offered again to buy this building. But he's not interested in selling. If he would, then we could build something permanent and much more attractive."

Mrs. Gooding folded her hands in her lap. "Do you remember the year of the big flood? It was 1938. That alley ran full of water. The current was almost as strong as the main Nezzac River, Frank said. Only a little exaggeration, of course."

Doris smiled. "Yes. He liked to exaggerate." She thought fondly of her father-in-law. She'd never had a moment's problem with him. He was as easygoing as Carl.

"And then the water ran in the back." Alice pursued her memories. "It flooded ankle-deep all through the store. Carl and Frank piled up sandbags while we splashed around, moving the goods to higher shelves. Do you remember that, Doris?"

"How could I forget? I remember that I slipped on something under the water—I'll always believe it was a fish, alive or dead—and I fell flat on my behind in that cold muddy water. Frank and Carl laughed so hard they almost cried. So did you."

Mrs. Gooding looked years younger as she laughed. "Yes, I did. You looked so funny. You should have seen the expression on your face."

"You'd look funny, too, if you'd just sat on a fish. And remember how the tin washtub, with the piggy banks in it, floated right out the door and away down the river before we could catch it? Frank said those little pigs probably sailed all the way to Tokyo."

"Rub-a-dub-dub!" Alice shrieked.

The two women howled together, releasing old tensions and resentments. Mr. Atchison, left out, chuckled politely.

"Oh, we had some fun," Mrs. Gooding said when she could speak. "Even during the early years, when times were hard and we all were so poor that we couldn't even buy a new pair of stockings. I remember how you worked in your garden and all those vegetables you canned. You and your mother. You fed us all for three years from that big garden." She regarded Doris for a moment. "You always were a hard worker, Doris. Whatever else, you work hard."

Briskly, Alice cleared her throat and stood up. "Let's go, Harold. The next time Warren Stonebraker comes to town, ask him again to sell the building. We can afford to make him a good offer. Whatever you think is fair, Doris. But a good offer."

She marched toward the front door. Doris followed her, like a greyhound pacing a bulldog, she thought, fighting back the urge to giggle some more.

"It was nice to see you, Alice. Stop in any time." She'd

never called her mother-in-law by her first name, except to herself, but today seemed a good time to begin.

Mrs. Gooding didn't slow or turn around, but she did waggle one hand over her shoulder as she left.

Amazing, Doris thought. It's twenty years since I married Carl and she finally said something nice to me.

A little after six o'clock, still bemused by Mrs. Gooding's visit, Doris locked the hardware store. She walked slowly to her car. The late May sun slanted warmly from the western sky. A certain softness in the air filled Doris with a familiar, undefinable pain. Somewhere, sometime, there had been other evenings like this, when in the midst of beauty, she'd felt herself touched by the melancholy hand of an irretrievable loss.

It was an old feeling, rooted in the distant past, long before Lee had come and gone, long before Carl, perhaps even long before the creation of the person known as Doris. It seemed to go back into another life, of which all recollection had been lost, except for the memory of a summery evening and the mingling of loveliness and sorrow.

A scene faded in and out at the back of her mind. It was clearest when she didn't focus on it, but dissolved when she tried to examine it closely. She saw a young woman—perhaps herself—with long hair coiled around her head. She wore a Biblical-looking, ankle-length white dress. The figure stood on a paved terrace, outside a house of stone, imagined more than seen. Soft sunset rays touched the hilltop. Beyond were other low rocky hills on which grew small gray-green trees, probably olives. Somewhere nearby, but not in sight, was a young man, his presence keenly imprinted on the atmosphere in an indelible mixture of love and longing. He had just left or could not come—some circumstance kept him apart from the woman. In the tranquility of early evening, Doris remember the sweet pain of love returned, but never fulfilled.

A wry smile twisted her lips as she unlocked the car door. Where did those thoughts come from and why did they have such power? The half-dream was as significant as anything else she'd felt all day. And yet it was only a fancy, wasn't it?

The mood stayed with her as she drove slowly home, the windows open so that the ambrosial air blew against her face. She wandered around the yard with the house keys in her hand. She pulled a weed here and there, not many, as she'd worked outside all the previous weekend. She liked yard work—spading, planting, pruning, cutting grass, raising flowers and vegetables. Even when Carl was alive, she'd done most of it. Doris lingered, putting off the moment when she must enter the empty house.

The phone rang faintly through the walls. She hurried to the door and thrust the key in the lock. The phone jangled on—five, six, seven times.

"Hello," she gasped, out of breath from her race across the yard.

No one answered.

"Hello? Who is this?"

She heard only silence. Yet the silence was full, heavy with the sense of someone listening. She put down the receiver. Kids, she thought. Why do they think this is so funny? Surely it was a child, even though there had been no giggle, no stupid joke about Prince Albert in the can.

An unsettled, restless feeling crawled through her in place of the melancholy tranquility of only a few moments before. What a day this had been—Warren first thing in the morning, Alice soon after, two odd phone calls, strange feelings and half-memories accompanying her home.

She made a fried egg sandwich. She usually ate her main

meal in a restuarant at noon, so that she didn't have to cook much at night. She took a photo album from the closet shelf and put it on the table to page through while she ate.

The first picture was of the little country church where she and Carl had been married, followed by other photos of her wedding. Her husband gazed serenely at her from out of the past. He looked so much himself: medium build, medium height, medium hair—this soon to disappear and leave him bald on top. He wore glasses even then. Hers came later.

Someone tapped on the door. Doris jumped. The door opened a crack and Anna's cheerful face peered in.

"Sorry to startle you. Am I interrupting your supper?"

"I've finished. Come in. Can I get you something to drink? Iced tea? A Coke?"

"No, I'll only stay a minute." Anna glanced at the photo album. "Oh, my. Look at Carl. He didn't change at all, did he? Well, maybe he lost a little hair." Anna turned another page. "And you haven't changed much, either. You still have that twenty-four-inch waist."

Doris gazed at the eighteen-year-old girl with Carl. Those large expectant eyes in the photos, so eager for life, were often tired now and always half-hidden behind silver-framed glasses. She felt little connection with the distant girl-bride in the pictures.

Anna closed the album after a moment. "Bette is going to call you. She wants you to come for dinner on Friday. You can ride over with Peter and me."

"That's nice," Doris said cautiously. "Will anyone else be there?"

Anna laughed. "No, just us. My sister, the demon matchmaker. But this time, no divorced and lonely dentist friends of George's. I asked, because I know you hate that."

"In that case, I'd love to go."

"Good. I wanted you to know, before she calls, that you'll be safe from her Noah's Ark pairing instincts."

When Bette called later on, Doris accepted the invitation. She put on her nightgown and got into bed with *The Black Rose*. She liked to read books that took her away from the confines of Woodbridge. Ancient China was an intriguing place to go after a day in the hardware store.

The phone rang after awhile. Who in the world would call at ten o'clock? "Hello?"

Silence.

A cold little chill ran down the back of Doris's neck. She listened. The silence stretched on for perhaps thirty seconds. Then whoever was on the other end inhaled—slowly, deeply, deliberately. He—and she knew absolutely that it was a man—held his breath for a moment and then exhaled in the same deliberate way.

Gently Doris replaced the receiver. On the opposite wall, she saw her reflection in the mirror on the dresser. Her eyes were wide and dark. Her neck and shoulders looked small-boned and vulnerable beneath the thin fabric of her gown.

Almost instantly, the phone rang again, a harsh and ugly sound. She snatched up the receiver and plopped a pillow over it. She watched for a few seconds, as if she'd covered a scorpion or some other nasty creature that might come crawling back out.

The calls were not the prank of a child, but something more disturbing. Had she offended someone at the store? She paged mentally through her customers, salesmen, suppliers, trying to find someone who might be angry and resentful.

Last year, Mr. Hauptmann had threatened to sue because his bathroom had flooded and leaked into the kitchen below after he'd remodeled it with plumbing supplies purchased at her store. But she'd worked that out, quite generously considering that he'd installed some of the fixtures improperly.

No, she didn't think it was a customer. More likely it was a pervert who was aware that she lived alone, someone who got a sick thrill from knowing that he'd frightened her.

She fell asleep, but it took a long time. In the morning, she didn't put the phone back on the hook until just before she left for work. She asked Keith to answer all phone calls that day. Just before they closed, she asked if there had been any wrong numbers.

He looked puzzled and uncertain.

"Did anybody call and hang up without speaking?"

"Yeah, twice." He looked at her curiously. He was nineteen years old, with sandy-blonde hair and the awkwardness of a puppy that had not yet grown into his feet. "Is something wrong?"

"I've had some strange calls, here and at home, too."

"Then I'll answer the phone for awhile."

"Thank you, Keith." She wondered who would answer at home.

It rang twice that evening. She didn't pick it up.

She had a new dress for the dinner party, a vibrant green that brought out sparks of the same color in her hazel eyes. A touch of black frogging decorated the bodice. Doris was tall and slender enough to wear a fashionably wide belt, as Alice had unsuccessfully attempted. The cinched belt and flared skirt accentuated Doris's small waist. Thank heaven, she'd never had to wear a girdle as many women did. She turned sideways. She was slim, but the best push-up bra in the world couldn't give her a voluptuous profile. Oh, well.

She checked doors and windows carefully to make sure all of them were locked. She closed the drapes in the living room and turned on a light before walking across the yard to the Stegners' house.

Anna's sister, Bette, had married a dentist with a successful practice. They had recently bought a home in the country club area. Glenn Draper, Doris knew, lived just around the corner. It was a pretty area with new homes nestled among lush, Pacific Northwest trees and shrubs.

Bette and George welcomed and settled them with drinks. They immediately began to talk about Milton Berle. Doris sipped her weak-by-request gin and tonic and looked out the window into the deep green of the back yard.

"Doris, have you bought a television yet?" Bette asked.

She shook her head. "No, I have so little spare time. I don't know when I'd watch it."

"It becomes addictive," George said. "Bette won't leave the house when Ed Sullivan is on."

"Soon every house in America will have TV." Peter Stegner swirled his drink and stared into it as if it were a crystal ball. "Have you ever noticed how hypnotic it is? Those flickering little images put you right into a trance."

"What he means is that it makes him fall asleep," his wife explained. "I can't decide if he's too intellectual for TV or if he's just permanently tired."

"If you had to try to teach physics to high school kids, you'd fall asleep early, too."

As Peter and Anna bickered amiably, a man in a white shirt moved through the shadowy trees behind the house. He stepped onto the lawn and strode across it.

"Oh, here comes Glenn." Bette jumped to her feet, glancing guiltily at Doris. "I know. I told Anna that no one else would be here, but I ran into Glenn this morning. When I mentioned that you were coming for dinner, he seemed so interested that I asked him, too."

Doris looked at Anna, who shrugged. Doris managed to greet Glenn in a reasonably friendly way, but a hard little knot of resentment burned inside her. Just because he was single (or soon to be) and next door, she didn't want Glenn Draper jammed down her throat. She didn't even understand why he was interested in her. She wasn't tanned and athletic as Phyllis, his wife, had been. She wasn't young and flashy like the women he'd been seen with outside of his marriage. The only thing she could imagine was that he considered "no" a challenge.

Resentment stiffened her spine and chilled her voice. It seemed that whenever Glenn spoke to her, which was often, the others in the room paused as though hoping for a bolt of electricity to arc back and forth between them. Doris felt more and more awkward as the evening wore on. At last, to her relief, Glenn seemed to give up. He ceased his attempts to charm her and turned his attention to the others.

She gulped at her wine and closed her eyes. She'd give a lot to have Lee or Carl—either one of them—beside her so that she didn't have to go through the humiliating process of being sold, like a heifer, by her well-meaning, but interfering, friends.

When she opened her eyes, she heard Glenn talking about fishing. ". . . and the best hole on the river is just below Mrs. Domingo's ranch. I've taken some beautiful four-pound trout out of there."

"You seem to know a lot about the Little Nezzac area," said Peter.

"I've spent a lot of time up there, although I don't go as much as I used to." He looked at his empty plate for a moment. "I could hardly wait for Tommy to get old enough so that I could teach him to fly fish and take him to all my favorite spots. That won't be easy, now that he's so far away."

Doris stood up. The chair legs squawked on the hardwood floor. "Excuse me." She went down the hall to the bathroom.

How cheap of Glenn to use sentimental appeal—the bereft father, missing his son. Did he think that would melt her heart? She splashed water on her face and blotted it with a towel. What a frightful evening. If only she had her own car so that she could go home.

Bette and Anna were clearing the table when she returned to the dining room. She picked up a stack of dishes and took them to the kitchen, setting them on the counter with a clatter. Bette glanced at her. Doris hurried out the back door to the patio.

The darkness and coolness soothed her flushed skin. The solitude eased the tension that piled up inside. She drew a deep breath and looked up. Stars flickered faintly, dimmed into insignificance by the proximity of the man-made lights of Woodbridge. She breathed again, deeply.

Then she heard Glenn's voice behind her in the kitchen. He said something to the women; Bette touched his shoulder, and then he opened the door to the patio. Doris wished she'd gone around the house and out of sight.

He stepped into the darkness beside her. "You don't have to get all stiff again. I know that the evening was not a success. I'm going home."

She couldn't think of a word to say. She couldn't see him clearly enough to read his expression, but there was a hard edge in his voice that she'd never heard before.

"Maybe part of the problem is that you don't believe you're attractive. You think 'plain' instead of 'pretty' and it makes you as prickly and defensive as a porcupine. Have you always been that way or did Jamison do it to you?"

"I can't see that it's any of your business."

It was a weak rejoinder, but she felt off-balance. She'd never seen even a hint of anger in Glenn. He was always the facilitator, self-deprecating and pliable, the perfect public relations man. He seemed different tonight, the sound of his voice, the way he moved.

He said, "You've made it perfectly clear that nothing about you is my business."

"Look, I was rude, I know. But . . ."

He stepped closer, a tall shadow against the lighted window at his back. She wondered if he would grab her and kiss her, make a show of his masculine strength.

"It makes me angry," he said. "It makes me really angry that a no-account like Jamison moved in and moved out. He left, but you have to live with the damage he did. I don't treat people that way. I took care of Phyllis when she got pregnant, even though things were pretty bad between us by then. I still take care of her financially. I take care of my son. As for you— you don't give a damn about any of that, do you?"

Abruptly, he turned and left the porch. She watched his white shirt disappear among the dark trees.

As soon as she got home, she peeled off her clothes, slipped into her nightgown, and toppled into bed. Her head felt muzzy. Either she was coming down with something or else she'd had too much to drink. She suspected the latter. A gin and tonic before dinner, a glass of wine, and then an after-dinner drink, were too much for one who rarely drank at all. She'd accepted the last drink out of guilt, after she'd apologized to Bette and her husband for being rude to Glenn. George had said, "Oh, he'll get over it. Let's have a drink." And so she had a drink. But she doubted that Glenn would "get over" her behavior.

Have I been a fool?

She burrowed into the softness of the pillow and closed her eyes. Maybe she was a fool, but she was beginning to wonder if a woman really needed a man to complete her. In stories and movies, the resolution was always marriage. Doris's friends kept trying to find a mate for her. Any unattached man, from the banker down the street to her landlord, assumed that they did her a big favor if they asked her for dinner.

She often felt lonely, but she'd experienced long periods of loneliness within her marriage, as well. She'd been happy with Lee, except for the knowledge always in the back of her mind, that it was not a permanent thing. Perhaps that intensified her happiness, the bittersweet realization that it was only a short-term love affair, not a lifetime commitment.

Her hands slipped down her body, over the smoothness of skin beneath the flimsy gown, remembering how Lee's hands had traced that same path. He'd understood sensuality, the pleasures of the flesh, whether it was sex, the first cup of coffee in the morning, or the silky feel of water on bare skin. Sometimes she missed him almost beyond bearing—him and the pleasures, the sharing he had taught her.

Drifting gently between waking and sleep, Doris recalled an incident from the years before she knew Lee, but which was linked with him in her mind. She and Carl had camped in the Sawtooth Mountains of Idaho. One day she felt too lazy to scramble along the creek, fishing with Carl. She rested on a soft patch of earth in the late morning sun. She wasn't aware of falling asleep. One moment she drowsed, lulled by the murmur of the nearby water. The next moment her eyes flew open. She knew that she had been asleep for an unknown length of time and that something had awakened her. She didn't move a muscle except her eyes.

A wolf sat on his haunches nearby. His ears pricked toward her and his tongue lolled out. Little drops of moisture dripped off the end of his tongue. He was big and rawboned, not starved, but rather spare as though there was no place in his life for anything superfluous, even flesh. His fur shone and his bushy tail curled neatly around his feet. No-color, black-pupiled eyes looked directly into Doris's with confident curiosity.

She was not afraid. The animal was not menacing, but had come to observe the stranger asleep in his territory. They regarded one another with mutual fascination. The wolf licked his muzzle with a long red tongue, a slurp on each side. He closed his jaws with a snap, averted his chilly eyes, and trotted off into the woods.

Doris was left with a deep sense of loss. He'd vanished too soon, that wild, intensely living thing. Later when she looked into Lee's pale gray eyes and, certainly, when he left her, she thought of the wolf. Some creatures cross our lives only briefly, but are remembered forever.

The phone rang. It's Lee, she thought sleepily, seduced by the touch of her own hands, bemused by mystic images. Her voice was low and dreamy. "Hello."

The other voice was also low and singsong. "Dor-isss." The syllables stretched out seductively. "Dor-isss. I'm here."

Her eyes flew open. She slammed down the receiver. Just as quickly, she snatched it off again and buried it under the pillow. She sat up in bed and hugged her knees to her chest, careful not to look into the mirror. She didn't want to see the frightened woman huddled in her bed.

The next day she met Vivian Jamison for lunch. They'd become friendly while Lee lived with Doris and still saw one another occasionally. Doris was never quite sure how to handle the subject of Lee. She didn't want to ask about him so much that it seemed she was still in love with him, yet it seemed churlish not to mention him at all. Worse, Vivian might believe that the subject was so painful to her that she could not bear the sound of his name.

First they talked about Bob and the children. Bob worked too hard, as always. At sixteen, Katie was still more interested in horses than boys, thank heaven. Justin was in Japan, although they feared that he would be sent to Korea if the border skirmishes escalated into outright war. Andy's new ambition was to become a pilot and he spent hours poring over airplane magazines and books.

Then Doris took the plunge. "Is Lee still staying with you?"

"He's still helping Bob on the ranch, which has been wonderful. There's too much work for one man to handle. Do you remember where the Browns used to have that little resort? Well, they called it a resort, but they were really just cabins on the water. He's rented one of them, now that he's back from Wyoming."

Doris nodded and yawned. She felt a dull ache, faint but constant, in her head. Her eyes were scratchy and her brain barely functioned. She slid her fingers under the lower frames of her glasses, lifted them a little, and rubbed her eyes.

Vivian said, "You seem tired."

"I am." She hesitated. "I didn't sleep well. I've had odd phone calls, at work and at home. Last night the man said my name, twice, in a very strange voice."

Vivian frowned. "That is upsetting." It was her turn to hesitate. "Lee had an anonymous phone call not long ago. I don't suppose there's any connection?"

"I don't know why there would be. I don't see Lee anymore. But . . . do you think there's a connection?"

"I don't know. I'll ask Lee what he thinks."

Doris heard the Mercury as soon as it turned into her driveway. Lee had called to find out if she would be at home on Monday. After work, she'd changed into an old skirt, loose shirt, and moccasins. She resisted an urge to wear nicer clothes. She did brush her hair and smooth on a little rouge. She dusted the living room and gave the bathroom a quick once-over. There was no time to do more, anyway.

She let him knock before she opened the door. Emotions fluttered through her—apprehension, pleasure at seeing him, regret at seeing him; a flood of memories, of pain, of sex, of the taste, smell, touch, sound of him. She took a deep breath.

"Come in. You're looking well." She used her customer voice, pleasant, controlled, well-modulated.

"So are you."

He sat in his favorite chair. He carried a parcel wrapped in brown paper, which he set carefully on the floor. He settled into the room, as though it were only the night before that he'd last been there. He looked more than well; he looked wonderful—relaxed, healthy, sleek.

"Ranching agrees with you."

He nodded. "I like it. It's good to be with Bob and Vivian and the kids. I'm even starting to like the idea of staying in one place." He cleared his throat. "Vivian told me about your phone calls. You know that I had one, too. Actually, Vivian thinks he called again while I was in Wyoming. I guess she didn't tell you what the man said? Or what happened in California?"

Doris shook her head.

"I met a woman in Redding—Joanne Johnson. She had a regular boyfriend who was very possessive . . . and had . . . some irregular habits."

It was obvious that Lee was picking his way, editing as he went. It was obvious, too, that he felt uncomfortable speaking to Doris about another woman. Good, she thought. It's

224

good for him to squirm a little.

"Joanne was terrified that Don—that wasn't his real name and she wouldn't tell me his real name—would find out about me. The last night I was there, she thought Don saw me in her house. She was so afraid that I told her I'd come back as soon as I dropped off my new mare at Bob's ranch. When I got back to Redding two days later, I found her dead—murdered."

Doris gasped. She couldn't help it.

Lee lit a cigarette, sucked in smoke, and blew it out again. The familiar scent drifted through the room.

He went on. "That was the end of March. Then a little over two weeks ago, he called me at the ranch. He said, 'I know who you are. I saw you with Joanne.' " Lee took another drag on the cigarette. "The thing that bothers me is that he's connected me to Bob. And if he knows that Bob is my brother and where he lives, maybe he knows about you, too."

"If he knows that much, he must know that we're not together anymore."

"You'd think so. But maybe he doesn't like our . . . our past relationship, for some reason. The man is obviously not normal. Who knows what goes on in a mind like that."

A mind like that. The phrase chilled Doris. It carried terrifying implications—of strange twists, of abnormality, of a psychological darkness far beyond her comprehension.

"I learned from a friend of Joanne's that this Don has a connection to the Woodbridge area. And there's more. Do you remember Charles Balleau?"

"The name is familiar."

"The family lives up the Little Nezzac near Bob. They're Indian. Charles's sister, Juanita, was murdered five years ago. She was dating someone who sounds the same—rich, secretive, perverted. He beat and strangled her, just as Joanne

225

was beaten and strangled."

"Oh, God." Doris felt sick. "I remember when that happened. And I do remember Mr. Balleau. He comes in the store sometimes, but he always pays cash. If he ran an account, I would have recalled him right away."

Lee said, "Charles, who was just a kid then, found his sister's body. He actually saw the man who did it, but it was dark, in the woods at night, so the killer was only a shadow. There was something about a belt buckle in both cases—a big, heavy, unusual buckle with a ram's head on it. Have you ever seen anyone wear a belt like that?"

"I . . . I don't know." Doris searched through her memory. "I could have. I don't think I notice belts."

"Well, from now on, maybe you'd better look at the belt on every man who comes into the store. You get a lot of traffic through there. You're in a good position to spot him. And if you do, for God's sake, be careful. Call the sheriff immediately. Or me."

They discussed the situation some more, but after awhile it became a conversation that went nowhere, just around in circles with no resolution.

Then Lee asked, "Doris, do you have a gun?"

"No. Carl never hunted, as you may recall."

"Do you remember the time that we went target shooting? I showed you how to use a pistol."

"Sort of."

Lee picked up the package by the chair. He unwrapped it and held a small revolver in his hand. "I want you to keep this. Not on top of the closet shelf, but somewhere you can get it in a hurry. I don't want to scare you, but I'd feel better if you had some protection."

He showed her how to use it. It wasn't difficult at all. So easy to end a life. Lee seemed to read her mind.

"Don't be squeamish about using the pistol. This guy isn't the least bit squeamish. He's already killed two women, maybe more. And if it comes to a situation where you think you need it, use it. It will be him or you. Do you understand that?"

"Yes." Even as she spoke, it seemed too bizarre, too unreal. These things simply didn't happen to ordinary people, certainly not to anyone as boringly ordinary as herself.

Lee went to the door, then looked at her without speaking. Once before, he'd stood at her door while she sensed the pressures of unspoken words behind his silence. The old longing rose in Doris, the hunger to wrap her arms around his familiar body, to hold him close, to try to keep him with her, just a little longer. She clasped her hands together, so she wouldn't reach for him.

"Doris . . ."

Her breath stopped. Maybe her heart stopped, too. Lee looked at his hands, work-scarred hands that knew her body as well as it remembered his touch.

"I still care about you. Please be careful. And remember to watch for the belt buckle."

Surely that was not what he had intended to say, those flat disappointing words. She watched the Mercury until it disappeared.

In the bushes across the darkening street, something moved quickly, furtively. Inside Doris, fear leaped in quick response. Then she recognized the blonde head of a boy who lived a few houses away. He retrieved a football from the bushes and dashed toward home.

She closed the drapes carefully, so that not even a crack was left between them. The pistol felt cold and dangerous as she carried it to the bedroom and placed it in a drawer by the bedside. Somewhat to her surprise, it was comforting to know that it was there, to know that she had a means of self-defense.

But it was ridiculous to think that she would need it, here in her own home, in her safe little town. Surely there was no real reason to be afraid.

Chapter 10

CHARLES

Fourth of July to September

Red, white, and blue bunting decorated the rodeo stands. The sun scorched the crowd, wilted but still enthusiastic after an afternoon of bronc riding, calf roping, and other events. Somewhere in the distant parking lot a string of firecrackers stuttered noisily.

"Damn fool," Bob Jamison muttered. "He'll scare the stock."

But the animals in the arena seemed too hot and jaded to react. Charles knew how they felt. Heat hung in the valley, trapped between the hills, speckled with scrub oak, that rose on both sides of the river. He couldn't see the water, but he knew it was there, no more than a mile or so beyond the fairgrounds. What bliss it would be to dive into the cool green depths.

Katie Jamison, blondish and cute, sat on one side of him. Charles had come to the rodeo with Wally Jenkins. As they'd looked around for a place to sit, they spotted the Jamisons, including Lee, who made room for them. Wally, on the other side of Charles, leaned forward to talk to Katie.

"What do you hear from Justin?"

She shook her head. "Nothing. As far as we know, he's still

229

in Japan. But we're afraid that his outfit will be sent to Korea."

Wally said, "I thought he'd go to college. Why did he join the army?"

"I don't know," Katie answered. "None of us know. He just did."

Charles didn't understand, either. While going to college didn't hold any appeal for him, the military held even less. Too many rules and uniforms, too much saluting, yes-sirring and snapping to orders. It was not the life for Charles. And he would have thought it was not the life for Justin, either. He didn't know Justin well, but he never would have figured him for a soldier.

Just a few days ago, on the twenty-fifth of June, Communist North Korea had launched a surprise attack on American-supported South Korea. And Justin might soon be in the fight, perhaps to kill or be killed.

Brahma bull riding, Charles's favorite event, was next. Justin was forgotten as he sat fascinated by the actions of the big dangerous animals. All too soon, the last rider was called: "Marvin Crawford from Missoula, Montana. He'll be coming out of chute Number Three on a bull named Bad News." The amplified voice of the announcer dominated the summer air as the metallic sound rolled off the sun-baked hills.

Charles saw the rider's head above the gate as he settled himself onto the back of the animal. There was a pause as he adjusted his handhold and seat. He nodded. The gate opened. For a split second both Brahma and rider were framed, motionless, in the loading chute.

Then the bull exploded out into the arena and bucked his way toward the grandstands. The large slick body twisted and plunged. The bell on the bucking strap fastened around his flanks clanged and clattered, adding to the bull's rage. He leaped high into the air, landed with jarring force, then lunged upward in another direction. The rider flew to one side and sprawled on the ground.

The clown had followed closely. Now he darted between the bull and the cowboy. The bull, distracted from the fallen rider, rushed at the clown. He scampered toward the safety of his barrel, but the Brahma wasn't really interested and had already turned away.

The thrown rider hobbled toward the chutes. The mounted hazers closed in on the bull and tried to herd him toward the gate that would take him to the holding pens behind the chutes. The bull charged between them and galloped around the arena. He passed directly in front of the bleachers, his big domed head held high. With his ghosty-gray color and wild, dark-circled eyes, he looked more like a spectre than an actual living animal.

"God, he looks mean," said Wally. "I'd never try to ride one of those devils."

In a few minutes, the riders had the bull safely back in the pens.

"My mouth is so dry, I can't even spit. Let's get a Coke," Charles suggested. The others clamored for a drink, too.

"I'll treat," said Lee.

A number of people waited in front of the refreshment stand as Lee, Wally, and Charles took their places at the end of the line.

"Sherry, is that you?" Wally asked in his loud, friendly voice.

The girl in front of them turned around. It seemed that the bottom dropped out of Charles's stomach. He'd seen her only once, at a distance, since he quit school in April. A fancy tooled leather belt cinched her small waist. She wore a

231

checked cowboy shirt and a jaunty western hat.

"Hello, Wally." There was a distinct pause as she saw Charles. "And Charles. How are you?"

She glanced quickly at him and then back to Wally. Charles felt his heart begin the old familiar hammering, all the harder because the sight of her was so unexpected.

"I haven't seen you since graduation," Wally said. "What are you doing this summer?"

"Oh, this and that."

"You should have tried out for rodeo queen," Wally told her. "You make a real cute cowgirl."

"I can't even ride a horse. These boots are just for show." Her voice sounded strained.

Charles took a long slow breath. He shouldn't allow the sight of her to disturb him so much. Sherry had broken off with Wally, too. Yet he talked to her easily, as if it didn't matter that she'd said she didn't want to see him anymore. It probably didn't matter to Wally. He dated other girls, but there had never been anyone else for Charles.

He tried to think of something to say, instead of just standing there as if he were made of wood. A wooden Indian, he thought sourly.

"Oh, here's Warren." Sherry turned toward an approaching man. "Warren, this is Wally Jenkins and Charles Balleau. We were in school together."

The man looked at them indifferently. His skin was pale, even in the heat, and his swelling flesh seemed stuffed into it as tightly as sausage into casing. While he wasn't tall, his shoulders were massive and reduced Sherry to a doll-like figure beside him.

"Hello, Mr. Stonebraker. I've seen you around, but we haven't met." Wally thrust out his hand. Charles followed his example. He and Stonebraker exchanged a brief, impersonal clasp. A wave of color washed over Sherry's face and then receded from her porcelain-perfect skin.

"And this is Lee Jamison." Wally included Lee who stood behind them. "Do you know Sherry Prentiss, Lee?"

"Hello, Sherry." Lee smiled warmly at the girl and then extended his hand to Warren. "How are you?"

Warren's rigid expression didn't alter as he exchanged perfunctory remarks with Lee. Sherry smiled brightly and kept her eyes firmly on Wally's face.

"Mother and Marlene are up in the stands." Her voice was high-pitched and gay. "We came down to get something cold for all of us to drink."

Warren Stonebraker's eyes flickered from Lee to Wally to Charles. There was a brief silence.

Wally came to the rescue again. "What are you going to do now that you've graduated—get a job or go to college?"

Another dark wave of color surged over Sherry's face. She looked away, off over Charles's shoulder to the tawny hills beyond. The blush faded, leaving her suddenly pale and stricken.

Charles impulsively extended his hand toward her to offer the comfort of a touch, but jerked it back before the gesture was complete. Sherry's eyes flashed to his. There was a look of such agony in them that his heart twisted. Their eyes held for a brief, startling moment, then she turned toward Warren, who stared fixedly at her with an unreadable expression.

"Oh, dear. It's our turn to order and I haven't even thought about what I want. It was so nice to see you both. And to meet you, Mr. Jamison. Good-bye," she chirped in her bright, unnatural voice.

Charles didn't say a word during the encounter or as Sherry and Mr. Stonebraker walked away. Wally and Lee ordered drinks and handed one to him. Lee went ahead, balancing the tray of paper cups, as Wally followed with Charles.

"Pretty tough, huh?" Wally asked after a moment.

"Yeah." Charles's throat felt rusty. He sipped at the Coke. It went down like something hard and lumpy.

"Sherry's always been different," Wally said. "When we dated, even when we held hands and it seemed like we should be close, I felt she wasn't really there. Or maybe I wasn't there. Do you know what I mean?"

"Yeah," Charles lied. He didn't know what Wally meant. When he and Sherry touched, she had been completely aware of him. He knew it by the way she looked at him, by the way her mouth clung to his and her hands caressed him. But it hadn't made any difference. She'd cast him off, the same way she'd left Wally and Jim Parrish. And what was the deal with the Stonebrakers? Charles couldn't shake the feeling that there was something hidden between them.

You're making yourself crazy, Charles admonished himself. Think about something else. Think about the rodeo and the damn dumb animals that spend their lives trying to buck off one damn dumb cowboy after another. Unblinking, eyes straight ahead, he stared down into the arena.

Later, after the rodeo was over, Charles coaxed the old Plymouth, which he'd parked down on the main road, up the steep climb to the shack. His father was still in Portland. He no longer worked, as far as Charles knew, but lived a hand-to-mouth existence on the streets. He seemed to be deliberately cutting himself off from Charles.

As the Plymouth lurched up the hill, Charles relived every second of his meeting with Sherry. Why hadn't he said something? Even "hello" would have been better than that stunned silence.

He couldn't forget the agonized look in her eyes when

Wally had asked what she was going to do now that she'd graduated. Her mother and the Stonebrakers must be making demands upon her. Maybe he should go to a pay phone and call. But what good would that do? She didn't want to see him anymore or she wouldn't have dumped him.

The sun sank toward the coast range behind him and long shadows pointed eastward. He turned the last corner below the cabin. A wispy plume of smoke rose from the chimney and faded in the evening air. Someone had built a fire in the cookstove. His father had come home, it seemed. What kind of mood would he be in? Charles walked warily toward the house.

The door was open and the smell of cooking food drifted through it. The interior of the room was in shadow and at first glance it appeared to be empty. Then he saw a woman sitting in a chair. Her long gray hair was braided into a single thick rope and pinned into a knot at the back of her neck. She wore a loose-fitting navy blue dress. Gnarled hands rested in her lap.

"Grandmother!"

She rose to her feet, smiling. Her small white teeth were as perfect as pearls in a necklace. They looked artificial, but Charles knew they were her own. She was barely five feet tall.

"Good evening, Charles," she said in her soft, precise voice. She'd learned English as a second language after she went to school and still spoke with the precision of the woman who'd taught her.

He hugged her a little stiffly. "How did you get here?"

"Some people I know were going to visit their son in Canyonville. I asked if I could ride along. They will pick me up Wednesday on their way back to the reservation."

"That's good. I'm glad to see you, Grandmother."

"You've grown into a fine-looking young man." She looked at him for a moment, smiling proudly. "Where is your father?"

"He's in Portland with his friend, Bill."

Her smile disappeared and she sighed. "Your father has changed, Charles. It was whiskey that changed him. Some men should never drink." Then she looked at Charles, almost hopefully. "But he stayed with you, didn't he? He stayed with you and Juanita until she died and you were grown. He did that, didn't he?"

"Yeah, he stayed." Charles answered reluctantly as he thought of his father's silent, ungiving presence. It hadn't been enough. If I ever have kids, I'll talk to them, he vowed. I'll listen to them. We'll do things together. I'll be there, really there, not just a body in the house.

Aloud he asked, "How are you feeling? How is your rheumatism?"

They talked while Grandmother dished up the stew she had made. Later, after the dishes were washed, they took the kitchen chairs outside and sat in the yard where it was cooler. It was pleasant in the summer twilight. Faint stars appeared overhead. An owl hooted somewhere off in the woods. Mosquitos whined around them.

Charles dropped his hand down beside the chair seat, half-expecting that Blackie would stick his wet nose against his fingers. It still seemed strange without the dog. He thought sometimes that he'd get another one, but just any dog wouldn't do. He wanted a really good one, like Blackie.

Grandmother had been silent for several minutes and Charles thought that she might have dozed off. She shifted on the hard chair and sat up a little straighter.

"Charles, I am going to tell you a story about your father when he was young. His best friend was named Lester. Although he was a good boy, Lester was sometimes careless and got into trouble."

Charles interrupted. "Grandmother, I've heard this before."

"I will tell you again. It is the duty of the old to tell stories to the young. Someday you can tell this and other stories to your children."

Charles moved restlessly and swatted at a mosquito as she began.

"The winter that Asa and Lester were sixteen years old, Lester went riding by himself. He had a new horse, a young mare not much more than a filly. Night came and Lester did not come home. His parents worried, but it was too dark to look for him. It rained and the rain turned to snow. They went to search in the morning. Asa went, too.

"They looked and looked, but could not find Lester. All the tracks were covered with snow which did not melt for two days. Other people joined the search, but Lester and his horse had disappeared as if the earth had opened beneath them.

"Everyone gave up. It is true that people sometimes disappear. They go out and never come back. It seems that it would be easy to find a person, but sometimes it is not."

In spite of the fact that he knew the end of the story, Charles felt himself caught up in it. Disappearances did occur. Just the summer before, two families from Woodbridge had gone picnicking only a few miles farther up-river. A boy, seven years old, wandered away from the picnic site. It was nearly dark by the time his parents missed him and it was the next day before a search could be organized. Volunteers, Charles among them, hunted for days. In spite of their best efforts, no trace of the boy was found.

Grandmother paused, as if realizing that Charles was distracted. She went on in her low precise voice. "For two days after the others, even Lester's parents, had given up, Asa searched alone. On the evening of the second day, for some reason, he went into a gully so narrow that he left his horse behind. A creek, just a trickle of water, ran along the bottom. There was no reason for anyone to go back in there. But Asa went on, farther and farther. And he found Lester, badly hurt.

"Lester had ridden along the top of the gully. He saw a bobcat creep out of sight below the rim. He jumped off his horse and ran to the edge to see it again. But he slipped on loose rock and fell far down to the creek bed. One leg shattered on the rocks.

"He had a little dried meat in his pocket and water in the creek, so he lived. But he could not crawl out. Lester's horse wandered away. Later a man said he saw her running with the wild horses. The horse was the same color and wore a hackamore, so probably he was right.

"Asa forced his horse into the gully and put Lester on his back. On the way out, the horse slipped on the rocks and sprained his leg. Asa made him walk as far as he could, but soon the horse was so lame he could not go on. Asa left the horse and carried Lester on his back. He carried him for miles—six, seven miles, maybe more. He carried Lester all night."

Charles could almost see his father, even younger than himself, but already stocky and muscular. He imagined him stumbling through a dark night lit only by stars while his friend clung to his back. He imagined Asa sinking to the ground, panting and exhausted. But as soon as he could, he picked up his friend and struggled on.

Charles finished the story himself. "Lester's leg didn't heal right, so it's crooked and he walks with a cane. And now he's a member of the intertribal council, an important man.

But he's never forgotten what my father did."

Grandmother smiled. "You do remember the story."

"Yeah." Asa had told it to him when Charles was little and it had impressed him that his father was so strong and determined, so faithful to his friend. But he'd stopped talking to Charles about the time he began drinking heavily and Charles hadn't thought of the event for years. Now his chest ached with a feeling of loss and regret for the man who might have been.

"Asa wouldn't give up," Grandmother said. "He saved his friend because he wouldn't give up."

"He's given up now. He's given up everything. Why?" The words sounded mean as Charles spoke them, but the bitterness in his heart overflowed and he could not hold back.

"That strength is still inside him. Someday he may find it again."

He looked at her dim profile. She was composed, her voice steady.

"You are the one who is strong, Grandmother."

"Any strength I have must also exist in my son and grandson."

A rush of feeling welled up inside him and he struggled to find words that would express some of it.

"I'm glad you told me the story again," he said at last. "I won't forget it."

She nodded. They sat silently together under the stars.

It was pleasant having Grandmother in the house. She cleaned the rooms and washed the windows. She pulled down and burned the drab curtains that were falling apart on their rods.

"You don't need curtains out here in the trees. Let the trees and the sun and the moon look into your house."

"You work too hard, Grandmother. Sit down awhile."

"I do not enjoy sitting too long. Besides, I do not want you to live in such a dirty place." Later she said, "I see you are not working. Did your father leave some money for you?"

"I had a little saved up from my last job," he lied. He didn't want her to know that he stole in order to obtain the things he needed.

Gas and oil were a more pressing need than food. Dried beans, potatoes and onions were filling and cheap. He knew what wild greens were edible. Berries ripened in the clearings. He fished, shot rabbits, squirrels and grouse. Once he killed a deer, but most of the meat spoiled before he could eat it. As it was poached out of season, he'd hesitated to share it with anyone else and the waste troubled him. But all in all, he ate quite well from the land.

The Plymouth, however, could not. He needed grain for the horses, too. There was plenty of forage for them, but the grain kept them close. Without it, with thousands of unfenced acres in the Cascade Mountain range, they could easily wander where he would never find them again.

"I'll look for a job next week," Charles assured his grandmother. Maybe he really would, so he wouldn't have to keep lying to her.

Wednesday arrived too soon. The people who would take her back to the reservation arrived in mid-morning. Charles carried her satchel out to the car.

She put her arms around him. "I am concerned about you, Charles. Neither your father nor your mother have given you much care. You are so alone. Come with me. The reservation may not be the best place to live, but we will be together."

"I'm fine," he told her. "I get by just fine. I'm glad you came to see me. I wish you could stay longer." The man and woman waited in the car, so he quickly kissed her soft wrinkled cheek. "Good-bye, Grandmother. Take care of your-self."

"Come see me soon."

"I will."

He stood in the yard and watched her ride away. She waved out the back window just before the car went around the turn. Charles wandered in the yard, looking for trash to pick up, but Grandmother had inspired him and he'd got it all several days before. It was so quiet in the heart of the forest. No trees rustled in the heat of the day. Only a crow squawked far off and out of sight.

He wished Blackie were here. It would be nice to have him panting and wagging his tail, trotting busily around, now and then looking at Charles to see what he was doing. Maybe he'd drive up and see Mrs. Domingo, although he didn't want to tell her that he still didn't have a job. Maybe tomorrow he'd look for one.

He'd thought about Sherry at intervals during his grand-mother's visit. At about four o'clock, tired of the empty house, he drove to the pay phone outside the Nezzac River store. Mrs. Prentiss should still be at work. Maybe Sherry would not mind that he called. Maybe she'd even be glad and would tell him what had put that expression of misery into her eyes. Or was it only his imagination that put it there?

The phone was picked up on the third ring. He recognized Mrs. Prentiss's voice. He hung up as quickly as if the phone had stung him. Why was she home from work so early? Maybe she was sick.

The next day, he drove slowly past their house. There was no car in the carport. He turned and drove by again. The thought of knocking on that blank white door filled him with apprehension. What would he say if Mrs. Prentiss opened it? What would he say if Sherry did?

He couldn't escape the feeling that something was wrong, that she needed him, whether she knew it or not. But she would probably tell him that it was none of his business. She'd say it politely, because she always tried to be nice to everyone, but she'd tell him just the same. He stepped on the gas and sped away.

He didn't look for a job. Instead he came across an out-of-state car with a handbag sticking out from under the front seat. He broke in and found nearly one hundred dollars. What an idiot, he thought. Anyone that careless deserved to be robbed.

A few days later, early in the evening, Charles split wood for the cookstove. He heard a vehicle laboring up the road. It was Wally Jenkins in his father's car.

They talked for a few minutes, but Wally seemed ill at ease. He kept looking at Charles in an intent way, as if he expected him to do or say something special.

"What's wrong?" Charles asked. "Why are you looking at me like that?"

"Do you read the paper?"

"Not very often."

"I didn't think so. There was some amazing news in it yesterday." He took a newspaper page from the front seat. "Brace yourself before you read it."

Charles skimmed the photographs and headings in the society section of the Woodbridge paper. There was a photograph of Sherry, her face trapped in flat, impersonal black and white. She smiled like a movie star, chin tilted, blonde hair smudged into darkness.

He looked at it a moment before he read the words beneath. "Mrs. William Prentiss, formerly of Whistler's Bend, announced the marriage of her daughter, Sherry Marie, to Warren Stonebraker, of Portland. The wedding, a private affair for immediate family only, occurred on June 15 . . . The couple will live in Portland where Mr. Stonebraker is in business."

Something like a two-by-four seemed to have struck Charles in his center. His fingers turned nerveless and his hand dropped to his side, the paper dangling.

Wally looked at him sympathetically. "Can you believe it? They were already married when we saw them at the rodeo. No wonder she acted funny."

"But he's too old," Charles blurted.

"I happen to know he's thirty-eight," Wally said. "That's sure as hell too old for an eighteen-year-old, like Sherry."

Nausea swirled slowly as Charles thought of Warren's cold eyes, the stuffed-sausage look of his chunky body.

Wally said, "I called Jim Parrish. His folks and Marlene's are pretty good friends. It seems this marriage has been arranged for years, since Sherry was about fourteen. But no one knew it, except the Stonebrakers and Sherry and her mother.

"Mrs. Prentiss quit her job and there's a 'for sale' sign on their house already. She's set up in an apartment in Portland and she'll never have to work again. She gets to play bridge and go to fashion shows all day. And Sherry gets creepy Uncle Warren."

Wally looked at Charles as if expecting him to speak. No words came, so Wally went on.

"He even let her date boys in high school so she could have some fun first. Isn't that crazy? All the time, while she was so cute and popular and all the guys were crazy about her—all the time she'd been bought by a rich older man, just like she was a dog or something. I didn't know things like that really happened."

They stood in silence for a few moments.

"I've got to go," Wally said. "I hated to be the one to bring you the news, but I thought you oughta know."

"It doesn't matter," Charles said heavily. "It's been over between us for quite awhile."

"Sure. Try not to take it too hard, though. See you around."

The car bounced away down the rough lane. The sun shone low in the sky with the soft retreating glow of evening. Soon it would drop behind the hills and darkness would cloak the forest. Charles stood where Wally had left him, eyes unfocused, unseeing.

He thought of the man he'd met at the rodeo. He imagined those fleshy hands on Sherry's body, the grim lips claiming her soft mouth, the thick body beside her, on top of her.

I'll kill you, you miserable bastard. You stuck-up son-of-a-bitch. For what you've done to Sherry, I'll kill you by inches and enjoy every second. I'll . . .

But reason hit him like a club. Stonebraker hadn't raped her. Sherry had agreed to marriage. Even if her mother had encouraged her, Sherry had done it herself. She'd said "yes."

How could she do it?

Almost two months later, Charles stood on a tall stump and squinted down the hill toward where the choker setters worked in the brush. One of them raised his hand in a signal. Charles beeped twice on the button at the end of the long electrical line that ran from his hand to the yarding platform on the hill above him.

The operator revved the motor. The 1 1/4" steel mainline cable snapped taut. Two logs, hooked on by shorter cables called chokers, lunged upward. They leaped over or smashed through wreckage left by other logs as they were dragged up-hill. They were soon hauled out of sight. Charles heard the motor ease off and idle as the logs were unhooked at the landing, nearly a thousand feet away. They'd be stacked until they were loaded onto the trucks that took them to the mill.

The sweet scent of warm fir needles mingled with the harsh odor of diesel. Sweat from the heat of the early September sun trickled down Charles's face. He shifted his hard hat and wiped his forehead with the back of his wrist. The old Plymouth had needed major repairs and he'd been forced to find a job with Carnes and Baylor.

As whistle punk, he acted as relay between the buckers and fallers in the brush and the men on the landing. After the trees were felled, buckers with chainsaws attacked the fallen trunks. They cut the 150- to 200-foot trees into mill-length logs, 16, 24, 32, or 40 feet long. The length of the cut was determined by the usability of the log, breakage from falling, or the presence of conk, wood fungus, or other defects.

The yarder, a diesel-driven winch mounted on a movable wooden sled, sat in a prominent position on a nearby hill. Heavy cable ran through an enormous pulley, called a bull block, near the top of the spar tree at the landing.

After the choker setters signalled Charles that they had hooked on the logs, he in turn signalled the "donkey" yarder operator on the distant landing. A horn mounted on the side of the platform bleated out a signal—two squawks for "go." The operator activated drums that reeled in the mainline. One blast on the horn meant stop, three meant reverse. Sometimes logs hung up on stumps or rock, and the drums had to be reversed in order to get slack into the line. After the logs reached the landing, a lighter cable called the haulback line completed the loop and pulled the mainline back to the logs where the process was repeated.

The horn blared for the noon break. Charles jumped from the stump and hiked up to the landing where he'd left his

245

lunch. He sat down by George Olson, the high climber and rigger.

George grinned as he unwrapped his sandwich, a thick slab of yellow cheese with a slice of salami on each side, all wedged betwen dark rye bread. He took a big bite and waved the sandwich toward a flat bench farther up the side of the canyon. An occasional crumb flew out of his mouth as he spoke.

"There she is, kid. See that big Doug fir sticking up? That's our next spar tree. Right after lunch, I'll top her out and that'll be your last lesson for awhile. You'll have to learn the rest by doing it yourself. And you'll make a high climber, as soon as you learn to come down a little faster. It ain't no farther coming down than going up."

He grinned and slapped Charles on the knee. Charles smiled agreeably, even though he'd heard the joke before. George had befriended Charles almost from his first day on the job. When the younger man expressed an interest in high climbing, George showed him how to use the spurs and ropes during their lunch breaks. He explained the intricacies of topping a tree. When Charles proved adept, he brought some old, but still serviceable, equipment for him to use. Charles practiced climbing as often as he could while George stood spraddle-legged on the ground below, yelling up instructions and criticism.

Charles liked climbing. He liked the satisfying thunk as he drove the spurs into the tree. He liked the slow recession of the ground beneath his feet. A feeling of exhilaration came over him as he went higher. There was no fear going up, just a sense of elation that rose along with his physical body. It felt good to stand far up in the air, feet firmly planted against the furrowed bark, and lean out into the rope that looped around the tree. He felt secure, as safe as an eagle on a perch. He grinned as he looked down at the faces below, all turned up toward him.

The moment of insecurity came when he had to start back to earth, to draw the steel spurs out of the wood and step down. Then he didn't look toward the ground, but kept his gaze on the tree directly in front of his eyes. He breathed steadily and carefully, inhaling the pungent scent of wood and pitch. George came down the tree like a monkey. Charles had heard of climbers who dropped down even more recklessly, driving their spurs in the bark just often enough to prevent free fall.

Charles looked toward the distant Douglas fir that George had indicated. The nearby logs were almost cleared out. It was time to move the landing and rig a new tree farther up the canyon. The first job was to take off the top of the spar tree that would serve as anchor for the mainline. The tree must withstand massive strain as it supported the weight of the great logs when they were reeled in. A spider's web of supporting rigging and cables went from the spar to the ground for additional mooring.

The spar would creak and groan as the massive logs bowed it in the direction of the pull. The whip-like action created under the strain could cause the top, if left on, to break off and perhaps fall on the men below. The day-to-day task of the rigger was to work around the landing, adjusting the network of cables, blocks, pulleys, and hooks, and to help with the loading. His most spectacular job was to remove the top of the new spar.

During the morning hours, George had climbed the tree and trimmed off all the branches to within about forty feet of the top. Men began gathering during lunch. In addition to the loading crew, as many fallers, buckers, and choker setters as were within walking distance of the new landing headed toward it. A driver left his partially loaded truck and hiked up the hill. George finished eating and lit a cigarette. A dusty jeep drove up and a gray-haired, heavy-set man in gray twill climbed out.

"Well, lookie here," George said with satisfaction. "Even the head push has come to see the show."

Karl Blessinger walked over to them. He squinted at the distant Douglas fir. "Looks like a pretty good day for the job. No wind to speak of."

"Should be all right." George blew a smoke ring. The two men talked while he finished his cigarette and Charles listened. At last George stood up, spit copiously into his palm, and stubbed out the cigarette in his hand. He would not be responsible for starting a woods fire by throwing away a smouldering butt. He buckled on his wide leather climbing belt and gathered up his ropes, saw, and axe. He jerked his head in a "come on" gesture to Charles, who followed him to his pickup. They jounced up the hill.

It was a showman's instinct that prompted George to time the topping so that it coincided with the noon meal. It was enough of an event so that all the woods workers within a convenient distance took time to watch.

George went up the tree quickly and easily, about 175 feet to where the cut would be made. He settled in his spurs and drew up the axe which dangled on a rope below him. He chopped a notch in the trunk to guide the direction of the fall. Of necessity, the axe blows fell close to his rope. Some careless climbers had been known to cut their own lines and send themselves plummeting to the ground. George was careful.

When the notch was finished, he lowered the axe, circled around to the other side of the tree, and pulled up the handsaw. The branches of the trees in the uncut forest not far away stirred in an almost inaudible warning. The rustling increased and the great trees shivered and sighed.

On the ground, Karl Blessinger shifted nervously and scowled. "I hope the wind doesn't come up."

The rhythmic insect sound of George sawing drifted over the woods. Charles leaned against the pickup, looking up along with the other men. It seemed unnaturally quiet in spite of the little breeze that murmured through the forest. The noisy yarder engine was shut down. The Cat rested silently in the brush. No logs crashed and gouged through the underbrush. There was no blare of the whistle punk's signal or incessant whine of the power saws. The only sound was the rasp of George's handsaw.

It was drowned by a great hissing from the distant trees. Their tops trembled and swished in agitation. George stopped sawing and looked up at the crown of the tree above him. The branches shivered and then were still again.

"Hey, George," Blessinger bellowed up. "Come on down. I don't like these wind gusts. You can finish later."

George didn't answer. He hung in the tree, staring off into the distance as though the wind were something he might see sliding along the ridges of the remote hills. The movement of air had dropped until it was almost imperceptible. The faintest of breezes brushed Charles's face. Normally he would not even have noticed it. George shifted his gaze down to the woods boss.

"I'm too near through," he yelled. "I can't leave the top standing half-cut to maybe fall on somebody below. I'll be finished in a few minutes."

Blessinger gave a sort of growl, jammed his hands into his pockets, and paced around in a little circle. George resumed sawing. In a few minutes, the tip of the tree trembled, just the slightest flutter of limbs against the sky. George paused and glanced up. He wiped his forehead and went back to work.

The tremor increased, a definite shuddering, and the crown swayed gently. He sawed on. He and the top floated together, high against the clear sunny sky.

A sudden gust of wind jolted out of the northeast. The crown tilted abruptly. George dropped the saw to the end of its rope. There was a great splintering crack as the tree split. The rent tore downward well below the cut line. The two halves opened skyward like the long jaws of a crocodile and then closed again. The severed top leaped off the trunk and plunged toward the ground with a whistling rush. Limbs flailed the air. The released spar sprang backward and then snapped forward in the other direction.

The amputated top smashed into pieces as it struck the earth. Small broken limbs flew in all directions. In the sudden silence, George hung in the ropes like a puppet with severed strings. His arms dangled. His head lolled as the tree whipped back and forth. The maimed tree rocked in a diminishing dance, each arc less than the one before.

"Great God! It split and squeezed him in the ropes," one of the men cried.

"Damn it! I should have made him come down," Blessinger shouted.

"George! Hey, George!"

"He can't hear you. He's out cold."

Charles opened the door of George's pickup and took out the practice rope and spurs. He buckled on the climbing belt with numb fingers. The excited voices of the men seemed to come from far away.

"The Balleau kid has been doing some climbing," he heard the head loader say. "Maybe he can get George down."

The men turned toward Charles as he walked down to the spar, carrying the spurs. Blessinger, his face as gray as his jacket, looked at him doubtfully.

"I don't know. You're new at this. We don't want another casualty." He turned toward the others. "Anyone else done any climbing?"

No one spoke.

Charles said, "I'll give it a try." He fastened the spurs onto his boots. Blessinger handed him a small pulley with a lightweight manila rope running through the eye.

"Here's the snatch block. Be careful, Balleau. And good luck." He thumped him on the shoulder.

Charles nodded. His face felt stiff. One of George's gloves lay like a fallen leaf at the base of the tree. His upside-down hard hat was nearby in a clump of ferns. Charles thought of the three little blonde kids George talked about, of the wife who made the thick sandwiches and rich slabs of cake and pie. Charles looked up the tree, up and up the long tapering stem, to the point where George hung suspended. His legs crumpled above his spurs still thrust deep into the wood. His body slumped against the tree.

Charles looped the climbing rope around the tree and flipped it upward. He climbed until he was level with the rope, leaned into the tree, and moved the rope up again. The ground slowly receded beneath his feet, but there was no exhilaration in this climb.

He paused to look up. George was almost directly above him. The pulley Charles carried dragged heavily at his shoulder. He shifted it to a new position and flipped the rope. Something warm and wet dropped onto his hand. It was blood. He crept on. More drops splashed down, splattering scarlet. He edged to one side to get out from under them. The saw dangled only a few feet above Charles's head. The jagged teeth glinted as it swayed back and forth.

The wind was rising. It thrummed around the tree and in his ears. The bark was warm from the sun. Charles felt a slight quivering against his body. Was it the wind or the movement of his climbing? Or was it the tree itself, trembling as it died? He felt a sudden rush of kinship and sorrow for this other life, now destroyed forever.

"Forgive us," he whispered. Then he felt foolish and surprised that he had spoken aloud.

For the first time, he looked down. The men gathered below, all faces upward, as featureless as mushrooms. He felt their tension and anxiety radiating toward him. He couldn't allow himself those feelings. He looked away and shifted the rope again, closer to the dangling saw. The axe swung in and out of sight around the curve of the trunk. Charles edged a little to the left and cautiously moved the rope, afraid that he would strike the tools and make them swing harder.

He drove in his right spur, pulled himself up, then the left spur. His eyes drew almost level with the dangling saw blade, freshly filed that morning, as jagged and sharp as the teeth of a predatory animal. He tossed the rope and raised himself. The wind gusted, a forceful blast. It caught the flat surface of the saw. It spun in the air and the ripping edge came straight at Charles's eyes.

He flung up his right arm. The teeth struck him. They punctured his shirt and then his flesh, driven partly by the wind and partly by the panicky movements of his arm. Flesh ripped from wrist to elbow. He swung to the left, off-balance, and the rope slipped down. He grabbed for it and missed. His fingers scrabbled at the bark. The saw came at him again.

He closed his eyes and turned his head. His fumbling right hand found a groove in the bark. He embraced the tree, leaned into it. The flat side of the saw clanged against his hard hat. He groped for the rope, found it and his balance again. The saw came spinning back.

He hunched his shoulder and leaned away as far as he

could. Razor-pointed teeth pricked him as he stepped up and around to the left. The saw swung past on an arc that missed him by inches. Relief lightened him and he moved quickly up the tree until the saw swung harmlessly just below his feet.

Charles's right sleeve was ripped and wet with blood, partly his, partly George's. He worked the rope carefully around the other man's slack body and eased upward until they were level. George's head rolled to one side, his eyes were half-closed and his mouth hung open. His face was pulped, smeared with blood from his nose and the lacerations he'd received when his head smashed into the tree.

Charles reached past George and fastened the pulley to the tree just below the cut line. When he had run the straw line through the pulley and secured it to George's climbing belt, he gestured thumbs-up to the men below. They hauled on the end of the rope that dangled to the ground. George's limp figure lifted until his weight was supported by the straw line rather than by his spurs and climbing rope.

Charles drew up the axe and cut through George's rope with a single sharp stroke. He lowered the axe again and kicked at the other man's spurs until they jarred out of the wood. Charles heard his own heavy breathing, as he panted like a dog with exertion. But not a sound from George.

Again, Charles signalled to the men on the ground. They carefully paid out rope and lowered George back to earth. Charles watched him go. He had to wait until the other man reached the ground before he could remove the pulley and begin his own descent. Now and then, George bumped gently into the tree trunk. His mutilated face was hidden by the angle of his head.

A queasy feeling rose in Charles. He looked away from the

dangling man and out to the panorama that spread serenely below him. The wind had dropped to a slight breeze. He concentrated on the land and tried to pour his sickish tension out into the indifferent hills.

Taller mountain ridges rose against the sky to the south. Untouched timber lay thick and close as feathers on their sides. Hills dropped in soft-looking mounds and shadowy draws down to the narrow river valley. The watercourse curved and twisted in strips of silver-gray. Much of the near side of the drainage had been logged over and it spread out in jumbled patterns of clear-cut and seed blocks.

Closer to him sprawled the littered wreckage of the cutting process—uprooted trees, gouged Cat trails, logs and limbs piled helter-skelter in a giant's game of pick-up sticks. Miscellaneous equipment added to the clutter—the yarder engine, the half-loaded truck, a yellow Cat parked at an angle in the brush, power saws, oil cans, hard hats, cables and hooks. The untouched forest began a short distance up the hill behind Charles. The trees stood in dark green ranks, only days away from destruction.

When he looked back, George was nearly to the ground. Charles took a deep breath and tried to hold the tranquility of the mountains within his own heart. He removed the pulley and began his descent. He didn't look at anything except the tree directly in front of his face. He didn't think about anything except the next careful move. It seemed to take forever. Hands stretched out to steady him as soon as he was within reach.

"Good work, Charlie!"

"You're okay now, kid."

He had to ask the question first thing. "How's George?"

Blessinger shook his head. "He must have been killed instantly. I'm sorry, Balleau. You did a great job bringing him down. Let's take a look at your arm. You're bleeding pretty bad."

Charles looked at his sleeve, soaked with mingled blood. "Aw, hell," he said unsteadily. "My dog's bit me worse than this."

Charles didn't work the rest of the week. The gashes on his arm were not severe, but when Blessinger said, "Take a couple days off, with pay," Charles certainly was not going to argue.

The next morning, he cooked oatmeal and topped it with a generous spoonful of sugar. He punched a hole in a five-ounce tin of evaporated milk and sloshed it into the bowl. He bought the little cans by the case. With no electricity in the cabin, the only way to keep things cool was to put them in the spring. Fresh milk soured too quickly in warm weather.

The Plymouth was running fairly well at the moment, thanks to the latest infusion of cash. Charles drove to Woodbridge, favoring his sore arm, and turned north on Highway 99. He reached the outskirts of Portland in about four hours. The name he wanted was in the phone book. It was so easy that it scared him. He got gas and a city map.

The town changed as he drove west and the streets curved upward into the hills. He passed through an area of large expensive homes tucked into hillsides and sheltered by trees. The street leveled out. He slowed down, reading numbers. He was close.

It was an apartment building on the other side of the street, pale gray and imposing. The dented Plymouth clanked to a stop. Charles sat inside, waiting for the tight feeling to leave his middle and his pulse to slow down. He looked at the windows, wondering which one concealed Sherry behind it.

Why had he come? There were dozens of reasons, none of

them good. He'd come because, like a lemming compelled toward the sea, he could not resist.

And now what? He had no idea. He didn't know how long he sat across the street from where she lived. Then a car came into view and stopped in front of the building. Two blonde women were inside. They looked much alike in that first instant. Sisters, he thought, maybe twins. Until one got out. It was Sherry. And her mother.

Sherry clutched several packages as she bent to the open window, still talking. Mrs. Prentiss fluttered her fingers and the car moved toward Charles. He sank down in the seat, but still had a good look at Sherry's mother as she drove past. Her face looked flushed and happy, almost pretty. He'd never before considered her good-looking, but a different expression changed her whole face.

Sherry crossed the sidewalk toward the apartments. One of the packages slipped. She clutched at it and others fell to the sidewalk, scattering in all directions. Without thinking, Charles jumped from the car and ran across the street. He helped her gather up the packages.

"Oh, thank you," Sherry said. "I have too many . . ."

In the long pause that followed, Charles straighted up and faced her.

"Charles, what are you doing here?"

"I came up to see my old man." The lie was already prepared. "As long as I was here, I thought I'd drive by and see how you're getting along." He hoped his voice sounded casual and friendly, the way Wally had sounded at the rodeo, not shaky as he felt inside.

"I'm glad to see you. Come in."

"No, I don't think so."

"It's all right. Warren is out of town and won't be back until Friday night."

She walked to the door, swaying on high heels. She wore a white wool suit and looked like a model. She turned and beckoned. "Don't just stand there. Come on."

Reluctantly, he followed her to the elevator. He didn't want to go into the apartment where she lived with Warren Stonebraker. But he didn't want to hand her the packages and drive away, either. He'd come this far, so he might as well go a little further.

The apartment door opened into a spacious hall that showed off the living room, two steps down. It was almost entirely white. The carpet was the palest of beiges, the large curved sectional couch an even lighter tone. There were white walls and a vast expanse of creamy drapery drawn back from wide windows that overlooked the city.

Charles felt as out of place as an inkblot. Everything about him was too dark for this room—his hair, his eyes, his skin. He was shabby, too, in a faded denim jacket, jeans and unpolished boots.

"Your . . . husband likes white, doesn't he?" The word stuck in his throat awhile before he got it out.

"Yes, he thinks blondes should have lots of white. He even wants me to lighten my hair, but I think it's blonde enough naturally. Here, give me the packages. And take off your jacket."

She dumped the packages in a corner of the sofa, then lay Charles's jacket on top of the pile. "What happened to your arm?"

He glanced at the bandage. "A woods accident. Nothing serious." He didn't want to talk about George, about his death, so he struggled to find something safe to say. He looked around the room, so carefully arranged, objects matched to other objects as precisely as the display window of a furniture store.

He finally came up with a remark. "It must be a lot of work for you to keep everything so clean."

"Oh, I don't do any cleaning. Warren's housekeeper, who's looked after him for years, takes care of everything. She's very fussy. She doesn't like it if I leave a magazine out of place or move a pillow from where she puts it. There isn't a thing for me to do, except a little cooking sometimes when Warren is home." She laughed. "Well, now that you're here, let's have a drink."

Charles tried not to show his surprise. After all, she was married to an older man and it was undoubtedly different in the city than in Whistler's Bend. He followed her to a small bar in an alcove off the living room.

"Is gin and tonic okay?"

Charles nodded. She mixed them competently and handed a glass to him. It looked good, with lots of ice cubes and a slice of fresh lime. Outside of his one bitter experience with whiskey, Charles drank only beer now and then. He sipped the drink and was surprised by its tangy taste. He'd expected something sweet like a cream soda.

"Sit down and tell me all the gossip from home. I'm dying to hear everything you know."

"I don't know much." Her gay, high-pitched voice and artificial speech bothered him. But he knew that he sounded wooden. She probably felt just as awkward as he did.

He tried to find something that would break the glass wall between them. "Justin Jamison is in Korea where the fighting's going on. And Wally is in college. His dad will pay for everything, so he can be a coach."

"Yes, I heard about Wally. Marlene told me. She's at the University of Oregon."

Charles took another careful sip. Sherry's eyes were hidden under her lashes and her fingernail, polished to a pale smooth pink, circled around and around the rim of her glass. It was already half-empty. There was a pensive set to her mouth. Her shoulders drooped. She looked tired and, somehow, older. She watched her finger moving in restless circles, like a small trapped thing that could not change its path.

The silence stretched out until Charles began to wonder if she had hypnotized herself with her revolving finger. He shifted uncomfortably and Sherry looked up, her blue eyes wide and bright. She smiled, that dazzling smile that had always been so much a part of her. Now it seemed the smile of a girl in a toothpaste ad who beams to show her perfect white teeth, not from any inner sense of joy. She tipped her glass and drank deeply.

"My, I really was thirsty. I think I'll have another one, since you're not finished with yours yet."

She held the little silver jigger over her glass and poured gin into it. The measure slopped over and she kept on pouring. Clear liquid splashed generously and dripped off her fingers. She added a little tonic, another piece of lime, and more ice.

"Mother is so happy now," she said as though he'd asked. "She has such a cute little apartment not far from here. Warren pays for it. He's very generous."

"It sounds as though everything has turned out just fine," Charles said heavily. "I hope you're happy, too."

Sherry's little laugh tinkled like ice cubes in the glass. "Haven't I got everything a girl could ever want? Just look around."

Charles looked at her. She didn't meet his eyes, but tilted the glass to her lips.

"When did you start drinking?"

She looked at him a second. "You make it sound bad, but

it's not. Warren expects me to go with him to all his dull business dinners and parties. Everybody else drinks, so he got me a fake ID so I could, too. It makes the time go faster."

She smiled brightly. "And Warren likes me to have a cocktail with him when he comes home. He says it makes me cuter and more affectionate. And he's right. I'm much cuter after a little drinkie.

"I'll confess, Charles. Marriage isn't what I expected. I'd never . . . I'd kissed boys, you know, but never anything else. Before we were married, Warren would never . . . but now, I have to sleep with him and everything . . ." She floundered to a stop and gulped at her drink. "Why am I telling you this?"

Charles closed his eyes. He thought he might throw up. "God, Sherry. It makes me sick to think of you with him."

She didn't look at him. "When kids are growing up, they imagine what they'll do when they're older. Wally always wanted to be a coach. Marlene wants to be in big business, some kind of finance. I've always known I'd marry a rich man. If not Warren, I'd have to find someone else. Mother did everything for me and I had to . . ."

"Damn your mother!" Charles jumped to his feet, jarring the glass cocktail table. "You don't owe her your whole life, for God's sake. And lay off the booze. You'll turn into a drunk like my old man."

He snatched up the glasses, not caring that the liquor slopped onto the pale immaculate carpet. He hurled the glasses into the fireplace. They smashed into a hundred glittering shards. If only Stonebraker were here. He'd smash him to a pulp, shove him out the window, pound him into . . .

Charles strode to the bar and splashed the bottle of gin into the sink. He jerked open the door of the cabinet and pulled out other bottles. He twisted off corks and caps and tilted them all upside-down. They gurgled, swirled, and bubbled together. A pool of Scotch, gin, wine, and sweet liqueurs, all disappeared down the drain.

He fought the urge to smash more glasses, kick furniture, rip down drapes, to wreck this coldly perfect room. Sherry watched with her hands folded in her lap. He pulled her to her feet.

"Get out of here, Sherry, before it's too late. You've made a bad bargain. I've got a job now and we can get by. Not like this, but we'll get by. We'll tell your mother and Warren to go to hell."

She smiled dreamily and lay her cool palm against his cheek. "You're so sweet. You always were, so sweet and so tough at the same time. Of all the boys I dated, you're the only one I ever . . ." She hesitated. A faint frown marred her porcelain features.

"Go on. I was the only one you ever—what?"

"I feel woozy. I had a teensy bit more gin than I should have, with drink at lunch and all. I need to lie down. I'll clean up this mess in the morning before Mrs. Brewster sees it."

He shook her roughly. "No, don't lie down. Get some clothes and let's get out of here."

She shook her head. "No, I can't. Mother would . . ."

"Forget your mother. You keep saying that your mother wants all this crap." He gestured at the surrounding apartment. "Is it your mother—or do you want it, too?"

She looked around vaguely. "I don't know. I'll think about it sometime, but not right now. You'll have to go, Charles. I don't feel well." She tried to smile, but her mouth quivered.

"Sherry . . ." He pulled her against him. She didn't resist, but everything except her physical self had already slipped away. He put his lips against her soft hair. He cradled her in his arms, willing her to become the warm and tender Sherry he had held in the past. But he might as well have tried to breathe life into a mannequin.

She stood lifelessly until he dropped his arms in defeat. She walked to the entrance hall, wobbling on her high heels. She opened the door and summoned up one of her toothpaste smiles.

"It was nice of you to come. Tell everyone in Whistler's Bend hello for me."

She spoke as though it were the end of an ordinary social visit. Now Charles knew what Wally meant when he'd spoken of how he felt "not there." Charles had an eerie feeling that Sherry had somehow made him disappear. He no longer existed for her, except as an object to be removed as quickly and tactfully as possible. It was the remote politeness that chilled him.

It was small comfort to think that she gave Warren Stonebraker only that sweetly smiling shell. Warren probably didn't care. Probably all he wanted was a perfect blonde ornament to complete his perfect blonde apartment.

Charles walked silently past her and pressed the button for the elevator. He stepped inside. He didn't want to turn around, but he did. Sherry leaned against one side of the doorway, with the light at her back and her face in shadow. She looked propped up, like something that had lost its life force. Her hair glowed golden in the late afternoon sun that shone through the big window behind her. He couldn't see her eyes—maybe they were closed.

He didn't want to go. Oh, God, he didn't want to go and leave her there.

Someone must have pushed a button, because the doors slid silently shut in front of Charles's face. The elevator went down. He got into his car and drove back the way he'd come, not paying attention. He soon discovered that he was lost. He pulled over and consulted the map. The process of concentrating, of thinking logically, somewhat restored him.

He'd planned to see his father, too. Even though he had no fixed address, it was easy to find him. Asa rarely ventured far from his regular territory where he felt safe and where he knew the other street dwellers. As soon as he learned that Charles had a job, he asked to borrow money.

"What do you want it for?" Charles asked.

"I need a new jacket."

"Okay, let's go buy one."

"It's after 6:00. The stores are closed. Besides, I'll pick out my own damn jacket. I don't need my kid to go with me."

"We can do it together. We'll find a place that's open."

"No, thanks. I'll probably die of pneumonia in the next rain." His voice whined like a tired dog. He wouldn't look into Charles's eyes, but turned and shuffled off down the street. He was forty-six years old and moved like an old man. What had happened to the determined boy who'd carried his friend on his back?

"Wait a minute." Charles ran after him and stuffed thirty dollars into his pocket. He'd probably spend it for booze instead of a jacket, but Charles guessed he was old enough to make his own decisions.

Asa's eyes brightened. "Thanks, kid. Let me buy you a drink before you go."

"Let's eat instead. I'm starving." Charles suddenly realized he was very hungry. Except for a package of cookies which he'd crunched on as he drove, he hadn't eaten anything since his bowl of oatmeal that morning.

They sat in a cafe with something sticky spilled on the table and flyspecks on the windows. Charles told him about Grandmother's visit, but Asa didn't seem much interested. She's your own mother, Charles thought, resentful on her behalf.

But he tried again. "Grandmother told me the story about you and Lester—how you found him after everyone else gave up and carried him home on your back."

"Yeah." Asa sipped coffee and looked out the window.

"She's proud of what you did, that Lester lived because of you."

"It was luck. Sometimes luck is good. Sometimes it's bad."

"Maybe sometimes we make our own luck," Charles said.

Asa shrugged.

Impulsively Charles asked, "What about my other grandparents? Do you know where they are?"

Asa shook his head. "Probably dead. Or crazy, like their daughter." A sullen note crept into his voice. He always refused to talk about Charles's mother.

"They had an Italian name, didn't they? Something like Peduzzi. Maybe they know where . . ."

"They aren't interested in us. They didn't want your mother to marry me. We both know you're half-white, but you're all Indian to them. And that's not good enough."

"Where did they live?" Charles persisted.

Asa stared at his hands clasped around the empty coffee cup, his face hard and resistant. Then he said grudgingly, "They had a nice little farm. They sold vegetables and fruit to markets in Portland. I worked for them one summer. That was where I met your mother. She used to bring water to me, out in the fields. She was seventeen. She was . . . really good-looking." He stood up abruptly. "I gotta go. I gotta meet somebody."

Charles paid for the meal as his father waited outside with his hands in his pockets. There was no point in asking any more questions. Asa had already said more than he ever had before. If Charles wanted to know about his mother's family, he'd have to look elsewhere for the answers.

When Charles came out, Asa said, "I'll pay you back in a few weeks, soon as I get a job and on my feet again."

"Sure. Don't worry about it."

They walked toward where the car was parked.

"How's the Plymouth running?" Asa asked, trying to be sociable in the few minutes they had left together.

"Not bad. I had to get a new timing gear. It cost me almost . . ."

Charles stared across the street to where a white Cadillac was parked by the curb. The man who had just gotten out talked with a red-haired woman in stilt heels, obviously a prostitute, who lingered in front of a bar. The man was thickset and bull-necked, with sparse reddish hair. His back was turned, but Charles had no doubt who it was.

"That bastard! He's supposed to be out of town."

Things exploded inside Charles—rage and a Vesuvius of other emotions. He often thought of ways that Warren Stonebraker might die. Sometimes he imagined accidents. Sometimes he imagined killing him. He amused himself while driving to work or waiting to doze off at night by inventing new and creative ways for Stonebraker to leave the world. Sometimes Charles was surprised and pleased at how creative he could be.

At the moment, however, Charles didn't think at all. He only felt and what he felt was murderous. He sprinted across the street, yelling.

"Warren! You son of a bitch! Why aren't you home where you belong? Goddamn you!"

Startled, the woman looked in Charles's direction. The man turned, too, not very fast. He seemed too massive to move quickly. Charles was only a few feet away, charging, when he turned far enough so that Charles could see his face.

He had slab-like jaws that pushed his pale eyes up into a mean little squint. He had a loose-lipped mouth open in surprise. He had huge ham-like fists that rose to protect his face. He was not Warren.

"Jesus!" Charles's 148 pounds shifted direction as quickly as a rabbit. He skidded to a stop. "You're not him. God, I'm sorry. You're not who I thought you were."

The man stared silently for a moment. When he spoke, his voice was a light tenor, but that did not mean that it was without menace. "You're lucky. You're very lucky that you're not looking for me."

Charles backed away, hands raised, palms out. "Sorry," he said again. He jogged back across the street.

Asa, openmouthed, watched him. "What the hell's the matter with you?"

"I made a mistake. I thought he was somebody else."

"You're crazy, kid. To run at a guy that much bigger than you. He's bad, I can tell. You're plain crazy, just like your mother." Asa scuttled around the corner and down a side street.

"Hey, the car's the other way."

"I don't care. I ain't going with you. I'll walk. You're too crazy. God, you got it from your mother. You're both crazy."

Charles's teeth clenched so hard they nearly cracked. The knuckles of his hand ached to smash flesh. The rage in him had to go somewhere or he would blow up, fly into a million shattered pieces and never be whole again.

A dented garbage can, lid tip-tilted, stood in an alley. Charles picked it up. He carried it a few running steps. "Bail bonds" said peeling letters on a dirty window. Charles hurled the trash can at the window. The glass cracked and the can clanged back to the sidewalk.

Charles grabbed it by the rim and smashed the glass with

266

the bottom of the can. A yell rose in his throat, a war cry, a primal scream. Glass crunched underfoot. Shards rained on his arms and hands. Spots of blood prickled his skin. Something sharp struck his cheek. Several people at the nearby intersection stared toward him.

"Fuck you!" he yelled. "Fuck all of you!"

He whirled and loped into the alley, seeking the shadows. His father had disappeared, also gone to ground. Charles ran in the opposite direction from his car, but it didn't matter. The street was so dark it was unlikely that any witness could identify him. He'd circle around to the car and stroll to it from the other side, innocent as pie.

He laughed. Maybe his old man was right. Maybe he was crazy, like his mother. Other people made them that way.

When Charles returned to work, a new whistle punk had joined the crew. Charles took over as rigger and high-climber-in-training, for which he received a substantial raise in pay.

The spar tree that killed George, useless because of the split, had been felled. The crew raised a substitute, supported with an elaborate system of guy wires, cables, and rigging. It was some time before Charles was called upon to top his first tree, on another site farther up the river. Karl Blessinger drove him between locations.

"You're going to be in pictures, Charlie," he told him as they raced along the narrow road.

"Oh, yeah?"

"Yeah. There's a man from an eastern newspaper who wants to do a story on logging. He was tickled to hear we're topping a new spar and he's going to take pictures of the operation. Hope that won't make you nervous."

"It doesn't matter." But he felt a stab of apprehension. He

already knew that the crew would watch him. Now a stranger would, too.

The reporter, a skinny man with receding hair, waited for them when they arrived at the landing. Two expensive-looking cameras hung around his neck. He approached as soon as they stepped out of the jeep.

"Are you the man who's going to climb that tree?" he asked the woods boss.

"No, not me. I'm Karl Blessinger and this is our high climber, Charles Balleau."

"Paul Emerson." He thrust out a sinewy hand and looked sharply at Charles. "I've been hearing all morning how dangerous it is to top a tree. I expected somebody older and bigger."

"It doesn't take size to climb a tree, just guts and skill," Karl said.

"That's a good quote." Emerson took out a notebook and scribbled in it. "Do you spell Balleau B-A-L-L-E-A-U? That sounds French, but the kid looks Indian. Is he?"

"Ask him," Blessinger said shortly. "He can talk."

Charles ignored Emerson and walked to the tree. His stomach twisted in knots, but he tried to act as though he did this every day. He and the boss discussed the direction the top should fall and other technicalities as the reporter listened.

"I hear that the last man who had this job got killed. How does that make you feel?"

Charles didn't answer. The man was as annoying as a gnat buzzing around his head. He wished that he could ask Blessinger to make him leave. There were many things that could go wrong when a tree was topped, especially when it was his first time. If he made a mistake, he sure as hell didn't want an article about it in the newspaper.

"Let's get a picture before you start up. How about a smile?"

Charles's anger rose. He had other things to think about besides grinning. He buckled on his equipment. Emerson took his picture, even though he didn't smile. Charles went up the tree as soon as he could.

His nervousness and irritation receded along with the ground. He gave himself over to the satisfaction of the climb. He'd already cleared the trunk of most of its branches and he soon took off the remainder, up to the spot where the cut would be made.

He thought about George. He told himself that loggers got killed all the time. Logs rolled on them. Cats tipped over on them. Cables cut off their heads or squeezed the breath out of their bodies. If a man thought every day about getting killed, he'd be selling shoes or pumping gas instead of working in the woods.

Charles finished the undercut and moved around the tree to make the back cut. He thrust in his spikes and anchored himself. He sawed slightly above the undercut. Soon the fir began the deep shuddering and swaying that meant the top was about to fall. God help me. Don't let it split. He made another quick pass and dropped the saw down to the end of its line. He leaned back into the ropes and held on.

The brushy top plummeted down, crackling and splintering. The decapitated tree lashed back and forth. Wind lifted Charles's hair. Something stung his eyes—wind, wood chips or excitement. Everything blurred around him. He found himself grinning through clenched teeth.

The arcing diminished until the tree stood still again. Charles looked down at his audience below. Emerson had one of his cameras pointed at him.

"I'll give you one more picture, city boy," Charles muttered.

He withdrew his spurs and eased himself up onto the flat top. The tree was about two feet in diameter at the cut. He slowly stood upright on the little perch. He stretched his arms over his head and reached for the sky, breathing deeply. Fragments of old legends that his grandmother told him flitted through his mind, stories of men who'd flown with the eagles or been lifted up to the heavens through the power of the Old Ones. At that moment, he almost believed them.

He revolved slowly, facing for a moment toward each of the four quarters of the wind. He had an absurd desire to do a triumphal dance on top of the tree, but he didn't want to look like a fakey Indian in a damned-dumb Hollywood movie. He stood quietly for a moment and then descended the tree. Going down didn't seem so hard this time.

Emerson waited with a big grin, holding a cigar in his hand. "Hey, Balleau, I thought maybe you were going to do a dance up on top for me."

Charles felt the blood surge into his face. How could an asshole like the reporter know what he had felt?

"Only kidding. Those were great action shots. You were terrific. You should smile once in a while, though. Might make a better picture." He threw his cigar into the brush.

"Hey!" Blessinger roared. "You get over there and stomp out that weed. No man with any savvy throws cigars or cigarettes into the woods. You could burn up everything for a hundred miles."

There was a triumphant note in his bellowing and Charles knew he had been hoping that Emerson would make a mistake, just so he could yell at him. Charles smiled then, his widest grin, as the newsman hurried after the cigar. He didn't seem at all chagrined, but made a big show of grinding and stamping the butt into the ground.

"Stupid jerk," Blessinger muttered and Charles chuckled.

Emerson hung around a couple of hours longer. He took pictures of Charles rigging the spar and some of the rest of the crew. At last he got into his rented car and drove away.

When quitting time came, Charles walked toward Blessinger's jeep. He saw something on the ground next to a stump. It was one of Emerson's very expensive cameras. Charles glanced casually toward the landing. The crew was gathering up their gear and no one looked his way. Karl Blessinger wasn't in sight.

Without hurrying, Charles slipped the camera into the canvas pack that carried his lunch and climbing gear. It would bring a good price from his contact in town. And he'd have the satisfaction of putting something over on Emerson. He got into the jeep, took off his hard hat, and closed his eyes to wait for the woods boss. He arrived several minutes later and they jolted down the road.

"Well, Charlie, you're a full-fledged climber now. You did a good job, although you'll have to go some to replace George. He was a fine man in every way, reliable, honest. If he were less conscientious, he'd probably be alive today. If you're half the man he was, I'll be satisfied."

"Maybe I can work up to half."

"It didn't make it any easier to have Emerson here, sticking his cameras into everything and yapping like a fool. What an idiot."

"He didn't bother me much," Charles lied.

A small silence followed during which Blessinger glanced around the interior of the jeep and then at Charles. He drove for a few minutes and then looked toward him again. Charles kept his gaze straight ahead as though he didn't notice. Soon Blessinger made a remark about the job. Charles replied. Another silence fell, which for some reason grew awkward. Blessinger began to whistle tunelessly through his teeth, a man feigning indifference to cover tension.

What's the matter with him? Charles wondered. What does he want from me?

He thought back over what they had talked about—topping the tree, Emerson, George. Blessinger had complimented Charles on his work, said he was glad to have him take George's place. It was right then that he'd looked around the jeep and started acting funny. He'd said George was a fine man, a reliable, honest . . .

Oh, God. The camera. Blessinger had seen him pick it up. Blessinger knew that he'd stolen the damn camera.

Charles reached into his pocket for a cigarette and stuck it between dry lips. There was a book of matches in his pocket, too, but he made his fingers fumble on past it and then into his other empty pocket.

"Do you need a match?" Blessinger asked. His voice was cool and remote.

"I should have some in my pack." Charles reached into the bag at his feet. He drew out the camera, laid it openly on his lap, and groped around inside.

"Here, use these," Blessinger said, his voice suddenly cheery again.

"Thanks." Charles took the matches and lit his cigarette, careful not to look into the other man's eyes. He picked up the camera and studied it, turning it over in his hands. "I found that jackass's camera laying by a stump. I been seriously considering taking it home and dropping it down my two-holer. But I don't suppose that's a very good idea. It's got pictures of me inside."

Blessinger laughed, hearty with relief, and slapped him on the thigh. "I wouldn't blame you much if you did, but he'll probably come looking for it tomorrow. Hey, let's stop at the store and I'll pick up a six-pack. A man oughta have a beer on the day he becomes a full-fledged high climber."

"Sounds good." Charles clenched his teeth to keep from laughing too loudly and giving away his own relief. That was close, much too close. He'd almost got caught, almost lost his job for a few lousy bucks. He'd told his father that people sometimes made their own luck. His would be bad if he weren't more careful in the future.

Chapter 11

LEE

Fourth of July weekend to September

After the Fourth of July rodeo ended and Charles and Wally left, the Jamison family went to a Chinese restaurant for supper. Lee's head ached from the long afternoon in the sun. His back was stiff from hours of sitting on the bleachers. He'd had a couple of beers at the rodeo and they'd made him feel sluggish and dull.

He needed a drink. He longed for the sharp taste of whiskey to cut through the stale beer residue in his mouth. Even more, he longed for the mellowness and easing of his mind that came along with a couple of stiff belts. But he'd have to wait until he got home for that. There were no bars in family-style restaurants.

A noisy group of cowboys sat in a big booth in a corner. One of them was Ed Graham, his friend from Santa Rosa. Ed raised rodeo stock. Lee had visited with him behind the chutes earlier in the day. Now he felt a twinge of envy. It was obvious that Ed and his friends had found hard liquor somewhere and felt a lot better than he did.

Soon Ed came over to Jamison's table, wobbling unsteadily on high-heeled boots. Introductions were made. After a bit of general conversation, Ed bent close to Katie in a confidential manner. He'd been good-looking when he was young, but age and hard living had coarsened him. Reddish-blue veins marred the skin on his nose. His eyes were both blurred and genial. He squinted in an effort to bring Katie into focus and she recoiled as a blast of whiskey breath blew into her face.

Ed tilted forward and nearly pitched into her lap. Katie flung up her arms to ward him off. Lee and her father gripped Ed from behind and pulled him back to a vertical position.

"Oops, my apologies, pretty little lady," he said gallantly. "I had a tad too much to drink at the last water hole. Food and coffee will help." He staggered back to his table.

Lee shook his head ruefully. "Old Ed has always been a little heavy on the sauce. He didn't used to slop over like that, but he gets worse as he gets older. I hope he didn't upset you, Katie."

"No, but he smelled awful. Whiskey really stinks, doesn't it."

Her father chuckled. "Especially secondhand. But I want to finish what I was saying, Lee. It gets harder all the time to make a decent living. I can't get reliable ranch help anymore. And taxes keep going up.

"Now there's talk of a freight strike that'll shut everything down. This country started going to hell when Roosevelt was elected and now Truman has escalated the process. What does a man who used to sell shirts know about running the government?"

"You're talking too loud," Vivian whispered.

"I don't care. The country is falling apart. And who can we trust? The State Department may be infiltrated with Russian sympathizers. My God! This is a scary time."

Lee didn't answer. Politics held little interest for him. When Bob got started on one of his the-country's-going-to-hell tirades, he didn't want discussion, anyway, only agreement. Lee suspected that Bob's real fear was for Justin, somewhere in Korea. Bob didn't want to talk about how much he feared for the safety of his oldest son, so he spoke of the terrors of Communism instead.

"Some say that America is the target of a worldwide conspiracy," Bob went on. "I don't care for McCarthy's methods, but at least he speaks up for what he believes in."

Vivian said sharply, "This is a public dinner with Lee and the children. It is not the time or place to discuss politics, especially if you can't keep your voice down. People are looking at us."

"You're right," Bob said stiffly. "I apologize."

An awkward silence fell. Andy looked from one to the other, bright-eyed and curious. Lee tried to think of a remark that would steer the conversation in another direction, but his head ached too badly. He wanted to eat quickly and retreat to the cabin he'd rented.

It was little more than a shack with two small rooms, but it got him out from under Bob and Vivian's feet. They insisted that he continue to stay in Justin's room, but Lee felt that a certain amount of distance was better for all. Vivian had furnished the cabin comfortably with "these old things we're not using, anyway." She was a whiz, he thought fondly, although a bit too organized and energetic for him to live with at close quarters.

Ed Graham had subsided into silence at the table in the corner. The rest of the group still talked and laughed, but his head tipped forward, slack-faced, over his coffee cup. His meal, nearly untouched, was pushed to one side. His eyes were closed, his mouth open. The lines of a hard life were etched cruelly into weathered skin.

Old Ed looks pretty tough, Lee thought tolerantly. Then

he felt Andy's eyes upon him. "You're looking at me sorta funny, squirt. What's up?"

"I was thinking that you look kind of like Mr. Graham." Andy spoke in the slightly shrill, attention-getting voice of an eleven-year-old. Everyone at their table turned to look at Ed and then toward Andy with varying degrees of shock and disapproval. The boy's expression of innocent revelation disappeared. He squirmed.

"I mean sort of. I don't mean that you get drunk and almost fall on people the way he did. And you don't have a nose like that, either. There's just something about him that reminds me . . . I'm sorry, Uncle Lee. I don't know what made me say that. It was stupid. It's not true, at all."

"Don't worry about it, squirt. One run-down old cowboy looks pretty much like another." Lee kept his voice light. "Pass me the shrimp, Katie. That tastes pretty good."

In fact, it suddenly had about as much taste as a mouthful of cardboard. Lee struggled through the rest of the meal and the drive home. As soon as he stepped inside his cabin, he reached for the whiskey bottle and tossed back a big jolt. While he waited for it to relax him, he looked at his face in the mirror that hung on the bedroom wall.

There was no electricity in the cabin and only one window in the room admitted the evening light. His skin was weathered, darkened by years of exposure to sun and wind. Sun wrinkles surrounded his silvery gray eyes and his lips looked dry. His hair had whitened years ago, but it was still thick. He peered closer, looking for the telltale blemishes of the drinker's nose. Then he stepped back and stared at himself, trying to see whatever it was that Andy had seen in his face.

God, that was a jolt. He thought of Ed as much older than himself and, yes, marked with signs of dissipation and an unhealthy lifestyle. To hear his nephew say that he looked like Ed . . .

His fingers fumbled in his shirt pocket. Then he dropped his empty hand to his side. He'd had too many cigarettes already today. He must cut down on smoking, at least. He collapsed into the big comfortable chair that Vivian had installed for him. He stretched out his long legs and stared without seeing toward the scuffed toes of his boots.

Things weren't going well. Things hadn't gone well for a long time, but he kept pretending that the setbacks were only temporary. Shit, his "temporary setbacks" had lasted most of his adult life. He'd been an adolescent to the age of fifty, with his priorities always on fun and a fast get-away.

But the fun had gone out of a lot of things, just as much of the excitement of wild horse chasing had been eliminated by machines. A woman he slept with but refused to take home to his family had been murdered, perhaps by someone he knew—certainly by someone who knew him. The years had slowed and stiffened him. And his little nephew noticed his resemblance to a man Lee had long regarded as an over-the-hill drunk. All in all, it had not been a good year.

Bob kept talking about how things were changing and how important it was to change along with the times, to live in the present instead of trying to live yesterday's life in today's world. That was only Bob thinking out loud, wasn't it? Surely he hadn't been directing those comments specifically at Lee.

He knew that he preferred the past to the present. He liked horses and cattle better than machines, wild land more than suburbs and a horse trail more than a paved highway. He couldn't even begin to imagine the future that lay ahead for his niece and nephews—a crowded, noisy, concrete-covered world of chrome-decked cars, jangling radios, of obsessions with halitosis and underarm odor. All that was bad enough,

278

but the real terror lay in atomic weapons, the terrifying Bomb that held inside its casing the most awesome power the world had ever known. How could anyone not fear the future, as one considered the horrors of such weapons and the almost certain knowledge that men would use them again?

Lee poured a dollop of bourbon into the water glass and screwed the top back on the bottle. That much and no more. He had some thinking to do and needed a reasonably clear head.

Night came quickly in the dark-timbered hills. The tireless voice of the river murmured behind him. He didn't light the kerosene lamp, but let shadows seep from the corners of the room and close around him.

What was he going to do with the rest of his life? Maybe a better question was, what could he do? His options were limited by his age (fifty), scarcity of funds (none), and his lack of marketable skills, beyond cowboying and a gift of gab.

He stumbled to bed just before one-thirty with no more sense of direction than he'd had when he'd first sat down in the chair. But the cap had stayed on the bourbon bottle and that was something.

Lee walked slowly down the steps of the courthouse. The September sun warmed his skin, but a feeling of autumn was in the air. Even if he had no calendar, an instinct deep in his body, attuned to the rhythms of earth, would have warned him that the seasons were about to change.

He paused and lit a cigarette. The Redding police had a possible lead on Joanne's killer and had wanted him to be interviewed again. Lee had spent the last hour reliving the discovery of her body, searching his mind and memory for any detail that might have been overlooked. He felt drained, frustrated that he couldn't remember more, regretful that he hadn't protected Joanne. He felt, more heavily than ever, responsibility for her death. There was no escaping the fact that, if he hadn't been in her bed that night, she would be alive today.

It was too late in the afternoon to return to work at the ranch, too early to have a drink, since he had imposed restrictions and limits upon himself. He'd cut back on smoking, too, and aimed toward a day when he might give up cigarettes entirely.

But not yet. He inhaled deeply and blew a smoke ring which hung in the quiet air in front of his face. When Katie was a little girl, she had tried to poke her tiny finger through the center. Now she was sixteen years old.

Last week he'd caught her puffing on an experimental cigarette. "Don't do it. Don't get the habit," he'd warned her.

"Are you going to tell Mom and Dad?"

Lee shook his head. "No, but don't smoke. Please."

Katie was growing up. Suddenly she had breasts and her legs had filled out from straight and stork-like to womanly curves. One of her classmates had a crush on her and he regularly called on the phone or came to the house, suffering the indignities of her indifference and Andy's smarty remarks. "He's a drip," Katie said scornfully. And Lee silently agreed that he was, a scrawny kid with pimples and straight slippery hair that kept falling into his eyes.

But Lee sympathized with the boy's feelings. It was hell to love someone who didn't love you back. Rosalind had taught him that. It could also be hell to have someone adore you when you could not reciprocate. He'd learned that lesson from Hallie. The regret he felt at the heartless way he'd used her too-willing body had increased, rather than decreased with the years. And Joanne . . .

Lee paused blindly in front of a shop window. He stared into the glass, but what he saw was Joanne's bloody face, her battered body.

He glanced left, then right. Suddenly he realized that he felt uneasy. He'd felt uneasy for two or three blocks, as he thought of past indiscretions and of murder. He studied the reflections in the window, searching for someone who might be staring at him. There were few pedestrians and none glanced his way. He turned to look up and down the street, but all appeared to mind their own business.

He drifted slowly on, all his senses alert. Why would anyone follow him, watch him? It was ridiculous to feel apprehensive. If he hadn't just come from the sheriff's office, if he weren't thinking about Joanne's murder. He was as jumpy as a child who'd heard a horror story.

Lee found himself in front of Gooding's Hardware. He went in. Doris sat at the desk in back, talking on the phone and writing with the other hand. She didn't look up. Lee turned toward the street. He searched the faces of passersby and studied those who lingered by windows or sat in cars. He didn't see anyone he recognized, except the bank vice-president, Glenn Draper, who strode briskly on long legs as he disappeared into the building.

Lee faced the back of the store again. Doris looked toward him, waved the pen, and continued her phone conversation. He moved slowly around, pretending to look at merchandise, but thinking about Doris. Another woman he'd treated shabbily. Was there any other kind?

He could try to make amends. She'd loved him once; she might love him again. She was good-looking, with her slender figure and large, expressive eyes. She thought of herself as plain and sometimes her demeanor made her so, but she was really quite lovely. And she was someone he could confidently take to Illinois and present to his elegant seventy-six-year-old mother. Vivian and Doris were friends. She would fit right into the family.

If she accepted him back, maybe he would give her the sapphire ring and relinquish his foolish memories of Rosalind. No, not the ring. It would always be a reminder of the only woman who'd broken his heart. He could sell it and . . .

His eyes focused. Doris stood in front of him, a questioning look on her face. He had the feeling that she'd been there for several moments, had even spoken to him and he had not heard her. A wave of color swept over his face. God, he hadn't blushed in years. What the hell had come over him, as he veered back and forth between incompetence and adolescence?

"Sorry, Doris. I was thinking about something else." That was a lie. He'd been thinking about her. He had their future half-planned and he wasn't even sure she was interested in him anymore.

"Yes, I noticed that," she replied coolly. "Can I help you find something?"

"No. I . . . I just came from the sheriff. The Redding office may have a lead in Joanne's death and they wanted me to go through things again."

Her face changed. "Oh, I see."

"Have you had any more anonymous phone calls?"

"No. How about you?"

He shook his head.

"I've looked at the waistline of every man I meet. I haven't seen a single belt that seems the least unusual. Sooner or later, every man in the community comes into this store. If the killer does live here and if he wears the belt, surely I'll see it eventually."

"Maybe he wears it only on special occasions," Lee said.

"When he's visiting his lady friends."

"Or when he plans to kill them?"

"Well, maybe not that. The killings may not be premeditated. But he likes to inflict pain. Maybe that's when he wears it, as some sort of ritual adornment."

"You didn't tell me that he tortures women."

"Didn't I?"

She studied him, frowning slightly. Lee could imagine her thoughts. What kind of woman was Joanne? What kind of man was Lee? He wanted Doris to think well of him. He hated seeing doubt and uncomfortable questions in her clear, honest eyes. She had once looked at him with love. It hurt unreasonably to see that measuring look replace it. Confused, feeling soiled and inadequate, he retreated to the cabin on the Little Nezzac River.

He called the sheriff in a few days. The new lead had fizzled out. Lee again asked about a possible connection to the killing of Juanita Balleau. The sheriff repeated that there was no evidence to link the two murders. The logical part of Lee's mind had to agree. But another deeper part, perhaps the same sense that divined the change of seasons before a single leaf turned color, knew that both women had died at the hands of the same man.

The door to Lee's rented cabin closed with a wooden latch without a lock. Most of the people who lived on the Little Nezzac River rarely locked their doors. As Lee prepared to enter with a bag of groceries, it occurred to him that perhaps he should put a lock on the door. The sense of unease that he'd felt in town was still with him.

He listened a moment before he stepped inside. He put the groceries on the table and looked into the bedroom, feeling like a nervous female as he did so.

I'll get a padlock, he thought. Some kid might sneak in and swipe my guns.

He did look in the closet. The rifle and the pistol were there. He slept lightly that night. He heard an owl hoot, heard the wind whoosh through the tops of the firs, heard a few vehicles pass on the gravel road, but no sound that did not belong.

During lunch break in the next day's harvesting, Lee and Bob sprawled under a tree in the shade. Lee gulped iced tea from a thermos and chewed on a roast beef sandwich that Vivian had made.

"Did I tell you that Harold Reuther wants to sell his place?" Bob asked.

"No, I hadn't heard that."

"Harold is almost seventy years old. He's been lonely since Frieda died last year and he wants to move closer to his son and grandkids. The place isn't officially on the market, but he asked if I'd be interested. It's only 120 acres, but more than half is bottom land."

"You could use more of that." Lee considered a moment. "You'd have to drive back and forth, but it's only four or five miles."

"I wasn't thinking about me. I wondered if you'd be interested. We might become partners."

"That's quite an idea," Lee answered noncommittally.

"I didn't realize how much work Justin did until he left. This place isn't a one-man operation anymore."

"You're doing real well, little brother. You've made good business decisions. Except you pay me a hell of a lot more than I'm worth."

"You're worth it to me."

Lee saw Bob arrange his thoughts before he went on.

"You know that Vivian and I struggled. More than once, I

wondered if we should sell, give up the idea of ranching. Her salary was all that kept us going in the early years. But the last three years have been pretty good. Expansion would only make it better. There's timber on the Reuther place. You could sell it to help pay for the property and clear that land for pasture at the same time.

"I know you've never liked the idea of settling in one place, so I wouldn't have suggested this partnership a couple of years ago. But I detect a change in you. Maybe I'm wrong."

"No, you're not. I've been thinking about making some changes."

"Then it's perfect timing. We can work the two places as one. We can reasonably expect to double my present income before long. I've some ideas to talk over with you. Now, I don't know how much money you have put aside or how much is easily accessible, but I'm sure we can work something out. Or Mother would—"

"I don't want to involve Mother," Lee interrupted. "Let me think about it. I really appreciate your offer and there's no one I'd rather have as a partner. I'm glad you've got that much confidence in me."

"Hell, you're my brother. I know you."

Do you? Lee wondered. There are many things I've never told you, little brother.

And never would tell him. His family heard only the expurgated version of his life. Could Bob read between the lines? Lee wasn't sure. Maybe it didn't matter. They were brothers and, as different as they were, the bond between them was strong.

Lee wanted to stay. His hesitation was not because he felt unsure of that. He had no idea where else he might go and the prospect of driving until something struck his fancy had lost its appeal. But he had no money. He couldn't tell his prudent brother that he had not one penny saved. Everything he owned in the world could be tossed into the Mercury in a few moments.

His mother would help. The safety net was there, if he could bring himself to use it. Maybe it was false pride that made him hesitate. Was false pride better than no pride at all? Bob offered an opportunity that would change his life and he was ready for the change, if he could figure out a way to accept it.

The jeweler squinted through his lens. "This is an exceptionally fine sapphire. A Kashmir blue, I believe."

"Is it? I don't know much about stones. I do know that I paid a pretty price for it about twenty-seven years ago."

"I'm sure you did. It's very high quality. Look at the platinum setting. Outstanding workmanship and lovely diamonds, too." He turned it longingly in his fingers. "But I can't buy it. There's no market in Woodbridge for a piece like this. I suggest you take it to Portland. I can give you the name of someone to see. She has a very different clientele than mine."

"Thank you. I'd appreciate that."

Mr. Knudtson wrote on his card and handed it to Lee. "If you like, I'll call Mrs. DuBois and tell her to expect you."

"That would be great. Can you give me a rough idea of what this might be worth?"

The jeweler shook his head. "I'd rather not hazard a guess."

Lee persisted. "Hundreds of dollars?"

"Several thousand. You can probably buy a nice little house with what you'll receive for the ring."

Or make a down payment on a small ranch.

★ ★ ★ ★ ★

The headlights of the Mercury sliced through the darkness ahead. The beams caught a pair of glowing eyes in the brush beside the road. Lee braked quickly. Deer were likely to dash into the road at the last moment, dazzled into stupidity by the blinding glare. The buck he'd spotted stayed put, but two other deer suddenly bolted from the opposite side to join it.

The Mercury slid on the gravel as he braked harder. "You idiots! Damn . . . Damn . . ." He heard . . . felt the right front fender strike the rear haunch of an animal, hardly more than a tick. The deer vanished into the shadows as magically as they had emerged. The car clung precariously to the curve of the road, then Lee wrestled it under control again.

"I'll get you in hunting season," he muttered. "If somebody doesn't get you on the highway first."

Tex Ritter stopped picking and singing and a news broadcast came on. General Douglas MacArthur had landed at Inchon, Korea, three days before, on September fifteenth. United Nations troops battled to retake Seoul.

Was Justin part of that battle? The military never told the families anything until it was all over. Was it better to know or not know? Those little North Koreans were tough. What was even more frightening was what lurked beyond them, the massed and mysterious hordes of Communist China. If they should decide to enter the war . . .

Lee turned off the radio. He'd heard the news several times on the drive from Portland back to the ranch. He carried a cashier's check in his pocket. It was a whopping sum. The ring intended for Rosalind had snuggled down in the safety-deposit box and quietly grown more and more valuable. He shuddered to think how casually he'd treated it. He'd worn it on a chain around his neck, stuffed it into his duffle or carried it in his saddlebag. He'd nearly sold it several times and thought of wagering it in poker games.

But he could never quite let it go. It was Rosalind's ring. Even though she had rejected it—and him—the faint, foolish hope had remained. Someday he would see her again. Maybe he could give her what she had once cast away. But now he admitted it was over. His throat closed up. Shit! It wasn't easy to give up on a dream that had lasted half a lifetime, even if it was the dream of a fool.

Once, during a late-night conversation with Bob, softened by the intimacy of firelight, shadows, and a generous amount of bourbon, Lee had spoken of her.

After listening, Bob said, "She must have been a remarkable woman, since you've kept those feelings for so many years."

"There's no doubt about it. Remarkable is a good word. Unusual is another. And mysterious. Maybe the mystery is the most intriguing part of all. She wouldn't tell me anything about her family or where she was from. 'Boring. Too boring,' was all she'd say."

"Maybe it was," Bob said. "Maybe she was a farm girl from Iowa and the mystery was part of her act, part of her stage persona."

"Maybe. I thought of that, but I don't believe it. She had expensive clothes, lots of them, plenty of spending money. Her fancy car. And there were the phone calls. She made phone calls from everywhere that we performed. We were all curious about them, but no one in the troupe knew who she phoned."

"Let's see." Bob took a sip and scratched the back of his neck. "Rosalind had a husband. A rich old man in his dotage. Almost ready to die. She kept calling to find out if he was dead yet, if she'd inherited the money."

Lee lifted his glass in his brother's direction. "That's

pretty good. And logical, too."

His brother swirled the liquid in his glass. "There's another possibility you might consider that has to do with you, not Rosalind."

"Oh? What's that?"

"You knew this woman for a couple of years, long ago, yet she seems to keep you from falling in love with anyone else. It's a way to avoid marriage. It's a hell of a lot easier to stay in love with a fantasy who never asks or needs anything, than it is to live on a day-to-day basis with a real woman."

"So, Doctor, you think that I'm using memories of Rosalind as an excuse to avoid the hard work of marriage?"

"I don't know. Are you?"

Lee hadn't answered. He didn't know then and he didn't know now. But he had taken one important symbolic step that he'd never managed before. He'd sold the ring.

Lee sighed and flipped the radio back on.

The announcer purred in a late-night voice. " . . . well over a million new homes constructed this year. Nineteen-fifty has been the busiest year ever for the housing industry, as suburbs spring up . . ."

He turned it off again. More bad news. More concrete, more fences, more crowding. Even Woodbridge had its new little subdivisions springing up like mushrooms. Some of the houses were about as substantial as fungus and not nearly as attractive.

He turned into the short driveway that led to the cabin. The headlights flashed over the parking area, the board-and-batten exterior, the growth of fir and tangled brush that shielded the cabin from the road. He turned off the motor, stepped out of the car, and stretched the kinks out of his six-foot frame. The gurgle of the river was the only sound he heard.

He opened the cabin door. He'd forgotten to buy a padlock. He only thought of it at night, when it was late and dark and all sinister things seemed possible. In the clear light of day, with sunshine spangling the surface of the water and the spaces under the trees empty of moving shadows, except friendly shiftings of birds and squirrels, the thought of a padlock never entered his mind.

It was dark as a cave inside. Faint oblongs of light fell through two small windows in the main room. He fumbled on the shelf to the right of the door, found the wooden matches, and crossed to the table in the middle of the room. Memory told him where it was, as he couldn't see a thing. He struck a match on his thumbnail. He removed the globe with his left hand and touched the match to the wick. The light steadied in a moment and a yellow glow washed the room.

There was something on the table that hadn't been there when he left. He stared at it, uncomprehending. It seemed to be a pile of clothing with something stuck through it. It was one of his shirts, with a sheet of folded white paper on top. A long-bladed kitchen knife pierced the pile and into the wooden tabletop.

Lee pulled it out and unfolded the paper. Large block printed letters read, "I SAW YOU WITH THE SHERIFF. DON'T FORGET. I KNOW WHO YOU ARE. WHO AM I?"

A photograph stuck to the paper with rubber cement. It wasn't very clear and Lee tilted it toward the light. It had been taken from a distance, perhaps from a moving car, and the features were blurred, but Lee recognized the girl. Katie.

"Jesus!" His knees went weak and he sank onto one of the wooden chairs. He looked at the photo again. Katie, in bright sunshine, walked with the dog along the lane between the house and the county road. It looked as though they were nearly to the ranch gate.

He slumped forward. One elbow bumped the neatly folded shirt. Shreds tumbled to the floor. The shirt had been slashed into pieces.

"He was there. The son of a bitch was right in the cabin."

Early the next morning, Lee sat in Bob and Vivian's kitchen. Bob was not shaved. Vivian wore a striped cotton robe and looked pale. Neither of them spoke for a moment.

Then Bob said, "I think it would be a good idea if you moved back into the house for awhile."

"Hell, no. I'd be delighted if the creep came after me. But he won't. Guys like him are cowards and bullies. He'd never face me directly."

"He might shoot you. Or set the cabin on fire." Vivian's voice was steady. She wore the intent look that came when she thought hard about a problem.

"He could shoot me in the yard here just as easily. Or set fire to this house. No, we've got to keep the kids out of it as much as we can."

"The kids are already in it." Bob's voice was heavy. "At least Katie is. Maybe Andy, too."

"We'll have to talk to them this morning," Vivian said. "They should be safe in school. But we have to make them understand that they can't go places by themselves anymore, even to the mailbox. And they can't trust anyone, even people that they've known for years." She covered her face with her hands. "Oh, it's so awful. I can't believe this."

"I'm sorry, Vivian. I'm really sorry. It's my fault," Lee said.

"No, it isn't. It's the fault of whoever is doing these terrible things."

"I have to face up to facts. None of this would have happened if I hadn't been involved with Joanne." Ugly memories of her battered body swirled in Lee's head, along with the words in the note, the phone calls to himself and Doris, what Charles had said of Juanita's murder. He felt sick with fear for Bob's family and for Doris. Perhaps worst of all was the sense of helplessness. What could he do about the terrible threat he'd brought upon the people for whom he cared?

If he were the hero of a book or movie, he'd start on a quest, ask a lot of clever questions and soon track down the killer. In real life, he didn't know where or how to start. Question Charles again? Go back to Redding and talk to Joanne's neighbors and friends? Since the mysterious "Don" seemed to keep tabs on Lee, he might know if he started an investigation of his own. And what would "Don" do then?

"Better call the sheriff," Bob said. "But not from the house. We're on a party line. Use the pay phone at the store."

"I'll do it right away."

Vivian stood up. "Have breakfast first. The kids are still asleep and we know they're safe right now. Do you want more coffee?"

"Sure." Lee held out his cup. What he wanted was to get into the Mercury and escape, drive to a distant place where no one could ever find him. If Lee got out of their lives, Doris, Bob, Vivian, and the kids would all be safe. It was as simple— and as hard—as that.

It was probably the best thing he could do for them now.

Chapter 12

CHARLOTTE

September

Charlotte awoke in the night to the sound of rain. It was not unwelcome. The woods were dry in mid-September and the fire danger high. A good soaking would cool things down and reduce the risk. She dozed off to the familiar patter on the roof.

A gray steady downpour, more like midwinter than early fall, beat against the windows when she awoke in the morning. She listened to the radio as she drank her coffee. The early-morning disk jockey in Woodbridge demonstrated his sense of humor by the song he played.

"Into each life some rain must fall,

"But too much is fallin' in mine."

You're playing my song, she thought. That could be my theme.

She squished through the rain to feed the ponies, the cow, the cats, and the chickens. The cow and the mares with their colts plodded into the barn with heads down, hides dripping. Their eyes seemed to admonish her as though it were Charlotte's fault that they were so wet. The chickens huddled in the henhouse and clucked querulously at her. Only the cats, cozy in the hay-filled corners of the barn, greeted her contentedly. They stretched and blinked as they awaited their share of milk. The familiar odors of damp hay and wet animal hide mingled together.

In spite of the rain, Charlotte set the milk pail on the ground on her way back to the house. She rested, breathing carefully. Her hand pressed against her ribs on the left side where the pain kept returning.

She felt squeezed-in, only partly because of the tightness in her chest. Thick clouds hovered just above the treetops. A curtain of falling water dimmed the trees along the river. The hillside pasture faded into mist not far above the house and the old forest massed darkly close beyond.

A keen sense of aloneness pierced her. No one lived to the east. Warren Stonebraker's cabin was there, but he only visited it now and then. The closest place downriver belonged to Mr. Fox, an unfriendly retired Austrian with a thick accent and a wife with the face and demeanor of a sheep. It was eight miles to Jamison's ranch, too far on a dank end-of-the-world day like this one.

Charlotte thought of death, of dying alone, and shivered, although the day was not cold. Resolutely she picked up the pail and winced as pain extended into her arm. Ridiculous that a pail with a little milk in it seemed so heavy when at one time she could lift and carry sacks of feed as easily as a man.

She trudged slowly to the house. Most of the milk was for the dogs. She mixed it with a big pan of oatmeal she'd cooked earlier and poured it into their dishes. They lapped it up hungrily, jostling for better position. She put the quart she'd saved for herself into the cooler on the back porch.

It was a good day to go to the store. She needed the comfort of a friendly face and groceries provided an excuse. She put her yellow slicker back on and eased the pickup out of the garage. The wipers snick-snacked at the water on the windshield.

Before she'd traveled two miles, a dark mass filled the road ahead. She stomped on the squeaky brakes and the truck rolled to a stop. A mudslide, with a red-barked madrone tilted on top like a pennant on a crumbling sand castle, nearly blocked the narrow road. She got out for a closer look. There was not enough room for the pickup to pass.

"I shoulda gone yesterday," Charlotte muttered. She turned the truck, which involved a lot of jockeying back and forth in the tight space, and drove home. Her sense of isolation, her feeling of being cut off from the rest of the world, deepened.

Her stomach hurt. She mixed bicarbonate of soda with a glass of water and drank it down. She belched loudly and felt briefly better. Pain had been at the edge of her consciousness for quite awhile, like one of the hawks hovering in the sky. Sometimes it swept in close enough to cast a shadow over her, then it retreated until it was no more than a distant point of awareness.

She'd thought about going to a doctor, but it seemed too much fuss to make when there was nothing seriously wrong with her, except that she was old. It was to be expected that she would hurt sometimes.

For weeks she had felt a loosening in herself as though, one by one, the delicate tendrils that held her to the earth were detaching themselves. The voices of nearby people came thinly to her, as over telephone wires stretched across a continent. Her hands seemed covered with heavy gloves. Familiar objects of everyday living had the static unreality of pictures hung on a wall. Her entire body ached with the terrible effort of living and yet she could not yield herself to death.

Part of it was fear. Part of it was the knowledge that Johnny Domingo and Alie, her precious boy, lived only in

295

her. When she died, they would also die and she did not want them lost from all memory.

Charlotte sat in the kitchen with the calico cat on the table beside her. The cat's paws were neatly folded and her eyes were closed. Her elegant plumey tail draped across a stack of washed dishes that hadn't made it to the cupboard.

Charlotte took a pen in her hand and opened a tablet of ruled paper. She printed neatly, "Last Will and Testament of Charlotte Blakely Domingo." Underneath that she wrote, "I, Charlotte Domingo, being of sound mind and body, do hereby will and bequeath . . ."

A child raced through her mind, a boy dark and exquisite as a deer, running with quick grace through a field of daisies. He came closer and looked up at her. His eyes were brown and laughter shone like sunshine in them. Before she could touch him, he whirled and was gone, running over a distant hill, leaving the sound of laughter spinning back.

And Johnny . . . he'd been young, too. They'd had so little time together before he was cruelly taken from her.

"Into each life some rain must fall . . ."

A heavy sigh, bearing old sorrows, escaped her. Her eyes drifted to the rain-streaked window, as she forced herself to think of what she might do. She had six hundred acres of land, a lot of it marginal hillside, but good fenced pasture along the river. There were the ponies; there was Mamie, the cow; the chickens; all the dogs and cats. They needed someone to look after them or to see that they went to other homes, if possible. She didn't expect anyone else to be crazy enough to live with a fluctuating population of almost a dozen dogs and half as many cats.

The house would soon be more liveable. The county had promised to extend the electric power lines to her property. A person could have a refrigerator and even a washing machine.

There were her investments. Although small, they enabled her to indulge herself and raise ponies instead of a more practical product like beef or sheep.

She owed Mr. Greeley a debt for his financial advice and there was only one way she could repay him. She was sorry she hadn't taken more to Francine, his granddaughter. They'd been polite to one another, but no bond had formed during the two or three times they'd met. It seemed odd, because Charlotte had been so fond of both Mr. Greeley and his daughter. But maybe it wasn't necessary that she like the girl. Maybe it was the passing on that was important. She'd known people who didn't like their own flesh and blood. After all, a will was the last opportunity a person had to remember or to help those who were left behind. A will was a final legacy of much more than money. She must not waste what would be her final gesture.

Charlotte sat quietly, her eyes wide, but she didn't see anything in the room. Images flickered behind her unfocused gaze as she thought . . . as she remembered. Suddenly she smiled. She wrote firmly, folded the paper, and put it in the drawer in the sideboard where she kept her accounts and receipts. The next time she went to town, she would find a lawyer and hand the document over to him.

She felt a little dizzy when she stood up. She said aloud, "It must be the flu." It didn't seem so bad to be sick in the rain, when outside work was almost impossible to do. She dozed on the couch until evening.

She managed the chores and fell into bed immediately afterward. She didn't even glance at the rocking chair by the window. Johnny hated wet weather and never came in the rain. Sometimes she thought about moving to the desert. Maybe he would come more often, but it was also possible that the move would sever the tenuous link that bound them together. She was afraid to risk it.

The pain came in waves and she tried to adjust her body to accept its rhythm. It would be so much easier just to give up, but she was the last custodian of Alie and Johnny. Besides, she believed in God and some said that He was a god of vengeance.

Charlotte was still sick in the morning and so weak that she couldn't get up, except to use the slop jar she kept under the bed. Rain lashed the windowpanes. The dogs whined and scratched outside the door. She thought of Mamie waiting by the barn with a full udder, but knew she could not walk that far. If she had a telephone, she could call Bob Jamison. He would willingly help her. But surely she would feel better by evening.

She dozed again and dreamed of baking cherry pie. She felt the heat of summer, smelled the warm sweet fruit bubbling up through the browning crust. If she looked out the window, she would see Johnny with Alejandro close by. Johnny would be whistling, that peculiar trill of his, like the song of an exotic bird. Her body was young and supple. Soon her beautiful man would come into the house and lie with her in love.

She awoke with a feeling of joyful expectancy, but the house was night black, damp and smelling of neglect. Layers of cloud smothered the moon and the unseasonable rain fell on the roof.

"But too much has fallen in mine."

Most of the time, Charlotte thought western Oregon was the greenest, most beautiful land imaginable. But sometimes she hated the rain. It soaked her soul like tears. To wake in the night in isolation, to hear the rain drum on the roof, was almost more than she could bear.

A single tear slid down the parched skin stretched across her cheekbone. Please, God, not tonight. I don't want to die in the rain, not when I'm alone.

In the fall of 1924, when she was fifty-five years old, Charlotte went through a spell where she thought she would go mad if another raindrop touched her skin.

I'll go home, she thought. Back to eastern Oregon where it rains only a proper amount. Just for a visit. I need to get out of the rain for a few days and I want to see the old places once more.

She took the train as far as she could and then rented a horse and buggy from the livery stable. There were a few automobiles on the street, but she did not drive. The town had grown. The dusty track that led to the ranches was now a gravel road. She recognized landmarks along the way—the shape of a butte, a cluster of rocks, the look of the land and the smell of dry grass and sage.

The sun shone, as she had hoped. There was little wind, no sound but the clop of her horse's hoofs and the single piercing cry of a hawk. Ahead of her, a cluster of trees marked the location of the Mosher house where she had lived and worked for eight years.

I'll stop and see Elsie. It would be a shame to come this far and not see her. She did answer my letters, after all. Charlotte had written a few times, the first about a year after her flight from the ranch and the last time when Alejandro was six years old and started first grade. She clearly recalled when Elsie's oldest daughter had entered school. It seemed an enormous step and Charlotte had wanted to share her child's progress with someone who understood how significant it seemed. But her Alie had never grown up.

Elsie also wrote to Charlotte to say, "I must tell you that Howard is dead. It was very strange and it is so sad to consider."

Charlotte should have been able to see the Moshers' house as she approached in the buggy from the livery stable. But the house wasn't there. Only the big post that had supported the corral gate, a few tumbled corral poles, and a weathered portion of what must have been the bunkhouse remained. The lane was overgrown with weeds and grass.

Charlotte stopped the horse. Where were they? William, Elsie, the three children—why had they left? And long ago, from the way the buildings had disintegrated. They must have moved soon after Charlotte last wrote. At the time, she'd wondered why Elsie hadn't replied, but her days were long and busy ones, and she soon ceased to think of Elsie. Now Charlotte wondered—what happened?

She looked around for a clue. A thin spiral of smoke rose against the skyline. She urged the horse on down the road. There was another house about a quarter of a mile away, where no house had been before. A name was painted on the gate: Deckers. It meant nothing to her. She had never heard of a Deckers in this part of the country.

A woman hung clothes on a line in the backyard. A little girl in a pinafore danced around her, singing in a shrill voice. Perhaps one of the Mosher girls had married a man named Deckers. Would the woman remember her if she went into the yard and said, "I'm Charlotte"?

She couldn't do it. She felt as insubstantial as a ghost. Maybe she was a ghost. Maybe she'd already died and the punishment for her sin was to always be separated from her family, to believe that she lived while they did not.

She clucked to the horse and he moved on. Soon the road began its gentle descent toward the river. Charlotte's stomach roiled uneasily. She drew a deep breath and then another. There was the roof of the house. But it wasn't quite where she remembered. And it was a different color, a different composition. It was a new house tucked into the trees and nearly hidden from the road. It looked big, even bigger than the original, which must have been torn down. The name was lettered on the gateway that arched the lane: Pope. Some of them still lived there, maybe Howard's younger brother. Perhaps even the parents were still alive.

Hannah Pope had been so kind to her, more than kind. She had embraced Charlotte warmly on the day that Howard told her they were engaged. She had said, "You will be my daughter now."

Charlotte knew of the two tiny graves along the riverbank, planted with flowers and carefully tended. Like Alejandro, Hannah's little girls had never grown up. Was that why her eyes were so sad? Did she forever miss those daughters who might have followed in her gentle footsteps? Or did the ever-present sorrow come from years of living with her bullying avaricious husband? Perhaps even more painful, did she recognize that her oldest son had grown up to be another bully?

Charlotte wished she could say to Hannah, "I'm sorry for what I did to your son."

But such words were beyond impossible. She kept the horse moving smartly until they were past Pope land. She'd go see where her friend, Sadie, had lived. And then on to the patch of charred earth that had once been the house her parents had rented and where Charlotte had lived as a child. It had burned down while she was in high school, after both of them were dead.

A cow bawled, a single hoarse "Bawww!" Charlotte recognized it as a cry of distress. She stopped the livery stable horse and looked around. "Don't you dare move," she warned him and stood up on the seat of the buggy for a better view. There wasn't a cow in sight.

"Bawww!"

301

It came from the brush along the river. She'd heard enough cattle bawling to know that something was the matter with this one. She steered the horse off the road. The buggy tilted and jolted over rocks and rough ground. She didn't want to break a wheel. When she'd gone as far as she could, she wrapped the reins around a good-sized rock, settling it firmly on top of the leather straps. The horse could pull away if he wanted, but she hoped he was well-trained enough not to try.

"You be a good fella." She patted him on the neck as she left him.

It didn't take long to find the cow. She'd slipped down the riverbank. Maybe she'd been after water or maybe walked too close to a crumbling edge. At any rate, she'd slid over the muddy bank and fallen onto her side. She'd slipped and fallen again when she tried to get up.

Then she'd churned persistently until she was thoroughly stuck in a slippery trench on the bank. Her ears flicked toward Charlotte when she heard footsteps. Her eyes rolled apprehensively. She hadn't been there long. She didn't have the dull, glazed-eyed look of an animal that had given up. She was bawling, so she still felt like living, if Charlotte could get her out.

The cow wore the Pope brand. If it were any ranch but that one, Charlotte could simply go to the door and pass the problem on to someone else. But she could not go to that door, nor could she ride off and let the silly cow die.

Could she push or pull the animal out using her own strength? It seemed doubtful. Cows are big and heavy. The ground was slippery. Her traveling shoes and clothes would certainly be ruined. She might plunge in at home, to save one of her own animals, but surely she could find another way.

She went back to the buggy. There was no rope, of course.

302

She studied the harness, wondering if she might rearrange the straps and buckles in order to fasten them to the cow and use the horse to haul the animal out. The bay gelding turned his head and looked at her quizzically.

The reins were long enough. If she unhooked them from the bridle, maybe she could fasten them to the single tree and tie the other ends around the cow's neck. Then the horse could pull her out. Would the reins be strong enough to take the weight of the animal or would they break?

She unhitched the horse and led him to the riverbank. Before she could do anything else, he looked toward the road and pricked his ears. A man on horseback jogged into view.

Charlotte's first impulse was to duck down in the brush and hide. What if it was Howard's brother? Or old Mr. Pope himself? She did not want to meet either of them. But it was too late. The man had seen the unhorsed buggy. He paused and looked at it curiously. In a moment, he would see her, too.

"Hello," she called, before she totally lost her courage.

He raised a hand in greeting as he came nearer. Relief grew in her with every step of his horse. It was not one of the Popes. It was a man she didn't know—young, rangy, with a bedroll behind the saddle and a canteen and other accoutrements tied on with saddle strings.

He touched a finger to his hat brim. "Good afternoon, ma'am."

"There's a fool cow stuck in the mud over the riverbank," she said without preamble. "I was just trying to figure a way to get her out."

"I'll take a look." He rode past her. It took a moment for him to assess the situation. Then he sent his horse over the bank to test the depth of the water. It was no more than belly-deep on his gray gelding. He shook out his rope. The cow, perturbed by strange horses and unknown people, bawled loudly. She lunged and floundered helplessly.

The cowboy flipped his rope over her head and dallied it around the saddle horn. The dappled gelding spun in the water and leaned into the rope. The heavy muscles in his haunches rippled and flexed beneath his shiny hide. The cow, bellowing in protest, oozed out of her almost-tomb and down the bank into the water. Her head went under as her numbed legs refused to take her weight. She was hauled, with much splashing, to a nearby sandy bank.

The rider dismounted and retrieved his rope. The cow struggled up and fell down a couple of times before her legs worked properly and she stayed upright.

"She doesn't look bad," the cowboy called to Charlotte. "I think she'll be all right."

He hiked up the bank toward her. Charlotte was taller than average. When she stood barefooted and face-to-face with Johnny Domingo, they'd looked almost exactly into one another's eyes. She looked up to this young man, long-legged in his high-heeled boots.

He's a real good-looking fellow, she thought as she met his startling light gray eyes.

"Is that cow part of your stock?" he asked.

"No. I just came across her. I'm . . . visiting. You're not from around here, either, I guess."

"Nope. I'm just passing through."

Charlotte found herself still staring at him. A brief involuntary smile moved across his lips, as though he might be used to such looks. She grinned back, unembarrassed, acknowledging his male attractiveness.

I was married to a man even better-looking than you, she thought with satisfaction. But she'd gawked long enough at someone half her age.

"That's a fine-looking horse," she said, admiring the graceful neck and the dish-faced Arabian head.

He smiled proudly and stroked his horse's glossy, dappled neck. "He is, isn't he? And as smart and strong as he is pretty."

They talked horses for a few minutes. Then Charlotte said, "Well, I gotta be going." He hitched up her animal and assisted her into the buggy.

"Thanks for helping," she said. "Have a safe journey."

"Thank you, ma'am. The same to you."

He jogged away toward town. Charlotte went the opposite direction in pursuit of childhood memories. After a bit, she turned to look after the man.

He was already far in the distance, as the gelding traveled with an effortlessly mile-eating gait. It was a familiar, but always poignant image to her—a single horse and rider, lonely but self-reliant, under the wide arching sky. So Johnny had traveled the trail that led from his birthplace in New Mexico northwest to Oregon. So thousands of other men had traveled back and forth across the west. Towns, ranches, railroads, an entire civilization sprang up in the dusty tracks of their horses.

I should have asked his name, Charlotte thought. But what does it matter? I'll never see him again.

She quickly concluded her visit. It had unsettled her. It was eerie to find herself already an unbelonging phantom in the country of her childhood. She never returned.

Charlotte roused to the dawn, years and miles away from where her recollections had taken her. She must tend the animals, no matter how sick she felt. She pulled on boots and slicker, a slow process that involved a wait between each movement for the dizziness to subside. A cup of tea would help, but she'd have to build a fire to brew it and that would take some of the strength she needed to get to the barn.

When she opened the door, the dogs leaped around in paroxysms of joy. She tottered across the porch and down the rickety steps. Her knees buckled and she sat on the bottom step to rest. The dogs licked her face and hands. She pulled herself to her feet, crossed the yard, and sagged against the gate post. The air, heavy with moisture, seemed ready to coalesce into raindrops at any moment.

The barn wavered at the end of her sight, far across a vast distance. The empty milk pail dragged at her arm like a bucket full of bricks. Mamie and the ponies waited in a huddle by the barn door, their hopeful heads turned toward her. The cow raised her muzzle and bawled.

A horse whinnied. The ponies nickered in answer and looked toward the road. A man on horseback rode along the fence, coming upriver. He turned in at her gate. A poncho, with an odd, hump-backed bulge, covered him from the neck down. He wore a beat-up old hat on his dark head.

Charles Balleau slipped off the barebacked horse and ignored the bellowing dogs as he approached her.

"I don't feel so good," Charlotte said. "I been sick for two days and didn't get the cow milked."

"I'll tend to it." He supported her on the long walk back to bed. Through the open door, she watched as he removed a packsack, which had caused the bulge beneath his poncho, and set it on the table. He built a fire and put on the kettle.

"Don't forget to feed the chickens. Give the cats some milk. And feed the damn dogs. Their dry food is in the barrel just inside the shed."

Charles smiled, nodded, and went out. She must have dozed because it seemed only a few seconds until he was back, moving quietly around the kitchen. He brought her a cup of tea, strong and hot. She sipped it slowly. It burned her lips, but she enjoyed the warmth flooding into her long-empty stomach. She was too embarrassed to tell him about the slop jar which badly needed emptying. He noticed it and took it outside in a matter-of-fact way.

Charlotte saw him take a loaf of bread from the packsack and spear a slice on a long-handled fork. He removed a lid from the cookstove and toasted the bread over the open flame. He put it on a saucer and carried it in to her.

"Mrs. Furman said you hadn't been to the store for awhile, so when I heard the slide had closed the road, I brought a few groceries."

"I appreciate this, Charles. You seem to know all about taking care of sick folks."

"I had some practice with my old man. He gets hung-over a lot."

Charlotte nodded without comment. "How do you like your job with Carnes and Baylor?"

"Pretty good. I'm learning to be a high climber, to take George Olson's job. He got killed. Maybe you heard."

"High climber, that's a good job."

"Yeah. Mr. Blessinger gave me a raise. Said I'd get another one soon."

There was a note of pride in his voice that she'd never heard before. "You're doing real good, Charles."

"Thanks." He talked a little about his job, then he said, "I drove up to Portland. I saw my dad."

That girl was in Portland, too, Charlotte knew—the one that married stiff-necked Stonebraker. They passed her place now and then in their fancy white Cadillac. There were many troubling things in Charles's life. Both his parents had been swamped by problems they couldn't handle and Charles had no one to teach him any differently.

If only we'd been friends sooner. Maybe I could have helped him. Maybe I wouldn't have been so lonely. But it was too late for all those wishes, all those might-have-beens.

"Charles," she blurted out. "You can do almost anything you want. Don't let your parents' mistakes or things from the past drag you down." Words of advice clogged her throat. There was so much to tell him, if he would listen, if there was time.

"I know. Lately I tell myself that every day. But you can keep reminding me." He grinned.

Charlotte feared to say more. Sometimes a few words were more effective than too many.

"You'll do just fine. I know you will." The teacup was empty and she put it on the little table by the bed. To change the subject she remarked, "I hear that Lee Jamison left. He seemed to be settling in on the ranch and I thought he might stay this time. I know Bob hoped he would."

"Yeah, I know he did, too. So you know Lee?"

"I've only talked to him a time or two at Bob's. He seems like an interesting fellow." Her head wobbled heavily. "I'll close my eyes for just a second," she said and sank into sleep like a stone into water . . .

"Mrs. Domingo, wake up. Mrs. Domingo."

"What? What's wrong? Who's that yelling?"

"It's you. You had a bad dream. You were yelling something about blood all over. And a shot. You said something about a shot that keeps going off over and over again."

"Yes, it does. In my head. I hear it over and over in my head. It's the shot that killed . . ." She couldn't complete the sentence. "Charles, have you ever seen anyone shot?"

"No."

"It's terrible. It's just terrible. I never could stand the sight of blood, couldn't even kill a chicken when I was a girl. And then . . . and then . . ."

Charles's voice was soothing. "It's okay now. You had a bad dream and it's over."

"No, it's not over. It'll never be over, not as long as I keep hearing that shot. I can never forget. It's too late for me, but maybe not for you."

She took his hand in both of hers and squeezed it tightly. "Charles, promise me. Promise me that you'll never kill anyone."

Charles blinked. He stared into her eyes.

"Think about it," she urged. "You can kill someone just as fast as you blinked. But think about afterwards. I can't forget the look on his face. I still hear that shot. All my life since, I've heard that shot."

The desperation faded. All she felt was an overwhelming sense of exhaustion. "Promise me," she whispered.

"All right."

"Say it."

"I promise I'll never kill anyone."

Charlotte released his hand and slumped back onto the pillow. Patches trotted through the door from the kitchen. She jumped onto the bed, purring, and curled up against Charlotte's neck. She stroked the cat lightly with her fingertips. Charlotte's eyes closed, but this time she didn't sleep. She remembered. It seemed like last week, but it had been nearly sixty years ago . . .

Johnny said, "I am finished with milking cows. Today I will tell Mr. Solonas that I will milk no more. I am not a dairy farmer."

"No, don't." Charlotte's voice was sharper than she intended. "If you quit the job, then we'll have to move."

"Why do you mind if we move? I cannot believe you love this house so much?" He gestured at the rough unpainted walls and bare floors.

"No, I don't like the house. But . . ."

"You don't like the house? You don't like this house?"

There was an edge in Johnny's soft voice, a note she'd never heard before.

She spoke placatingly. "I don't care about it, one way or another. But I don't feel like moving . . ."

"You do not feel like moving. I do not feel like milking cows. Which feeling is more important?"

Charlotte swallowed. She felt as though she would throw up. Again. She'd managed it the first time, discreetly, by slipping out the back door and around the house. All she wanted at the moment was for Johnny to go to work so that she could lie down until the nausea subsided. Tonight, when she felt better, when there was more time, then she would tell Johnny why she didn't want to move right now. But Johnny had to ride horseback for nearly half an hour to reach the dairy and he was late already.

"You'd better go," she said.

"Yes, I had better go. And leave you in the cabin. Which you do not like. You could have lived in a fine big house by the river. No doubt you are sorry that you followed me."

"No, I'm not sorry." Her voice sounded flat and unconvincing even to herself. "I'm sick this morning."

"Now you are sick also. Of me? Of this poor cabin? Of the poor choice you made? I am sick of milk cows, Charlotte." He snatched up his hat. The door banged shut behind him.

She looked out the window as he swung into the saddle. The buckskin tossed his head; Johnny loosened the reins and they galloped away. Charlotte flung open the front door. She rushed to the railing, hung over it, and vomited.

It was not Johnny's nature to be bad-tempered for long. He flared up quickly, but it passed just as quickly. This evening he would be loving again. Then she would tell him that he was going to be a father. She wanted it to be a special moment, not a hurried disclosure while she was ill and he must leave immediately for work. They would decide if it would be better to move at once or for him to milk cows a few months longer.

It was a little over a year since they'd left the Mosher ranch. They lived in an agricultural community south of Portland, in a remote cabin that belonged to the owner of the dairy. While it wasn't much, it was rent-free. Their dream was to buy a place of their own and every penny they could manage was saved toward that goal.

In mid-afternoon, Charlotte untied the clothesline rope that stretched between two trees behind the house. One end was frayed and she feared that it might snap under a heavy load of wet clothes and drop them on the ground. Dreaming of babies, she coiled the rope in her hands as she walked inside. She hung the coil over a chair and sat down with a pile of mending.

She sewed up a three-cornered rip in one of Johnny's shirts and stitched a button back on his pants. She repaired a hem in a skirt. She thrust her hand inside one of Johnny's socks and looked critically at the heel. Was it worth darning again? Maybe. Yarn was cheaper than new socks. She turned her hand dreamily back and forth, thinking of babies, of Johnny's face as he looked at the child that was theirs. Her lips curved in a smile.

The crows that stayed in the big-leaf maple grove in front of the house cawed noisily. The ruckus went on and on. They were as good as watch dogs. Charlotte looked out the window, but didn't see anything. The racket persisted. She stepped onto the porch. Something moved in the trees. She waited a moment. Maybe she'd seen one of the crows flapping from limb to limb. But they still squawked, annoyed or alarmed at whatever—or whoever—had intruded upon their quiet place. She felt uneasy that no one showed himself.

Charlotte went to the bedroom and took the rifle out of the closet. She levered a cartridge into the chamber. From where she stood, she could see through the front window to the maple grove. A man rode out from the concealment of the trees. Charlotte's heart thumped in her chest. She knew that rider. She'd seen him come toward her a thousand times, ever since she was a child. She thrust the rifle back into the closet and walked slowly to the porch. They looked at one another for a moment without speaking.

Then she said, as though it had been only a few days since she'd seen him, "Hello, Howard."

"How are you, Charlotte?"

"Elsie must have told you where I live."

"She did."

I wish she hadn't, Charlotte thought. I wish I'd asked her not to tell him.

She didn't like the idea that he'd concealed himself in the maple grove and watched the cabin, until he realized that the squawking crows had alerted anyone inside. Howard dismounted.

"Don't . . ." But it was too late. His right boot had already touched the ground. He dropped the reins and stepped up onto the porch. She'd forgotten how big he was, tall with heavy shoulders and head. His eyes were intent and red-rimmed. It was like being in close quarters with a large male animal, perhaps a bull, of uncertain disposition. She resisted an urge to move away.

"You haven't changed." He spoke in the thick, choked

312

way his voice sounded when he was upset.

She didn't answer.

He sucked in a deep breath. "I didn't come all this way to beat around the bush. I came to say that you can come back. It was my fault you left. I drove you off when I broke our engagement, so I don't blame you for leaving."

"You came all the way from eastern Oregon for me?"

"I'm going to buy cattle in Portland. That's what I told everyone. I came by train and then got a horse from a stable. I didn't say I was coming here."

He looked around at the rough exterior of the cabin, the expanse of weeds, grass and hoof-trampled ground that passed for a yard. His measuring look traveled over her worn cotton dress and scuffed shoes.

"It doesn't look as though you're doing too well."

Her chin lifted. "We're doing fine. We're saving all we can to buy a place of our own. We don't spend foolishly on things we don't absolutely need."

"I can see that. Christ, Charlotte, you could have had better with me than you'll ever have with him."

"But I love Johnny."

"You'll get over it. It's infatuation, not love. When I was your age, I thought I was in love with Iris May from McCullough's saloon. It lasted a couple of years, but it wasn't love. You aren't the same calibre as Domingo, any more than I was like Iris May. It'll pass."

"No, it won't. This is different than what you felt for that woman."

"I'll tell you what. Come to Portland with me for a few days. We'll stay in a nice hotel, go to some musicals or the opera. I'll buy you some pretty dresses. We'll have fun. Maybe we should have done that more and not been quite so proper."

She shook her head. "I'm married, Howard."

"I don't give a damn. You can get unmarried. Or you can stay married and we'll just . . . spend some time together, as long as we want, no strings."

She stared at him in disbelief. "You expect me to run off with you when I'm married to another man?"

"You're not so prim. You ran off with that half-breed while we were engaged." His voice had risen.

Hers rose in response. "Engagement is not the same as married. Besides . . ."

"It was the same to me. God, I couldn't believe it when William told me. Even after he showed me the note, I could hardly believe it."

"As you reminded me, you broke it off. You told me you didn't trust me."

"And with good reason."

"Then why do you want me back?"

"Because I can't stop thinking about you. Because I never wanted anybody as much as I want you. Because you're like a disease I can't get rid of. Because I'm absolutely crazy about you and I think of you every single day."

A brief silence fell. He passed his hand over his jaw. "Oh, God."

"I'm sorry you feel that way, Howard. But if you do feel like that, then you'll understand when I tell you—that's exactly how I feel about Johnny."

The air seemed heavy between them, every molecule charged with emotion.

Thick-voiced, he asked, "Did you ever love me?"

She thought about it, as deeply and seriously as she could. Exactly what had she felt for Howard? Infatuation or . . . His hand smacked against the side of her face, knocking her off-balance.

314

"You bitch! You didn't! Why did you say you'd marry me? Why?"

"You hit me." It was the most shocking thing that had ever happened to her.

"Answer me. Why?"

She struggled, through the shock, to find an honest answer. "Other women wanted you. That was part of it. You're a catch and you wanted me. But most of all, I like your mother. I thought you might be like her, inside, where it matters. But you're not." She yelled in outrage. "You're mean. You're a big bully, Howard. You always were a bully, mean and nasty."

"You make me mean. You drive me crazy. But if you'd take me back, I'd be so good to you . . . ."

She struck at the hands that reached for her. "Keep away from me. You make me sick." She hated the thought that she had once embraced this man, that she had kissed his tight, ungenerous mouth. She despised the cajoling look on his face, the smell of him when he came near.

He grabbed one of her hands in each of his and pulled them above her head. He forced her back against the wall of the house and jammed his knee between her legs. He bent his head to hers. She bit his lip.

He jerked away. "You're a real wildcat, honey. I always suspected you were, beneath that fake lady manner you picked up somewhere." He spoke almost without emotion, without rancor. "And you're a fool. You could have had everything.

"Do you know what I've decided, Charlotte? We are going to spend some time together. Maybe here, maybe someplace else. A few days, just the two of us alone. Plenty of time to do whatever we want. And then we'll decide what to do next."

It was the calmness that chilled her. For the first time, she realized that she was in danger.

"I'm pregnant. I'm going to have a baby."

One heavy hand moved familiarly over her waist and flat stomach. "You're lying."

"No, I'm not. I just found out."

He studied her a moment. "Well, then I won't have to worry about getting a bastard on you, will I?"

"God, I hate you, Howard!" she screamed. "Whatever made me think I liked you?"

He smiled, not pleasantly, and pulled her toward the door. She resisted. "Johnny will be home any minute."

"No, he won't. He doesn't get home until after six."

"You've been spying on us."

"Just enough to figure the lay of the land. It's only fools that rush in, you know."

They stumbled through the door together. Her skirt ripped as it snagged on something.

Charlotte tried again. "He'll be home early today. He's going to quit his job. He hates milking cows."

There was enough truth in this so that it got Howard's attention. "That's not a real big problem," he said after a moment.

Howard was not only large and strong, he was used to handling recalcitrant animals—branding, de-horning, castrating. It was a simple matter for him to force other creatures to do things they were determined not to do. He grabbed the clothesline off the chair. In a few moments, Charlotte was trussed up like a calf. Her hands and feet were bound together, wrists and ankles in front of her. Johnny's unmended sock was jammed into her mouth and held there by a dish towel cinched around her head.

He carried her into the bedroom, kicked the partially open closet door so that it sprang wide, and dumped her onto the floor. She landed on top of Johnny's chaps, extra boots, a blanket, and other items piled in the cramped space. Howard closed the door.

There was too much sock in Charlotte's mouth. She thought she would strangle. Frantically, she worked at it with her tongue until she could breathe a little more easily. The rope cut into her wrists. She struggled until she could peek out the crack between the ill-fitting door and the wall.

Howard was not in sight. She'd heard his footsteps leave the bedroom as she struggled with the sock. She held her breath and strained her ears. She heard the soft thump of hooves on grass on the other side of the uninsulated wall. Howard had taken his horse around to the back of the house. Something bumped against the rear wall. In a few moments, footsteps clumped in through the back and crossed the kitchen. Howard appeared in the bedroom door. He had a rifle in one hand and a small flask in the other.

"Are you okay, Charlotte?"

She sank back against the wall. He opened the door and looked in at her. She knew her eyes were stretched wide and frightened. He grinned and twisted the lid off the bottle. He laid the rifle on the bed behind him. He sipped the whiskey and rubbed his lower lip which looked slightly swollen where she'd bitten him.

"It stings a little, Charlotte." He bent toward her and tested the gag. "Is that too tight?"

Frantically she nodded yes. He thrust the tip of his finger between her cheek and the cloth. "Oh, it's not so bad. Now, we'll just wait for Johnny to come home." He shut the door in her face.

Charlotte turned to look at Johnny's 30.06 which had slid down the wall and lay on the floor behind the jumble of clothes and blankets. If she were neat about the way she kept the house, Howard would have seen the gun. But she never minded things piled around and, because of that, the rifle had gone unnoticed.

But she couldn't use it as long as her hands and feet were tied. She peered through the crack again. Howard had pulled a chair in front of the window. He sat with his back to her, looking out. The rifle and the whiskey flask lay on the table beside him.

Charlotte rooted awkwardly around on the floor until she found one of Johnny's spurs. It was not an everyday spur, but a fancy silver Spanish colonial with long spiky rowels. He wore them only for show, and very gingerly, for it was easy to hurt a horse with such barbaric ornaments.

Her arms were tied by the length of rope to her ankles. She couldn't raise them above her waist while sitting down and she would not be able to stand without bending almost double from the waist. She managed to grip the spur between her knees and slipped the rope that bound her between the rowels. She sawed back and forth, pulling down as hard as she could. She kept her eyes on Howard's broad back.

Now and then the chair creaked as he shifted his weight. He took off his hat and put it on the table; twice he sipped from the flask. Occasionally his hand caressed the rifle beside him.

He turned his head. "How are you doing, Charlotte?"

She froze. Howard stood up and stretched. Quickly, she thrust the spur under the blanket and her hands into the folds of her skirt. He opened the closet and looked down at her. She felt her long hair tangled damply around her face and neck. He stooped and touched a finger gently to her cheek.

"You're going to have a bruise. But I'll be able to untie you soon. It's after five o'clock."

Oh, God, so late. Johnny would be home soon. He would

ride, unsuspecting, directly into the muzzle of Howard's rifle. She closed her eyes in despair. She heard Howard move away and opened them again. He had not closed the closet door. All he had to do was turn around and he would see her sawing at the rope.

Now what? Maybe she could close the door. She struggled to her knees. Something clinked, perhaps the spur. Howard turned.

"Oh, oh." He swaggered back into the bedroom. "Are you trying to get out, little girl? I don't trust you at my back, even tied up. Sorry about that." He put the sole of one boot against her chest and tipped her backwards into the wall. The door clicked shut.

What a relief! As soon as he was in the chair, she grabbed the spur. Her hands whipped frantically back and forth as fast as she could move and still pull down with any force. It hurt and a rusting of blood soon stained the rope. Pain increased along with the size and depth of her abrasions. She had no idea how much time passed as she looked alternately from Howard's back to the fraying rope. But she saw the light change in the room as the sun slid westward.

At last the strand separated. Some of the nagging pain eased. "Ahhh." The sigh escaped her lips before she could stop it. Howard's head turned. He listened. He stood up.

Oh, God. Oh, God. It was too soon. Her hands were numb. Although one strand of the clothesline rope was severed, other strands still tightly wrapped her wrists.

All at once, she heard a crow. It squawked a warning and another echoed the cry. Then the flock joined in the raucous cacophony with which they greeted anything that moved near their maple grove kingdom, from a passing coyote to a wandering cow to a rider coming home.

Howard exclaimed, a soft explosive word. He turned to

the window and picked up his rifle.

Charlotte worked off the cords on her wrists and picked up the other gun. Awkwardly, because her feet were still tied together, she raised herself to her knees. She unlatched the door and nudged it so that it swung open.

She could not see out the window from her position, but she knew what was there. The image was clear in her mind—a slim, black-hatted rider on a buckskin horse. They jogged around the grove and toward the cabin. Howard raised his rifle and sighted along the barrel.

Charlotte lifted the 30.06. Her hands trembled so she could barely find the sight. Her voice trembled, too, when she spoke. "Howard, put down that rifle."

He turned his head. His eyes were cold and flat. The harsh lines of his face seemed unfamiliar, as though he were an ugly stranger whom she'd never seen before. Contempt iced his voice.

"Charlotte, you can't even kill a chicken."

He turned to the window and lifted the rifle. A shot exploded in the small cabin. It was the loudest sound Charlotte had ever heard. It rolled around and around the walls, out the open window and bounced back from the hills. It filled her ears. It rang and echoed endlessly the way it would echo for the rest of her life.

The barrel of the rifle she held dropped. Howard turned slowly. His gun barrel pointed up. He had an odd look on his face.

"Why, Charlotte . . ." His voice was soft. A bright red gush of blood sprang from his mouth. It dribbled down his chin and splattered onto his shirt. Slowly, carefully, he placed the rifle on the table. He coughed. His hand flew to catch the blood that spewed from his mouth. He looked at his hand in a puzzled way.

Howard reached for the back of the chair as though he would sit down, but he missed and sat on the floor. His head thumped against the wall.

Charlotte scrambled awkwardly toward him. Johnny appeared in the door before she reached Howard. For once, she barely noticed him. Nor was it Howard she thought of as she held his heavy head against her body.

"Hannah, I'm sorry. I only wanted to stop him. I didn't want to kill him. I'm sorry, Hannah. I'm so sorry."

"I didn't want to kill him," Charlotte said. "I only wanted to stop him from killing Johnny."

Charles shifted in the chair beside the bed. "It don't seem you had much choice," he said softly. "It was either him or your husband."

Charlotte didn't know when she'd begun talking, when memories had turned into confession. She'd never told anyone else. Charles had listened without speaking. His dark eyes remained impassive and the remote expression on his face did not change throughout the narrative. It marginally comforted her that he did not appear shocked or surprised.

Johnny had been both. He'd stared from her to Howard with a look of disbelief. Later that night, his expression was something like awe.

"How you must love me," he whispered. "You, who are so soft-hearted and cannot bear the sight of blood. You must truly love me."

Oh, yes, she did. And he never doubted that for a second, during the few years that were left for them to be together. But she paid a high price for that love.

Charlotte had told Charles enough so that she might as well finish. "We got Howard on the horse. He was so heavy, I was afraid we couldn't do it. Then Johnny took them somewhere. I never asked a single question. I don't know what happened to the horse. Maybe he turned it loose. Maybe he killed it. I don't know. I didn't want to know.

"Johnny quit his job and we moved to the Woodbridge area. We were afraid for a long time, but there was no reason for anyone to think we'd ever seen Howard. I think people disappeared easier in those days. Elsie wrote me later. She said Howard went on a cattle-buying trip and never came home. Hannah suffered dreadfully. She kept hoping he'd come back. I can't forget that. I know how it feels to lose a son.

"Then Johnny died when he was only thirty-three. It was lockjaw. We didn't know it at first. We thought he had influenza. We never connected the way he felt, the stiff neck and aching, with that little gash on his leg from the nail. I took him to the doctor, finally, but it was too late. Maybe he could have been saved in 1950, but not then, not by a country doctor in 1901."

She sighed. "God has punished me my whole life for killing Howard. First He took Johnny and then He took my son. And likely He'll send me to Hell after I die."

Charles didn't say anything for a moment. Then he asked, "Do you think soldiers go to Hell? Soldiers who kill in battle, in wars?"

"I don't know. I never thought about it."

"It wouldn't seem fair if they did, would it? Men kill in wars because they have to, not because they want to. You and Howard were in a war, over Johnny."

"I guess so." She thought about that. Did it make a difference? When Johnny was dying, he'd prayed to his Catholic God. He was sorry to die so soon, to leave Charlotte and Alie behind. But he felt no fear. He had absolute faith that his God would accept him and he'd died as trustfully as a child. But

Johnny's sins were not as great as hers.

Charles stayed with Charlotte that night. She felt better by the time he returned from work the next evening.

"If you think you'll be all right, I'll go home after work tomorrow. I should feed my horses. I'll ask Vivian if she'll come up and check on you on Saturday."

"You go on," she said briskly. "I'm okay now. And don't bother Vivian. I'll be fine."

That's what she said aloud. To herself she whimpered, Don't go. I've been alone so long. I don't want to die alone, too.

She walked slowly to the barn the next morning. The ponies shifted restlessly at their mangers, stirring up dust, bits of old hay, and the heavy smell of manure. She measured grain from the big metal barrel and moved slowly down the line. She doled out portions to each one and spoke to them all by name.

She filled the measure for Mamie and milked her, then fed the clamouring dogs. Endless chores awaited her. Simply thinking of even the most pressing ones exhausted her. The barn roof needed repairs before winter and she'd have to hire someone to do it. She couldn't climb that high anymore. All of her clothes were dirty and that meant either driving to the laundromat in town or doing them by hand with a washtub and metal plunger. And those chores were only the beginning. Every year it was harder to maintain the basics of living.

As she mentally stared at the mountain of work awaiting her, the dogs began their hullaballoo. It was Vivian.

"The county finally got the slide cleared away. I'll drive you to the doctor," she said in her brisk, take-charge manner.

"I appreciate that. But I'm not going. There's not a thing the matter with me, except I had the flu. And I'm eighty-one years old. No doctor can fix that."

Vivian smiled. "It wouldn't hurt to have a checkup. How long has it been since you've seen a doctor?"

"It's been awhile. I'll go," she said to stop Vivian from pestering her. "I'll let you know when I'm ready."

"All right. But don't wait too long. There's no point in being uncomfortable, if you don't have to be. I'll put this meatloaf right here. It's left from what we had last night. It'll be fine if you eat it this evening. I'll bring you some ice for your icebox tomorrow." She shut the cupboard with a firm little thump and kneed two drooling dogs out of the way.

"Thanks, Vivian. You're a good neighbor."

"Now, let's get busy with your chores."

Charlotte was grateful for her capable help. As soon as the work was completed and Vivian had gone, Charlotte lay on the old couch in the corner of the big kitchen. Her head rested on a lumpy, grease-spotted pillow. She picked a dead leaf off one of the potted plants growing on the shelves that crossed the window above her. Dirt crusted the glass, diffusing the sunlight. It filtered through the cloudy pane and the green leaves like light falling under water, shadowy and wavering.

Memories flooded her in warm and comforting profusion, of Alie, of Johnny. She'd always loved his name . . . Johnny Domingo. Domingo. It had a rhythmic jangling music, like the sound of a Spanish spur. When he was alive . . . when they were young . . .

The calico cat jumped onto Charlotte's chest, startling her to wakefulness. It had started to rain again, a soft rain of early autumn. The drops whispered against the window and ran down in spasmodic crooked rivulets. The kitchen clock indicated a few minutes before five. She had not been aware of the hours passing, but had lain mesmerized as the ghost of Johnny Domingo rode shining through the past.

Patches's paws tramped up and down, kneading her shirt.

The cat purred noisily. She thrust her face into Charlotte's and wiped her whiskers against her chin.

"It's getting late, Patches."

Charlotte pushed the cat away, swung her feet to the floor, and sat up. As she did, the hawk that had circled so long in the sky descended with a rushing of wide dark wings. It struck her full force. She slipped to the floor and lay on her back. A draft blew against her, as though a door had cracked open to another place. Above her, she saw rain splashing behind the green plants.

It's happening. It's happening. And there's nobody with me but Patches.

She couldn't move. Hands . . . fingers . . . head . . . nothing responded. Only her eyes moved and they flickered here and there around the empty room.

The dogs barked in the distance. A rapping came from somewhere. The cat bolted out of the room. The knocking sounded again and a man's voice called to her.

"Mrs. Domingo." Boot heels thumped on the bare wooden floor.

It was Charles! Oh, thank God. It was Charles.

A man came into the kitchen, but not Charles. Was it Daddy? He was tall, his face shadowy under a broad-brimmed hat. He wavered in and out of her sight so that she could not see him clearly. He lifted her from the floor and lay her on the couch.

No, it was not Daddy, but she knew him. She'd known him all her life, from the time she was a baby. He was one of the lean, quiet-voiced range riders of her youth. He'd been neighbor, friend, teacher, guardian. He'd taught her to ride, to handle cattle, to read the weather. He'd told her stories of days that were old when she was young. He'd danced with her at neighbors' houses, swung her high and whirled her fast.

She knew him well, the smell of him—cigarettes and horse-hide. She knew the unflinching eyes, the feel of the work-roughened, capable hands that took hers in a warm grip.

"I know you," she whispered. "You're . . . you're . . ." She couldn't quite recall his name, but it didn't matter, because he was there, because she knew him well. "I'm so glad you came."

"Of course I came, Charlotte. You rest easy now."

"You stay with me. Don't go away."

"I'm right here. I'll stay, Charlotte."

How lovely the sound of her name, to know that she was not alone, but with someone who'd known her for years. She listened to the comforting tone of his voice. She gripped his warm hand. When she could hold on no longer, he still held tightly to her.

She rose from the couch. She floated towards the ceiling, drifting gently. Below she saw the figure of a gaunt old woman and a man beside her. Above was darkness. She moved toward it, going into it. She no longer felt the man's hand, but she knew that if she went back, he would still be there. That assurance gave her the courage to go on, the knowledge that he would be there for as long as she needed him.

She felt a wonderful sense of release, an immense flooding of joy. Something inside her resounded. Yes. Yes! There was no reason to be afraid. There never had been reason to be afraid. Everything was as it must be. All was well.

A light emerged from the darkness. She flowed toward it. We wait for the coming of the light. Godspeed the light. It bloomed like a glorious flower, brighter and more beautiful than any light she'd ever seen before. There were figures ahead of her; people waited for her. She knew them. She knew them all. Exultantly she rushed on, like a swallow winging home in evening flight.

Chapter 13

DORIS

Early September to October

Doris's head ached dully. The phone had rung regularly all day long. Now she listened to a voice in New Jersey tell her that there'd been a factory increase in the price of one-inch tile. They couldn't let her have them for what she'd paid last time, but instead they'd have to charge . . .

"That's all right. Just send me an invoice."

"You understand we don't want to raise our prices, but manufacturing costs have skyrocketed . . ."

Doris yawned. Running a hardware store was not a choice she had made. When she'd been asked, as a little girl, what she wanted to do when she grew up, she'd never said, "I want to own a hardware store." She'd married it, along with Carl. If she could have done what she really wanted . . .

Lee Jamison appeared in the street outside. He paused and looked around as though searching for someone. Then he came in.

There was silence on the other end of the phone. New Jersey obviously expected a reply. "I understand, Mr.—ummmm." She looked at the name she'd scribbled on her notepad. "DiPaulo. I'll make a note of the new price right now."

"Part of it's the unions," Mr. DiPaulo complained. "The unions have done a lot of good, but . . ."

Doris waved her pen at Lee. He strolled around the store, looking at things on the shelves. Vivian said he seemed to enjoy working on the ranch and they thought he might actually settle down. Doris doubted it. When he'd had the saddle shop a few years ago, she'd been sure that he would stay in Woodbridge. But instead he'd gone to Mexico. When he'd returned to Oregon and she'd asked him to move in with her, she'd hoped—oh, how she'd hoped—that he would stay. But he'd gone to California. Where would it be this time? Alaska? He'd talked about Alaska and she knew it was someplace he'd never been.

"Thank you, Mr. DiPaulo. Good-bye." She found Lee staring at gas cans, but he obviously wasn't thinking about them. He looked intent, serious. His lips moved slightly as though he were talking to himself, perhaps rehearsing something. She felt a rush of affection for him, followed instantly by anger at herself for being so susceptible.

"Damn you," she whispered. Was she cursing Lee or herself?

His eyes focused on her. A wave of color swept over his face. Was that a blush, for some odd reason?

"Sorry, Doris. I was thinking about something else."

"Yes, I noticed that. Can I help you find something?"

"No, I . . ." He looked at her intently. He was going to say something important. She held her breath. What? What is it? But the moment fled. She felt it evaporate before his words were spoken.

". . . I just came from the sheriff. The Redding office may have a lead in Joanne's death and they needed to ask me some more questions."

The murder again. She'd begun to hope that it would fade

away as though it had never happened, as though it were only a nightmare. As they talked, Doris thought about that woman. What kind of person was she? How many others like her were in Lee's life? A feeling of distaste, of coming in contact with something soiled and unpleasant, crept over her as she thought about the murder, the belt, the weirdness of it all.

Lee looked at his watch. "I didn't realize it was so late. Take care of yourself, Doris."

As the door closed behind him, she was left deflated, disappointed. It wasn't that anything unusual had happened. It was that something had not happened. She felt that Lee had come to a corner and almost turned it, but at the last moment he'd gone in another direction.

The contradictions in him had always baffled her—sensitivity combined with selfishness, intelligence with intellectual laziness, and his persistent refusal to consider consequences. Or maybe he was purely independent and refused to live life by standards of society with which he did not agree.

On the other hand, Doris had always done the proper, the expected thing, except when she'd invited Lee into her bed and her life. Before that, she'd drifted into marriage with Carl and so into the hardware business. Now she drifted again, still in the store, still in Woodbridge. If she weren't careful, she might drift into a romance with Glenn, simply because he was unaccountably infatuated with her.

Although maybe it wasn't as inexplicable as it had seemed at first. If the rumors about Glenn were true, he had sought solace with "wild" women when his marriage went bad. Perhaps it was Doris's less than sterling reputation which drew him to her.

Not long ago, Glenn had been shamelessly flirting with her, apparently having forgiven her for the awkward evening at the house of Anna's sister. Two young women of Doris's acquaintance were shopping in the store. After Glenn left, Doris walked down an aisle to ask if she could help them. She wore soft-soled shoes and they didn't hear her approach.

One said to the other, "Well, of course, there's only one reason why the vice-president of the bank is interested in a woman like her." They saw Doris then and knew that she had overheard. The woman who spoke stared at Doris in a smug and challenging way. The other, whom Doris had considered a friend, flushed guiltily. But it had been months since she'd included Doris in any invitation. It hurt that a woman who had once entertained Doris and Carl in her home now judged her so harshly.

She thought about the doubtful progression of her life, from a naive young bride full of self-importance to a dull and reliable wife and business partner to an equally dull and virtuous widow. Then suddenly, by the simple act of having sex without a license, she'd gone from being an object of pity to one who threatened the sanctity of the community.

There were women—and men—who no longer spoke to her except when they must, inside the only hardware store of any size for fifty miles. At first it had amused her. She'd made a little game of trying to figure out who would censure and who would allow a bending of the rules. Now, more than a year after Lee's departure, she was no longer amused. He was gone, but the disapproval was not.

She needed to think of something else, something less disturbing. In the last few weeks, she'd become obsessed with the desire to travel. Neither Doris nor her parents had ever been out of the state. As a young wife, she'd fantasized that she and Carl would go on trips together. Later she'd imagined that Lee might take her. Now . . .

She opened a drawer in her desk and drew out a brochure: "New England Inns." What could be safer, cozier, for a woman traveling alone than New England inns? They looked so picturesque, so quaint. She'd go by train to Boston. She'd never been on a train, so that in itself would be an adventure. She'd take some easy trips and then, when her confidence and coping skills were up to it, she'd go—

The phone rang. She finished the thought before she answered.

—anywhere in the world.

"Good afternoon. Gooding Hardware. Oh, yes, Mr. Ivarson. Yes, I believe we still have some of that wood stain to match. Just a minute and I'll check."

In early October, the phone rang as Doris unlocked the store in the morning. She raced to the back.

"Doris, this is Betsy Arness." Mrs. Arness was one of Alice Gooding's friends. She was also most overt in her disapproval of Doris. If they met on the street, she clutched the arm of her elderly husband and pulled him away as though she feared that Doris might seduce him in front of her eyes.

Mrs. Arness said, "I thought you should know that Alice had a stroke. She's in the hospital."

"Oh, dear. Is it serious?"

"Dr. Whitney said it's too soon to tell. Alice called me this morning. It was only a little after five-thirty and we weren't awake. She said she couldn't find her glasses, that she couldn't see to find her glasses. Her voice sounded so funny, sort of slurred, just like my mother right before she died. I called the ambulance immediately. I called you at your house about seven, but you didn't answer."

"I was out walking."

"Walking where?" Mrs. Arness was puzzled.

"For exercise. I've begun walking three or four mornings a week. It makes me feel better."

"Oh." It was obvious that the idea of exercise making anyone feel better was quite foreign to Mrs. Arness.

"I'll go to the hospital right now," Doris said. "Thank you for calling."

"I was sure you'd want to know. Norman and I are just leaving. We're going to get some breakfast."

And you must keep skinny, potbellied Norman away from the scarlet woman, Doris thought uncharitably.

She hurried up the outside steps and into the hospital lobby. Her heels clicked on the polished floor. The gray-haired receptionist looked up with a smile. "Good morning. I'm here to see Mrs. Gooding."

The receptionist looked at the chart. "Mrs. Gooding can see only immediate family."

"I'm her daughter-in-law."

The woman pursed her lips.

Doris said, "There's no one else. I'm all she's got."

"All right. Room thirty-five. Down that hall and to the left. But she's not conscious. Please don't stay longer than fifteen minutes."

I'm all she's got. Doris repeated the words as she went down the hall. That's pathetic.

In spite of Alice's bold talk of strong stock, her only sister had died in California several years before. She rarely saw her niece and nephews. Her deceased husband's relatives were either dead or far away. And Carl, her only child, was also gone.

I'm no better off, Doris realized. Who would visit me if I were in the hospital? After my parents go, who really cares if I live or die?

She opened the door of Room 35 and stepped quietly inside. The blinds were nearly closed. Alice looked unnaturally small. Her doll-like face appeared crumpled and defenseless without glasses and her usual expression of self-confidence. Her gray hair went every which way.

Why didn't someone comb her hair? She'd hate to look so frowsy.

Doris pulled a chair close to the bed and sat down. She took Alice's limp clammy hand. "Alice, it's Doris. Can you hear me?"

There was not a flicker of response.

"I'm very sorry that you're ill. You've had a slight stroke, but there's every reason to expect you'll soon be as good as ever." Maybe that wasn't true, but it wouldn't hurt if she believed it. Knowing how her mother-in-law fretted over unplanned expenditures, Doris went on.

"You've got a wonderful insurance policy and don't have to worry about a thing except getting better." That was true. Doris had checked the store copy of the policy before she came to the hospital. Her father-in-law had insisted that one could not have too much insurance. Doris sometimes cringed at the premiums, but now it was comforting.

She cast around for something else to say. "Do you remember that funny little Mr. Karadzic? He has such a heavy accent that I can barely understand him. Yesterday he came to the store and . . ."

She talked on, wondering if Alice heard or understood any of it.

"If Mrs. Arness doesn't attend to it, I'll go by your apartment and pick up a few things—a comb, a toothbrush. I'll also call Dr. Whitney for more information on what we can expect. And I'll come back this evening. You rest now."

She squeezed Alice's hand. There was a slight tremor in her fingers that might have been an attempt to respond, but the expression on her face did not change. Doris squeezed again and immediately the little tremor was there in return.

"You hear me, don't you. I'm so glad." Doris surprised herself by bending forward and brushing her lips across the older woman's forehead. She left the room quickly. An odd feeling of embarrasment accompanied an unexpected prickling in her eyes. She couldn't remember that she'd ever intentionally touched her mother-in-law before.

I can't believe that I'm actually feeling sentimental about the old lady. Maybe it's because I just had my thirty-eighth birthday. I'm almost middle-aged and getting soft, I guess.

Several days later, Doris waited in the lobby for the doctor to complete his examination of Alice. She held a book that Anna Stegner thought Alice might enjoy. Doris thumbed through it. Another novel in which the smart, successful working woman proved to be scheming and promiscuous. Anna hadn't noticed the stereotyping.

If a man showed ambition and aggressiveness, he was admirable. If a woman exhibited the same characteristics, she was a bitch. If a man entered into sexual adventures, he was a devil with the ladies, wink, wink. A woman who followed the same moral code was a tramp. No understanding winks for her.

Popular magazines warned women against the perils of trying to combine marriage and a career. Yet men did it all the time. Doris thought back to the movies that had entertained her during the thirties and forties. They featured smart, sassy, aggressive women such as Rosalind Russell and Katharine Hepburn. They had careers and were proud of them. No advice columnist told them to play dumb so that their males would feel smarter nor were they told to talk only of the men's interests, so as to flatter them.

What happened to us? Doris wondered. All the defense workers, the women in the military, those who managed businesses and farms while the men were away at war—why are we being stuffed back into the Victorian box? And why are we going—without a fight, like lambs following one another into the pens?

Anger stirred deep inside Doris, like a living thing far beneath the waves. "The kraken wakes." The sentence popped into her head. It suggested the rousing of a creature of great power and mystery, one that might soon surface.

She thought of women she knew—Vivian who could have mobilized armies, Charlotte Domingo who did hard physical labor that would tax many men. Her mother-in-law, in spite of frivolity and occasional silliness, had a good business head and a sharp mind.

Doris told herself not to be too modest. The hardware business had more than doubled since she took over. Some of it could be attributed to post-war prosperity and the building boom, but she'd done a good job. A damn good job. She'd done it alone and could continue that way. If she did remarry, it would have to be a man who recognized her abilities and accepted her as a full partner. She would never step back into the shadows again.

Doris stared into the future. For the first time in a long while, her heart surged with excitement, with possibilities.

"Doris."

"What?" Startled, she looked up at slender Dr. Whitney.

He sank into the chair beside her. "Alice is doing pretty well. Tomorrow we'll transfer her to Ridgewood Center. She'll need physical therapy. And she must exercise and lose weight. She'll probably need a walker for awhile, but I anticipate a full recovery."

"I'm happy to hear that."

"She wants to get better and that's important. She's tougher than I might have guessed. Although since I play bridge with her occasionally, I should have known."

Doris smiled. "She loves her bridge games."

"Bridge is good for her. It keeps the mind alert." He stood up. "You can see her now. She can hardly wait for you to get there."

Doris watched him stride away. He'd made that up. Alice had never looked forward to seeing her.

But she smiled warmly when Doris entered the room. She began to talk about her transfer to the nursing home. Her voice was slurred and in a somewhat different pitch than before her stroke.

Doris said, "I brought you some magazines. And these books. Paperbacks, so they'll be easier to hold."

"You're very thoughtful, Doris. Sit down. Betsy was here this afternoon and she told me something absolutely unbelievable. Carrie Allison went to . . ."

Doris sat down. She listened to the bridge table gossip that Alice loved and repeated with relish. Such revelations never failed to surprise Doris. People rarely told her scandalous tales and she was amazed that so much intrigue and drama occurred all around her.

After awhile, Doris glanced at her watch. "I must go. It'll be after seven when I get home and I still have to write copy for the ad in Friday's paper." She stood up.

"Wait a minute, Doris. I've made a decision and I want you to know."

"What's that?"

"I'm going to change my will."

Somewhere inside Doris, something went *thump*.

"I'd left my share of the store jointly to Nancy's children. They're the only blood relatives I have left, so it seemed I should. And then you and I—well, you know, we didn't always understand one another. But I've had time to think while I've been in the hospital.

336

"It wouldn't be good for the business to divide it up, with my share split three ways between people who don't know or care anything about it. They've hardly even set foot in the building. So I have an appointment with Leon tomorrow afternoon to rewrite the will. Nancy's children will get my insurance and the house and any personal things they may want. But the store is yours."

"Why, Alice, I'm . . . I feel quite overcome. And grateful. Very grateful."

She waved a plump hand. "Now, let's not get all maudlin. Sam Whitney says I'll be around for years yet, plenty of time for us to provoke one another again. But I won't change my mind. I promise that. I know that Carl and Frank would both agree with my decision. Now, run along. And come see me tomorrow at Ridgewood."

Doris paused in the door. "May I say that . . . you've changed recently."

"Have I? Well, so have you. You were always so stand-offish. As stiff as a poker. Do you know that you've actually begun to laugh at some of my bridge club stories? Think about it."

Doris thought about it all evening. It had never occurred to her that the lack of harmony between them might be her fault, too.

Doris glanced hopefully at the wall clock. Ten minutes to closing. Keith had left early and she was alone in the store. A new order of decorative kitchenware was stacked, unopened, in the back room. She was eager to unpack and put it on display. She'd found that certain non-hardware items, displayed in the street-side windows, brought in extra customers.

She was still dazed by Alice's revelation of the previous day. The store was to be all hers! Of course, it was the most practical, the most sensible thing, to do from a business standpoint. But she'd never expected such generosity from her mother-in-law.

She wondered when it had first entered Alice's mind. Perhaps she'd begun to think about it even before her stroke, as she was not given to rash decisions where finances were concerned. Doris felt as though a weight that she'd carried for years—and become so used to feeling on her back that she sometimes forgot it was there—had been lifted. The weight was suddenly conspicuous by its absence and she felt as though she might float right up to the ceiling.

Five more minutes. She turned the page of the newspaper and her eyes drifted to the obituary column. The first name jumped out at her.

Charlotte Blakely Domingo.

Oh, dear. That remarkable old lady was gone. She'd been so striking, with her lined leathery skin and eyes the color of dark summer-gold grass. Feelings of regret and loss twinged through Doris. I wish I'd talked to her more, asked more questions. I'll bet she had stories to tell.

Doris read that Charlotte Blakely had been born in 1869, near Baker, Oregon, not far from the Oregon Trail which her parents had followed west from Ohio. Preceded in death by her husband, Juan Ignacio Domingo, and a son, Alejandro Juan. A death from natural causes at her ranch near Whistler's Bend.

Eighty-one years summed up in a few lines. But it was the story behind the lines that would have been interesting. Perhaps Vivian knew more. Doris hadn't spoken to any of the Jamisons for some time and she should inquire about Justin, too. General MacArthur and his troops were fighting in South Korea and Justin was likely in the middle of it.

All of the Jamisons seemed to have suddenly dropped out

of sight. Busy, Doris supposed, with haying and harvests of various kinds.

She wondered if she would ever see or think of Lee without a lingering sense of loss. They'd come close—she still believed that. But there was a distance in him, a barrier that protected him against emotional risk. Had anyone ever penetrated that shield, been loved enough that the barriers came down? That was an interesting thought with an answer she'd never know.

She sighed. Whatever scars Lee might carry, she had never found a place at the center of his life or heart. She had no choice but to accept that and move on.

Work helped. She looked at the clock again. Three minutes after six o'clock. Good. She could close up and get busy with the new merchandise. The sample had been wonderful and she knew exactly how she wanted to do the display, using red wax apples, autumn leaves, and sheaves of dried grass which she'd gathered the night before. Thank goodness, no one had come in during the last few minutes.

She hurried to lock the front door and turn over the "Closed" sign. Just as she started to the back again, someone tapped on the glass behind her. She paused, prepared to shake her head: You're too late. We're closed.

A massive shape leaned toward the glass. Small eyes peered demandingly at her. Her heart sank. Oh, no. It was her landlord, Warren Stonebraker.

Reluctantly, she opened the door. "I didn't expect you until tomorrow morning."

He crowded her as he stepped in, his bulk filling the doorway. Doris retreated as he re-locked the door.

"I'm at the cabin for a few days with Sherry and Lila. I have another appointment in town this evening and if I can handle both at once, I won't have to drive back again in the morning."

"That makes sense. But I'm in rather a hurry. Alice had a stroke and was moved today to Ridgewood. I want to make sure she doesn't need anything."

Warren looked appraisingly around the interior. He wasn't one to waste time in conventional small talk. "I hear your business is doing real well. The taxes went up this year and you'll remember that you asked for some repairs. When your lease comes up for renewal, I'm going to have to raise the rent."

Doris was not surprised, but her heart sank just the same. She wasn't ready to negotiate a new agreement this evening. "Alice and I would very much like to buy the building. We're prepared to offer more than last time."

He shook his head. "That's not an option. This is prime retail property, right on the corner, exposure two ways. If you can't manage a rent increase, plenty of other businesses will be glad to step in."

As Doris thought about her reply, Warren smiled. "Besides, I have hopes for our future relationship. It's always been good and I hope it will get even better."

At the insinuating tone in his voice, she looked him firmly in the eye. "We've had a reasonable business relationship. I don't expect that to change in any way."

He didn't stop smiling. There was something smug and self-satisfied in his manner, as though he gloated over a secret.

"You're a smart businesswoman in most ways, Doris. But you could make things a lot easier for yourself. I've acquired a new property in Woodbridge. Do you know Sally Roush?"

"Slightly."

Sally was a realtor, an over-dressed, raven-haired divorcee

addicted to jangling jewelry.

"I've just added her to my inventory."

"You mean that you bought the Zeiger Building?"

Warren's eyes stayed fixed on hers. "I bought the Zeiger Building, yes. And in about forty-five minutes, Sally and I will finalize our arrangement. She's a very generous woman. I can be generous in return."

You bastard, Doris thought. You're married. To an eighteen-year-old girl. The ink is barely dry on the wedding certificate and you're already after Sally Roush.

Warren said, "You don't need to purse your mouth and look so prim. You defied convention, too, for something—or someone—you wanted outside of marriage."

"There were no husbands or wives involved in my—"

"In your affair. You can say it to me. You've taken the first step. I've taken a few steps more. We don't need to pretend. I think we understand each other very well."

He moved closer to her. Doris resisted the impulse to retreat. She didn't want to move away from the front window. Even though there weren't many passersby at this time of the evening, Warren made her feel uneasy and she preferred to remain in view of anyone who did chance by.

He might have read her mind. "Let's sit down where we'll be more comfortable."

"I'm perfectly comfortable right here."

One of Warren's meaty hands closed on her elbow. At that moment, someone thumped on the window. She glimpsed a fluttering hand and a dark jacket, as the hurried greeter dashed past. But it served to remind Warren that they were in a fishbowl of sorts and he released her arm.

"Doris. Doris. You do me an injustice." He almost crooned. "I have no intention of forcing myself upon you. We'll continue our discussion another time. Right now I have an appointment with lovely Mrs. Roush."

He'd suddenly begun to pronounce the letter *s* with an exaggerated emphasis, a hissing sound. Realization jolted Doris.

"You made those phone calls, didn't you?" The accusation popped out in an angry burst.

"What phone calls?" But there was satisfaction in his eyes and in the way that he hooked his thumbs in his belt loops. The movement drew Doris's eyes to his thick waist. They locked on a heavy silver belt buckle, shaped into the head of a ram. She stared at it, feeling a sluggish sense of surprise, feeling a warning like a distant drumbeat. At last, she managed to pull her gaze away from the belt and up to meet Warren's eyes.

"Is something wrong?" he asked.

"No! Nothing." Her answer sounded too vehement. Her hands clutched each other. She forced them to her sides and felt the tension in her neck and a slight hunching of her shoulders. Pretend. Pretend everything is all right. She tried to smile, but her lips were stiff.

Warren's brow wrinkled faintly. One finger moved back and forth, tracing the bulge of the ram's forehead. "You seem intrigued by my belt buckle."

"It's . . . it's unusual." Where should she look? At the belt? At his face?

"Yes."

He considered her with an intent, slightly puzzled gaze. She clearly read the questions in his mind. Does she know something? What does she know? How does she know it?

Doris glanced toward her watch without seeing either hands or numerals. "I've got to go. Alice expected me by now."

Neither moved for a moment. Doris's purse, with her car

342

keys, was in the back. But she was afraid to move out of sight from the window.

Warren spoke casually. "Have you seen Lee Jamison lately?"

"No. Not for weeks. Excuse me, please."

He didn't move. When she attempted to step around him to reach the door, abandoning thoughts of the purse, only wanting to get out, he blocked her way.

"Warren, we're right in front of the window." She tried for a mild tone, but detected shrillness in her voice.

As if to prove her point, little Mr. Karadzic appeared beyond Warren's broad shoulder. Doris waved wildly at him. He paused and waved back. Warren glanced in his direction, then quickly unlocked the front door, and flung it wide as he stepped through.

"Since you have another appointment, I won't keep you any longer." His voiced boomed loudly enough to be heard across the deserted street, if anyone had been there. Rain was beginning to drizzle. "I'll see you in a couple of months."

He beamed at Mr. Karadzic, who smiled uncertainly back. "Good evening, sir. And how are you?"

Mr. Karadzic replied unintelligibly.

"That's wonderful. Good night, sir. Good night, Doris," Warren shouted. He hurried off.

What in the world? Doris stared after him as he vanished around the corner. What was that all about?

Mr. Karadzic said something. Doris struggled through an exchange of gestures and smiles, baffled by Warren's hasty exit, and longing to get to the telephone. With a final nod and smile, she sent Mr. Karadzic on his way.

She hurried to the phone at the back to call the sheriff to tell him about the belt, to tell him that she believed her landlord was guilty of the murder of two women. She picked up the receiver.

The lights went out. A board creaked. One board in front of the door that led to the alley and the lumber annex always creaked when it took weight. A bulky figure, featureless in the shadows, rushed toward her.

Without even seeing his face, she understood the charade that Warren had played out in front of his witness, Mr. Karadzic. The ostentatious departure with a reference to Doris's non-existent appointment with someone else, the comment that he would see her in two months, gave Warren an alibi. A witness would say that Doris was fine when her landlord left and that an unknown person must be responsible for her murder. And she knew that murder was what Warren intended. Somehow he'd connected her reaction when she saw the belt to the realization that she knew what it meant.

All this flashed through her mind in an instant, as quickly and completely as a bolt of lightning illuminates a landscape. The thoughts occurred in the tiny crack of time between the moment when she saw the dark figure rushing toward her and the second that the telephone dropped from her fingers.

She darted from behind the desk, quick as a cat in her crepe-soled shoes. The layout of the store was such that Warren had the more direct path to the front door and the display windows. Even if she managed to outrun him, she wouldn't have time to unlock the door before he reached her. As she ran between the high shelving, she heard the thump of Warren's feet in another aisle as he raced to cut her off.

She stopped before the end of the aisle. She tried to control her breathing, too loud in the silent store. It wasn't exertion, but fear that set her panting. Like a trapped animal, she waited for Warren's next move. Then he came around the end of the shelves. He paused, filling the space, looming from out of a nightmare.

He was a monster. She felt it in the chilling of her blood, in the hollowness of her stomach, in the trembling, awful knowledge of the nature of the man who confronted her in the darkened store.

He slowly pulled his head back, as far as it would go on his thick neck. Doris felt something come over him—a sense of distance, as if he had moved away from normal human feeling. There'd always been something vaguely nonhuman about him. He lacked an essential component that most people possessed—a sense of empathy, of connectedness. She felt that separation intensify as he stared at her, as if from a great height. Had he looked that way at the woman in California before he killed her? And at Juanita Balleau?

Doris tried reason, though her voice trembled with terror. "Your alibi may not hold up. Mr. Karadzic barely speaks English. He probably didn't understand a word you said."

"He understood enough. You're the one who doesn't understand. What a disgusting piece of trash you are—women like you and Joanne, without any moral sense at all. Fornicating bitches. You don't deserve to live in the same world with a pure and innocent girl like Sherry, like my wife." He took a step toward her.

"You creep! You freak!" She surprised herself by yelling. "You're a horrible creep."

It surprised him, too. He flinched as though he'd been slapped, but then advanced again. She thought of the pistol in the bedside drawer at home. She'd never considered that she might need it at the store. But Doris knew her stock. The aisle she had chosen, the place where she'd stopped, displayed yard tools. Deftly, Doris snatched one off a hook.

"Stop!" she cried. She slashed a pruning saw back and forth. It had a heavy, two-foot-long curved blade, crowded with wickedly sharp, serrated teeth as nasty as those of a shark. She handled it with skill and confidence, backed by years of using it in her yard, sometimes while balanced on a ladder or in the tree itself.

Warren halted. She could not clearly see his face, only a bulking, bullet-headed shadow. But his voice spewed at her ugly words she'd heard only once before, whispered when she was in high school by a perverted classmate who was thrilled if he could shock and offend.

"Get out of my store," she yelled. She advanced, slashing the blade recklessly back and forth.

He looked around, probably hunting for a shovel or rake with which he could parry her attack, but those tools were all behind Doris. He snatched something off a shelf and flung it at her face. She ducked to one side and it whizzed harmlessly past. He reached for something else, aimed deliberately at her body, and threw. It struck her ribs with numbing force. She felt breathless. Pain spread and panic instantly followed. Not hurrying, he reached for another missile.

Doris knew that he could soon pummel her to a pulp. All he had to do was stay out of the reach of the pruning saw and he could force her into retreat, pounding her with one object after another until her numbed arms dropped and the saw was no longer protection. He would drive her back into the shadows, disarm her, and she would die as the other women had died, in pain and humiliation.

As the panic washed through her, it was followed by a great flash of rage. She screamed—in anger, in fear and desperation. She charged at him, still screaming, a long wordless cry of defiance. The pruning saw slashed ahead of her. She glimpsed shock on his face and the upflung movement of his arms. She sliced furiously, felt contact, heard the tearing sound of Warren's jacket as fabric ripped. A sleeve suddenly flooded red.

Inspired, she reversed the blade and slashed upwards toward his genitals. Warren stumbled backward. He crashed into a shelf, spilling goods to the floor. Objects thumped, tumbled and rolled around their feet. Doris pressed forward, jabbing and hooking with the shark-toothed tool. Warren floundered backward, bloody hands held at the joining of his legs. He shouted something that she couldn't hear over the sound of herself screaming.

"Getoutgetoutgetout!"

He turned and ran. He twisted the lock and slid through the door, surprisingly fast for his size. He jerked it nearly closed behind him, leaving only a crack to speak through. Blood smeared the glass. His eyes seemed barely human in their malevolence. His voice was raspy, breathless.

"I'll be back, Doris. No matter how long it takes, I'll be back. And you'll be sorry when I come."

He whirled and his broad back retreated down the street. She slammed the door and re-locked it. She flew to the rear of the store to lock the alley door. She dialed the lumber annex with a shaky hand. She must warn her employees in case he looked for vengeance there. But no one answered. They'd gone home.

Quickly, she called the sheriff's office. "This is Doris Gooding. I was just attacked in my store by my landlord, Warren Stonebraker. I believe that he killed a woman in California named Joanne Johnson and also Juanita Balleau at Whistler's Bend. You've talked to Lee Jamison about this.

"No, I'm not injured. When I last saw Warren, he was going south on Main Street. He drives a new white Cadillac. He said that he was staying in his cabin on the Little Nezzac River. I don't know exactly where it is, but the Jamisons will know. Call Bob Jamison at Whistler's Bend." She hung up and dialed the ranch before the sheriff could call them and tie up the line. It was busy. She kept dialing, but it was a long time before she got through.

"Bob, this is Doris." She told him what had happened.

Bob said, "Lee is here. He just got back from Redding, where he tried a little amateur sleuthing. The police there told him that Joanne's 'friend' drove a white Cadillac. We never thought of Stonebraker. We thought of someone who lived here, not just visited. And we had no idea that Warren owned property in Redding."

"Warren has property everywhere," Doris answered grimly, thinking of Sally Roush and how lucky she was that he would never keep their date. "Warren said that Sherry and Lila are up at the cabin. I called as soon as he left here, but your line was busy."

"That was Katie, talking to a girlfriend. I'm thinking that we should run up to the cabin. There's no phone. Maybe we can get Lila and Sherry out before Warren gets there. I know Sherry is his wife, but it's hard to say what he'll do now."

"He's dangerous, Bob. He's a very dangerous man."

"We'll be careful."

Someone pounded on the front door and Doris saw two men beyond the glass.

"The police are here. I'm not going home. I'd be sure Warren was in the closet. I'll stay at Alice's place tonight. Call me there later."

She hurried to open the door for the police. A quick search of the downtown area had turned up no trace of Warren or his white Cadillac. They questioned her briefly and then headed for the Little Nezzac River.

Later, as Doris drove toward Ridgewood Center, she thought about Alice. What she would tell her mother-in-law would fuel bridge table stories for months to come.

But mostly, she remembered the look on Warren's face as

he threatened her at the door. He was indeed a dangerous and unbalanced man. The fragile facade that he'd maintained was shattered beyond repair. What might he do now?

She prayed that her call had gotten through in time, that Bob and Lee could warn Sherry and Lila and that they would be safely away before Warren reached the cabin. She felt sure that was where he would go, to claim his most prized property—his wife.

Chapter 14

CHARLES

October to November

Charles took the 30.30 Winchester that Bob handed him.

"It's loaded."

Charles nodded. So it was always assumed. That understanding prevented a lot of stupid accidents, followed by the lame excuse, "I didn't know the gun was loaded."

Katie stood by the window, looking at the road beyond the field. "There's a white car going upriver. It's going fast," she said excitedly.

Bob hurried over. "Is it a Cadillac?"

"I can't tell."

"Damn! Those bushes are too high. I can't tell, either. But if Warren drove like a bat out of hell, he could be here by now."

"Let's go." Lee's voice was businesslike. "If we're lucky, we'll get in and out with the women before Stonebraker shows up."

The men trooped through the door. Charles was the last. He glanced at Katie, who met his eyes with an expression that he clearly read: I want to go, too. It's not fair.

Her father had told her that she was needed to answer the phone, to give directions to the law officers if they asked. But

Charles felt a twinge of empathy. He and Katie were almost the same age. She was competent and also familiar with guns. Of course, she'd never fired a shot at another human being, but neither had he. Nor Bob. He wasn't sure about Lee. Those chilly gray eyes hinted at all sorts of experiences. But Katie was a girl and it wouldn't have been right or expected that she would come along. So she must stay home—alone, as Vivian was away working on one of her community projects.

Charles sat in the back seat with the rifle across his knees. He thought about killing Warren Stonebraker. How satisfying to avenge himself upon the man who had murdered his sister. And Sherry—my God! Sherry was married to a killer. What an awful shock to learn that the man she lived, ate, slept with, was a murderer. And not just killing, but torture. Charles could hardly believe that a big shot businessman could hide such secrets.

Anyone could be a killer, anyone at all. Even an old neighbor woman, who'd also concealed her secret for years. Emotions and thoughts circled like bees in Charles's head. He'd impulsively stopped at the Jamisons' after he heard of Mrs. Domingo's death. He wanted to talk with someone who knew her, to share his sense of loss with someone who would understand. Instead he'd found Bob and Lee preparing to visit Warren's cabin.

Bob seemed to be thinking along somewhat the same track. "This is going to come as one hell of a shock to Stonebraker's pretty little wife."

Lee nodded as he lit a cigarette. "No doubt."

"And Lila Prentiss," Bob went on. "She's all puffed-up over her rich son-in-law. I never much liked either of the Stonebraker brothers, but murder . . ." He shook his head, awed at the enormity of it.

Images crowded Charles's memory—Juanita's eager,

pretty face; Sherry fair and remotely smiling. Both of them lay under the massive shadow of Warren Stonebraker. A killing shadow. That's what he longed to do to Warren, kill the bastard . . . the man who'd ended Juanita's life and the same as raped Sherry. It was rape, for a man like him to use a young girl. Charles had never felt such hatred. It consumed him like a fire. He generated so much hate, so much heat that he wondered that the entire back seat of Bob's car didn't spontaneously combust along with him.

Lee turned around. He caught Charles's eye and stared hard at him. "Let's keep in mind that we're not a posse. Our only reason for going to the cabin is to get the women out of the way before Stonebraker gets there. We agreed."

Charles could barely make out Lee. A vision of Warren with a bullet hole in the middle of his forehead obscured the older man's face.

"Charles, are we agreed?"

"Yeah. Sure."

Lee's eyes continued to bore into him. "If you do something stupid, you'll go to jail. You won't do yourself—or Juanita or Sherry—any good. The best thing you can do for everyone, yourself included, is to stay within the law."

With an effort, Charles obliterated Warren's dead and bloody face and focused on Lee. "Do you always stay within the law?"

"Damn right. I went to jail once, a long time ago, for getting drunk and smashing up a bar in Cheyenne, Wyoming, but that was it. I'm not a criminal. Don't you turn into one. I'll beat the shit out of you."

"Before or after I go to jail?"

"Both."

Their eyes clashed. You're nobody to me. Who are you to tell me what to do? But Charles didn't speak aloud. Lee was perfectly capable of bashing his head with a rifle barrel before he even got a chance to get Warren. Charles would gladly take a beating, even a jail term, for the pleasure of killing Stonebraker.

"Slow down, Bob," Lee said. "You promise, Charles. Or you're getting out of the car right here. Promise—nothing outside the law. And remember—there are few things more important than a man's sworn word."

Charles crossed his fingers. "I promise."

It was easy for the words to sound as though they were reluctantly dragged out of him. They were. He liked Lee enough so that he didn't want to disappoint him. But he hated Warren more. He hadn't realized until today how very, very much he hated Warren—his thick ugly body, his toad-like face, his money, his arrogance, every fucking thing about him.

"I promise," he said again. You're a fool if you believe me, Lee Jamison.

Lee stared at him. Charles could tell that he wasn't reassured.

Bob slowed the car. "There's the lane to the cabin."

Charles leaned forward and peered up the narrow track that wound off into the shadows of the great trees. The early evening glow thickened into twilight under the canopy of the forest. Full dark would not be long in coming here. Bob left the car in second gear. It rocked sluggishly from side to side as it crawled over humps and rocks in the dirt track.

"He ought to spend a few dollars and fix his road," Lee muttered.

"He likes it this way. He says a bad road discourages trespassers," Bob answered.

"It's discouraging me." Lee ground his cigarette butt into the ashtray. "How far is it?"

"A mile and a half, maybe."

It was slow going. Charles's sense of unreality increased. He had entered one of his dreams, as he drove into the approaching night to kill Warren Stonebraker. He was always alone in his dreams, but now he had two men with him. Of course, they didn't know why they were going. They thought it was a rescue mission.

"We're almost there," Bob said. He eased back on the gas a little.

The knot tightened in Charles's stomach. He smoothed his palm over the satiny rifle stock, seeking reassurance in the promise of its power.

The car bobbed around a curve and stopped. In front of them, a clearing sloped gradually upward to a log structure. It stood with its back close against the forest wall. The place was two-storied and seemed a house, not a cabin, to Charles. A porch extended across the front, reached by five or six steps. Light gleamed through windows on either side of the door. A big white Cadillac was parked near the steps.

"Shit!" Bob and Lee swore in unison.

Quietly, without so much as a click, Charles opened the back door and stepped out. He inhaled the resiny scent of Douglas fir needles, a sweet contrast to the rifle, cold and heavy in his hands.

"Get back in the car," Bob whispered. "We've got to talk this over before we . . ."

The door to the cabin banged open. Sherry was propelled through it, pushed by Warren from behind. She looked small as a child in comparison.

"But I don't want to go," she protested. Her voice was high and querulous. Neither of them noticed the car at the edge of the woods.

Lila followed closely behind. "Warren, what's the matter?

What happened to your arm?"

The figures on the porch froze as they saw the car. Bob and Lee had quietly eased out, holding their rifles. There was a moment of silence.

Sherry recovered first. "Why, hello, Mr. Jamison. What a surprise." She struggled to attain a hostess voice. At the same time, she tried to pull away from Warren, but he did not release her. "We were just . . . we were going to . . ." Explanations failed her. It was obvious that she didn't know what they were doing.

"Good evening, Sherry. Mrs. Prentiss." Bob's voice was polite, soothing. "We thought you might need transportation. We'll give you ladies a ride anywhere you want to go."

"That's not necessary," Warren said. His right hand, half-hidden behind his wife, emerged with a pistol in it. "Get in the car," he barked at Sherry. He shoved her toward the steps.

She resisted. "Warren, don't be so rough." Apparently she hadn't seen the pistol.

But Lila did. "My God, he's got a gun. Everybody has a gun! What's going on?" Her voice kept rising as she spoke, until the last words were a shrill near-shriek.

"Don't try to be heroes," Warren said. "All I want is to get in the car and get out of here."

"That's fine. You do that," Lee said. "But leave your wife. All we want is to make sure the women are safe. The sheriff is right behind us."

"I don't believe you," Warren said. "No sheriff would send you ahead. Doris called you."

"She also called the sheriff. Let's be reasonable about this." Bob's voice was as level as though he commented on cattle prices.

"Tell me what's going on," Sherry cried. "Charles, tell me."

"Warren killed my sister." Charles's voice shook in spite of the fact that he tried to sound as self-possessed as the Jamison brothers. "And he murdered another woman in California. One of his girlfriends."

His fingers trembled on the rifle, not from fear but from eagerness to lift the barrel and send a bullet right where he'd dreamed it would go—between Warren's piggy little eyes. But no one yet had raised their gun. Even Warren's pistol pointed at the ground and Charles did not want to be the one to escalate the situation.

"Get in the car," Warren commanded Sherry.

She didn't respond. She seemed shocked into immobility. He pushed her down the first step. She stumbled and nearly fell.

"She's not going with you," Charles yelled. "Let her go."

Sherry began to struggle against her husband as he pushed her ahead of him down the steps. The rage Charles had held so long exploded. He whirled toward the Cadillac and fired twice. The rear end dropped as the two back tires went flat.

Swearing, Warren retreated across the porch. He stumbled into Lila, who stood frozen in front of the door with her hands pressed against her mouth. Warren swung the hand with the pistol in it and knocked her to her knees. He wrenched open the door and backed into the house, pulling Sherry along with him. The door slammed.

Lila floundered to it and clutched at the knob. "He's locked it. Sherry! Sherry!"

Charles sprinted up the slope and around the side of the house. Warren, dragging Sherry with him, had come out the back door and was already at the edge of the trees. Charles raised the rifle and sighted at the retreating back. Once before this killer had fled through the forest and escaped. He would not get away again. Warren flickered in and out of the tree trunks, yanking Sherry along like a puppet. He was larger than a deer and not nearly as swift. Charles had brought down several in shots more difficult than this one. He took his time, aimed with an intense feeling of satisfaction, and prepared to kill Warren.

"Charles! You promised me!"

He blinked. It was Mrs. Domingo's voice. It was so clear and sharp that she might have been right beside him. As he stood frozen, he heard Bob and Lee, older, slower and hampered by cowboy boots, coming up behind him. Warren fired off a shot over his shoulder, too hastily to aim but clearly sending a warning.

The sound of the shot did something to Sherry. Her resistance had been feeble, but now she struggled and scratched like a wildcat. Charles heard her screeching, "Let me go! Let me go!"

Warren tried to pull her along, but she fought back. Charles sprinted toward them. Warren saw him coming and got off another quick shot as Charles dodged behind a tree. He peered around it and saw Warren drive a meaty fist into Sherry's face. She collapsed. Charles ran forward, as Warren hoisted his wife over his left shoulder like a felled deer.

"Back off!" Warren yelled.

Charles ducked behind another tree. Bob and Lee also took shelter. Warren shambled into the brush with Sherry's head hanging against his back.

"Damn!" Lee said. "We can't shoot. We might hit her."

"Keep him busy," Charles said. "I'll get ahead of him."

"Don't be a hero," Bob called.

Charles loped through the woods, circling to the right. He tried to imagine Warren's likely path, to stay to the right of it and to be as quiet as possible. He kept brush and tree trunks between himself and where he thought Warren must be. Behind him, the Jamison brothers made a big racket, yelling at Warren to stop, thrashing through the undergrowth. One of them fired his rifle – a shot in the air, Charles guessed—just to—keep Warren focused on the pursuit from the rear.

He glimpsed a moving light-colored shape to his left—Sherry's white blouse showing between the dark tree trunks. Warren couldn't go nearly as fast, carrying his burden, as Charles could move. The twilight deepened. Bushes and small trees clumped into shadows.

He stopped and listened. He heard Warren a little behind him, panting and blowing. The man stumbled over something and cursed. Charles trotted on. His feet touched softly on the forest floor, matted with fir needles, cones, small twigs, fragments of centuries of shedding from the trees above. The detritus was damp from the recent rains and no dry sticks cracked under his woods-wise feet.

He tracked Warren with his ears, pausing now and then to listen, occasionally glimpsing the telltale bit of white in the brush. The Jamison brothers whooped it up, making as much noise as an entire posse.

A stick popped, startlingly close. Warren had veered toward him. They were separated only by the trunk of a huge fallen tree, higher than Charles's head as it lay across the slope of the hill. He froze, barely breathing, as Warren's footsteps came closer. The man slid clumsily down the hill and against the tree. Sherry mumbled something.

"Hold still," he said harshly. "Stop wiggling."

Charles silently crept along the lower side of the trunk, wanting to reach the butt end before Stonebraker did. Charles tucked himself into the shadow of the gnarled root wad and waited for him to come into sight.

A few loose pebbles rolled down the dirt pile that had been lifted up by the falling tree. Broken roots of varying lengths thrust out like the twisted arms and splayed fingers of a Halloween monster. They created a barrier between Charles and the man coming down the hill. Charles leaned against the tree, trying to be invisible, thankful for the shadows in the almost-dark.

Warren's foot slipped as he moved past Charles. Stonebraker exclaimed softly and leaned the hand with the pistol in it against a root for support.

Charles lunged forward. With the full weight of his body and the slightly downward motion, he drove the rifle barrel into Warren's ribs. A sound somewhere between a cough and a bellow erupted from him. His feet slipped out from under him. The pistol fired twice as he sat heavily on the ground. Sherry rolled to one side and up on all fours like a cat.

Without a pause, Charles whipped the rifle in a loop and clubbed Warren on the side of the head. The pistol dropped from his fingers and slid downhill. Stonebraker toppled to one side like a sack of grain and sprawled at Charles's feet.

He retrieved the pistol and stuck it through his belt. He knelt beside Sherry, who had slumped into a sitting position. Blood smeared her face and her upper lip puffed out. He whispered her name. She looked at him with dazed eyes, as though she had never seen him before.

Later, after the police had come and gone, taking Warren with them, Charles, Bob, and Lee lingered on the porch of the cabin.

Mrs. Prentiss cradled her badly bruised arm. Her voice trembled when she spoke. "I can't stay another night in this place. I'm going to pack. You, too, darling."

"In a minute." Sherry didn't move from where she sat on the porch settee.

The day's overcast partially obscured the sky and only a few faint stars were visible in the night. Hesitantly, Charles sat beside her. Lee and Bob smoked and talked in low tones at the other end of the porch.

After a moment, Sherry said. "I'll have to get a divorce."

"Yeah, you should."

She twisted off her wedding ring. It clinked to the boards of the porch, but she didn't seem to notice. "Warren was always nice to me. Years ago, Mother made him promise that he wouldn't take advantage of me just because he was older, that he would respect my innocence. And he did. He liked it." A secretive expression, almost a smile, flitted across her face. It was gone so quickly that Charles wondered if he'd imagined it.

Sherry went on. "He took advantage of me in other ways, though. He pretended to be someone he wasn't. It makes me sick to think of it."

"You'll soon be free."

"Yes, I can do anything I want. I won't have to listen to anyone, even Mother. Especially Mother. She's not so smart. She made a bad choice for me." Her voice had grown stronger.

Not for the first time, Charles wondered what went on between the two women. What did they talk about together? And what had Warren and Sherry talked about? What passed between them during daily life in that chilly white apartment? The question unsettled him, as he looked at Sherry's unfamiliar, puffy-lipped profile. A little shiver passed through him. He didn't know this girl at all.

She said, "I'll be rich. I'll never have to listen to her again. I'll give her money, like Warren did, but I'll be free of her."

The sky pressed down on Charles, heavy with the weight of clouds and moist darkness. Every last star was obscured.

"You've been a good friend, Charles. Maybe you could visit me in Portland sometime."

"Maybe." He recognized a crumb when he saw one. "I hope you'll be happy, Sherry."

He stood up quickly and joined Lee and Bob at the other end of the porch. Lee handed him a cigarette. In a moment, Charles heard Sherry's footsteps pass behind him as she went inside and up the stairs, but he did not look around. Instead he searched the sky for stars and, finally, he found one . . . and then another as the clouds shifted and the sky changed.

Charles looked around with a feeling of satisfaction. He'd spent the weekend cleaning the house, remembering what Grandmother had done and doing the same chores. He'd washed windows, wiped cobwebs out of corners, scrubbed the wooden floor with a broom dipped in water. The place looked pretty good. It was well over a month since Mrs. Domingo's death and he was still astonished that she'd willed everything to him.

He took an old photograph from a drawer. Charlotte, young, stern, and beautiful, looked back. Her husband, beside her, didn't appear to be an ordinary next-door-neighbor kind of man, but more like a barbarian prince from another time.

I wish I knew more about them. A melancholy pang came along with the thought, as he looked at the vanished young woman in the high-collared, old-fashioned dress. It was too late.

But maybe not for him. Charles's parents had almost no records or pictures of any kind. But Grandmother knew at least some of the stories. She was the keeper of memories, the teller of tales. It was important that he listen and remember, while she was alive and he could ask questions.

A lot of things were different now. Charles hadn't stolen since Karl Blessinger had nearly caught him with the camera. There'd been opportunities, but he let them pass. The comment he'd made to his father about making your own luck had taken root in his mind. He had too much to lose, too much to risk on silly kid stuff, ever again.

Two dogs slept on the rag rug. He'd gotten rid of the rest, as well as half the cats, and built a pen for the chickens. He couldn't live like Mrs. Domingo, with animals all over the house.

He went after the milk pail. Time for the evening chores.

"Come on, you damn dogs." He smiled as he heard the echo of Mrs. Domingo's words in his voice. The dogs followed him outside. Mamie, looking toward the house, mooed softly. One of the ponies pranced toward Charles, head lifted and tail pluming out behind.

Two hawks came down from the hill, sailing through the early evening sky. One called out as they slanted off toward the trees along the river. Charles couldn't see the water, but he knew how it looked and sounded, as it passed in its long journey to the Pacific Ocean.

The old-growth forest behind him awoke with a deep whooshing sound, as though a living force moved among the trees. Charles turned and glimpsed a shadow like a cloud pattern pass through the woods. But the evening sky was clear.

Something inside him awoke in response, part of his new sense of possibilities. Without even knowing it, for all his life, he'd teetered between the separate worlds of his mother and father. They had come from different directions, converged for a brief time to produce him, and gone their separate ways again. He didn't need to follow either one, but could find his own path.

Charles watched the motion in the trees as it rippled up the slope and vanished around a curve of the hill. It stirred his blood with almost-memories of ancient days. It reminded him of his fundamental connection to the trees, to all other living creatures, to Earth herself.

His lips moved in what might have been a prayer or a plea for guidance. "Spirits, listen. I am between . . ."

Epilogue

LEE

November

Lee drove slowly as autumn skittered around him in the form of leaves swirling across the road. So many changes—in the seasons, in the lives of people.

Warren Stonebraker, in jail, awaited trial for two murders. Doris, who'd never traveled, was in San Franciso with Anna Stegner. Charles was a property owner.

Although he hadn't known her, thoughts of Mrs. Domingo brought a twinge of sorrow. He'd just returned from California, where he'd gone in a fruitless attempt to gather information about Joanne's mysterious "Don," when Vivian sent him to check on the old lady. He'd found her collapsed on the floor and quickly figured out that she believed he was someone she knew, someone from her past. He'd tried to be that person for her. He'd spoken her name, held her hand, and offered as much comfort as he could.

He'd watched her eyes change and saw her lose sight of him during those awesome moments when the spirit departed and only the husk remained. Almost at once, her body lost its Charlotte-ness and became a shell, not at all as it had been when animated by the spirit of the woman. He'd continued to hold her hand, to murmur her name and speak reassurances, until he was certain that she'd gone beyond the reach of his voice.

During those moments, strangely, he'd thought of Smoky, his favorite horse from long ago. He'd imagined the dappled gelding with Charlotte, liking her, putting his beautiful Arab head down to snuffle at her hand. It was odd, the thoughts that sometimes came to mind.

At his back, a late sun slid toward the hills in the west, as the spinning wheels carried him on. The road curved and he slowed to make the turn into the lane. The old ranch house sat comfortably on a little rise, back near the base of the forested hills. It overlooked the barn and sheds, the pens and corrals, the fenced and promising bottom land.

Lee glanced at the mailbox as his new pickup passed it. The box was freshly painted with bold black letters: Lee Jamison. He grinned and stuck a cigarette between his lips. For the first time in his life, he wasn't portable. He couldn't throw everything he owned into the transportation of the moment and take off down the road. For the first time, the road led him home. And it felt good. Scary, but good.

He entered the house with his arms full of groceries. Slanting afternoon sunlight illuminated bare wooden floors and worn, faded upholstery. He'd bet that Reuthers hadn't spent a nickel on furniture in the last twenty years. Lee could manage two or three new pieces right away and the rest would come gradually.

He went to the kitchen and put a quart of milk into the refrigerator. Harold had left his cow, but she wasn't fresh and Lee hadn't decided whether or not he wanted to breed her and turn her into a milker again.

The dingy kitchen badly needed paint. He'd do that right away. In fact, he should have bought paint today. Something cheerful to lighten it up, Vivian had said. But what color?

He'd ask Doris when she came to see the place.

His boot heels clicked as he wandered around. The house was bigger than he needed and his footfalls echoed through the rooms, all half-empty after Harold had moved what possessions he wanted to take along with him. The sun would soon set behind the high dark ridge beyond the river. Evenings came early as winter drew in. Nights stretched long and silent with only the murmur of the radio, the sound of his footsteps, the pages turning in his book.

The convivial cowboy bars were all too far away for a weeknight drive. They'd lost their appeal, anyway, now that he'd cut back so much on drinking.

Lee looked out the window at the fields in front of his house. Pride of ownership was firm, as well as the conviction that he'd made a good choice. But loneliness remained and so did a sure sense that this would increase with time.

He would ask Doris for dinner when she got home from San Francisco. She hadn't yet seen his place, even though he'd invited her twice. He was eager to show her around, but she'd been too busy at work. She was completely absorbed in the hardware store. It was doing better than ever, partly because of post-war prosperity and partly because of her own business and marketing abilities. It was astonishing how Doris had changed in the last months. She'd lost that hesitant insecure manner that had sometimes charmed him and sometimes made him impatient. She'd become direct, confident, obviously capable.

Poor Glenn Draper was in her store almost every day, wagging his tail like a hopeful puppy. He didn't have a chance, even though he didn't seem to know it yet. Doris brushed him off in such a friendly, unassuming way that he didn't even realize what had happened.

A surprising sense of uneasiness came over Lee. Surely

Doris wasn't evading him, too? She really was busy. It wasn't that she didn't want to come. After all, she'd loved him for years. And even though he was no longer her lover, he counted on her as a good friend, one who was always there.

And what that boiled down to, he recognized with a sudden sickish feeling, was that he'd taken her for granted. From the very beginning he'd assumed that she would be content with however much—or little—he chose to give. It was good that he had a few days to think this through while she was out of town. It was important that . . .

But he had never allowed Doris any real importance in his life. A sense of shame flooded him—shame and regret at being so careless with her feelings even as he protected his own. It jolted him to realize that he no longer knew how she felt about him. He also realized how often he'd pictured her on his ranch—admiring the view from the front porch, riding with him to the upper meadow, completing the table for meals with Bob, Vivian, and the kids.

As though she belonged. Part of the family.

And now it was possible that she had no intention of ever setting foot on his place.

Lee lit a cigarette and sank into one of the lumpy chairs. He stared out the window without noticing anything beyond the glass. But there was much that he did see as he began to look, as honestly and deeply as he could, at himself.

He was still there when darkness filled the valley. His self-examination had been long and painful and was far from over. But he could see a small glow like the distant flicker of a candle. It came from a future that he hoped, and believed, he could bring into being—one with Doris in it.

He knew that she would want to hear words of love and they would not come easily to him. He was afraid that . . . He was afraid. A startling idea for a man who prided himself on not being afraid of much of anything—not of other men, nor of unfamiliar surroundings, nor the solitude of mountains and deserts with only the company of a horse. He counted on his own resources to get through whatever might arise. To count on another person, to risk those feelings that he'd once given so freely—that was terrifying.

But this was Doris. He'd be safe with her. She was true-blue. And even if she wasn't—what the hell? He'd survived once. Better to take a risk than remain a coward all his life.

He stood up. He paced around the room, his footsteps quick and purposeful. What could he say to Doris to close the distance he'd created between them? Something not too serious at first. He might begin by saying, "Now that I'm a property owner, I need a partner. We were always good together and I want to keep you in my life . . . I just realized . . . can you? . . . will you? . . ."

The words piled up, propelled by a flood of emotion. It seemed that they would come easily, after all.